A DANCE TO REMEMBER

sequel to
Dancing in the Light

OTHER BOOKS AND AUDIO BOOKS
BY ANITA STANSFIELD:

First Love and Forever

First Love, Second Chances

Now and Forever

By Love and Grace

A Promise of Forever

When Forever Comes

For Love Alone

The Three Gifts of Christmas

Towers of Brierley

Where the Heart Leads

When Hearts Meet

Someone to Hold

Reflections: A Collection of Personal Essays

Gables of Legacy, Vol. 1: The Guardian

Gables of Legacy, Vol. 2: A Guiding Star

Gables of Legacy, Vol. 3: The Silver Linings

Gables of Legacy, Vol. 4: An Eternal Bond

Gables of Legacy, Vol. 5: The Miracle

Gables of Legacy, Vol. 6: Full Circle

Timeless Waltz

A Time to Dance

Dancing in the Light

A DANCE TO REMEMBER

sequel to
Dancing in the Light

a novel

ANITA STANSFIELD

Covenant Communications, Inc.

Cover image photographed by Picture This... by Sara Staker

Cover design copyrighted 2006 by Covenant Communications, Inc.

Published by Covenant Communications, Inc.
American Fork, Utah

Printed in Canada
First Printing: November 2006
12 11 10 09 08 07 06 10 9 8 7 6 5 4 3 2

ISBN 987-1-59811-169-9

For those who live in darkness.
May you find your way into the light.

You can't jump the track, we're like cars on a cable.
And life's like an hourglass, glued to the table.
No one can find the rewind button . . . so cradle
your head in your hands.
And breathe, just breathe.

Anna Nalick

Chapter One

Salt Lake City, Utah

Wade Morrison glanced down the long bench in the chapel where he was sitting. For a moment time felt as if it had stopped, while his mind and spirit both attempted to grasp the enormity of all that had changed in his life—and all that had remained constant. On both counts he felt incomprehensibly blessed. He clearly recalled a day much like today, two years earlier. He'd been sitting in the same spot, and many of the same people had been on the bench with him. But that day had been filled with a grief so tangible that Wade had barely been able to breathe. He remembered being relieved to have his infant daughter, Rebecca, start fussing so that he could take her out. And when he hadn't been able to get a handle on his emotions, he'd just taken her home. Rebecca's mother, Elena, had not been gone many weeks at that point, and the loss had still been raw. She had died in her sleep from a cerebral hemorrhage, and even though Wade and Elena had both felt spiritually prepared for her death, he hadn't felt emotionally prepared at all when it had finally happened.

But now Wade felt a joy so perfect that the grief of two years ago was almost impossible to imagine, even if he could remember how horrible it had been. Today, just as then, his half-brother Alex was sitting farther down the row. Alexander Keane sat beside his wife, Jane, and they were surrounded by their four children. Ruthie was two and had been dubbed Rebecca's twin; they looked nothing alike, but they were only two weeks apart in age. And since Wade had been living with the family prior to Elena's death, the babies had grown together, side by side. Alex and Jane's other children included Preston, who was five and had just started going to afternoon kindergarten, and Katharine, who was eight. And then there was Barrett.

Barrett was ten years old and one of the lights in Wade's life, and he made no qualms about declaring the child as his favorite nephew. Wade caught Barrett's eye, and they exchanged a smile; little in life could warm Wade's heart like a smile from Barrett. He was an amazing kid with the insight and sensitivity of someone much older, but then he'd been diagnosed with leukemia at the age of four, and the bone marrow transplant that had saved him had also left him sharing Wade's blood—quite literally. But that was the least of Wade's reasons for feeling so close to Barrett. Their age difference of eighteen years felt almost irrelevant. They were friends, and Wade loved him. Of course, there was also nearly a fifteen-year age difference between Wade and Alex, and they were the best of friends. Clearly, the span of years was overridden by an invisible bond that couldn't be denied.

Wade pondered for a moment how blessed he'd been to have Alex in his life, especially when he'd not even known of his brother's existence until not so many years ago. The old adage that good things can come out of trials and adversity was both pertinent and personal for Wade. He'd become an adult before he'd discovered that the ideal Mormon family he'd grown up in had once had some serious challenges. Brad, his father, had not been a very good husband, and his mother, Marilyn, had given up on trying to point that out. She had left him and lived with another man for a couple of years before she'd returned to a very humble Brad, and they had put the marriage back together. But

Wade had resulted from that affair. Brad and Marilyn—as well as Wade's biological father—had all gone through the deepest pits of grief and repentance, and they had all worked their way back to become some of the most amazing people he had ever known. But Wade had learned that no amount of repentance or forgiveness could take away the natural consequences of sin—and in this case, that meant his own existence. Initially he'd been horrified and had nearly ended his own life over the matter, but he'd long ago come to terms with his unique family, and he'd gained a warm relationship with his biological father and the half-brother he'd not known existed. Looking at Alex now, he wondered how he had ever survived without him. He could never begin to list what this man had done for him; their father, Neil, was equally good and kind.

As Wade considered that moment two years ago when his grief had been eating him alive, his focus turned to the person sitting closest to him, the one holding his hand. She was the reason for his perfect joy. And he loved her for it—and for a thousand other reasons. Laura had been his wife a little longer than twenty-four hours, but as he watched his little daughter, Rebecca, climb onto her lap with a storybook, it felt as if they'd been a family forever. He would always love Elena, and her impact on his life was eternal. No woman could ever replace her, but Laura had filled the hole that Elena had left in his life—and she had done it brilliantly.

Wade just luxuriated in observing Laura for a long moment, amazed that someone so beautiful could be so wise and spiritual and sensitive. Her long, curly blonde hair was twisted into a clip at the back of her head, and she wore the same tiny pearl earrings that she'd worn yesterday in the temple.

As sacrament meeting progressed, Wade watched his wife and daughter together and felt as if his heart would overflow. He'd actually met Laura about two years earlier, but it had only been two weeks ago that he'd worked up the nerve to ask her on a date. And now they were here, husband and wife, mutual parents to Rebecca, embarking on a life together in the best possible way. She turned to look at him, her eyes sparkling as if they shared some great secret. And maybe they did. The love they shared felt like magic to him, and while their twenty-four-hour honeymoon had gone way too fast, he felt confident that the magic would last forever.

When the meeting ended, Barrett said to Wade, "Do you want me to take Rebecca to nursery when I take Ruthie?"

"That would be great, buddy, thanks," Wade said, and Rebecca went eagerly with him. She loved Barrett, and she loved her nursery class at church. The other children left as well to go to their Primary classes, but the adults remained seated, since the gospel doctrine class was held in the chapel. Wade had been teaching teenagers in Sunday School, but he'd gotten a substitute for today, not certain if he'd make it back for meetings or not, and since he was moving out of the ward, the responsibility would now fall to someone else.

"How was the honeymoon?" Alex asked.

"Way too short," Wade said, holding tightly to Laura's hand, "but marvelous—even though Laura snores."

"I do not," she said and laughed, making him laugh as well.

"Are you coming over for dinner?" Jane asked.

"Are we invited?" Wade asked.

"That's the stupidest question I've ever heard. You've lived with us for more than two years. Just because you'll be sleeping and keeping your clothes at Laura's house now doesn't mean you're any less a member of the family. The door—and the kitchen—are always open."

"We'd love to," Laura said. "I'm still on my honeymoon, so I had no intention of cooking, but I could help wash the dishes."

"It's a deal," Jane said.

Laura turned to look at her husband as the Sunday School class began. She felt her surroundings become distant; all she could see was him. She still had trouble believing this was real. She'd fallen for him the first time she'd seen him, nearly two years ago. But never in her wildest dreams had she really believed that he would ever take a second glance at someone like her. And now she was his wife. He turned to look at her and smiled. The adoration in his eyes had been there from that very first date, even though he'd since then seen her at her absolute worst, and he knew everything about the difficulties of her life—past and present. He was the kindest, wisest, most sensitive man she'd ever known. And he certainly wasn't bad to look at. Until two days ago, she'd never seen him without a beard. But with or without it, he was more attractive to her than any man ever had been. He was six foot two, with sandy brown hair and hazel eyes, and a smile that lit up his face—and warmed her heart. As he leaned over to whisper something to Alex, she couldn't help thinking how the two of them together were so intriguing. In spite of being half-brothers, they technically shared no resemblance in features or coloring, since Alex's hair was much darker. But they were exactly the same height, and their mannerisms and behavior were so much alike that no one could watch them interacting without realizing they were brothers.

Ironically, Laura was actually near the same height and coloring as Jane; they both had blonde curly hair, but they too looked nothing alike. Still, in the brief time she'd come to know Jane, Laura had found in her the kind of sister she'd only dreamed of having. Her own dysfunctional upbringing had made her doubly grateful to be warmly accepted by Wade's family, when they were all such wonderful people.

Laura was startled from her thoughts when the elderly gentleman teaching the class said, "Brother Morrison, I see you have a visitor with you today. Please introduce this lovely young woman."

Wade chuckled and stood up, clearly taken off guard. "Actually," he said, urging Laura to stand beside him, "this is my wife, Laura." A pleasant rumble went through the room. "We were married yesterday in the Salt Lake Temple."

"That's wonderful," the teacher said. "Congratulations! I'm sure that everyone in the room is as happy for you as I am."

"Thank you," Wade said.

"Will you be staying in the ward?" the teacher asked as they sat back down.

"Uh . . . no, I'll be moving into Laura's home."

"Well, we're going to miss you," the teacher said, "but we're sure glad you found someone."

"Thank you," Wade said again and winked at Laura. She was glad when the attention was drawn away from them, except that she found Wade looking at her with a familiar dreaminess in his eyes that tempted her to melt. She felt sure they had to be a spectacle to anyone who cared to take notice. They probably looked conspicuously like newlyweds, but she really didn't care. She was the happiest woman alive.

After church they had a wonderful dinner with Alex and Jane and the kids, then they gathered up some of Wade's and Rebecca's odds and ends that needed to go to Laura's home, where they would now be living. Wade still had a few things he needed to come back and get from his room, and he would still be storing some things in the garage, but most of their things were already at Laura's house.

Alex and Jane both became very somber when it came time to say goodnight. But Barrett actually started to cry.

"Hey there, buddy," Wade said, pulling Barrett onto his lap. They'd talked a couple of days earlier about how difficult this was for both of them, but it still made Wade's heart ache to see Barrett's sadness. "I'm still going to see you a lot. We're family, and you're my favorite nephew. Your mother is going to tend Rebecca tomorrow, and she will do that a few days every week."

"And we'll have them over for dinner at least once a week," Jane said.

"It's not the same," Barrett insisted.

"I know, buddy," Wade said, hugging him tightly. "But one day it will be you leaving, and I'll be the sad one left behind." Barrett looked confused, and Wade said, "What do you expect me to do when you go on your mission?"

They talked a few more minutes before more hugs were shared by everyone, then Wade took his wife and daughter home. It only took a few minutes to set up Rebecca's crib in the spare bedroom, while Laura arranged the rest of Rebecca's things and talked to her about how fun it was going to be for them to live in the same house.

"You got that right," Wade said, and Laura laughed.

After Rebecca was in her pajamas, the three of them sat together on the couch while Wade and Laura took turns reading pages in a storybook. After the baby was put to bed, Wade found Laura in the kitchen watering plants.

"Guess what?" she said without looking at him.

"What?"

"I don't have to sleep alone tonight." She smiled at him. "And you don't have to leave."

He smiled back. "It's a miracle. And one of these days we'll have a real honeymoon."

"Just having you here is like a vacation. It makes everything better."

"You got that right," he said again and wrapped her in his arms, kissing her the way he'd wanted to for hours. He agreed completely. Being with her made everything better.

* * * * *

Before they went to sleep that night, Wade told Laura there was something important that needed to be done. Laura felt a little in awe as he told her they needed to start their marriage out right. They took turns reading from the Book of Mormon, then they knelt together to pray. When that was done he said, "And there's one more thing." They sat close together and he held both her hands. "The day before we were married, you told me it was hard for you to be alone in this house."

Laura looked down, almost ashamed by the memories of that day. She'd warned him previously that she struggled with depression, but that day she had sunk into it hard and fast. He'd talked some sense into her, had given her a priesthood blessing, and she'd been able to take hold of the light he'd brought into her life. She'd not given it a second thought since she'd become his wife. Now, just as then, she couldn't help wondering why he would still be so committed to her, why he would love her so completely when he'd seen how pathetic she could be when she got like that. But the acceptance and adoration in his eyes were impossible to miss. She had promised him that she would take note of depression symptoms before they got out of hand, that she would talk to him and allow him to help her. She only hoped that when it hit her again, and she knew that it would, she might be capable of keeping her promises, and that he wouldn't regret bringing her into his life. She feared that he simply had no comprehension of how it could take hold of her with such debilitating force. And she prayed that he would not become a casualty of problems that were hers.

"Yes, that's true," she said, recalling the conversation well. She felt the need to repeat what she'd told him then. "I *don't* like being alone here, especially at night. I love this house, Wade; I really do, but . . . Randall lived here with me. You know the marriage only lasted a month, but it was horrid. This is where he . . . yelled and screamed at me, and . . ."

"Hit you?" he said to fill in the blank, preventing her from having to say it. She nodded and looked down, unable to comprehend the difference between her first husband and her second. Randall's idea of dealing with her depression was to slap some sense into her—quite literally. It had only happened a couple of times, and he'd not left any bruises, but the things he'd said to her had mingled with the words her drunken mother had said over and over throughout Laura's childhood. The scars from both relationships were deeply ingrained in her spirit, but Wade seemed to understand. At the very least, he loved her in spite of all she'd been through.

"And," Wade went on, his voice tender, "this is where you got the news of Tina's death, and where you had all those long conversations with Rochelle that were so hard for you."

Laura looked up at him, amazed that he would remember what she'd said, and that he would show such compassion. She had lost both of her best friends, and the impact had been devastating. Tina had committed suicide not so many weeks ago, and long before that Rochelle had jumped off a spiritual cliff, immersing herself in a lifestyle that had distanced her from Laura. She and Rochelle kept in close touch, but they had lost the deep emotional connection they'd once shared. Many times as Laura had struggled to deal with her own loneliness and chronic depression, she had felt tempted to follow Rochelle's example—or Tina's. But Wade had changed all of that. He was living proof that God loved her. How could she not be grateful? And now that he was a part of her life, she could put all of that behind her and start over.

"Anyway," Wade said, "I thought that since we've started a new life as a new family, we should give the house a fresh start as well."

Laura was struck anew with what a marvelous man she had found when he knelt and dedicated their home, by the power of the priesthood, to be a place where the Spirit could reside, and where they could be guided through the challenges of life that might lie ahead. When his prayer was completed, Laura looked into his eyes and felt distinct evidence of the transformation that had taken place—in her home and in her life. The very idea of ever being depressed again was simply incomprehensible.

* * * * *

Wade fell asleep with Laura in his arms, and his next awareness was coming awake with a gasp, startled by the noise that had come out of his mouth, as well as the peacefulness of the dark surrounding him. It only took a moment to assess that Laura was sleeping soundly beside him, but it took much longer for his heart rate to return to normal. In all his life he couldn't recall ever having a dream that intense, that vivid, that *horrible.*

He sat up and swung his legs over the edge of the bed, then he had to lower his head when he felt a little woozy. The images from his dream flashed into his mind, and he groaned, pressing his hands into his hair only to realize that he was sweating. He stood carefully and went into the bathroom where he splashed cool water on his face and blotted it dry before he sat down on the edge of the tub and tried to convince himself that it was just a nightmare. He wasn't going to lose Laura the way he'd lost Elena, and entertaining such a fear for even a moment was ludicrous. He forced the images—of finding Elena dead and then seeing her face turn to Laura's—out of his mind. *It was only a dream.* Duly convinced, he went back to bed, finding reassurance in Laura's nearness while she slept peacefully beside him. But it still took a long while and a great deal of prayer to feel peace enough to sleep again.

Laura woke to hear Wade in the other room with Rebecca. Embarking on her day, she found joy in simply having them in her home. She'd become so accustomed to her lonely, quiet existence that she couldn't stop laughing for no apparent reason as she and Wade worked together to get each other and Rebecca some breakfast, get the baby dressed, equip her diaper bag, and get everything ready for the day ahead. Wade left before Laura to take Rebecca to Jane's house before he went to the family practice clinic where he was presently doing a rotation as part of his medical training. Once he'd given her a savoring kiss and had hurried out the door, Laura quickly put the kitchen in order, made the bed, and laughed again as she picked up Rebecca's pajamas and toys off the floor of the room that had become hers.

Driving to work, Laura couldn't help thinking of how she loved her job. Working as an LPN at a pediatric clinic had been the one solid thing in her life. She loved children and liked the people she worked with. And this was where she had met Rebecca—and her father. She recalled fondly that day two years earlier when she'd first seen his face. Rebecca had been two months old, and Laura had asked Wade why he'd brought the baby in for her checkup without her mother, since it was so rare for a father to come alone. He'd told her of his wife's recent death, and when tears rolled down his face, she had cried too. She'd fallen for him in that moment, and had secretly harbored feelings for him while she'd felt certain a man like that would never be interested in someone like her. And then one day he had come into the office under the false pretense of Rebecca needing to see the doctor. He'd asked her to go out with him—and that had been two weeks ago today. They'd connected so quickly and so deeply that it still left her breathless to think about it. He was everything she'd dreamed of and more. And while the present still felt far too good to be true, how could she not relish the joy she'd found and make the most of every moment? For now, she felt deliriously happy. With any luck, it would last longer than a heartbeat.

* * * * *

Wade followed the family practice doctor he'd been assigned to from one patient to another, sometimes watching, sometimes doing some of the basics while the doctor supervised. While it felt tedious at times, his passion for becoming a doctor made much of it fascinating and enjoyable. But all that he was learning paled in contrast to the changes that had taken place in his own life over the last two weeks. Laura was so prominent in his mind that he often had trouble keeping his joy from erupting in bold laughter. Just recalling their somewhat chaotic morning made him smile. She'd commented more than once on how nice it was not to be alone. For him, he'd not been alone in the same way that she had, since he'd been living with Alex and Jane and their children. But he'd been lonely still the same. He'd spent two years observing his brother's interaction with a wife, while Wade had longed for that kind of companionship in his own life. And now he'd finally found it. The memory of last night's dream momentarily invaded his serenity, but he forced it away.

Wade shouldn't have been surprised when the doctor noticed his good mood. "Why the perma-grin?"

Wade chuckled. "It's that obvious, huh?"

"Uh . . . yeah."

"I got married over the weekend, actually."

"Is that so?" the doctor said, pleasantly surprised. "Well, congratulations."

"Thank you," Wade said, and the day moved on.

When Wade found a few minutes for a break, he called the clinic where Laura worked.

"Is Laura available?" he asked.

"May I ask who's calling?" the woman asked.

Wade just couldn't resist. "This is her husband."

The woman snorted. "That's a good one . . . or wishful thinking, maybe."

"Just tell her that her husband's on the phone," he said. "I'm certain she'll know who it is."

Laura came out of an exam room and closed the door just as Sally approached her, saying, "Some joker on the phone says he's your husband, and that you'd know who it was."

Laura just smiled and held up her left hand, saying, "That would be my husband, then."

"You're *married?*"

"Sure am," Laura said, moving toward the phone.

Sally laughed. "When did you get married?"

"Saturday."

"What did you do? Run off to Vegas or something?"

"No, we stayed right here in town. We got married in that magnificent granite building right in the center of the city."

Sally laughed again, walking alongside her. "So you . . . what? Eloped to the temple?"

"Something like that. Although there were probably too many relatives there to really justify it as an elopement."

"That is so awesome," Sally said, and Laura picked up the phone.

"Hello, Mrs. Morrison," Wade said, and her stomach fluttered just to hear his voice. "How's married life?"

"Even at work, it's blissful. And you?"

"Ditto. I just had to hear your voice. I'm cooking dinner tonight. Will you pick up Rebecca if I get the groceries?"

"I would love to," she said, and he laughed. "What's funny?"

"We sound like married people."

"So we do. I guess you realize now that everyone I work with knows I'm married."

"Is that a problem?"

"Not in the slightest. There's only one problem, as far as I can see."

"And what's that?"

"I'm getting black and blue from the way I have to keep pinching myself."

He laughed, then said, "I love you, Laura Morrison."

"I love you too. Thanks for calling."

She ended the call and had to just stand there for a long moment and absorb the reality of her happiness. The very idea of ever having been depressed felt completely impossible.

* * * * *

Wade found that being married to Laura was the easiest thing he'd ever done. Perhaps it was the time they'd both spent on their own that had given them each such a deep gratitude for being together. Doing the simplest tasks, coming and going and coordinating their schedules, working together to care for Rebecca—it all seemed to be surrounded by some formless kind of magic.

They quickly worked out a schedule where they rotated grocery shopping, cooking, laundry, and getting Rebecca to and from her daycare with various loved ones. Jane took her three days a week. Elena's parents and her sister each took a day, wanting to maintain a close relationship with the child. And Wade's mother and other family members were available as backup. Wade and Laura made a point of spending some time with Alex and Jane regularly, and the four of them always had a marvelous time together. Wade also made a point of connecting with Barrett frequently, and a few weeks after the wedding, Barrett had a sleepover at Wade's new home. Wade could see that as his nephew and Laura spent time together, they were growing to care for each other.

Wade quickly made a habit of interrupting Laura in the kitchen, regardless of whatever she might be doing, long enough to escort her through a minute or two of waltzing her around the tiny floor, whether there was any music playing or not. It was something he'd seen Alex and Jane do frequently, and he'd often envied the spontaneous togetherness it seemed to bring into their relationship. They'd given Wade some dance lessons after he'd learned that Laura liked to dance and he'd wanted to impress her. Since Alex and Jane had come together through a ballroom dance team, they were certainly qualified teachers. At their suggestion, he and Laura had shared a waltz at their wedding luncheon, and now that they were husband and wife he loved impulsively dancing with her, no longer envying what Alex and Jane had shared, but reveling in his own happy marriage. Laura always laughed when they danced, and he loved surprising her with an unexpected turn or dip. And their dancing always ended with a kiss before they would go back to whatever they'd been doing.

They had some announcements printed that simply read: *Rebecca Elena Morrison is gleefully happy to announce the marriage of her father, Wade Moses Morrison, to Laura Isabelle Dove. The marriage was solemnized in the Salt Lake LDS Temple. No gifts are necessary. We have each other*. There was no date or any other information; it was simply the means to let friends, loved ones, and colleagues know that the marriage had taken place. A copy of a picture was included with each announcement. Laura had picked out what she considered the best pose of her and Wade sitting on the temple steps, with Rebecca on his lap. She had the same picture enlarged and framed, and when she hung it on the living room wall, she felt certain her home was perfect.

* * * * *

Laura couldn't help laughing when Rebecca picked up her bowl of spaghetti from the high chair tray and plopped it upside down on her head.

"Oh, that's marvelous," Wade said with sarcasm, but he couldn't keep from laughing too. "We shouldn't laugh," he added with forced sobriety. "We certainly don't want to encourage her."

"Sorry," Laura said, but she couldn't suppress another giggle.

Wade leaned over the table and kissed her before he said, "I think your spaghetti is marvelous, Mrs. Morrison, but I prefer to eat it, as opposed to wearing it." He stood up and shook his head as he looked at his daughter, who was grinning up at him. "Pathetic," he said.

"No, adorable," Laura said. "I bet her mother is looking down on her right now, thinking how adorable she is."

Wade glanced at Laura. *"Both* of her mothers."

Laura shrugged. "You have two fathers. Rebecca can certainly have two mothers."

"Lucky girl," Wade said and kissed her again.

"Lucky stepmother," Laura said and kissed him.

"Yeah," Wade chuckled. "Do you feel lucky enough to clean up the high chair while I give her a bath?"

"I did promise for better or worse, didn't I?"

"Yes, you did," Wade said and gingerly got as much spaghetti off the child as possible before he carried her at arm's length to the bathtub. He actually stood her in the tub before he stripped her down, and she was soon playing in the water and giggling up a storm.

Laura listened to the distant laughter and couldn't help smiling as she put the kitchen in order. The phone rang, and she reached for the cordless handset.

"Oh, hi," she said, hearing Rochelle's voice. Not so long ago she had dreaded her friend's calls, when hearing about her promiscuous life had only contributed to Laura's own depression. But now she felt confident enough in her own life that it actually felt good to hear from Rochelle.

"How are you?" Laura asked.

"I'm good," Rochelle said. "How are you?"

"I'm fantastic, if you must know. I'm cleaning spaghetti off of a high chair." She laughed.

"And you find this exciting, why?"

"Because it means I have a family."

"So, things are going well, I take it."

"Yes, very," Laura said, knowing there was a hidden agenda behind the question. Rochelle had shown up two days before the wedding, trying to talk Laura out of it, certain it was headed for disaster. Of course, Laura and Rochelle had witnessed a lot of disaster in marriage. But Laura had assured Rochelle that she knew what she was doing and that Wade was a good man. Since the wedding, Rochelle had called every week or so for a brief conversation. Laura had told Wade that she felt sure Rochelle was almost disappointed to hear regular evidence that Laura was happier than she'd ever been. She sensed that Rochelle would almost like to be proven right—even if it meant that Laura might be unhappy. It was a pleasure for Laura to say, "I never imagined that life could be so good."

"Well, I'm glad to hear it."

Rochelle went on to catch Laura up on her latest boyfriend, who was occasionally spending the night. Laura kept her mouth shut, knowing from experience that reminding Rochelle of the values she should be living would have no effect beyond creating an argument. Rochelle had a very good job with an accounting firm in Chicago, and her life was apparently great—at least from Rochelle's perspective. She was bringing in a lot of money, wearing designer clothes, living in an elegant downtown apartment—and partying with the wrong crowd. Laura could only listen to the regular updates and pray that when Rochelle fell she wouldn't fall as hard as Tina had. Of course, Tina had lived the gospel. She'd just married an abusive man who had eventually put her in the hospital, convinced a judge that Tina was delusional, and had taken custody of their son—all of which had contributed to her final decision to end her own life. Laura hoped that Rochelle could eventually find her way back, and the biggest reason she endured listening to the details of her friend's sordid life was the hope of keeping a bond between them that might give Rochelle something to hold onto when the inevitable crash came. Laura knew a person couldn't live that way forever and not feel the effects.

While Laura was listening, she went into the bathroom and leaned against the counter to watch Wade while he shampooed Rebecca's thick, dark hair—so much like her mother's. The baby giggled as Wade made a game of rinsing her hair.

"What's all the racket?" Rochelle asked.

"Oh, Wade's just washing the baby's hair. It's very entertaining."

"Whatever floats your boat," Rochelle said, and kept talking. Laura just listened, finding deep joy in the tender way that Wade wrapped his daughter in a big towel and fluffed the water out of her hair. He picked Rebecca up and gave Laura a warm kiss while she put a hand over the mouthpiece of the phone.

"I love you, Laura Morrison," he said.

"I love you too," she whispered and silently thanked God for sending Wade into her life before she'd resorted to following Rochelle's path—or Tina's.

* * * * *

Wade came home from a long day at the clinic and got Rebecca out of the car before they shared the ritual of getting the mail. He found a piece of junk mail she could carry into the house and color on, then he found a letter from his younger brother, Brian, who was serving a mission in England. He was currently living in London's inner city and loving every minute of it. They exchanged emails regularly, but those were usually brief and hurried, since Brian only had minimal time each week with access to a computer. But Brian had declared before leaving that he liked *real* mail, and he expected his loved ones to send a paper letter once in a while. And in return, he did the same. Wade loved the occasional letter that came from his little brother, but this was the first to arrive at his new home, and he couldn't help chuckling when he came across it.

Wade took Rebecca into the fenced-in backyard and let her play in the shade of the large, old trees there, while he sat on a little bench beneath one of them and read his brother's letter. The September air was pleasant and warm.

So, you're married again. Wow! That's great. I sure wish I could meet her. She must be amazing to have snagged a guy like you. I'm certain you'll be deliriously happy. He went on to tell about the investigators they were working with in the heart of London. The British people weren't very receptive, but they were working with immigrants from South America, Africa, Eastern Europe, and even Afghanistan. He talked of the cultural challenges and the ethnic food he'd been eating. *And I thought I'd be eating meat pies and figgy pudding,* he wrote. *I've yet to find out what figgy pudding is.* He wrote casually of the difficulties in the area, as if they were nothing. He told of getting off a bus because it was stuck in a traffic jam. While walking to their destination, they passed an area that had been taped off by the police because of a shooting in the streets. His point was to tell about the investigator they'd found in the crowd, but Wade couldn't help feeling unsettled. He reminded himself that he'd served a mission in Africa, and he'd been exposed to similar things, but it felt different hearing about it from Brian.

Brian went on to say, *Dad tells me that Mom is doing better. I'm glad to hear it. I've worried about her. It's nice to hear she's got the whole cancer thing behind her, and that she's doing better with the depression too. I hope she stays on top of that.*

Wade shared his brother's sentiments fully. Their mother had been through some rough times, both physically and emotionally, since Brian had left. Marilyn *was* doing better, for the most part anyway. He hoped it would continue.

Brian went on to write, *I want you to tell her something for me. It's very important. I've told her myself but I want it to come from you as well. You tell her that I know beyond any doubt that whatever trial might come into our lives, no matter how difficult or unfair it might seem, that God is mindful of us, that He holds us in the hollow of His hands. I know it, Wade. Tell her that no matter what happens, I will always love her and admire her for what a good woman she is, and for all that she taught me. Promise me that you'll tell her.*

"I promise," Wade said aloud to the letter.

As soon as he'd read it, he took Rebecca inside and went to the computer to send his brother an email. It simply said, *I got your letter. Thank you. I promise I'll tell her. More to come via real mail. I love you, and I'm proud of you.*

Wade then sat down and handwrote a lengthy letter, telling Brian about the changes in his own life, and how happy he was. Adding one of Rebecca's scribble drawings, he put it out in the box to be picked up the following morning. Then he called his mother in order to keep his promise. She cried when he read what Brian had written, but she was often emotional over such things. Sending her youngest child out on his mission had been difficult for her. But she was an amazing woman, and Wade admired her greatly. They shared small talk for a few minutes, and Wade told her he loved her before he hung up. A few minutes later, Laura came home with some groceries that he helped her carry in, once he'd given her a proper kiss in greeting. Oh, life was good!

Chapter Two

One night, after being married for a month, Wade asked Laura over supper, "Have you told your parents yet that you're married?"

She scowled at him. "No, and I don't want to."

"Don't you think they could be ticked off to find out you've been married a month and you never told them? The more time that passes, the more unhappy they could be."

Laura sighed and leaned back in her chair. Beyond a very rare phone call from one of her parents, she had practically no connection with her family at all, and she preferred it that way. Still, she had to admit, "You're probably right."

"Have you sent announcements to any of your relatives at all?"

"Not yet. I was just . . . going to give some to my parents and let them do it if there was anyone they wanted to tell."

"Okay, well . . . I should meet your family, don't you think?"

She moaned and threw her napkin to the table.

"What?" he asked lightly. "You're ashamed of me?"

"Hardly. It's the other way around, I can assure you."

"Laura, it's you I love, you I married. I just think you need to let your family know you're married, and I think it would be good if we met each other." He chuckled. "Surely they'll love Rebecca, even if they hate me."

"They won't hate you. They'll probably be smitten with you—but not for reasons you would likely appreciate."

"*What* reasons?"

"Oh, you're tall, good-looking, and you're going to be a doctor. My mother will probably flirt with you if she's been drinking. My father will treat you like some kind of god because you actually went to college. My siblings will fall into one of two distinct categories."

"Which are?"

"Well, my father always took a stand of self-righteousness, believing that since he didn't drink and swear like my mother, and he usually went to church, that his yelling and verbal abuse were justified and okay. My mother just took the course of being rebellious and proud of it. My siblings have, for the most part, fallen into one of those two categories. There are the ones who tell crude jokes, swear, and drink. And the others who are so boldly disgusted with them that they're always yelling their judgment and condemnation. On top of that, my nieces and nephews are all just totally out of control. And *you* want to *meet* them?"

"Yes, I do." He leaned toward her. "So, how about this? We'll take Rebecca, get a room in Vegas for two nights, make a little vacation out of it, and we'll offer to take all the *adults* out to dinner. We have the money my dad gave us for a wedding gift; that ought to about cover it. So we can meet somewhere public, where everyone is more likely to be on their best behavior. We'll visit over the meal, then hurry away, declaring that we have important plans—which of course, we will. And then you can stop dreading the inevitable. What do you say?"

Wade was relieved to see her smile. "I think I can live with that."

The following day Wade made reservations at a hotel in Las Vegas, where Laura was from, and she suggested a restaurant that was nice without being too tacky or too expensive. As soon as she got home from work she called and reserved a private room there. Then she realized that it would probably have been better to call her parents first and make certain someone could actually be there at that particular time. She debated whether it would be easier to call her parents with Wade there—or absent. Impulsively, she decided to hurry and make the call before he came home with Rebecca. But the phone was busy. She tried four times and only got a busy signal, then Wade came home, so she just started fixing dinner once he'd greeted her the way he always did—with a tender kiss and a glow in his eyes that made it clear his love for her was real and deep.

"Did you call them?" he asked, once she'd greeted Rebecca, who by then had run off to play in her room.

"I tried. It was busy."

Wade handed her the phone. "Try again. If they can't be there, we need to change the reservations."

"Okay," she said and punched in the number, hoping it would still be busy. But it rang, and her stomach tightened.

Wade leaned against the counter and folded his arms over his chest. The look on Laura's face made it clear she might prefer he leave the room, but he felt compelled to make sure she followed through. While he understood her reluctance, he also believed she needed to confront the issues that bothered her, rather than hiding from them.

"What if they're angry?" she asked with her hand over the phone while it was still ringing.

"Remember how you stood up to Rochelle when she thought you were making a mistake in marrying me?" he asked, taking her hand. "You can do this."

"Okay," she said, then into the phone, "Hi, Dad. It's me, Laura. I'm great. How are you?" She listened for a minute then said, "Well, that's good then. Is Mom sober? Well, that's good too. I've got some news. Why don't you put her on the other phone?" She whispered to Wade, "Okay. Here goes."

Wade kissed her hand and smiled at her, offering silent encouragement.

"Hi, Mom," Laura said into the phone. "How are you? Well, I'm great. Dad, are you there? Okay, well . . . I've been pretty busy. I'm sorry I didn't call sooner, but . . . I wanted you to know that I'm married." She listened for a minute, then said, "Well, it was kind of impulsive, but I'm absolutely certain it was the right thing. Yes, absolutely. I've never been happier." Again she listened, and Wade saw disgust come into her expression. "No, Mom, I'm not pregnant. We were married in the temple." Again she was silent, her expression growing more agitated. "Mom, listen to me. I don't need your approval, and I apologize if you're offended by not knowing sooner. I'm not going to argue with you. We're coming to Vegas this weekend, and we would like to treat all of the adults in the family to dinner, so that he can meet all of you. Consider it kind of a belated wedding dinner. Would Saturday evening work? Okay, well . . . can you let the others know?" She told them the restaurant and the time, then said, "Listen, Mom . . . Dad . . . I'm asking you to set aside all of that and just be happy for me. He's a good man. He wants to meet you. I'd like it to be a pleasant experience for everyone. Is that possible? Okay, thank you. His name is Wade. Wade Morrison. Yes, that makes me Laura Morrison. Yes, same address. He's moved in with me. He's going to school." She mouthed silently to Wade, *Here it comes; now they'll love you.* Wade just smiled at her, and she went on with her conversation. "He's going to medical school. Yes, that means he's going to be a doctor. Yes, Dad. He's certainly got a lot going for him."

"I've got *you,"* Wade whispered and made her smile.

"Well, he was married before," Laura continued. "His wife passed away. He has a two-year-old daughter; well, she's mine now too. She already calls me Mommy. She's adorable. Yes, we're bringing her too so you can meet her. Okay, great. We'll see you Saturday."

Laura hung up the phone as if it were contaminated.

"Very good," Wade said. "Now you don't have to dread *that* anymore."

"No, I just have to dread dinner on Saturday."

"Just think how lovely Sunday will be when it's over," Wade said and kissed her.

* * * * *

On Thursday Wade was given some news that felt almost eerie by its apparent coincidence, and perhaps a little bit frightening. He hoped it was more good than bad, but he wasn't quite sure how he felt about it. He was anxious to share the news with Alex, since it had more to do with him than anyone else. He called the ER at the U of U Medical Center where Alex worked, and was pleased that he was available to come straight to the phone, and that he was also overdue for a break.

After leaving the clinic, he phoned Laura to tell her he was stopping to see Alex at the hospital before he came home. She offered to pick Rebecca up from his mother's and told him she'd see him later.

Wade met Alex in the ER waiting room, and they walked a short distance to a Starbucks that was located in the hospital. It was open and spacious and a place where they commonly met, usually after purchasing soft drinks from a vending machine. They found an empty table in a far corner, and Alex said, "So, what's up?"

"I've just been given my next rotation assignment."

"Really?" Alex sounded amused. "What horrible thing do you have to face now?"

"Well . . . you know the one place a med student will never be able to avoid?"

Alex's eyes lit up. "You're doing an ER?"

"Yes, I am," Wade said. "Now your expertise can really help get me through . . . big brother. I'm doing *this* ER."

Their eyes met for a long, silent moment, almost reminding Wade of the first time they'd met. There they'd stood, face-to-face, each attempting to accept that they were brothers when they'd not known of the other's existence a minute earlier. The bond between them had been almost immediate, and all they had been through together since that time was only made more profound by how much they found they had in common, and how they understood each other so completely. Wade would never forget how he'd felt when he'd realized that Alex was a doctor. No one else in his family had ever shown any interest in medicine, but it was something he and Alex had spent endless hours talking about. The field Wade wanted to pursue was a long way from Alex's expertise of emergency medicine. Neither of them would have ever expected a coincidence such as this. But then, Wade didn't really believe in coincidence, and he knew Alex didn't either. There were a lot of hospitals around here, and even though not all of them were teaching hospitals; the likelihood of his doing an ER rotation in this one was something he just hadn't expected.

"Wow," Alex said, breaking the silence. "That's awesome."

"Is it?" Wade asked, needing to know how Alex *really* felt about it.

"Why wouldn't it be?"

"Do you really think we can still like each other if we have to work together?"

Alex chuckled. "Little brother, you and I can survive *anything!* Besides, there are a lot of doctors here. What are the chances that our paths will really cross that often? But I hope they do. I think we could do great things together."

Wade made a scoffing noise. "No, I could watch *you* do great things."

"You seem upset. Is there a problem with this?"

Wade sighed. "I think it's just the whole emergency medicine thing that scares me more than anything. It's no surprise to me that you can't get through medical school without being exposed to trauma, but I have to admit it's something I've dreaded facing."

"Then it's good to be able to face it and get it over with," Alex said. "But most of the time it's really not that bad."

"*Most* of the time?"

Alex sighed and folded his arms. "You know what? I think you need to just take it one day at a time, keep an open mind, and not worry about what you have to face until it's there."

"So, maybe it's a blessing that I get to work in *your* ER?"

"We'll see," Alex chuckled. "Maybe our paths won't cross at all."

"Yeah, we'll see."

"So," Alex changed the subject, "you're off to meet the new in-laws tomorrow? That should be an adventure. Is Laura still dreading it?"

"Excessively, yes. I keep telling her there's nothing they can say or do that will make any difference in how I feel about her, but she doesn't seem convinced."

"So, now you have a chance to prove it."

"Yes, I suppose I do."

They went on to talk of trivial things until Alex had to return to work, and Wade forced his mind to the pending trip to Vegas, deciding to cross the bridge into the ER when he came to it.

* * * * *

They left for Vegas on Friday just as soon as they both got off work, stopping in Cedar City for supper. Rebecca was difficult to keep entertained through the drive, full of two-year-old wiggles. But Laura was patient and calm with her while Wade drove. At one point he kissed her hand and said, "You are such a good mother."

"She's easy to love," Laura said, as if it were nothing.

"Yes," he agreed, "but she's still two. They call it terrible twos for a reason."

Laura looked at Rebecca and laughed. "It's all a matter of perspective. She's just got an overload in her little brain. It can't get information quickly enough to keep up with her desire to discover the world."

Wade glanced back at his daughter to see her trying to open the tube of hand cream Laura had given her to play with. He chuckled and said, "So that's it. I thought she was just trying to act like her father."

Rebecca became quiet and wide-eyed in her stroller as they went into the Excalibur Hotel. Wade had come here with Alex's family and their father and stepmother on vacation once. They had some wonderful food and great stuff for kids. They managed to avoid the casino area completely as they went up to their room and got settled in. The view from the window was amazing with the castle-like towers of the hotel, and beyond them a likeness of the skyscrapers of New York and the Statue of Liberty.

Rebecca slept relatively well for being away from home and her own bed. The following morning they had breakfast at the buffet in the hotel, then did some sightseeing and had lunch in the midst of their excursion. Laura remained relaxed and at ease until late afternoon; then she kept glancing at her watch, appearing anxious and concerned.

"Hey, it's going to be okay," Wade said, but she didn't seem convinced. Her nerves grew steadily more jangled as the hour for dinner approached. They arrived at the restaurant before anyone else, and the rest of the family all arrived together about five minutes later. Wade noted that Laura did well at appearing composed and indifferent as she introduced him to each member of her family, then they were seated and ordered their meals. Overall, Wade felt that the gathering was fairly successful. They all made a fuss over Rebecca, saying how cute she was, and teasing Laura about becoming an instant mother.

The family gave them a wedding gift, which was a nice set of bed sheets and several high-quality bath towels.

"We figured you could always use more of that kind of stuff," Laura's older sister said, "even though you've had a household for a long time."

"Thank you," Laura said. "That's true. They certainly do wear out."

"They're very nice," Wade said. "Thank you."

Laura's parents gave Rebecca a gift as well, which was a set of hardboard storybooks that she immediately became enthralled with. Laura's father seemed especially taken with the child and called himself grandpa when he talked to her.

Wade only heard one crude joke and a couple of mild cuss words. Laura's mother appeared to be sober—at least she was at the beginning of the meal. She ordered alcohol with her meal and drank it zealously.

Wade was asked many questions about his education and his goals, proving what Laura had warned him about. These things were obviously very important to Laura's father, and consequently to most of her siblings. Wade didn't feel the strong aversion to being with these people that Laura did, most likely because he had no personal experiences with them that had caused him any grief. Still, he couldn't deny being grateful that they lived out of state. They all lived very close to each other, obviously comfortable with being involved in each other's lives.

"So, how are your friends doing?" Laura's father asked, and Wade felt Laura go tense beside him.

He turned to see fear in her eyes, and he realized she hadn't told them about Tina. She looked at him with a silent plea, and he whispered, "Just say it and get it over with."

She nodded and cleared her throat, saying unsteadily, "Um . . . Rochelle is the same. Tina . . . died a couple of months ago."

Everyone at the table was stunned into silence. Laura's mother said with a slur in her voice, "Your best friend dies and you can't call and tell your mother?" Wade squeezed Laura's hand under the table.

"Sorry about that, Mom. I was pretty upset at the time."

Her father asked, "What happened?"

While everyone waited for the question to be answered, Wade saw Laura squeeze her eyes closed, and her hand began to tremble. He hurried to speak so she wouldn't have to. "I'm afraid it was suicide."

"That's horrible," a sister-in-law said; Wade couldn't keep track of their names.

"Yes, it is," Wade said, noting the relief in Laura's eyes that he was speaking for her.

"Well, I guess it's fire and brimstone for her, then," Laura's mother said.

Wade felt as startled as Laura looked. He was most surprised to see that everyone else at the table seemed silently resigned to agreeing with her. He was grateful for the personal study he'd once done on the issue. His own attempt at taking his life had prompted him to understand the ramifications spiritually and doctrinally, if only to find peace for himself.

"Actually," Wade said, and all eyes turned to him, including Laura's, "that's not necessarily the case. While suicide is technically considered a sin, Church leaders have made it clear that a person's state of mind is taken into consideration. A person whose mind is distorted due to . . . say . . . depression, or chemical imbalance, or physical pain, would be judged accordingly. Only God would know the state of mind and the motivations behind such an act. That's why the outcome is in His hands, not ours."

Wade noted that Laura's mother looked mildly angry, as if his challenging her didn't sit well. Everyone else looked intrigued. Laura's father simply said, "Well, I didn't know that." He added toward Laura, "That certainly adds some comfort now, doesn't it."

"Yes, it does," Laura said, looking at Wade as if he were some kind of knight in shining armor. He just smiled and kissed her hand, surprised at how quickly the topic went elsewhere, as if no one wanted to talk about something as uncomfortable as the self-inflicted death of one of Laura's best friends. But perhaps that was best.

They all stayed and chatted long after the meal was over, then good-byes were finally shared as they stood and hovered around the table. Most of them were appreciative toward Wade for the meal, and for making the effort to drive to Vegas to meet them. Laura's father lightly told Wade to take good care of his little girl, and her mother made an inappropriate comment about Wade and Laura being newlyweds, letting him know that she was definitely no longer sober.

Once they were back in the car, Laura immediately said, "I'm sorry about that."

"About what? I thought it went pretty well."

"I suppose . . . overall. But there were a few . . . awkward moments. That last comment from my mother was—"

"Disgusting, I know. But it has nothing to do with you or me, and we're going to let it roll off. We've made a genuine effort toward bridging international relations. Now we'll go home and remain politely in touch with them."

Laura heaved a long, deep sigh and took Wade's hand. "You are so good to me."

"Vice versa."

"You were great back there. You were kind and appropriate, no matter what they said. I hate to make comparisons, but . . . Randall treated them with a certain amount of contempt."

Wade tossed her a surprised glance. "I'm sure that only . . . what? Made them defensive?"

"Mostly, yes. Or just angry."

Wade felt the need to clarify one point. "I hope I didn't speak out of line . . . about Tina's death."

"On the contrary," she said, "you saved me. I couldn't have said it without falling apart. And the explanation you gave them—it was perfect. I knew all of that, but I couldn't have said it." She sighed and added, "I know I should have told them before now, but . . . I knew that's how they'd respond. And I just couldn't handle them telling me how Tina would inevitably rot in hell. My mother would probably call her a selfish coward if given the chance. Now they know, and I hope it never comes up again."

She kissed his cheek while he drove. "Thank you, Wade. I really am glad to have that over with. And you're right, it wasn't so bad. At least with you there, it wasn't."

He chuckled. "I think it was Rebecca who had them bewitched."

"Probably," Laura said, and turned to look at her in the backseat.

"Moozah, Mommy. Moozah," she said. She'd grown up with a father who listened to loud music in the car, and his favorite CDs were now her favorite as well.

Laura laughed and said, "Turn on the *Collective Soul,* Daddy. We must keep Her Majesty happy."

Wade stuck in the CD and turned up the volume, filling the car with a buoyant beat and jubilant lyrics. *Break the news out; I got to get out. Oh, I'm feeling better now . . . The world's done shaking me down.*

* * * * *

Wade's first shift in the ER was an all-nighter while Alex was home sleeping. He didn't see anything that felt too traumatic. The only death was an elderly man who was DOA from a stroke. After a few nights in the ER he was almost beginning to feel semi-comfortable being there, even if he hadn't adjusted to sleeping during the day. And he never felt like he got enough sleep. Alex reminded him that was the life of an ER doctor. It gave Wade some empathy for Alex and made him glad he'd chosen a field with more consistent hours. Treating kids with cancer would have its drawbacks, but emergencies wouldn't be the norm.

Following a couple of days off, Wade arrived at the hospital late in the afternoon to begin a twelve-hour shift. He'd only been there a minute when the ER administrator told him she was assigning him to one of their best doctors. "For the next few weeks, his shifts will be your shifts, and you can be his shadow. He's one of the best, so you can learn a lot. If it works out, you can probably stick with him through your entire rotation, however long that may be. I guess we'll see. You let me know how it's going."

"Okay," Wade said and followed her to the staff lounge. She pushed open the door and Wade couldn't believe it. There was only one person in the room, and it was his brother.

Alex was sitting at a table, reading from a patient's file. He didn't bother to look up, even when the administrator said, "Dr. Keane."

"Yeah," Alex said, still focused on the file.

"I'm giving you a student. Meet your new shadow."

Alex's eyes shot up, then they sparkled with amusement even though he managed to keep a straight face.

"This is Dr. Keane," the administrator said. "Doctor, this is Wade Morrison."

Alex stood and stepped forward, holding out a hand. "It's a pleasure, Wade," he said, shaking his hand firmly. Wade noted he didn't say exactly *what* was a pleasure. He felt a little bit like a mouse meeting the house cat. He had a feeling Alex was enjoying this very much.

"Indeed," Wade said, following his lead. "I've been told you're one of the best and that I can learn a lot from you. I'm looking forward to that."

The administrator hurried away as if she had a tight schedule. "I'm sure the two of you can figure out what to do from here. He's your baby now, Doctor. Try not to be too hard on him."

The door closed, and Alex laughed. "Now what makes her think I would be hard on you?"

"Maybe she sensed that sadistic glint in your eye," Wade said and chuckled. "I'm just afraid you're going to try and make up for all you missed out on by not growing up with the opportunity to torment a little brother."

"I hadn't thought about that," Alex said. "But now that you mention it . . ."

Wade glared at Alex, and he chuckled. "This is just too weird," Alex said, motioning for Wade to sit down as he took his seat again. "At this point I would ask you to tell me about yourself, but I don't think that's necessary."

"Probably not," Wade said, "but do you know what just occurred to me? What if this had happened independent of any other aspect of our lives; what if we were sitting here right now having no idea that we were brothers? *Or,*" he paused dramatically, "what if I knew my biological father had the last name Keane, but I'd never met him—or you. How weird would *that* be?"

Alex was somber as he said, "That would be pretty weird. But it makes me wonder if . . . well, sometimes I think that maybe God has a back-up plan. If we hadn't come together one way, he would have brought us together in another."

"Well, I shudder to think where I'd be now if you hadn't been holding me up these past few years. For the record, I'm glad it happened the way it did. And when it did."

"Me too," Alex said, "and maybe moments like this are just to remind us that God *does* have a back-up plan."

"So," Wade said, "are you ever going to tell her—or anybody else around here—that we're actually brothers?"

"Maybe," Alex said. "Maybe not. It's more fun this way." He chuckled. "Besides, not telling could prevent some people thinking we might have politicked this, or that I might give you undue favoritism. We'll just go with the flow."

"You're the boss," Wade said. "And for the record, I don't want you to treat me any differently than you would any other student. If you need to say something to me, say it."

"It doesn't work any other way around here," Alex said, "but I'm glad you understand that."

Through that first shift of following his brother around, Wade began to see a completely different side to Alex. He wasn't surprised with his efficiency, his knowledge, or his compassion. It was just different to see him in this environment that was so comfortable for him. To every patient who was conscious, Alex introduced himself and then said, "This is Wade. He's a medical student." Then he'd add something light like, "He's just here to learn; maybe we can give him something really exciting."

Alex diagnosed infected ears on a baby, then had Wade look inside the ears and see the evidence. He found enlarged lymph nodes and had Wade feel them as well. He looked at the results of X rays and a CT scan and meticulously pointed out what he saw on the film. Wade watched him stitch up a laceration on a forehead, and another on a hand, and he was present when an older lady came in with chest pain and then went into cardiac arrest. Alex brought her back to life as if it were nothing, then he went to the next exam room where a sixteen-year-old girl was enduring some extreme pain while her mother looked terrified. Alex asked questions, probed, and ordered tests. After seeing two other patients, Alex looked at the results of the tests and cursed under his breath. It wasn't the first time Wade had heard him swear, even though it was rare, and if Wade hadn't been standing right next to him he wouldn't have heard it. But he knew it was a good indication that something was wrong.

"What?" Wade asked quietly.

Alex just shook his head and spoke to the woman behind the desk, who wore an ID badge that read Sandy. "The girl in room three is going to need surgery, stat."

"I'm all over it," she said and picked up the phone.

Wade followed Alex into room three, certain he was about to get the answer to his question. He didn't know what was coming, but he knew Alex didn't like it. Once inside the room, Alex sat on the stool and wheeled it close to the girl's bedside. The mother was in a chair, holding her daughter's hand. Wade leaned against the door, trying to be invisible. He wondered if this girl had cancer or some other horrible disease. The very idea made him sick.

"Do you know what's wrong, Doctor?" the woman asked.

"I do," Alex said. "She has an obstruction in one of her fallopian tubes. It will have to be removed surgically. They're arranging that right now." Wade watched Alex look hard at the mother as he added, "It's commonly called a tubal pregnancy."

Alex's behavior over this now made perfect sense as the mother's eyes widened, and she gasped. "What are you saying, Doctor?"

"I'm saying that your daughter is pregnant, Mrs. Webb."

The mother turned horrified eyes toward her daughter, who looked shamefully away. She then looked back at Alex as he went on. "The embryo did not attach in the uterus as it should have; instead it attached in the tube, and therefore it must be removed. It's a relatively simple operation. I'll be turning you over to a surgeon who can answer your questions about that."

Alex stood up to leave, and the mother stood as well. "Could I talk to you alone for a minute, Doctor?"

"Of course," Alex said in a voice that Wade recognized as a diplomatic mask for preferring a root canal over such a conversation.

They all stepped into the hall, leaving the girl alone in the room. Mrs. Webb looked more angry than concerned as she said in a low voice, "There must be a mistake, Doctor. She's a good girl. She just wouldn't do something like this."

"Mrs. Webb, I can assure you there is no mistake," Alex said gently. "I know this must be a shock to you, but—"

"Maybe the obstruction is something else," she said, crying now.

"Mrs. Webb," Alex said with firm patience, "the blood work showed positive for pregnancy. There is no mistake."

Mrs. Webb's tears increased, and Wade caught a discreet glance from Alex that let him know how difficult this was. Alex waited a moment, then said, "I know this is hard for you, Mrs. Webb, but—"

"I don't know what to do," she muttered, then looked up at Alex as if he should have the answer. "Tell me what to do."

"I'm just the doctor here and—"

"If it were your daughter?" the woman asked, her eyes pleading.

Alex sighed. "If it were my daughter, I would want her to know above all else that I love her no matter what. If it were my daughter, I would try to remember that anger and disgust would only drive her further away, and I would try to focus on the fact that if a kid ever needed love and understanding, it would be now. That's my opinion; you have to do what you feel is best."

Wade saw Mrs. Webb's countenance soften, and she took a deep breath as if to sustain her own emotions. "Thank you, Doctor," she said and went back into the room.

As soon as the door closed, Alex let out a loud sigh. "Very good, Doctor," Wade said quietly, and Alex almost looked startled.

He spoke as if Wade were nothing more or less than a student under his tutelage. "It's not my job to offer beliefs or opinions. If I'm asked, I try to trust my instincts and say what's appropriate, making it clear that it's *my* opinion. You find a lot of spiritual and emotional trauma as well as physical trauma in a place like this. Unfortunately, we can't do a whole lot for those aspects of the job. We can try when it's appropriate, but for the most part we have to stick to medicine and facts."

"But some appropriate compassion and a bedside manner can go a long way, can they not?" Wade asked.

"Yes, they can," Alex said with eyes that were almost hard, "but there's a fine line there, and nothing but experience can teach you where and how to draw it. Sometimes you have to draw it wrong before you figure out how to do it right."

"What are you saying?" Wade asked, sensing something deeper.

"Don't get emotionally involved; don't think you can fix the broken hearts and shattered spirits, or it will *kill* you. No matter how tempted you are to wonder how that girl is doing and what the outcome might be for her emotionally, just push it away and move on."

Wade sighed again, saying with sarcasm, "I'm already loving the ER."

Alex looked hard into Wade's eyes. His voice became gravelly, almost angry as he said, "This is nothing, kid. You have not yet begun to see the casualties of medical horror. And if you can't handle it, you'd better consider delivering babies or something. You tell me you know you're destined to practice pediatric oncology. That will make you the man who has to tell people that their innocent children are going to suffer and die for reasons that you can never explain to them. Appropriate compassion and a good bedside manner are important, but don't go deluding yourself into thinking that you can fix the broken hearts."

Alex walked away as if he feared that some level of anger might overtake him otherwise. Wade watched him go, wondering about the scenes Alex had encountered that might be classified as medical horrors—both personally and professionally. Nearly losing his son to leukemia was a sore point; Wade knew that. But obviously there was more. Still, Alex knew what he was talking about. He'd been there, and he wouldn't say such things if he weren't trying to help.

Wade hurried into the men's room to splash cold water on his face and try to accept that everything he'd just been told was true. He wondered how he might have taken it from some doctor he'd just met, as opposed to his brother, who just *happened* to be the doctor guiding him through the ugly side of a medical career.

He forced his mind to focus on the moment, and to let go of the emotional aspects of a promiscuous teenager and her concerned mother. Then he found Alex signing paperwork at the central desk.

"You okay?" Alex asked without looking up.

"I'm fine," Wade said.

"Sorry if I was too hard on you," Alex said, tossing him a brief glance.

Wade looked the other way. "I'm here to be educated. I guess that entails *every* aspect of the job. It's not exactly like becoming an accountant or a computer programmer."

"No, it's not," Alex said, now giving Wade his full attention. "But when it's in your blood you just know it's what you're supposed to be doing, and that's what gets you through the day." He put a hand on Wade's shoulder. "Come on, I'll buy you some lunch."

Wade glanced at his watch. "I think that's more like a late dinner."

"Whatever. It's in the middle of a shift. It's lunch."

Wade was relieved to be talking only to his brother while they shared a meal in the cafeteria, and he was pleased that nothing about medicine came up at all. Then Alex got paged, and they had to hurry back so that he could assist with three victims from a car accident. Alex insisted that Wade put on the sterile gloves, mask, and gown that went over the hospital scrubs he was wearing. A minute later Alex had Wade applying pressure over a bleeding wound until other, more serious problems were under control.

After the other two accident victims had been sent to other areas of the hospital for extended care and observation, Alex said to Wade, "Okay, you get to stitch that up."

Wade felt his eyes go wide. He'd observed stitches more times than he could count, but he wasn't sure he felt ready to do it on a real person, especially on a laceration that was deep and slightly jagged. As if Alex had read his mind, he said, "The patient is unconscious, and beyond him there's no one else in here. Better to learn on someone who's not watching. Get to it. You know what to do."

Alex sat close by and guided him, making an occasional suggestion and showing perfect patience with Wade's slowness.

"Very good," Alex said when Wade had finished. And he seemed to mean it. For the first time since he'd begun his education, more than seven years ago, Wade almost felt like a doctor.

"I learned from the best," Wade said and stripped off the bloodied gloves, pausing long enough to point out the scar on his wrist from a self-inflicted wound that Alex had once stitched up.

"Such tender memories," Alex said facetiously, and they moved on to a woman with pneumonia who they sent to the ICU. Then Alex alleviated a debilitating migraine, and sent someone to an emergency surgery for a hemorrhaging uterus. Wade was longing for the shift to end if only to let his brain catch up with everything he'd seen and felt since it had begun. And then Alex had to treat a rape victim, and Wade felt like something inside him would implode as the physical evidence was assessed so that charges could be pressed. It was his first exposure to the ER connection with the police department. Then he watched Dr. Alex Keane sit at the bedside of this woman, who was clearly crumbling and in shock, and tell her in a gentle voice that this was not her fault, that she should never let it keep her from living a good life, and she should do everything in her power to do just that, if only to prove to whoever had done this that she would not let him win by allowing herself to become a victim. He told her that before she left, someone would give her some information to guide her in getting the help she needed to get past this. The woman thanked Alex with tears in her eyes, and Wade followed him out of the room. He wanted to compliment Alex on his "appropriate compassion and good bedside manner," but he just gave him a warm smile instead and was glad to have the shift end.

"I guess you can go now," Alex said to him. "I need to sign off a couple of things first."

"Okay," Wade said. "Thank you . . . for a very educational experience."

"You're doing great, kid," Alex said.

Wade just forced another smile and hurried home.

Chapter Three

Wade arrived at the house in the middle of the night and tried to be as quiet as possible while he heated up the dinner Laura had left for him. He felt as exhausted emotionally as he did physically, with so many thoughts rolling around in his head that he just wanted his brain to shut down completely for a while. He was rinsing off his plate at the sink when he heard Laura say, "Good morning, Doctor."

"Not yet, I'm not," he said, wishing it hadn't sounded so terse.

"Bad shift?" she asked, moving closer.

"Yes and no," he said, and she lifted her lips to his, at the same time wrapping her arms around him. "Ooh," he said, holding her tightly, "I think it's all better now. I should say I'm sorry if I woke you, but it's really good to see you."

"I never sleep as well when you're not here," she said, and kissed him again.

"Now that I'm here you'd better get what sleep you can, because you have to go to work in a few hours."

She flipped off the kitchen light, and he followed her down the hall, where he had to slip into Rebecca's room and watch her for a long moment while she slept. He couldn't sleep without knowing that all was well with her.

He found Laura still at his side and whispered, "Was she a good girl this evening?"

"An angel, as always," she said with a smile.

"You only say that because you are a very patient mother," he said, and she just smiled again.

A few minutes later, Wade slipped beneath the covers, and Laura settled her head against his shoulder. Just having her in his life made everything easier, and he told her so before he kissed her once more and drifted to sleep. He became vaguely aware of some noise in the house when she got up to get ready for work, then he drifted off again until Rebecca bounced onto the bed, all dressed and ready to go spend the day with her Aunt Jane. He hugged her and talked to her for a few minutes before Laura came to kiss him good-bye, and they both left for the day. He quickly went back to sleep and woke up to an alarm. He hurried to shower and get dressed, then he met Laura on her late lunch break so that they could see each other before he did a few errands and went to the hospital to begin another shift.

The next couple of days didn't feel quite so strained for Wade. He truly enjoyed the opportunity to see his brother work, and couldn't deny that he was learning a great deal. Wade had followed other doctors around through his previous rotations, but Alex was very good at explaining what he was doing and why, and Wade liked the way he was warm and personable with the patients—even if he did have to cut himself off emotionally once an episode was over.

Wade got to know a number of the other staff members. With the way that shifts changed and crossed, he barely met some, and others he got to know a bit better. He felt certain that the more time he spent there, the more comfortable he would become with the many people who worked there. Most of them were good people, clearly gifted in their professions. There were the people who manned the central desk, coordinating every detail with amazing efficiency; and there were the nurses who often left Wade in awe by their ability to be tender with an emotional patient one minute, and effectively assist with a gruesome trauma the next.

And there were the other doctors, some of whom were more pleasant to work with than others. It was relatively easy to tell who was LDS and who wasn't, but even the ones who weren't often joked about Mormon culture, well aware that they were in the center of the Mormon capital of the world. But there was a general attitude of respect, and Wade liked the atmosphere.

Wade was thrilled with a few days off and the opportunity to have a normal schedule for a while. Following a three-day break, Alex would be doing a stretch of four six-to-six day shifts, and Wade would continue to be his shadow.

Once they'd both caught up on their sleep a little, Alex called to say that he and Jane wanted to take them out for a nice dinner—just for fun and to get away from the kids. Alex had arranged for their father and stepmother to watch all of the children. Neil and Roxanne loved being with the kids and were looking forward to it.

When Wade mentioned it to Laura she was thrilled with the opportunity. Alex's favorite restaurant was up the canyon, which was beautiful this time of year with the fall colors coming on. They both felt sure it would be a delightful evening and a nice break from the normal routine.

On the specified evening, Wade had expected Alex and Jane to be waiting for them, since they were a little late, but instead they found Alex talking quietly with Barrett, who had come home from a neighbor's house upset over a tiff he'd had with a friend. And Jane was cleaning up the Kool-Aid that Katharine had attempted to pour herself from a pitcher that had been way too full for a child to handle. Neil and Roxanne hadn't arrived yet. They'd called from a cell phone to say they were in some heavy traffic.

By the time they actually left the house, with Alex driving, they were more than forty minutes behind their intended schedule, but Alex called the restaurant from his cell phone to adjust their reservations, and they all relaxed, visiting comfortably and enjoying the drive up the canyon.

Alex felt mildly concerned when he realized that some distance ahead, beyond the car in front of them, a truck was in their lane, attempting to pass another vehicle. His concern heightened when it became evident there was no way the truck would make it in time to miss an oncoming vehicle. Adrenaline pumped through his veins as he backed off, praying the car in front of him would do the same, but then there wasn't a whole lot of leeway on this road. Seconds became eternal as he waited for someone to swerve to the shoulder or *something,* anything to prevent the oncoming horror. He was vaguely aware that the others in the car were talking, oblivious to the problem until he had no choice but to screech the car to a halt. He heard himself swear.

Laura heard Jane scream at the same moment she did. For a moment she felt certain they were doomed. Instead they just watched in stunned horror as the head-on collision occurred a short distance ahead. The truck that had been in the wrong lane hit the car in front of them, mostly on the driver's side, and almost went up over the top of it before it flipped and rolled more than once. She was grateful to realize that Alex had been alert enough to prevent them from becoming a part of the accident. A stark silence followed the collision while they all seemed to be assessing that they had come to a safe stop and that they were only witnesses, not victims.

The silence was broken by Alex saying calmly, "Jane, call 911. Wade, you're with me."

The men were both out of the car and running in an instant. Laura turned to see Jane's hands shaking as she pushed the buttons on the cell phone. She listened to Jane giving the report with a trembling voice, then it took Laura a minute to remember that she was a nurse and she should be using her skills in the midst of such a crisis.

Alex approached the car first, perhaps thinking he was more likely to find someone alive in that vehicle. As he came closer, the sound of an infant screaming was a good indication of that. A glance at the adults in the front seat let him know it was bad, but he had no trouble opening the back door on the passenger side to find a baby, dressed in boy's clothing, wailing with terror. Alex was quickly able to tell that the baby wasn't hurt at all before he got back out and said to Wade, "He's okay. Get him out and take him to Jane." He was grateful for a good excuse to keep Jane from seeing any of this. But he looked up to see Laura on the other side of the car, checking the pulse of the woman who had gone halfway through the windshield and was laying chest-down over the hood of the car. Alex came around the car to see that the woman was conscious and looking at Laura, clearly in shock. He did a quick visual assessment of what the damage might be and immediately knew nothing could be done without an extrication team to get her out of the car, and by then it would likely be too late. The pool of blood in the car, mostly coming from her midsection, was quickly growing bigger. He saw Laura notice it, and her eyes went wide with panic.

Laura realized how bad the situation was and felt sick. She was a nurse, and she'd survived some pretty gross stuff to become one, but she'd never before seen anything like this. But Alex was a trauma physician. She turned to meet his calm demeanor that didn't cover the alarm in his eyes.

"What can I do?" she asked him quietly.

He motioned her a little farther away from the woman and whispered firmly, "Talk to her. Tell her help is on the way. Don't lie to her, but don't say anything that doesn't have to be said. Hold her hand. Stay calm and positive. Do you understand?"

Laura nodded and wondered if he'd read her mind—or her eyes—when he added sternly, "You can cry later."

"She's going to die, isn't she?"

"Yes," he said and hurried to the other side of the car where Wade was prying the door open with a piece of a tire jack. He got it open, and Alex knelt beside the man, who was unconscious, and started a thorough check of his condition. He had a couple of head lacerations that were bleeding a great deal, but they were probably not serious. Judging from the way his seat hadn't been damaged but the window had, he guessed the guy probably had a concussion, but the spine was likely okay. He was thinking that beyond the obvious, he might only have a broken bone or two. Then he got a look at his left arm. It had apparently gone through the windshield, perhaps in an attempt to keep his wife from going through it. He shouted at Wade, "Get me a rag, a shirt, anything I can use for a compress. Now!" Five seconds later a disposable diaper was slapped into his hand. "Very good," he said with some exaggerated glee, if only to keep himself from screaming. But the diaper was perfect. He opened it and pressed it around the gash in the man's arm, saying to Wade. "You get your hand over that, right on top of the laceration. Hold it with all the strength you've got, and keep his arm elevated. Otherwise he could bleed to death in minutes. Do you understand?"

"Yes," Wade said, and they traded places so that Wade could lean into the car over the top of the unconscious man.

"I'm going to check the other vehicle."

Jane stood a safe distance away and held the crying baby close, wishing that she could stop shaking. She saw several cars slow down while their occupants stared, then they hurried on. Only one other vehicle stopped to help, and Jane was approached by an older couple who asked her what they could do.

"I've called for help, and my husband's an ER physician," she said, nodding in the direction of the accident.

"That's certainly a blessing," the gentleman said.

"Yes, I'm sure it is," Jane agreed, watching her husband, grateful and amazed. "I'm sure he'll let us know if he needs any more hands. It might be better if we keep our distance."

The woman took a turn at holding the baby, who calmed down somewhat, and Jane was grateful for their calm assistance, if not their company. They talked quietly, and Jane told them everything she knew about the accident and her family members who were on the scene.

Laura fought back her own emotions as she eased close to the woman who had gone through the windshield and took hold of her hand. She was desperately wondering what to say when Alex appeared again at her side.

"Hi," he said with a smile and pressed a gentle hand over the patient's head. "I'm Dr. Keane. I'm an emergency physician. We were right behind you. What's your name?"

"Megan," she said weakly, while Laura felt awed by his calm ability to handle this so well.

"Okay, Megan," he said gently, as if they had all the time in the world. "Are you in any pain?"

"No, not really."

"That's good. I want you to know that your son is fine. He didn't get so much as a scratch. Your husband has some injuries, but he's going to be just fine. My brother is with him, and he's a medical student. This is Laura, his wife. She's a nurse, and she's going to help keep you comfortable until an ambulance gets here, and they'll take care of you. Do you understand?"

"Yes," Megan said and gave a weak smile. "It's my lucky day, eh? Who gets in an accident with all this medical help right behind them?"

"Yes," Alex said, as if he completely agreed with her, "it's your lucky day. You just relax and try not to worry. We'll do everything we possibly can, and help is on the way."

Laura was amazed to hear how he didn't lie to her, but his words were soothing and full of comfort. It seemed he was well versed in helping a person die without fear and hysteria.

Alex gave Laura a firm gaze as if to repeat his earlier instructions, then he hurried away.

"You're married?" Megan asked, her eyes focused on the wedding ring on Laura's hand that was holding Megan's hand. Laura was grateful for something to talk about.

"Yes, just a little more than a month ago." For the sake of conversation she went on to say, "My husband has a beautiful little girl named Rebecca; she's two. Now I get to be a mother as well as a wife."

"What happened to . . . her mother?" Megan asked, her strength waning visibly.

Laura swallowed hard and regretted the course of the conversation when she had to say, "She died unexpectedly."

Megan murmured in little more than a whisper, "Maybe . . . your husband . . . can help mine." Laura knew then that Megan realized she was dying, and it took everything she had to keep from sobbing and screaming. She noticed a CTR ring on the woman's hand and knew she was LDS, likely married in the temple.

"Tell him . . . I love him," Megan said and closed her eyes.

Laura frantically searched for signs of life and could hear Megan's ragged breathing. "I will," she said gently, while inside she felt hysterical. And then she just talked about nonsensical, trivial things, aware from subtle changes in Megan's expression that she was listening. All the while, Laura prayed inwardly that some miracle would keep this woman from dying.

Alex hurried to where the truck had landed after rolling a couple of times. He found two men inside, and he didn't even have to check to see if they were dead. He knew they were. But he checked anyway. He had to admit he was glad that someone like him, who had been exposed to such trauma thousands of times, had come upon the scene, and not some tenderhearted person who had never been exposed to the horrors of head-on collisions. Habitually he looked at his watch and stated the time out loud, even though no one was there to hear it. He was walking away from the truck when he looked up to see Jane approaching him. He glanced past her to realize that someone else who had stopped was holding the baby.

"What can I do?" she asked.

"Nothing," he said. She looked confused, and he added, "Wade is doing very well at saving the only life that can be saved."

Jane glanced to where Laura was talking to the woman on the hood of the car, then back to Alex, her eyes wide with horror. Realizing she needed a task, he said gently, "You keep the bystanders calm and at a safe distance. Okay? No one needs to see this close up."

"Okay," she said and hurried back to where a small crowd was gathering, since other cars had now stopped.

Alex checked on Wade's patient, pleased to see that the bleeding in his arm had slowed significantly. "You want me to take over?" he asked, putting the compress back in place.

"No, I'm fine," Wade said, pressing his hand back where it had been before Alex had checked the wound. Looking at the blood in the car that had come out of this guy's arm, Wade said, "Now I know why you said that I didn't do a very good job cutting my wrist if I wanted to die."

Alex called on his skill of trying to behave normally when people were dead and dying and there was nothing you could do. "Yeah," he said nonchalantly, "it's amazing how that heart can just pump blood all over the place when it has an outlet. Maybe you could get some extra credit."

Wade wasn't amused. "What about the others . . . in the truck?"

"They're dead." He couldn't keep the anger out of his voice as he added, "Lucky for them."

"Why is that?"

"The beer cans and the aroma in the truck are a pretty good indication of the reason for their lack of judgment." He glanced at the unconscious man. "You may have just made a new friend; this guy could probably use some support on what it's like to be left alone to raise a child. But at least in your case, there was no one to be angry with."

Wade gained a quick lesson in perspective as he grasped what Alex was saying. He thought of the grief he'd dealt with in losing Elena, and wondered how he ever could have coped if it had been something like this, where someone else's negligence and irresponsibility had caused the death. He couldn't even imagine!

Laura watched Megan take her last breath, then she found it difficult to breathe. She told herself she should let go of her hand, that she needed to ease away, get some distance, but she couldn't move. Her next awareness was seeing Alex's fingers against Megan's throat, and then his gentle words, "She's gone, Laura. There was nothing we could do."

"I know," she murmured. "I just . . . need a minute."

"Okay," he said, and left her with Megan before he found Jane sitting in the backseat of their car with the motherless child. He told the people gathering that everything was under control and they should leave. Most of them did. Others hovered, but at more of a distance. It was easy to figure who was genuinely concerned, and who just wanted a glimpse of the gore. He got in the backseat of the car with Jane and the child, taking notice of a diaper bag that had obviously come with him. Jane was feeding him a bottle and said with a quavering voice, "At least there was formula . . . this time." He met her eyes and knew she couldn't help recalling when Wade had lost Elena, and Rebecca had been accustomed to nursing. He realized he couldn't comment on that right now.

"Do we know his name?" Alex asked.

"Andrew," Jane said, her voice trembling. "It's embroidered on the corner of the blanket." He could tell she was choking on emotion as she added in a whisper, "And he's lost his mother."

"Yeah."

"Wasn't there anything that could be done for her?"

"Jane," he said gently, knowing she expected an explanation, but not wanting to be gruesome. "The injuries were too severe. She was bleeding profusely. Even if I'd had her in the ER, I don't think I could have saved her."

"And the father?" she asked, crying now.

"He's going to be fine."

They heard sirens approaching, and Alex got out of the car. He quickly assessed that Wade's patient was still the same, then he approached Laura, who looked up at him, clearly on the verge of completely falling apart. He tried to take her hand out of Megan's but had to pry her fingers open. Then she grabbed onto him and started to sob. "It's okay," he muttered and guided her around the car, saying quietly to Wade, "Trade me places, little brother." Wade hurried to take hold of Laura and guided her away from the scene as the ambulance and rescue vehicles arrived. Alex quickly assessed the bleeding and put the compress back in place. He found a strong pulse in the neck with his other hand and waited for the paramedics to approach. He was glad to realize he knew one of them, which meant he had less to explain. He was also relieved to know the patient would be going to the U of U. He made eye contact with the paramedics, but no greetings were exchanged before Alex said, "The two in the truck died on impact. The woman in the driver's seat died a few minutes ago." He then explained the apparent injuries of the man and what they'd done with the arm.

"Good thing it was you, Doc," the paramedic said.

Alex just said, "I'll see you at the hospital."

The extrication team set quickly to work to pull the car apart in order to get the patient and the body removed, but it was evident it would take a while. Alex spoke with the police about what he'd seen, and what he'd done, then he got little Andrew from Jane and turned him over to them. By then they almost had Andrew's father out of the car. Alex was glad to know he was still unconscious and wouldn't have to see his wife like that.

Alex found Jane waiting in the front seat of the car, and Wade and Laura in the back. The women were crying. He got in and started the car, pulling quickly out onto the road and driving back down the canyon. He speed-dialed the ER on his cell phone.

Laura wondered who on earth Alex might be calling, and why he seemed in such a hurry. Then she heard him say, "Hey, this is Dr. Keane. You got somebody close by who's in charge that isn't busy? Thanks." He was silent a long moment. "Hey, Myers. I'm glad it's you. I was just on the scene of an accident in the canyon. They're bringing this guy in, and I'd like to work on him. So far, I'm ahead of the ambulance. Okay, thanks. I've got Wade Morrison with me, my medical student. Why? Because we were taking our wives out to dinner. And I want him there when this guy comes around." Alex paused. "Because they've both lost a wife. Yeah, I owe you one. See you soon."

He hung up the phone and handed it to Jane. All was silent for a few minutes until she said, "We were supposed to be there, weren't we." Alex just glanced at her, and she added, "If it was this woman's time to go, then God knew this guy would need someone like Wade, who has been there."

"That's the least of it, Jane," Wade said, and she turned to look at him with the same expectation Laura was feeling.

"What do you mean?" Laura asked.

"That guy would be dead right now if somebody hadn't found him who knew what to do."

"You saved his life," Jane said to Alex.

Alex didn't take his eyes from the road, didn't change his expression. "It doesn't take a rocket scientist to put pressure on a bleeding wound and get it higher than the heart."

"No, it doesn't take a rocket scientist," Jane said. "It takes a doctor. Some people might know that kind of logic, but most wouldn't. And if you hadn't been there, Andrew would be an orphan."

Alex sounded almost angry as he said, "I'm glad the guy is going to live, but don't go making me out to be some kind of hero or something. I did what I do. I couldn't do a blasted thing for the guy's wife. And somebody's got to tell him what happened when he wakes up."

"You volunteered for that," Jane said. "You could have left it to somebody else this time."

"Yes, I volunteered. Just because you know you need to do something doesn't make it easy."

"How do you know you need to do it?" Jane asked.

"I just know." His voice softened, and Laura saw him take Jane's hand and kiss it. "The same way I knew the first time I saw you that I wanted you to be the one by my side for the rest of my life, keeping my head on straight."

They exchanged a wan smile, and he kissed her hand again. Laura turned to see Wade looking at her in the same way. He kissed her hand too, then said, "How come you're so ticked off, big brother?"

Alex let out a humorless chuckle. "So now you're going to get all analytical and make me talk about my feelings? Is that it?" There was a hint of humor in his voice that kept the question from sounding too harsh.

"You bet I am. I learned it from you. What are brothers for?"

Alex sighed loudly. "I'm angry because some idiot who had too much to drink just left a man without a wife, and a baby without a mother."

Laura felt compelled to say, "Okay, but . . . I believe it's possible that a righteous person is not taken before her time. Megan was obviously a good person. She knew she was going to die, and she was at peace. If it hadn't been a drunk driver, it could have been something else. Perhaps if it hadn't been her time to go, she would have been protected."

"You might possibly be right," Alex said. "I try to remind myself of that, but it's hard to keep perspective sometimes when it's in your face. I believe it's also possible that the wrongful actions of others can cause the untimely death of an innocent person whose time to die has not necessarily come."

"I'm sure that is sometimes the case," Laura said gently. Silence followed until she added, "Maybe there's a lonely woman somewhere, wondering if she'll ever find a good man, and God's been keeping her for Andrew's father."

Wade looked at Laura abruptly, feeling the concept settle into his heart. He hugged her tightly while Alex said, "Okay, you got me there. That's perspective if I've ever heard it."

Alex was grateful to hit every light green once they got into the city. They were only a couple of blocks from the hospital when a siren approached behind them, and Alex pulled over for the ambulance to pass. He pulled up in front of the ER just as the patient was being removed.

"Okay, you ladies just go home. We'll call when we need a ride."

"No, we're staying here," Jane said.

Alex gave her a brief glare and said, "Okay, but . . . go get something in the cafeteria. It'll be a while."

Alex and Wade rushed into the ER. A paramedic who had been on the scene passed by them and said to Alex, "His name is Cole."

"Thanks," Alex said, and they hurried into the trauma room where Cole had just been brought. Wade knew that Alex always preferred knowing a patient's name, which made the fight more personal. The paramedics could have gotten the name off the car registration, or from a wallet.

Wade felt deeply grateful for the circumstances that allowed him to be here at Alex's side, actually participating in the assessment of this man's injuries and repairing them. He felt comfortable with the routine, but in this case, he felt some personal investment. Once the bleeding was under control, Cole was sent to radiology to determine the extent of internal injuries. Alex looked at the results and determined that Cole had a broken leg, which would not require any surgery, and a mild concussion. Everything else appeared to be in order, but he would be hospitalized for observation for at least twenty-four hours.

Cole was taken to a room upstairs, and Wade and Alex went with him. Alex insisted that Wade go get something to eat, and then he could sit with Cole while Alex did the same. Wade did as he was told, aware of his stomach rumbling but feeling no appetite. He felt more than a little sick as memories of losing Elena left him anticipating this man's reaction to the news that awaited him. If that weren't bad enough, the baby crying in the car had heightened the reality of those memories. Rebecca had been little more than two weeks old when her mother didn't wake up to feed her. How could he ever forget the baby screaming in the room while he'd tried to accept that his wife was dead? Laura had filled the emptiness left by Elena's death, but there were just some moments in a person's life that would forever be tough to swallow. And one of the worst had just been dredged to the surface.

Wade returned to the room and waited with Cole while Alex got something to eat. He guessed that Cole was near his own age, with hair that was darker than his own and lighter than Alex's. And the two of them shared an unmistakable bond. While his thoughts rolled, the memories of his own loss became more clear. He wondered what he would say to this guy and felt downright panicked. His breathing became sharp, and a tight pain gathered in his chest. He started to see spots and put his head down abruptly.

"What's wrong?" Alex demanded, coming into the room.

"I . . . don't know. I . . . I . . . can't breathe."

"It's panic," Alex said gently. "Come on, breathe. Just take a deep breath." He talked Wade through it until he was breathing evenly and the pain in his chest had let up.

"Talk to me," Alex said, and Wade let his thoughts spill while his hands shook.

When he'd said it all, he concluded, "I'm supposed to be strong and help this guy through? Look at me. I'm a wreck. No pun intended."

"A very poor pun at the moment," Alex said. "I'll do the talking. Just be here and go with the flow, okay?"

"Okay," Wade said, and they waited in silence.

When Cole finally came around, he looked disoriented at first, then his look became panicked. Alex put a hand on his arm and looked at him closely. "Hey," he said gently, "I'm Dr. Keane. I was driving the car right behind you when the accident happened. Do you remember the accident?"

"Yeah," he said. "Megan, the baby . . ."

"Stay calm, Cole. It's Cole, isn't it?" Cole nodded slightly. Alex went on, speaking in a calm, even tone. "I've been where you are right now, and I know you're scared and needing some questions answered." Wade had almost forgotten that Alex had once been in a car accident, and Jane had been in a coma for many weeks afterward. Cole was getting some much-needed empathy from several sources.

"I'm going to do my best to answer them for you, okay?" Alex said. "But I need you to try to stay calm." Cole nodded again, somewhat gingerly, no doubt due to pain from head injuries. "You have a mild concussion and a broken leg, but it's not serious. You're going to be fine, but you need to take it easy. You had a pretty nasty cut on your arm, and you lost a lot of blood." He glanced at the bag of blood that was feeding into the IV, then back at Cole. "Your son is fine. He didn't get a scratch. The police contacted your bishop, and the baby is with his family for the time being."

"Okay," Cole said, showing visible relief.

"Your parents have also been contacted, as well as your wife's. They're on their way from out of state and will probably all arrive tomorrow sometime. Okay?"

"Okay," Cole said again, then a moment of silence brought a question to his eyes before he asked with a tremor in his voice, "Where's Megan?"

Wade noted Alex moving his hand to take hold of Cole's before he said with firm compassion, "She didn't make it, Cole."

Wade saw the enlightenment envelop this man's expression, only to be replaced by horror—a horror that Wade knew well. He had to keep a hand over his own mouth to silence his emotion while he observed Cole's response to the loss of his wife. Alex just held his hand and gently tried to keep him calm. It took nearly half an hour for Cole's volatile grief to settle into visible shock, something else that Wade knew all too well.

After a few minutes of silence, Alex said to Cole, "There are some things I need to tell you, if that's okay."

"Okay," Cole said, looking at Alex with hollow eyes.

"I'm a man who does not believe in coincidence. So, with that in mind, I want to tell you what happened this evening from my perspective. I know it's difficult for you, but there are some aspects that I believe you need to know."

"Okay," Cole said again, looking more intrigued than concerned.

"I told you I was driving the car that was right behind you. I'm an ER physician. We were on our way up the canyon to go out to dinner, but we were more than forty minutes behind schedule. In the car with me were three other people. My brother, who is a medical student, held your arm with applied pressure until the paramedics got there, and that kept you from bleeding to death. His wife, Laura, is an LPN. She held Megan's hand and spoke with her." Cole's eyes tightened on Alex, asking silent questions. "She wasn't in any pain, but there was nothing we could have done. Even if we had been at the hospital, the damage was too extensive. But she was calm, and she didn't suffer. She wasn't in pain. She told my sister-in-law to tell you that she loves you."

Cole squeezed his eyes closed, and tears leaked from beneath his eyelids. Alex went on. "Laura stayed with her even after she was gone, until the emergency crews got there." Cole nodded and opened his eyes. Alex said, "The other person in the car with us was my wife, Jane. She held your son and calmed him down and fed him. Now, that might not sound like such a magnanimous thing, unless you know that she's done it before."

Wade straightened in his chair. Cole's intrigue heightened visibly. "You see," Alex went on, "a little more than two years ago, my brother's wife died in her sleep. Their baby was barely two weeks old. While my brother was struggling to accept that his wife was gone, my sweet wife was holding the baby and feeding her." Alex sighed. "Now, I don't know about you, but I'd say that's a little too much to chalk up to coincidence. I just want you to know that God sent us to help you through this, Cole, because we've been through it." He motioned toward Wade, who stood up and moved to Alex's side. "This is my brother, Wade. He kept you from bleeding to death today, and two years ago he lost his wife. I'm going to leave the two of you to talk for a while."

Alex eased away, and Cole said with new tears showing in his eyes, "Thank you."

"Don't thank me. God put us in the right place at the right time."

Alex briefly pressed a hand over Wade's shoulder as he said softly, "I'm going to find the women and take them home. I'll be back."

"Okay," Wade said and moved a chair close to Cole's bedside. His heart was beating so hard that it hurt. For a few minutes nothing was said, then Wade admitted, "My brother thinks I'm an expert or something, but . . . honestly, I don't know what to say. There's nothing anyone can say that will take away the pain. Sometimes it hurt so bad I could hardly breathe." Cole's tears increased, and Wade said, "You go ahead and cry, buddy. I'll just . . . cry with you."

Chapter Four

Laura realized she was shaking as she watched Jane drive to the visitors' parking lot after leaving the men at the door of the ER.

"Are you okay?" Jane asked.

"No, I don't think I am. How about you?"

"I'm a little shaken, but I didn't watch that woman die. I'm the only one there who was spared the gore, because I didn't choose a medical career."

Fresh tears rushed out of Laura's eyes. Jane put the car in Park and turned to wrap her in a tight hug. They cried together for a few minutes, then Jane said, "Come on. What we need is a distraction."

Laura followed Jane through the patient entrance into the ER. They walked through the waiting room, past a Starbucks off the main hall, and around a corner. They got into an elevator and went down as Jane said, "This is what Alex calls the well-beaten path."

"Why is that?" Laura asked, then the elevator doors opened, and Jane didn't answer. They stepped into a long skywalk that went from the basement of the U of U hospital to the fourth floor of the hospital next door, corresponding to the slope of Hospital Hill.

About halfway across, Jane said, "It's the path from where he works to where we lived for a very long time."

"Primary Children's," Laura said as it came together in her mind.

"The food is much better here," Jane said, and they went down the elevator to the cafeteria.

Laura found it difficult to eat, even though the food was good. She'd certainly been here before, occasionally visiting a patient of the doctor she worked for. But she'd never come in through the other hospital, and she'd rarely had a meal here. Jane talked about the countless meals she'd eaten in this place.

A memory occurred to Laura, and she said, "I saw Wade here once. He was with Alex. His mother was in ICU, and they'd come here to eat." Laura laughed softly, grateful for the distraction. "I remember it so well. Wade was sitting there crying, and I was afraid something had happened to Rebecca. But I could only stand there and stare for I don't know how long. The first time I'd met him he'd cried, telling me about Elena's death. I realized I loved that about him, that he wasn't ashamed to cry."

Jane smiled and said, "Yes, I heard about that. He thought you were still married, and he was chiding himself for having feelings for a married woman. Funny what lack of communication can do to us, isn't it?"

"Yes, it certainly is."

Once they were finished eating, Jane said, "Well, I'm sure we won't be seeing any sign of the great doctors for a while. Let's take a walk."

Laura followed her back up to the fourth floor, in the opposite direction from the skywalk. Approaching a large set of double doors, Jane said, "You don't have any sign of a virus, do you? Anything at all?"

"No. Why?"

"We don't take germs in here," Jane said, going through the first set of doors. "Even though they have an incredible air-filtering system, we have to be careful."

"This is the isolation unit."

"Yes, it is," Jane said and picked up the security phone. She said into it, "Hi, who's this? Oh, hi! I'm glad you're on shift.

This is Jane, Barrett's mom. I've got a friend with me and some time to kill. Is there anything we can do? Okay, let us wash up. Thanks."

Laura followed Jane's example of washing up before they went through the second set of double doors, where Jane was met by a couple of nurses who were ridiculously excited to see her. They'd obviously come to know each other very well. Laura had seen the scrapbooks and photos related to Barrett's time spent here, fighting to survive leukemia. But being here put a sense of reality to all that the family had been through.

"This is my sister-in-law, Laura Morrison," Jane said, introducing her to the nurses, Felicia and Susy. They exchanged greetings, then Felicia said, "This would be Wade's wife, then."

"That's right," Jane said.

"He's a big hero around here," Susy said. "We were ready for a party when he showed up with his bone marrow."

"Yeah," Felicia added, "but then we just couldn't hardly get him to go home. He just has a gift with these sick kids, you know."

Laura smiled. "He's a hero to me, too."

"Hey," Jane said, "we've got some time on our hands. You got anybody who could use a listening ear?"

"Boy do we," Susy said. "We've got a BMT mother who's about to lose it." She took Jane's arm. "Come on, I'll introduce you."

"What's a BMT?" Laura whispered to Jane as they walked.

"A bone marrow transplant," she whispered back.

Laura caught glimpses of bald-headed children and felt tempted to cry. She reminded herself that she was a pediatric nurse and that she could handle this. But giving shots and taking temperatures was nothing compared to this kind of work. She thought of Wade's goal to become a pediatric oncologist, and her admiration for him deepened. It wasn't a goal he'd set lightly; he'd spent a lot of time here during Barrett's illness, and he wanted to make a difference.

Susy went into a room and came back with a visibly weary young mother. She was introduced as Della, whose daughter, Lynnsy, had just received new bone marrow two weeks earlier, and they were still waiting to see if it would take hold.

"This is Jane," Susy said. "Her son Barrett had two transplants; he's now doing well. She thought the two of you might have something to talk about. We'll keep an eye on Lynnsy. Take as long as you need."

"The waiting certainly gets torturous, doesn't it," Jane said.

Della got tears in her eyes. "Yes, it certainly does."

Jane introduced Laura to Della, then the three of them started walking back through the two sets of double doors to a quiet room with a pleasant atmosphere. Laura just listened as Jane talked freely of her experiences with nearly losing her son, then she asked Della questions and got her talking—and crying. Jane openly shared her testimony of God's hand in the lives of their children—and themselves—in helping them get through these things. Laura had no idea if this woman was LDS, and Jane said nothing specific about her beliefs, but she spoke of faith and hope and trusting in God. She also spoke, however, of going through a time when she'd felt betrayed by God, when she'd lost her faith, and then of how she'd reached a point where she knew that whether her son lived or died, somehow she would survive it and move on.

Jane asked Della if she had any questions, which Jane answered with straightforward candor and compassion. After nearly two hours, Della thanked Jane profusely and gave her a long, tight hug. She hugged Laura too, even though she'd hardly said a word. Jane and Della exchanged phone numbers and email addresses and promised to keep in touch. Della hurried back to be with her daughter.

Laura turned to Jane and said, "You didn't choose a medical career, but I think you've got an honorary degree in what counts."

Jane made a scoffing noise as they walked slowly back toward the skywalk. "All I've got is empathy and a listening ear."

"That's what I mean," Laura said, but Jane changed the subject, speculating over whether the children were behaving themselves. Back at the ER waiting room she used a courtesy phone to call home. She told Roxanne what had happened and where they were, then she sat down next to Laura and said, "They told me everyone's fine, and we should stay as long as we need to." She glanced at her watch. "I wonder how it's going."

They sat there for another forty minutes before Jane went to call home again. While she was on the phone, Laura saw Alex approaching.

"Jane's on the phone," she said. "How is he?"

"Wade or the patient?" Alex countered, sitting beside her.

"Both, but I meant the patient. I was going to ask about Wade next."

"His name is Cole, and he's going to be fine. He's got a broken leg, a bad cut on his arm, and a mild concussion. He's been given the bad news, and Wade's with him now. As for Wade, he's gotten past a mild panic attack. I think he's pretty shaken up but holding it together rather well." He paused and asked, "How are you?"

"I'm pretty shaken up too, to be truthful."

"That's understandable."

"You see people die every day."

"Not every day," Alex said.

"But a lot."

"Yeah, I've seen a lot of people die."

"Do you ever get used to it?"

Alex sighed again. "I think I've learned to separate myself from it emotionally—most of the time anyway—but I don't think I'll ever get used to it. I never see death without wondering about the ones who are left alive to mourn the loss. I think that's actually become harder since we almost lost Barrett."

He turned to look at her, and she asked, "How are *you?*"

"I'm fine. But you must be sick of sitting here."

"Actually, we haven't been here terribly long. We went to the other hospital."

"They do have better food," Alex said.

"So I hear," Laura said. "Then Jane went to talk to a struggling mother in the BMT unit."

Alex looked momentarily surprised, then he smiled. "She can't stay away for long. Somehow she manages to get there on a regular basis."

"She really made a difference; I could tell."

"She has a way of doing that," Alex said as Jane approached them. He stood to greet her with a kiss.

"The kids are all asleep. Your dad said to stay as long as we needed, but I told him that at least one of us would be home soon."

"We can all leave soon," Alex said. "Wade's talking to this guy, but he's going to be out on pain meds pretty quick. We can check on him tomorrow."

"What about Andrew?" Jane asked.

"He's with the bishop's family, and the grandparents are on their way. I'm going to take the two of you home and come back for Wade. He'll be—"

"I'm right here," Wade said, and they looked up to see him approaching. "The bishopric arrived. I told Cole we'd check in on him tomorrow. Let's go home."

In the car Jane said, "Why don't you just leave Rebecca at our house; she's already asleep, and then you don't have to bring her on your way to work."

"I don't have to work tomorrow," Wade said.

"But Laura does, and you should go see Cole. Just come and get her when you're ready. I don't have anywhere to go. Alex can go buy groceries since he has the day off."

Alex made a comical noise of disgust. "Apparently I *don't* have the day off."

When they arrived at Alex and Jane's home, they all shared tight hugs before Wade and Laura got into their car and drove toward their own home.

"Are you okay?" Laura asked. When he didn't answer right away, she added, "Alex said you had a panic attack."

Wade looked at her sharply, but his voice was light when he said, "With him around, who can keep a secret?" More soberly he added, "Yeah, it shook me up pretty badly, I admit. The baby crying brought it all back."

"I'm so sorry you had to go through all of that, Wade."

"Well, it was tough, but . . . it was worth it." He took her hand and kissed it. "I never could say that I was glad to lose Elena, but I'm very grateful to have found you. And I couldn't have had it both ways. God knew you needed me. He knew what He was doing. But I don't think Cole's ready to hear that yet."

"We just need to keep him around enough that when he *is* ready to hear it, you're there to say it."

"Yeah, I think that would be good." He shook his head. "I can't stop thinking about him, what he must be feeling. Those first days . . . hours . . . were such a nightmare. But if nothing else, it's making me grateful I'm where I am now, instead of back there."

"I love you, Wade," she said. "And I'm grateful too."

The following morning Wade went to see Cole. He admitted to being in shock most of the time, and Wade empathized with that, expressing some of his own experience. They talked for nearly an hour, and more than once Cole expressed appreciation for God sending him a friend who understood. Wade learned that Cole and Megan had actually been married seven years. They had a four-year-old daughter, named Natalie, who had been left with a sitter the previous evening. And little Andrew was less than a month old.

Wade didn't leave until Cole's parents showed up, but they exchanged contact information. Wade promised to check on him after the dust settled, knowing that *after* the funeral could be the most difficult. And Cole promised to call, any time, if he needed someone to talk to, or anything else. Seeing evidence of Cole's parents' support, Wade knew he was leaving him in good hands.

A few days later, Wade and Laura and Alex and Jane went to the evening viewing for Cole's wife, Megan. Wade had a hard time seeing Cole near the casket with the baby in his arms. Again it brought back images of his own nightmare.

For Laura, seeing Megan in the casket brought back the fact that she'd been with her when she'd died. She managed to stay composed long enough to meet Cole, and to tell him herself of what Megan had said. But she cried all the way home.

The following day Wade was glad that he and Alex both had to work, which gave him a good excuse to not go to the funeral. He knew they could have probably traded a shift if they'd wanted to badly enough, but it would have been difficult. And truthfully, Wade didn't think he could handle it. He felt sure that Cole could use more support once the relatives all went back to their lives, and he was left alone to face the reality of raising his kids by himself.

That night, Wade had trouble going to sleep. He woke in the dark gasping for breath, cold with sweat. He'd forgotten all about the dream he'd had right after he and Laura had been married. But now it had recurred, exactly the same. The very fact of its recurrence made it difficult for him to breathe. He sat up abruptly, as if that might separate him from what sleep had assaulted him with. Then he had to drop his head when he saw stars. He wondered if he'd been working too hard, or if there was some level of suppressed grief hiding in the recesses of his mind that was trying to get out. He lumbered into the bathroom and repeatedly splashed cold water on his face, while images of seeing his wife dead hovered relentlessly in the foreground of his brain. He sat on the edge of the tub and pressed his hands into his hair, again finding it difficult to breathe.

"Are you okay?" he heard Laura ask, but the way he jumped at the sound of her voice made him realize how edgy he'd become.

"Yeah, I'm fine," he said, forcing a smile.

"You don't seem okay," she said gently and stood beside him, urging him close. He wrapped his arms around her and pressed his face into the soft nightgown fabric covering her belly. He could hear her heart beating, feel her breathing. The evidence of her being alive soothed him far more than he wanted to admit.

He sensed expectancy in her and hurried to explain, "I just . . . had a bad dream."

"Anything you want to talk about?"

"Not really," he said.

"Maybe you should tell me anyway," she said, looking down at him, pressing a hand over the side of his face.

Wade considered his own convictions about not keeping secrets between them, but he couldn't bring himself to admit aloud what he'd seen happen to her in his dream. He settled for a partial truth. "It was . . . like the accident. I could hear the baby screaming, and then . . . it was Rebecca screaming, like I'd gone back in time. It all came back to me. I was holding her in my arms. She was crying because she was hungry, and I found Elena dead." Wade didn't add that in the dream he'd rolled Elena over, and her dark hair had turned blonde, and her face had turned into Laura's. But Elena had looked peaceful, even though she'd looked dead. He remembered it well. In his dream, Laura's countenance had been tortured and filled with fear, as if she'd died in a moment of terror, and her expression had been emblazoned in stone.

"I don't know how you ever survived it," Laura said, easing him closer.

"People have survived much worse, I'm sure," he said. "I knew it was her time to go."

"Still, it was horrible for you."

"Yes, it was." He tightened his arms around her. He wanted to say that he could never live through it again, he could never bear to lose her, but he couldn't put his voice to the words. Instead he murmured softly, "But now I have you, and everything is okay."

She made a noise of agreement and pressed tender fingers through his hair. He looked up at her, and she bent to kiss him. He eagerly became lost in it, reminding himself of what he'd just said. Everything *was* okay.

Wade never went back to sleep before he had to leave for the hospital. He kissed Laura good-bye and peeked at Rebecca before he left just past dawn. He kept hoping the images of his dream would fade as most dreams did, but it wouldn't leave his mind. He was only an hour into his shift when Alex asked, "Is something wrong?"

"It's that obvious, eh," Wade said, trying to sound nonchalant. The ER was quiet, and the other staff members were all killing time elsewhere.

"You seem . . . down . . . distracted. Is there trouble in paradise?"

"No," he said firmly, "being married to Laura is a relatively blissful existence."

"Really?" Alex chuckled. "Not that I'm surprised, but . . . more blissful than being married to Elena?"

"That's a loaded question."

"And knowing each other as we do, I'm sure you can answer it honestly. Or you can tell me to mind my own business."

"Mind your own business," Wade said severely.

Alex looked a little taken aback but said, "Okay. I'll just—"

"I'm kidding." Wade chuckled. "I had you there for a second."

"Yes, you did, but . . . you really can tell me to mind my own business."

"I know. And you can do the same. Believe it or not, I don't tell you *everything*. Almost, but not quite." He sighed and considered the question. If nothing else it was a distraction from the reasons for his sour mood. "It probably goes without saying—but I'll say it anyway—that comparing two good women would be like that comparing apples to oranges thing. They're both amazing women, but they are more different than they are alike. I once believed that to be happy I needed someone just like Elena. And that would have been fine, I suppose. Elena was a wonderful woman. I felt completely happy and content. I had no complaints. But I look back now and feel grateful that it wasn't the other way around."

"What do you mean?"

"If I'd lost Laura, and then married Elena, I don't know if I ever could have been content. Laura has this way of looking at life that constantly keeps me thinking and wondering. She's deep and analytical and charmingly unpredictable. She cries harder, and laughs deeper, and sees everything around her with . . . complexity and . . . appreciation. She doesn't invest herself in something unless she's passionate about it, and that makes her passionate about everything in her life. The conversations we have always leave me in awe. Discussing gospel principles with her . . . that's the most amazing thing. Her testimony and her knowledge are . . . unbelievable. Elena appreciated life; she was spiritual, and sensitive, and everything a man could ever want in a wife and mother. But . . . Elena was like . . ." He chuckled and shook his head. "How do I explain it? It's like . . ." He struggled for a metaphor. "Being with Elena was like sitting on the beach and watching a sunset. Being with Laura is like surfing the waves, snorkeling in the tide pool, and *then* sitting on the beach watching the sun come up. Her qualities do not diminish the love I will always feel for Elena, and the gratitude I have for what we shared—and that it's eternal. And truthfully, I think that somehow Elena knows and understands the differences between herself and Laura, and she rejoices in them; she respects them. Bottom line, Laura is more amazing than I would have ever believed a woman could be. Just having her in my life makes me thank God daily for such evidence of *His* love for me, that He would bless me so richly."

"Wow," Alex said, and Wade turned to see his brother looking a little stunned. Then he smiled.

"What?"

"Nothing. I'm just happy for you. You deserve to be happy."

Wade turned the other way, wishing his thoughts would stop straying to nightmarish images. He felt as if he'd seen a movie he shouldn't have—twice—and it wouldn't leave his mind. But all he'd done was go to sleep. And he'd studied the scriptures and prayed before doing that.

"What's wrong?" Alex asked. "If you'll recall I asked that a few minutes ago. I think you're trying to evade the question."

Wade reminded himself that this was Alex. Had he ever gotten through *anything* difficult in his life without him? Not since he'd met him, anyway. He cleared his throat tensely and spoke his most prominent thought. "Maybe it's too good to last."

"Where did that come from?" Alex demanded, appalled. Wade said nothing, and he added, "Is this just . . . habit because you had inklings about losing Elena?"

"No."

"How long have you been feeling this way?"

Wade glanced at his watch. "About five hours."

Alex tightened his gaze on Wade, and his brow furrowed. Wade added quietly, "I had a dream—a nightmare. I had the same dream once before, right after I married Laura. I'd forgotten about it, but now it's happened again. I've never had a dream affect me this way. It's not fading; it's becoming more vivid in my mind. It's like . . . my every nerve is raw. I feel like some kind of . . . animal . . . like I have to be completely alert or some . . . predator will . . ." His voice broke, "take her from me."

Alex apparently had nothing to say until he'd had a minute to digest the implication. "So, what are you saying? You think this dream is some kind of premonition? Some . . . warning?"

"I don't know. But I feel scared out of my mind."

"So, tell me about the dream. Was it—"

"Dr. Keane," a nurse approached them, "we've got a burn victim coming in; one minute out."

"Okay, we're there," Alex said, and Wade followed him down the hall.

"Don't think you're getting out of the rest of this conversation," Alex said.

Wade didn't comment as they both put gowns over their scrubs and pulled sterile gloves onto their hands. He was actually relieved to be faced with some trauma—even as gruesome as it was—to distract him from his own thoughts. It wasn't until their lunch break that Wade was able to talk to Alex again, but not until he'd called Laura to make certain everything was okay with her.

"I love you so much," he said, once he knew she was fine.

"I love you too, Wade," she replied, and he knew she meant it. "You're the best thing that's ever happened to me."

"It's the other way around," he said. "Don't you ever forget that."

"How could I?" she laughed softly. "You treat me like a queen; I'm just trying to figure out why."

"How could I treat you any other way?" he asked. "You're the most amazing woman in the world."

She made a light scoffing noise to laugh off the compliment, even though his voice was completely serious. He felt compelled to add, "I mean it, Laura."

"I need to get back to work," she said. "Rebecca and I will anxiously be waiting for your shift to end."

"Ditto," he said and ended the call.

"Now, tell me about this dream," Alex said once they were seated over their meal in the cafeteria.

"It's not just the dream," Wade said, "but the way it made me feel, the way it won't stop haunting me."

"Maybe you need a priesthood blessing."

"Maybe I do," Wade admitted and went on to repeat the content of the dream, but unlike when he'd told Laura, he told Alex all of it.

"Well, I can see why you'd feel shaken," Alex said, "but I don't think you should give it too much credence. What would you do beyond doing what you already do, anyway? You live close to the Spirit, you don't take what's good in your life for granted, and you're careful. In my opinion, it's just a nightmare. That accident was pretty traumatic—especially for you, given the parallels between you and Cole. If it keeps bothering you, let me know. Dad and I can give you a blessing."

"Okay," Wade said and tried to force it out of his mind. "Thanks for listening."

"What are brothers for?" Alex said with a wink.

A minute later Wade said, "Just for the record, I want you to know . . . and I'm not just saying this . . . I've followed a lot of doctors around, and were you not my brother, I would truthfully admire you more than any other I've worked with. What you do is amazing, and the way you do it . . . your conviction, your passion for your work, your genuine concern for the patients and their families . . . you're amazing."

Alex stared at him a long moment, looking dumbfounded. He finally chuckled self-consciously and looked down. "I . . . don't know what to say."

"You don't have to say anything. I just want you to know that I mean it, and I thought it should be said."

"Well . . ." Alex chuckled again, "it means more coming from you than anyone else. I love my work, Wade. Sometimes it's tough; and sometimes it's *really* tough. But there's nothing else I would rather be doing."

"It shows," Wade said. "If I ever had to end up in an ER, I'd want you to be my doctor."

"Let's just hope you stay off the receiving end."

"I'll do my best."

* * * * *

A few days after Megan's funeral, Alex and Jane had Cole and his children over for dinner. They invited Wade and Laura as well, along with Neil and Roxanne. Natalie quickly became comfortable playing with the other girls, even though Rebecca and Ruthie were younger, and Katharine much older. The women all took turns holding little Andrew and making a fuss over him. Cole was getting around relatively well on a walking leg brace, and Wade was pleased to see that he seemed to be doing rather well with his grief, all things considered. Neil and Roxanne were up to their usual par with making Cole and his children feel completely comfortable and at ease. Cole enjoyed hearing a somewhat comical version of how Wade and Alex had discovered that they were half-brothers, and then he heard the serious side of it. He seemed touched by their story and declared firmly that he still wanted to hang around with them, even though they had such scandal in the family.

Wade talked privately with Cole for a few minutes; Cole's struggle was evident, but his faith was strong and his attitude as good as it possibly could be. Cole felt strongly that it had been Megan's time to go, and he found peace in that, even if the separation was difficult. Wade knew exactly how he felt.

Cole and Wade helped Barrett work on a large jigsaw puzzle. Following a minute of silence, Barrett said to Cole, "I'm sorry that you lost your wife. You must be very sad."

Cole looked at Wade, who shrugged and smiled discreetly. "Yes, I am," Cole said, "but I know she's in a better place."

"Yes, she is," Barrett said, focusing on the puzzle. "It's very beautiful there."

"So I've heard," Wade said. To Cole he added, "Barrett's a pretty amazing guy. His spirit is about three thousand years older than mine, which is why he's always giving me advice."

"You're so weird," Barrett said without breaking his concentration.

"No, it's true," Wade said. "But don't go getting a big head over it. You're still just a kid, and I can take you down."

"Give me ten years," Barrett said nonchalantly, and Wade chuckled.

Compelled to get back to a certain point, Wade said to Cole, "When Barrett says that it's very beautiful where Megan is, he really knows. He's seen it."

Cole looked intrigued. Barrett just kept working on the puzzle. "Just for a minute," the child said.

"I'd like to hear about that," Cole said, but Barrett said nothing.

Wade opted for the factual parts of the story. "Barrett got leukemia when he was four. He had two bone marrow transplants, and we almost lost him a number of times."

"Yeah. Wade only thinks I'm cool because we have the same blood."

Wade tapped Barrett lightly on the head and said like a child, "You weren't supposed to tell him that part."

Barrett chuckled, then he turned serious eyes toward Cole and said, "It's very beautiful there. And it feels more happy there than it could ever feel here." He stood up and moved toward the door, saying, "I forgot to take out the garbage. Mom'll be on my case."

Wade's eyes connected with Cole's, not surprised to see emotion there. "Yeah," Wade said, "Barrett has that effect on people."

A while later when Cole was getting ready to leave, Alex and Jane made a point of telling him that they expected him over for dinner at least once a week, and that any member of the family was available for him. Most of his and Megan's family members lived out of state, although he did have a couple of wonderful women in his ward who were more than eager to watch the children while he worked. He promised to be back for dinner the following weekend and thanked all of them with hugs, while he expressed tearful gratitude for God giving him another family.

After Cole left with his children, Wade turned to Alex and said, "He's going to be okay."

"Yes, I believe he is. I mean . . . look at you. You're the happiest man alive."

"Yes, I am," Wade said.

"Actually," Alex countered, "*I* am the happiest man alive."

Chapter Five

On their six-week anniversary, Laura woke up late and relished the fact that they had nowhere they had to go, nothing that had to be done. She could see a blue sky through the slant of the blinds, and autumn-colored leaves clinging to the tree outside the bedroom window. She turned her head with the intent of watching Wade sleep, but instead she found him watching her.

"You get more beautiful every day," he said, touching her face, and then he kissed her. His kiss became deep and passionate until they heard Rebecca calling from her crib in the other room.

"I wake, Daddy!"

Laura just laughed and said, "I'll make waffles if you'll get Rebecca dressed."

"Deal," he said and headed to his daughter's room to find her bouncing up and down in her crib, making him laugh.

Laura put a robe on over her pajamas and went to the kitchen. She took a bag of garbage out the front door and put it into the garbage can at the side of the house. Back inside, she plugged in the waffle iron and started mixing the batter. As the first portion of batter went into the iron, Rebecca ran into the kitchen, dressed in little blue jeans and a striped shirt, her hair in little pigtails. Wade followed her and set to work making some orange juice and setting the table. They talked and laughed over Rebecca's antics while they shared breakfast, then Laura cleared the table while Wade put dirty dishes into the dishwasher. He kissed her mid-task, reminding her of the joy he gave her every day in the midst of normal, everyday life.

"Let's go to the mall," he said. "We're overdue for a visit to the carousel."

"Sounds delightful," she said. "If we can pick up a few groceries on the way home, then we're set for Sunday."

"Okay, I'll take a shower while you keep an eye on the queen."

Wade went into the bathroom, and Laura peeked into Rebecca's bedroom to see her diligently playing with a baby doll, trying to put a play bottle into its mouth. Laura hurried to the basement to get some clean laundry out of the dryer. Coming back up, she heard a knock at the door. She set the laundry basket down in the kitchen and headed toward the door, but before she could get there it came open, and she heard a once-familiar voice call, "Laura? Are you here?"

She stopped halfway across the front room, astonished and upset to see her ex-husband actually standing there. "What are you doing?" she demanded.

"Oh, you *are* here," Randall said as if she should be thrilled to see him.

"What are you *doing?*" she repeated. "You don't just . . . walk into someone's house because they don't answer the door."

"It used to be *my* house," he said as if that justified the way he had just invaded her privacy—and her sense of safety.

"Well, it hasn't been for a very, very long time. How did you know someone else doesn't live here now?"

"I saw your car in the driveway," he said with a triumphant smirk that made her want to slap him.

"Well, what do you want?" she demanded, wrapping her robe more tightly around her, as if it might protect her.

"I was . . . in town," Randall said. "I just wanted to see how you're doing."

"I'm fine," she said firmly. "But I would appreciate it if you'd leave."

"Can't we just chat for old time's sake?" he asked.

"Not when you walk into my house as if you have the right to do so. Please go."

She absently pushed her hair back with her hand, and his eyes went wide before he grabbed her hand and pulled it close to his face, as if he couldn't believe his eyes. "You're *married?"*

"Yes, actually."

"You got married without telling me?"

"I didn't tell anybody," she said, pulling her hand away. "I don't know what difference it should make to you, anyway."

"I would think with what we've shared that you'd have let me know something that important."

"I would think with what we've shared that you wouldn't want to ever hear from me again, any more than I ever wanted to hear from you."

"Oh, so that's the way it is," he said, as if she'd done something wrong. His tone of voice, his stance, his expressions brought it all back. The horrible arguments, the degrading and cruel things he'd said to her, the way he'd slapped her when he hadn't liked what she'd said. "This was just supposed to be a friendly visit, Laura."

"A friend with any respect would have waited on the front porch until the door was answered," she stated firmly.

"I don't know why you're making such a big deal of it. You'd think I had—"

He stopped when Rebecca came running into the room and went straight to Laura, wanting to be picked up, as if she too felt disconcerted by the presence of a stranger. Randall looked as if he'd encountered an alien.

"This is my stepdaughter."

"You married a man with *children?"*

"One child—and, as you can see, she's beautiful. I'm her mother now, and I have a wonderful husband, and I think it would be better if you just leave. Whatever you came here to talk about is likely irrelevant. You are no longer welcome here."

Wade was getting out of the shower when he heard voices in the other room. He couldn't make out who Laura was talking to, or what was being said. But the agitation in Laura's tone was evident. He hurried as fast as humanly possible to get dressed and pushed his hands through his wet hair, leaving his feet bare as he crept quietly down the hall. He moved into the doorway to the front room without being noticed. He didn't know who this guy was, but the fragments of conversation he'd just heard gave him a pretty good idea.

Laura felt herself starting to tremble and wondered what she would have to threaten to get Randall to leave. She could feel a familiar power struggle building. She wanted him to leave, and he was very good at combating whatever she might want.

"Oh, come on, Laura. Can't we just—"

"Something wrong?" Wade asked, startling Laura as much as Randall. She almost melted with relief. For a moment she'd honestly forgotten that her husband was in the house.

"Not at all," she said, amazed at how steady her voice sounded. "I was just having a friendly chat with my ex-husband. I'd introduce the two of you, but I don't see the point when you're never going to see each other again."

Laura was amazed at how Randall's entire demeanor and tone of voice changed as he said to her, "So how are Rochelle and Tina these days?"

Laura fought to cover how the question bristled her every nerve. She looked hard at Randall and just said it. "Rochelle is living like some kind of harlot, and Tina's dead."

"What happened?" Randall asked. It was the first genuine thing he'd said since he walked through the door.

"She shot herself in the head," Laura said tonelessly.

Wade felt distinctly uneasy at this contradiction in what she'd told *him* about Tina's death right after they'd started dating. He wondered if the discrepancy in the story was due to some effort at shock value for Randall's benefit. Right now he was more concerned with just getting this creep out of the house.

"Why?" Randall asked breathlessly.

"That is the million-dollar question, Randall. Why does a woman spiral downward so completely that she would do something like that? It's been delightful catching up." Her voice reeked of sarcasm. "Could you please go now?"

Randall looked at her with a pleading in his eyes that seemed manipulative to Wade. "Laura, I just want to—"

"She asked you to leave," Wade said. "Any man worth his weight should know the importance of respecting a lady's wishes."

"Fine, I'm going," he said. "I wish I could say it had been a pleasure."

"The feeling is mutual," Wade said, and Randall left, slamming the door behind him. Laura set Rebecca down and hurried to lock it. She leaned back against it, and Wade could see her trembling. He crossed the room and took her in his arms. She clutched onto him and started to cry. "It's okay," he murmured.

"No," she sobbed. "No . . . it's not. He just . . . walked into my house. He knocked, and I was . . . slow getting to the door and . . . he just . . . *walked in!* How can I ever . . . feel safe . . . if he can just . . . walk in . . . like that?"

"He won't do it again," he said.

"How can you know that?" She stepped back and glared at him. Something in her eyes reminded him of the day before they were married when he'd found her sinking in depression. But there was something else in her eyes, something he'd never seen before, and it frightened him.

"He lives out of state, right?" he asked, attempting to convince her.

"As far as I know. He said he was in town. But what if he—"

"We'll keep the doors locked, even when we're home. I don't really think he wants to hurt you, Laura. He's just trying to be macho. It's okay."

"I need to take a shower," she said and hurried from the room, as if she were angry with him for trying to convince her there was nothing to be afraid of.

Right after he heard the water start running, the phone rang. It was Alex asking if they wanted to join the family for an excursion to the zoo. Barrett loved the zoo, and Wade always loved going with them, but he said, "I'm afraid Laura's not feeling very well, but thank you anyway." He wondered for a moment if getting her out would be better, but instinctively he knew it wouldn't. He wanted her to talk about this while it was fresh, and that wouldn't happen if they were out and around other people. He felt deeply concerned for Laura in ways he could never put into words. It was as if his instincts had all just bristled, warning him of danger. But it wasn't Randall he felt afraid of. It was whatever he might have triggered inside of Laura.

Given the train of his thoughts, Wade was hard-pressed to express his relief when Alex added, "Well, let us take Rebecca then. Laura can get some rest, and you can take care of her with some peace and quiet."

"Okay, you talked me into it," Wade said.

"You're not going to protest and let me beg you?" Alex asked lightly.

"Not this time."

"Okay, we'll pick her up in less than an hour."

After hanging up the phone, Wade checked on Rebecca, then he started pacing the house while the water in the bathroom continued to run. When he realized it had been running nearly twice as long as Laura's standard shower, he stopped trying to talk himself out of checking on her. He found his wife sitting in the bathtub, hugging her knees to her chest, sobbing uncontrollably, while the water spraying over her was turning cool.

"What are you doing?" he demanded, turning off the water.

She gasped but said nothing as he threw a terry-cloth bathrobe around her and helped her out of the tub. He put a towel over her head and rubbed the water out of her hair.

"Come on," he said in the midst of her ongoing tears. "I think we need to talk."

"I can't go out today," she said, sitting on the edge of the bed.

"I know," he said, "but I'm proud of you for declaring yourself."

She asked cynically, "Are you proud of me for falling apart in the middle of a shower?"

"If you need to cry, then you should cry," he said. "But I'd appreciate it if you'd talk to me about it."

"Okay," she said, "but . . . I need some time . . . to sort my thoughts."

"That's fine," he said. "Alex and Jane are taking Rebecca to the zoo. I'll be back in a little while." He touched her chin, looked into her eyes, and kissed her before he left the room, closing the door behind him.

Waiting for Rebecca to be picked up, Wade sat near where she was playing, and he prayed fervently on behalf of his wife. He prayed that she could navigate her way out of this morning's trauma and what it had apparently done to her spirit. And he prayed for himself, that he would know the right things to say, what to do, how to let her know that the love they shared was strong enough to get her through this.

When Alex came to the door to get Rebecca, Barrett came with him, hugging Wade tightly. He talked with his nephew for a couple of minutes while Alex put Rebecca's car seat into their vehicle. Wade hugged Rebecca, and Barrett took her to buckle her in. Wade handed the standard bag to Alex that always went along with Rebecca.

"Thank you," Wade said.

"What's wrong?" Alex asked firmly.

Wade sighed, grateful for his brother's perception. "Laura's ex-husband showed up this morning. He was just obnoxious enough to upset her pretty badly. Given her history of depression, I'm a little . . ."

"What?"

"Scared," Wade admitted. "Thank you for taking Rebecca. I think we could use some uninterrupted time."

"Well, you probably don't get it very often. It can't be easy having a two-year-old and being newlyweds."

"It has its challenges," Wade said. "Thank you again. We're not going anywhere. Just bring her back whenever."

"Okay," Alex said. "Let me know if there's anything else we can do."

Wade watched them drive away, then went inside and locked both the doors before he went to the bedroom to find Laura curled up on the bed, wearing jeans and one of *his* sweatshirts, which was huge on her. Since she was facing the other direction, he walked around the bed and sat on it. She looked up at him, showing a wan smile, but something in her eyes looked downright terrified. But of what? If she was truly that afraid of Randall, then there was more to their relationship than what she'd told him. Considering what she'd said about Tina's death this morning, he had to wonder what else she hadn't told him. Or had she actually lied to him? The very idea provoked sick knots in his stomach. But he wasn't going to jump to conclusions, and he knew he needed to tread carefully.

"Talk to me, Laura," he said, pushing her damp hair back off her face.

Laura *wanted* to talk to him, but there were so many thoughts whirling around in her mind that she didn't know where to begin. It was as if Randall's visit had opened a floodgate, allowing a vast array of horrid memories and images into a part of her brain that didn't know what to do with them. The most prominent were related to Tina's death. She felt as if she'd just now learned of the horror that had occurred. It was as if everything she'd done related to the incident had only been some kind of dream, and only now did it feel even remotely real. She looked up at her husband, feeling as if some kind of fog suddenly existed between them. And she didn't know how to reach past it.

"Laura?" he said gently. "Just . . . tell me what you're thinking . . . anything."

"How can I when it sounds so crazy?" she asked, pressing a hand over her forehead, as if she could physically will her thought processes to slow down.

"You can say anything to me that you need to say," Wade said gently. "Just talk to me. Don't shut me out."

Wade took in her confused and frightened countenance, wondering what horror from the recesses of her mind she'd been confronted with. Her eyes were distant, her gaze obscure, then she turned to look at him, penetrating him with a hard stare. "There was a funeral," she said. "My best friend died. She understood me better than anyone ever had. And she died. We had a funeral. We ordered flowers, and they were beautiful. And it was raining at the cemetery. It was wet and cold and I . . . I . . . I . . ." She clamped a hand over her mouth and whimpered. Wade pulled her into his arms. She took hold of him fiercely and muttered close to his ear, "How can it feel like . . . I just figured that out? It happened weeks ago, and . . . and . . ."

"Laura," Wade took her shoulders and looked at her closely, "the same thing happened to me when I lost Elena. It was like my mind was in some kind of fog for weeks. I did what had to be done. I had times when I cried like a baby. Then a day came when it was like . . . one part of my brain had lived through it, but the other part of my brain hadn't accepted it. I had to take myself through the whole thing again, every step of what had happened and why. You're not crazy, Laura. You went through something unspeakably horrible. You lost your best friend."

Laura felt a tiny degree of relief from his explanation and the validation it gave to her reaction. But she still felt a smoldering uneasiness that frightened her.

Following some minutes of silence, while she kept her head against his shoulder, Wade asked quietly, "What brought it up now, Laura? Was it telling Randall what had happened?"

He felt her tremble, and she clutched onto him more tightly. She said nothing, and he felt he had to say, "Laura, you told me she overdosed on prescription drugs. You told Randall she shot herself. Which was it?"

Laura let go of him abruptly and backed away. "What are you saying? You think I *lied* to you?"

Wade swallowed hard and measured his words carefully, reminding himself that any anger or defensiveness would only make the problem worse. "Laura," he said, his voice even, "you have never given me any reason to mistrust you. I'm not accusing you of anything. I'm not Randall, and I'm not angry. I'm just wondering why you told him one thing, and me another. I'm sure there's a good reason for that. I just need to know what it is. If you think I'm being unreasonable then—"

"No, of course not," she said, hanging her head. "Forgive me. You're right." She sighed loudly and looked up at him. "I'd never said it out loud before." The words came on a stilted sob. "Not that there was anyone around to say it to, but . . . I couldn't say it . . . until Randall . . . made me so angry . . . and it just . . . jumped out." She sobbed again. "What I told you was true, Wade. She *did* overdose, but her neighbor found her, and she had her stomach pumped, then she . . . she . . . went home and . . . and . . ." she groaned and wrapped her arms around her middle, "she shot herself . . . in the head." Her sobbing broke past any effort to maintain control.

Wade put his arms around her and held her while she cried so hard he almost feared she would pass out or throw up. He held her tightly, whispering words of reassurance, praying silently on her behalf. Her tears gradually merged into a silence that was equally startling. Wade felt certain it was good for her to be venting all of this emotion, and he felt compelled to say, "Talk to me, Laura. Where are your thoughts now?"

"She took all those drugs," Laura said tonelessly, without emotion. "We'd been talking on the phone every couple of days. I knew she was struggling, but we talked it through. We talked about making a new life, setting some goals, making some changes. She seemed eager to move forward. I tried to talk her into coming to stay with me. She said she'd think about it. She sounded good. Then I couldn't get hold of her, and I was worried. She didn't leave her apartment much. She called me from the psych ward, told me what she'd done. She told me she was glad it hadn't worked, that she was getting some help. I talked to her the day after she came home from the hospital. She assured me that everything was fine, but I felt uneasy—like she was just saying what she thought I wanted to hear. I offered to take some time off work and go there to spend a week with her. She thanked me, but insisted that I shouldn't come. Then I couldn't get hold of her. After two days I was really scared. I was a thousand miles away, and she wouldn't answer the phone."

Laura's voice remained quiet and toneless, as if she were reciting the events from a part of her mind that didn't connect at all into her emotions. Wade just listened with growing horror over what she'd had to deal with. "So after three days I called the police and told them she'd been suicidal, and I couldn't get hold of her. They called me back a couple of hours later to tell me they'd found her. With all the evidence tallied, they figured she'd been dead three days. She probably told me everything was fine, hung up the phone and did it. I had to call her family, her friends, and tell them. I had to talk to the police, the medical examiner, and the mortuary. People who loved her were fine with coming to the funeral, but no one seemed to want to help plan it. Rochelle and I went through her things, and . . . and . . ."

Emotion crept again into her voice, and Wade wondered why going through Tina's things would provoke it, after everything else she'd said.

"What?" he urged gently.

She sobbed quietly and held to him more tightly. "The landlord hired some . . . disaster cleanup company to . . . take care of . . . the mess. The neighbors had complained about . . . the smell . . . before the body was . . . found. The couch was removed, and . . . they cut out the carpet . . . and they put some kind of . . . acid on the floor . . . over the bloodstain . . . but . . . the smell. Oh, Wade . . . all those hours in there . . . going through her things . . . sorting through her life . . . with the smell of death."

"Oh, Laura," he muttered, holding her closer. "I'm so sorry."

"I boxed up some things of hers that I wanted to keep. I shipped them home. I opened the box and it . . . smelled that way and . . . I closed it. It's in the basement. I can't even touch it." Her grief escalated dramatically, and she cried with fervor, "She shot herself in the head, and she bled all over the floor, and she laid there dead for three days, and no one even noticed she was gone."

"*You* noticed," Wade said, but she just cried harder.

Wade held her and cried with her until she cried herself to sleep. Then he just held her, praying for strength and guidance, praying she could find peace, wondering how she had ever managed to keep going after such an experience—especially when she'd been so completely alone, with no one to talk to about it except for Rochelle, who had become more a thorn in Laura's side than a friend.

When Laura awoke, she had a dazed look in her eyes that left Wade uneasy. He offered to fix her something to eat, but she refused, insisting she wasn't hungry and that she just needed to be alone and let her mind catch up with her. Wade respected her wish to be alone, even though he could hardly keep from worrying about her while he tried to read and flipped through TV channels.

Alex called around eight o'clock to say that they were taking Rebecca home with them for a sleepover; she could use Ruthie's things. Wade just thanked him, certain that giving Laura some time would probably be good. Although he wondered if Rebecca might help bring her around a bit.

About nine o'clock, Wade took some soup and a grilled-cheese sandwich to the bedroom, insisting that Laura eat, whether she felt like it or not. He felt like a tyrant, talking her into taking nearly every bite until it was gone. She went into the bathroom while he took the dishes to the kitchen. He found her back in bed, and she said simply, "Thanks for supper. I'll see you in the morning."

Wade left her to sleep, but in the bathroom he found a prescription bottle on the counter. It was dated a few weeks before he'd first taken her out, which would have been soon after Tina's death. He checked on Laura and found her sleeping deeply in spite of having spent most of the day in bed. He called Alex and asked about the prescription.

"It's an anti-anxiety drug," he said. "Why?"

Wade recounted the day's events in detail. Alex offered compassion and concern, and he said that all things considered, her using a prescription like that in order to get some sleep wasn't a bad thing.

"Would you help me give her a blessing tomorrow?" Wade asked.

"I would love to. Why don't you just . . . come over for dinner. We'll keep Rebecca until then."

"If I can get her to come, that would be great. Thank you."

A few hours later, Wade felt tempted to take one of the pills that was allowing Laura to sleep so deeply. The images of Tina's death haunted him, and he couldn't even imagine how they had plagued Laura. He felt sure she'd been holding a great deal of her grief inside, but now that it had come forward, how were they supposed to cope? He hoped that her talking and crying had been cleansing and that she might be able to press forward. But Sunday morning she insisted that she was exhausted, and she hovered close to her bed. Wade had to go into tyrant mode to get her to eat, and she adamantly refused even attempting to leave the house, either to go to church or to dinner at Alex and Jane's home. Wade left long enough to go teach Laura's Sunday School lesson, but he felt concerned about leaving her alone too long. He called Alex as soon as he knew they'd be home from church to say, "We won't be coming to dinner. I'll come and get Rebecca in a few—"

"I'll bring Rebecca home when I come to help you give Laura that blessing—as soon as we're finished with dinner."

"Okay, thank you," Wade said.

Alex and Jane came together with Rebecca, bringing two plates of dinner that could be heated in the microwave. Wade greeted his daughter eagerly, grateful for the light she brought into a house that had quickly become so dark and dismal. She ran to find Laura and crawled onto the bed, saying, "Mommy wake."

Laura actually smiled when she saw Rebecca, and she hugged her tightly, saying how much she'd missed her. When Wade told Laura that Alex and Jane were here, and that he and Alex wanted to give her a blessing, she put a robe over her pajamas and came to the front room.

"I'm sorry you're not feeling well," Jane said, giving her a hug. "I'll watch Rebecca while these guys do their thing."

Jane took Rebecca into the other room, and the men gave Laura a blessing that gave Wade great hope and comfort. But it also led him to believe that this problem would not be easily solved. The context of the blessing was more centered on the need to stay close to the Spirit in order to endure the struggles that would eventually bring Laura to a place of healing and peace.

When the blessing was finished, Laura said, "Thank you," and she hugged both Alex and Wade before she went back to the bedroom and closed the door.

"I don't know what to do for her, Alex," Wade admitted, finding tears close to the surface.

"Just love her, and let the Spirit guide you, little brother."

Wade thanked him, and both Alex and Jane offered to do anything they could before they each hugged him and left. Wade checked on Laura, who insisted she just needed to be alone. He found some balance in spending time with Rebecca, but after she went down for the night, Laura was sleeping soundly, no doubt aided by medication, and Wade had nowhere for his thoughts to go that didn't feel frightening or disturbing. He read from the Book of Mormon until exhaustion put him to sleep. He woke with the hope that Laura's need to go to work would snap her into some level of normalcy, but he overheard her calling someone to let them know she wouldn't be coming in.

Before leaving with Rebecca to begin a shift at noon, he found the courage to say, "It's really so bad that you can't go to work?"

She almost glared at him. "It really is."

"Okay," he said gently, not wanting her to feel that he was being judgmental or careless. "Will you be alright alone?"

"Of course," she said, squeezing his hand. "I just . . . need some time to sort all of this through. Be patient with me."

"I love you, Laura," he said and kissed her. "Call if you need anything. I'll check my messages as often as I possibly can. Call the ER if you have to."

"Okay," she said, and he left the house, locking the door behind him, wishing he could believe she was going to be alright. He took Rebecca to his mother's and gave her a two-minute explanation of Laura's present struggles. She offered compassion and insisted he let her know if she could do anything. That was the problem, he thought. It seemed there was nothing to be done.

A week later, on Sunday evening, Wade had to admit that Laura had shown no improvement whatsoever. If anything, she'd only seemed to sink deeper into a place where Wade couldn't find her. She managed to get through her daily personal hygiene, but she ate very little, and that was only at Wade's insistence. As usual, when Wade didn't know what to do, he called his brother.

"I think she needs some serious professional help," Alex said. "The sooner the better. This is obviously not going to fix itself."

"So . . . how do you suggest I go about that?"

"If I were you, I might start with Dr. Hadley—the one who helped you when you hit rock bottom."

"But . . . he mostly works with suicide prevention. She's not suicidal."

There was a long pause before Alex said, "Are you sure?" Wade sucked in his breath and staggered to a chair. Memories of that horrible dream rushed into him, when he'd not given it a thought for several days. His stomach churned, and his palms turned sweaty. Before he could respond, Alex went on to say, "You're talking about a woman who has hardly come out of her room for a week. She doesn't want to eat, doesn't read, doesn't turn on the TV—at least not when you're around. How can you possibly know what's going on in her head?"

"I can't," Wade squeaked, feeling so sick and so utterly terrified that he could hardly breathe. "I can't bear to lose her, Alex—especially not like that."

"Do you want me to call Hadley for you? He's still my stake president."

Wade felt scared and hesitant. "I . . . don't know. I think . . . I need more to go on. As bad as it seems, I can't just . . . check her into a facility because she's not talking to me, can I?"

"You tell me," Alex said.

"I hate it when you do that," Wade said somewhat facetiously. "You always turn it back on me when I'm trying to get you to tell me what to do."

"Sorry, kid," Alex said. "She's your wife, and you're the only one with the stewardship to get the answers on her behalf. Give it some thought and prayer; you'll know what to do."

Wade did just that. He pondered, he prayed, he tried again to get Laura to open up to him, but she just wouldn't. He truly felt that getting some serious help for her was the right thing, but he didn't know how to approach it. He considered Alex's suggestion that she might be suicidal, and he couldn't even fathom the possibility. Surely she could see that she had much to live for, that their life together was good.

Around six o'clock he was surprised to have Jane show up at the front door. "I came to get Rebecca," she said. "You have a shift at three, and you need to get some sleep. Just pack her bag, and don't give me any grief." She smiled and gave him a quick hug before she found Rebecca and said in an animated voice, "You want to come and play with Ruthie?"

Rebecca giggled and found her shoes while Wade put some of her things into a bag.

"Thank you," he said to Jane and hugged her again.

"Glad to help," she said as if the thousand times she'd done it before were nothing. She touched his face and added, "It's going to be okay, Wade."

He wanted to believe her, but he found it difficult to sleep as his fears haunted him. He prayed fervently that if there was something he needed to do to prevent a disaster that he would be guided. And if not, that he would feel some peace. With that he *did* sleep and woke in the dark to his alarm. He got ready to go, keeping the same prayer in his heart that he would be guided, while he felt certain it couldn't really be that serious. Surely his own fears were blowing it all out of proportion in his mind.

Chapter Six

Wade felt apprehensive to leave Laura alone, but he kept a prayer in his heart for her and went to the hospital for his scheduled shift. He was grateful to be working with Alex when his level of concern was distracting, and he didn't want to try to explain it to anyone else. Through the early-morning hours he continued to pray and ponder the situation, feeling an urgency he couldn't explain. Mid-morning Alex said, "Maybe you'd better go home."

Wade thought about it for a moment. "No, it's okay. I need to be here."

But by late morning an uneasiness had come over him, and he admitted to Alex, "I think I do need to go home."

"Good. Go. I'll cover for you. If I'm tricky they might not even notice you're gone."

Once in the car, Wade was overcome by the memory of his dream to such an extent that he had to struggle to keep his breathing steady. And then he remembered what he'd told Alex that day. *My every nerve is raw. I feel like some kind of . . . animal . . . like I have to be completely alert or some . . . predator will . . . take her from me.*

"Heaven help me," he muttered and prayed aloud all the way home. He called home on his cell phone but got no answer. That wasn't unusual, since she rarely answered the phone these days, but it still scared him. By the time he arrived home, his heart was pounding with fear. What would he find that required such an urgent prompting? Memories of finding Elena dead mingled with his present concerns.

Wade parked the car and rushed into the house, where he found Laura asleep on the couch, clearly breathing and alive. Then why the prompting? he asked himself and looked around the room as if it might give him the answers. He still felt that undeniable urgency, as if he had to be fully alert to protect her. But protect her from what? Herself? He found himself wishing with all his soul that she would just open up to him the way she used to, that he could know where her head was. He thought of their early conversations, how open she'd been with him; she'd even let him read her journals. *Her journals.*

Wade said a prayer and quickly weighed the invasion of her privacy with the problem at hand. He felt no qualms about going straight to the bedroom in search of her current journal, praying that she might have written anything at all to give him some insight. A white, business-sized envelope was tucked as a marker between pages, guiding him to the most recent entry, dated that very day. He quickly surmised that it was the only entry written since Randall had shown up. Wade felt his insides smolder as he read words that expressed the whirlpool of darkness she was living in. She spoke of her regret in being such a horrible wife to him, and a useless mother to Rebecca, and her certainty that it was only a matter of time before her husband realized what a mistake he had made. The entry concluded with a statement that implied some kind of resignation, as if she had no more left inside of her to battle the darkness surrounding her. She clearly felt crippled and incapable of functioning. And Wade felt sick to his stomach. He again noticed the envelope that had been stuck between the pages. He turned it over and found his name written there. His heart beat painfully hard as he opened it and pulled out a single page, the paper having been torn from the journal.

Dear Wade, it read. *There are no words to describe the regret that I feel over what I have done to your life. By the time you read this I'm relatively certain you'll be wishing that you'd never met me. You've been so completely good to me, and you need to know that this has nothing to do with you. My reasons for doing what I have to do were inside of me long before I met you, and again I'm sorry for bringing this horror into your life. I beg you not to waste time or energy over this. I only want you to move on and find the happiness you deserve. I beg your forgiveness and understanding. Regretfully and with all my love, Laura.*

Wade's breathing became so sharp that he could hardly draw air. With a combination of terror and fury he rushed to where she'd been sleeping, wondering if the minutes since he'd last checked on her might have pulled an overdose too deeply into her system to counteract. Fear overrode the anger until he was reassured of her breathing, but that didn't mean she hadn't already done something stupid.

"Laura!" he shouted and grabbed her shoulders, pulling her to a sitting position. She immediately opened her eyes, looking startled and disoriented—but not drugged. *He wasn't too late.* Then he recalled in an instant his own suicide attempt. Alex had found him, and he'd been clearly angry. Wade felt a deep empathy for his brother's behavior that day. He also understood what Alex had meant when he'd said that it wasn't so much the cut in Wade's wrist that concerned him as his state of mind. If that had failed, would he have tried something else? Well, at least he didn't have to wonder if he had justifiable cause to get her some serious help. She'd just frightened him so badly he could still hardly breathe. But as the full circumference of what could have happened filled his mind, unadulterated fury rushed in to squelch every other emotion.

"What is this?" he demanded, holding the letter in one hand and her arm in the other.

Wade watched her eyes widen, first in terror as she met his angry expression, then in shame as she turned to see the letter in his hand. Her countenance then became angry and defensive as she said, "You read my journal?"

"You bet I did," he said. "And don't go turning this on me with some offense to your privacy, when you haven't hardly spoken a word to me for a week, and you once shared *everything* with me. Now answer the question. What is this?"

She looked down and tried to squirm out of his grip, but he wouldn't let her. "I should think it's obvious."

"So, am I to assume this really means what it implies? That you had no intention of my finding this letter until you were dead?" Her silence verified her guilt, and his anger rose. "It's dated today, Laura. If I had come home when I was supposed to, what might I have found?"

She winced visibly, and he wondered if it was his accusation or his anger that frightened her. Did she fear he would hit her the way Randall had? Or was she simply upset that he'd foiled her plans?

"Answer me!" he shouted.

Laura hung her head and once again attempted to break free of his grasp. "Maybe it would have been better that way," she said, her voice barely audible.

"Better?" he countered. "Better for whom? How dare you even imply that I could *move on?* That I could . . . what? *Not waste time and energy over this?* How could you even find it remotely possible to believe that I could *ever* recover from something like this? Maybe you think I did such a good job at finding my first wife dead that I could do it again." She looked horrified at the implication, and he knew the connection hadn't even occurred to her, which made him even more angry. "Yeah, you think about that, Mrs. Morrison. In the meantime, you come clean with me. What were you going to do? Tell me. Tell me now." She looked cornered and terrified but said nothing. "Was it going to be an overdose? A handful of whatever you could swallow? Or did you want to eliminate any possibility of failure and do it the way Tina did it? As far as I know there isn't a gun in the house, but maybe you've been holding out on me. *Is* there a gun in the house, Laura?"

"No!"

"Should I be locking up the kitchen knives and the sleeping pills and prescriptions?" She shook her head and started to cry, looking intentionally away from him. "Tell me what to do to keep you alive, Laura!" he shouted.

"I don't know," she muttered, then sobbed.

"What were you going to do?" he demanded more quietly. He felt her start to tremble. She said nothing, but her eyes shifted guiltily, and he glanced over his shoulder to see what she was looking at. The hall? The *bathroom?* He hurried in that direction, taking her along with a tight hold on her arm, not willing to let her out of his sight for a minute. She moaned in protest like a child facing unwanted discipline. Wade flipped on the bathroom light and felt his heart drop to the pit of his stomach. There on the counter was a handful of empty prescription bottles, laying on their sides, the caps scattered around them. And a haphazard little pile of pills. A colorful combination of anti-depressants, anti-anxieties, and sedatives. Laura whimpered and strained against his hold on her arm. Wade felt his anger flush out of him like water being sucked down a drain. And in its place came the horror—and the sorrow. The moment felt briefly distant and veiled by shock as his mind took him back to finding Elena dead. He heard himself sob before he felt hot tears running down his face. He tried to tell himself that she really hadn't meant to go through with it, that this was just a cry for help, or a means to let him know how desperate she really felt. But instinctively he knew the truth. He'd come home hours before he'd been expected. He recalled the feeling earlier that he'd needed to stay at work, and then he recalled how his feelings had shifted. If he'd come home too early, perhaps he wouldn't have the evidence before him of how serious she really was. He didn't know why she'd been asleep on the couch while the pills were waiting, but he knew there was a reason; something had prevented her doing this long enough for him to get home. And in his heart he knew that his coming home early had saved her life—and his own. He turned to look at her, silently pleading for an explanation that could possibly counteract the images in his mind of finding her dead. He sobbed again and saw regret in her eyes that gave him the tiniest degree of comfort. He knew he should feel compassion and concern for her and her state of mind, but the only words that could get from his brain to his mouth were a broken, "I never would have gotten over this, Laura. Never. How could you even consider doing this to me? What happened to all those things you promised me? That you would talk to me? Ask for help?"

"And what could I have said?" she retorted sadly, resigned.

"How about, 'I'm feeling suicidal, Wade. I'm scared and I need help.' You *promised* me."

She looked down. "One more reason you would be better off without me," she said.

He took her upper arms into his hands and shook her gently until she looked up at him. On the wave of a sob he muttered hotly, "Don't you *ever* say or even *think* something like that again. I *need* you, Laura. I *love* you!"

"How can you?" she asked and sobbed as well.

"How can I *not?"* She looked so utterly confused that he had to admit, "You know what, Laura? It's obvious that I have no idea how you're feeling right now, because you're not saying anything that makes any sense to me. But I'm not letting you out of my sight until I figure it out, and you will not—"

The doorbell rang and startled him, but Laura didn't look surprised. "Who is it?" he asked.

"It's probably . . . one of my visiting teachers."

"You knew she was coming?" he asked, and she nodded.

Wade walked toward the door, holding her hand tightly in his. She resisted and whispered, "Please . . . tell her I'm not feeling well. I can't talk to her right now."

Wade hesitated, looked at his wife long and hard, then guided her to stand behind the door, keeping a tight hold on her hand as he opened it. He saw a woman he recognized from church, but he didn't know her name.

"Hi," she said brightly. "I'm Sister Williams. Is Laura here?"

"She is," he said, "but she's not feeling very well."

"That's what she said on the phone," Sister Williams said, "but I was really hoping to see her." She became a bit nervous. "I don't want to be . . . pushy . . . or anything, but . . . I just couldn't shake the feeling that she needed a visit today; like maybe she needed a friend."

Wade swallowed carefully and struggled for composure. He wanted to just hug this woman and tell her the truth. He knew now why Laura had been waiting to take the pills. This woman had called and insisted she was coming over for a visit, and Laura hadn't wanted to be ungracious or cause her any alarm. Well aware of Laura's trembling hand in his, Wade forced words out of his mouth, noting they sounded a bit shaky. "I can't tell you how much your insight is appreciated. She very much needed a visit today, and I'm absolutely certain you were prompted. I want to thank you for acting on it. But since I'm home now, I'll see that everything is okay." He looked sternly into her eyes, hoping she would perceive something of what he wasn't at liberty to say. He saw her brow furrow and knew she'd picked up on the undercurrent of the conversation. "Please . . . don't ever be afraid to call her or visit any time you feel that you should. I'm absolutely certain that your efforts are no small thing."

In a cautious voice she asked, "Is there . . . anything I can do?"

"Not at the moment, thank you, but . . . I'll call if anything changes."

"Please do," she said. "I mean it."

"Thank you," Wade said, and Sister Williams held out a small gift bag.

"Will you give this to her?"

"I'd be happy to," he said, his voice more steady. "And again . . . thank you."

She left reluctantly, and Wade closed the door. He leaned against it and met Laura's frightened eyes. "She's the reason, isn't she? That's why you hadn't taken the pills yet."

She looked guiltily away. "She sounded so concerned when she called. I was afraid . . . if I didn't answer the door she'd break it down, and . . . I didn't want her to find me."

"Oh, you wanted *me* to find you? Me and Rebecca?"

"No!" she insisted, then hesitated.

"Just tell me and get it over with," he said.

"I . . . was going to . . . leave a message on your cell phone, and . . . tell you not to pick her up, and not to . . . come home alone. And to . . ." tears spilled down her face, ". . . to tell you that I love you."

Wade sighed loudly. "Forgive me if I'm not wholly convinced of that at the moment." He heard anger in his voice again and knew it wasn't going to help matters, but at the moment he didn't have the strength to navigate around it. "You love me, and therefore you were going to leave me alone—again. Is that it?"

She said nothing, hung her head, and sobbed.

Not knowing what else to say—or do—Wade handed her the gift. "Here. Open it."

"You open it," she said. He let go of her hand to do so, and she moved to the couch, slumping onto it, huddling at one end.

In the bag he found a tube of high-quality hand cream, which he handed to Laura, and a card in an envelope. He held that out to her, and she said, "You read it. I don't want to."

"So after she left you would have just . . . what? Tossed this on the couch and taken your own life in spite of her efforts?"

"Probably," she said, sounding mildly angry. But angry at what—or whom? Angry with Sister Williams for impeding her plans? Angry with him for actually caring that she was alive? Or just angry at life in general?

Wade opened the card and tossed the envelope aside. Printed on the front were the words, *Love Beareth All Things*. Inside Sister Williams had written a lengthy note, which Wade read aloud.

"'Dear Laura, I realize that you and I don't know each other very well, but I'm looking forward to getting to know you better, which is one of many reasons I'm glad they assigned me to be your visiting teacher. I want you to know that I've admired you for a long time. I know your divorce was difficult, but you always handled your struggles with such dignity and a positive attitude. I was so thrilled when I heard that you were married again, and it's good to see you so happy. I'm not sure why I felt so strongly that you needed me today, but the reasons don't really matter. I just want you to know that I'm absolutely certain your Heavenly Father loves you, because I have no doubt that He sent me to tell you that. Whatever might be wrong, I want you to know that you are in my prayers, and I hope that you will know that you can call me anytime of the day or night if you need someone to talk to.'"

Wade closed the card and found Laura holding a hand tightly over her mouth, while tears streamed from beneath her closed eyelids. "It would seem," he said with only a slight edge, "that God didn't want you to die today. But I wonder how Sister Williams would have felt to realize that in spite of her visit you had still ended up dead." She just kept crying.

Wade watched her cry for several minutes while the horror settled into him. He fought to keep his anger at bay and remember that it was simply a mask for the hurt and fear exploding beneath it. Forcing a calm voice, he said, "Just tell me one thing, Laura. What exactly did you believe this would solve?"

She wiped her face, then pushed a hand through her hair. Her voice was raspy as she said, "I just don't want to feel this way any more."

"And do you really think you would *feel* any differently once you get to the other side? It's your spirit that's hurting, Laura, your emotions. You take those things with you."

"But . . . it's different there."

"Yes, I'm certain it is. Maybe some things would be easier to overcome, and some would likely be harder. But consequences of our actions are eternal."

She sniffled loudly. "God would forgive me; He would understand."

Wade had to swallow hard. Hearing the depth at which she had thought this through made him increasingly sick. "I'm certain He would forgive you, Laura, and He would understand. I would have forgiven you too—eventually—even though I *never* would have understood." He leaned his forearms on his thighs and looked at her hard. He couldn't help the terseness in his voice as he added, "But no amount of forgiveness or understanding will *ever* take away the consequences of our choices. You were prepared to make a *choice,* Laura; a choice to *die*. A choice that is irreversible. I'm absolutely certain that God understands your state of mind, and that the repentance process for making stupid mistakes over there is probably much the same as it is here." Anger crept into his voice. "But you'd *still* be on *that* side of the veil, and I would still be *here*—without you! And I'd bet my heart and soul that eventually you would have come to your senses, and you would have wondered what on earth made you do something so stupid, and you would be wishing to be back here with me and Rebecca. Clearly, this is *not* the solution to your problems, Laura. And it sure wouldn't solve mine."

She looked as if she simply didn't believe him, and he wondered why he was wasting his energy trying to talk some reason into her. She turned to stare at the wall, and he wondered what to do now. The answer was obvious. He grabbed the cordless phone and sat down across from Laura while he dialed the ER.

"Could I speak with Dr. Keane please, if he's available."

Laura gave him a subtle glare, then sank further into the couch, looking away. The woman on the other end of the phone said, "He's close by. Hold on for just a moment. May I tell him who's calling?"

"His brother," Wade said.

A minute later, Alex said into the phone, "What's wrong?"

"You know that call you offered to make?"

"Yes," he drawled.

"I need you to make it; consider the situation extremely urgent. I'll do whatever it takes."

"Okay," Alex said cautiously. "I take it your need to get home was no small thing."

"You got that right."

"Oh, good heavens," Alex said. "Anything you want to tell me?"

"Can't at the moment."

"She's right there?"

"Yeah. If you could call me back as soon as you have anything to tell me, I'd appreciate it, and I think I could use your help for a few minutes."

"Priesthood blessing?"

"That's the one," Wade said.

"Okay, I'll make the call, and then I'll be over."

"It can wait until you get off."

"I'll see if I can get someone to cover for me," Alex said.

"That's really not—"

"I'll get there as soon as I can," Alex interrupted.

"Thank you," Wade said again and hung up. He said to Laura, "Alex is coming over."

"Is it really necessary for him to know about this?"

"When it comes to surviving the struggles of life, there are no secrets in my family. How exactly did you think we might get through something like this without some help? If I'd just found you dead, and Alex came over to scrape me up off the floor, would that be okay?"

She cried harder, and Wade moved to her side, setting the phone beside him before he pulled her into his arms. She clutched onto him tightly and sobbed uncontrollably. How could Wade not remember crying the same way after Alex had found him bleeding all over the floor when he'd tried to end his own life?

"Forgive my anger," he said, holding her closer. "You scared me, Laura. I can't live without you. I can't lose you."

"I'm so sorry," she muttered and cried even harder. Her tears settled into an eerie silence while he just held her, unable to fathom the horror of what might have been. He silently thanked God for sending him home, and he prayed fervently for guidance and strength to get them through this.

The phone rang, and Wade looked at the caller ID to make sure it was Alex; he had no desire to talk to anyone else. Alex immediately said, "He thinks you should check her in as soon as possible." Wade took a deep breath and considered the option. He had spent time in this facility a few years ago, after he'd tried to take his own life and had failed. He knew it was staffed twenty-four-seven with competent and caring people. "He'll meet you there in an hour or so if that's what you want."

Wade took a deep breath, briefly pondering his instincts—or more accurately, attempting to feel the guidance of the Spirit through the fog of his own fears. It only took a moment for his heart to agree unanimously with his head.

"Yes, I do," Wade said.

"Okay, I'll call him. I'll be right over."

"Thank you," Wade said and hung up the phone.

"I need to use the bathroom and lie down," Laura said.

Wade walked her to the bathroom door, saying, "You've got one minute, and don't be touching those pills or opening the medicine chest." He actually glanced at the pills to take note of how they looked so that he could tell if they were disturbed. She glared at him and closed the bathroom door, coming out a minute later with another glare before she headed to the bedroom. He felt confused by her vacillation between sobbing regret and her anger with him. She laid down on the bed, and Wade started looking through drawers.

"What are you doing?" she demanded.

"Searching for contraband," he said.

"Now you're just being ridiculous."

"Don't even go there," he said and searched the room for another ten minutes before he left her to rest, keeping the door open.

Alex came a minute later, and Wade let him in, barely closing the door behind him before he hugged his brother tightly. Alex returned the embrace, muttering quietly, "What happened?"

Wade was suddenly too emotional to speak as reality rushed to the surface. He took a few steps to retrieve the letter Laura had written and handed it to Alex, who looked concerned as he focused and began to read. He didn't get far before he asked incredulously, "Where did you find this?"

"I think I was prompted to read her journal; it was tucked in there."

Alex finished reading the letter and said, "Well, that certainly gives you something to go on, now, doesn't it."

"Oh, that's not all," Wade said. He put a finger to his lips to indicate they needed to remain quiet as Alex followed Wade down the hall and into the bathroom. He flipped on the light and motioned toward the counter.

Alex gasped, then picked up the bottles to look at the labels. "Yeah, that would have done it, alright. Looks like you were just in time."

Now that Alex had seen the evidence, Wade scooped up the pills and threw them in the toilet, then he flushed it. Then he felt suddenly frozen; he couldn't move, didn't know what to say.

"You look terrified," Alex said.

"I am," he admitted. "Terrified of losing her, wondering how I'm going to handle getting her the help she needs."

"Wade," Alex said, "there's something Hadley told me that you need to know." Wade riveted his attention on Alex, certain he wasn't going to like what he was about to hear. "Legally, you have the right to take her there without her permission. She can be held against her will for seventy-two hours if you have any cause to believe she could be a danger to herself or anyone else." Wade put a hand over his mouth, almost fearing he would throw up. He willed himself to remain detached as Alex added, "Once she's evaluated, she can be held as long as necessary, according to the doctor's judgment."

"So . . . what are you saying, Alex? That I should . . . have her committed against her will to . . . to . . ."

"Save her life—yes. If that's what it takes."

Wade thought for a moment. "I really don't think she'll resist going."

"That's good then. I just think you need to know how it works."

Wade nodded.

"Where is she?" Alex asked.

"She's lying down in the bedroom. Just give me a minute."

Wade found Laura curled up on her side, staring at the wall. "Alex is here," he said quietly. "We're going to give you a blessing . . . if that's okay."

"Okay," she said, sounding indifferent.

Wade briefly examined the gamut of emotions he'd been through since he'd come home and had to say, "We'll . . . be back in a few minutes." He left the room and motioned for Alex to follow him into the front room. "I don't know if I can do it," he admitted.

"You can't leave her alone like this, Wade. You've got to get some help to—"

"Not that," Wade said. "I don't know if I can give her a blessing." Alex waited for an explanation. Wade sighed loudly, then gave him one. "Remember how you were when you found me . . . after I'd cut my wrist?"

"You mean ticked off?"

"Yeah, that's what I mean. Well . . . I was pretty ticked off; still am to be truthful. I don't know that I'm in the proper frame of mind to do this."

"Okay, but . . . you're not unworthy to do it, Wade. You're just upset. I'll do the majority of it, if that's what you want. I really think she needs it before you go."

"Yeah, I know you're right. Okay."

Laura gave Alex little acknowledgment as she sat up on the edge of the bed. Wade realized his hands were trembling as he put them on her head. *He'd almost lost her!* He couldn't believe it. He was grateful for Alex's soothing voice and calm confidence as he spoke the words of the blessing. Laura was told firmly but with compassion that her time on this earth was not finished and only God had the right to give life and to take it. She was told that there were children waiting to be born to her, who would need the strength and guidance of their mother through the course of their lives. And she was promised that as she trusted in God, and in those around her, she would be guided to healing and peace. But she was cautioned that the path through this valley would be long and treacherous and she needed to rely heavily on the things that would keep her close to the Spirit. She was promised that God would always be with her, and that His power was far greater than any power that might encourage her negative thoughts and feelings.

When the blessing was finished, Laura seemed numb and emotionless. She thanked Alex and gave him a quick hug. He kissed her cheek, saying, "You take care of yourself, little sister. We're going to get through this." She nodded but wouldn't look at him.

She hugged Wade as well, but it felt withdrawn and apprehensive. He eased back and said, "You rest. I'll be back in a few minutes."

Wade walked Alex out to his car, briefly filling in the gaps of what had happened, and thanking him, as always, for his support.

"Do you want me to go with you? Do you need some help with this?"

Wade glanced back toward the house. "No, it's okay. Thank you. Keep your cell phone handy. I'll call if I have a problem."

"Hey," Alex said, "why don't you and Rebecca stay with us tonight, so you won't have to be alone."

"Thanks," Wade said. "I think we will."

As soon as Alex left, Wade hurried back to the bedroom, drawing courage and uttering a silent prayer. "Laura," he said, urging her to a sitting position.

"What?" she asked, sounding lethargic.

"Enough of this. We're getting you out of this house."

He started packing some of her things, which made her more coherent. "What are you doing?" she asked, sounding more curious than alarmed.

"I'm taking you to stay at a facility that can help you work through this."

"What are you talking about?" *Now* she sounded alarmed.

"I can't fix this, Laura. And obviously you can't either. I was tempted to do this yesterday when I realized that you've lost a week of your life, and mine too. I should have done it then. Now there are no other options. I can't leave you alone, and we can't go on like this. We're going to get the help you need—whatever it takes."

"But I . . . I'm sure that . . ."

"Stop stammering, Laura." He crammed her things into an overnight bag. "You don't have the answers. Put your shoes on."

Laura didn't protest; in fact she said nothing at all as he helped her into the car. A few minutes into the drive she started to cry.

"Laura," he said, attempting to explain why he had to do this, "you haven't spoken hardly a word to me in a week. I don't know what's going on inside of you, and it scared me before today. But today I almost lost you. We can't live like this, Laura. We have to do something about it. Do you understand?" She didn't answer. "I love you, Laura. We're going to get through this—together! Do you understand?" She nodded, and more tears fell. "I'm taking you to the place where I stayed when I hit rock bottom. They're good people. They'll take good care of you. I will come and see you as often as I possibly can. Okay?"

Again she was silent, and he just drove, wishing he could stop the cracking of his heart as they arrived at the facility where Alex had once taken Wade. As he parked the car, Laura asked tearfully, "You're going to leave me here?"

"No longer than absolutely necessary," he said and kissed her hand.

She jerked her hand away and turned to look out the window. "I don't blame you for wanting to call it off now that you've seen what I'm really like, but—"

"Call *what* off?"

"The marriage," she said as if they were talking about a social event needing to be canceled due to bad weather.

"Call it *off?"* he countered, not even caring that he sounded angry. He *felt* angry. "Laura, I *love* you, and I—"

"Don't say any more," she said without looking at him. "If it's easier for you to just . . . leave me here like that, fine. But don't try to spare my feelings. Just give it to me straight. If you never want to see me again, just say so."

"Who *are* you?" he asked. "Who is this woman impersonating my wife?"

"Maybe your sweet wife was just a cover for the real me," she snapped, turning defiantly toward him. "Maybe this is the best you'll ever get. Maybe I'm just a psychotic shrew that you're better off without."

"I hear Randall talking, or maybe your mother."

"No, it's *me* talking, Wade. And I'm tired of pretending."

"Is that what it's been? Pretending?"

She said nothing, and once again Wade wondered why he was trying to reason with her. He got out of the car before he said something he *really* regretted. She didn't speak as he took her arm to help her out of the car, and he kept hold of it as they went inside.

Chapter Seven

Once inside, it was apparent they'd been expected. A kind woman urged Laura away from the front office, saying, "Let me show you to the room where you'll be staying. Your husband will come and talk to you before he leaves. I promise." Laura glared at him as she was led away, and he wondered what he'd done to end up in this position.

When Laura was gone, Dr. Hadley entered the office, shaking Wade's hand. "It's good to see you again, young man," he said. "I wish it could be under better circumstances."

"Yeah, me too," Wade said.

"Come, sit down. Let's talk."

Hadley guided him into a room where they sat facing each other. "So, tell me what's going on," he said kindly. "But first, tell me how you've been doing since you lost your first wife."

Wade said, "It was pretty rough, off and on, until I had the good sense to ask Laura to marry me. Everything's been great—until a week ago." He went on to tell Dr. Hadley what had happened concerning Randall's visit and how she had been behaving since then. The doctor asked a few questions about Laura's upbringing, the situation with Randall, and her friend's suicide. Wade told him what he knew, and what had happened today, embarrassed by the emotion that came with it. But then, Dr. Hadley had certainly seen him cry before. He had to ask, "How do I know she won't try it again? How do I know if she'll be safe?"

"That's why you brought her here."

That wasn't good enough for Wade. When he'd come here himself, he'd already gotten past the urge to take his own life. He couldn't comprehend how they could insure Laura's safety when he knew her frame of mind.

"Wade," the doctor said gently, "when we get a patient who is at this level, they will not be left alone for even a moment. A woman will be with her constantly. She will wait just outside the bathroom stall, and stand on the other side of the shower curtain, and if Laura wants to shave her legs, this woman will watch her. The mirrors are not made of glass; there is nothing she can get her hands on that is sharp enough to inflict any personal damage. I can assure you that as long as she is in our care, she will not be able to take her own life."

Wade felt both relieved and a little sick to hear the report. But at least he could sleep at night and put in his shifts without feeling terrified.

"Do you have any other questions right now?"

"Uh . . . I don't know. I . . . how often can I . . . should I . . . see her?"

"Just call and check before you come. It really depends on her state of mind and what's going on at this end. Sometimes visits help; sometimes they make it harder."

"Okay," Wade said and swallowed hard.

Dr. Hadley took him to the room where Laura would be staying. The place felt eerily familiar to Wade, but it was a place where he'd felt safe and well cared for. He was grateful for Dr. Hadley's kindness and expertise. He knew Laura was in good hands. He stood back while Hadley introduced himself to Laura and told her they'd talk some more tomorrow. Then the doctor stepped back and motioned for him to say his good-byes, but he made it clear he intended to stay. Did he fear some outburst? Maybe he wasn't the only one. Wade felt his every instinct bristle as he stood in front of his wife, searching for the right words. He saw her anger fade into a desperate fear. She took hold of his arms and pleaded, "Don't leave me here like this, Wade; I beg you. I'll get out of bed, and I'll go to work, and I'll talk to you if that's what you want. Please, Wade."

Wade glanced toward the doctor, hoping for some guidance here. Dr. Hadley motioned with his hand and said softly, "Say what you have to say."

"Laura," Wade said, looking directly at her, holding her shoulders in his hands, "you tried to die today. I can't live constantly wondering if I'm going to find you dead. I can't. We need help to fix this problem, Laura. This is the only thing I know how to do."

"Please, Wade," she repeated. "Don't leave me."

"I'll visit when I can," he said and tried to step back, but she held to him more tightly.

"Please," she whimpered.

"You need to go," Hadley said firmly.

"Good-bye," Wade said and kissed Laura's forehead before he took her hands and forced her to let go of him.

It suddenly became a physical struggle as she tried to hold onto him and he tried to move away. Dr. Hadley moved behind her and took her shoulders into his hands, saying gently, "It's okay, Laura. He'll be back, and we'll take very good care of you and—"

"No!" she cried and strained against the doctor's hold.

"Just go," Hadley said to Wade with a firm nod.

Wade stepped back and resisted his every instinct as he turned his back and left the room.

"No!" he heard her scream as if he'd just abandoned her to fire and brimstone. He gasped for breath and pressed a hand over the burning in his chest as he quickened his pace and she screamed his name. Before he reached the door, he distinctly heard her plea turn to anger as she cursed him and declared her hatred for him. Wade stepped outside, grateful to be beyond hearing range, but too weak to take another step. He pressed his back to the brick wall of the building as heaving sobs erupted into the autumn air. He started to feel lightheaded and pressed his hands over his thighs, hanging his head while he struggled to catch his breath. He was grateful to be alone, but no sooner thought it before a car pulled up nearby. He cursed under his breath and hurried to his own car where he sat for twenty minutes, struggling with an inability to take a deep breath or slow his heart rate. He gripped the steering wheel and pressed his head there, wanting to pray but unable to put together any thought beyond a repeated, *God help me.*

A sudden need not to be alone spurred him to start the car and drive. He cried all the way to Alex and Jane's house, then he had to force some composure so he could go inside without making a spectacle of himself. He went directly to the room where Rebecca slept when she stayed here, needing to connect with his daughter. He found Barrett there, putting her into her pajamas.

"Hey," he said, and they both looked up.

"Daddy!" Rebecca squealed and ran to him. He squatted down and held her close for as long as she would tolerate it.

As she squirmed away and left the room, Barrett asked with wide eyes, "What's wrong?" Wade hesitated, wondering how to explain this nightmare to a child. "Mom said you were staying here for a while, and . . . I can tell you've been crying. And . . ." He looked down as if he'd reconsidered saying whatever he'd intended to say.

"What?" Wade insisted.

"And . . . Mom's been crying ever since Dad got home. All she told me was that she was worried about Laura . . . and you."

Wade sighed to think of bringing more trauma into his brother's family. They had been nothing but good to him, helping him through one crisis after another. Now, here he was again. He couldn't deny his gratitude for their caring, but he hated to see them upset by this. Knowing it wasn't fair to leave

Barrett ignorant and concerned, Wade cleared his throat and simply said, "Laura is in a . . . hospital of sorts. She's very sick, and I'm very worried."

"What's wrong with her?" Barrett asked, clearly more concerned than curious. Again Wade hesitated, and Barrett added, "And don't tell me I'm too young to understand."

Wade reminded himself that Barrett was wise and sensitive beyond his years. So he just said it, "She's depressed, Barrett. They call it emotional illness. It's like . . . she's lost control of her thoughts and feelings. But now she's in a place where they can help her." He forced a smile, hoping to lighten Barrett's mood. "The good news is that I'll be living here again for a while."

He expected Barrett to be pleased, since he'd had such a hard time when Wade had moved out when he and Laura married. But Barrett got tears in his eyes and said, "It's not the same without Laura."

"No, it's not," Wade said, "but . . . all we can do is . . . pray for her, and . . . wait." He tousled the child's hair. "Hey, there was a time when we did a lot of waiting and praying for you; that turned out okay, right?"

"I'm still here," Barrett said.

"Yes, you are," Wade said and hugged him tightly. "And I bet you're supposed to be getting ready for bed. Thanks for helping Rebecca with her jammies."

"I'll pray for Laura," he said, and left the room. Wade slumped onto the edge of the bed that was in the same room with the spare crib.

A minute later he was startled when Jane carried Rebecca into the room. "Oh, you're here," she said. "I was just going to put Rebecca to bed."

Wade stood up. "I'll take care of it. Thank you."

"Are you okay?" she asked, and he couldn't miss the unmistakable signs that indicated she'd been crying. But from the way she looked at him, he knew she could see that same evidence in him.

"No," he said. "And Barrett's already tattled on you, so I know *you're* not okay."

Her eyes teared up, then they heard Ruthie crying down the hall. "We'll have to talk later," she said and left the room.

Wade tried to force thoughts of Laura out of his head while he read a story to Rebecca, said prayers with her, and put her to bed. He managed to present a normal demeanor for the sake of his daughter, but in his mind he could only see flashes of those pills on the counter, the letter telling him good-bye, the hollow look in Laura's eyes. He closed his eyes in an attempt to block out the images, but he could only hear her begging him not to leave her, then screaming as he'd left. It all felt too dramatic, too surreal to actually be happening. Things like this happened on TV, not in real life, not with people who exchanged eternal vows. Obviously he needed to get a grip on reality and let go of whatever degree of idealism he'd been holding on to. He would have thought that his own unconventional family circumstances were pretty high up on the list of "things least likely to happen to a good Mormon boy," but this one topped it. He wondered at what moment his life had crossed into the realms of reality soap opera. And he wondered how many other people in the world—in the Church—were feeling the same way about their own lives and the sometimes-stark chasm that separated a worthwhile goal from a harsh reality that had to be conquered in order to get there.

Once Rebecca was down for the night, Wade left her room and quickly debated where to go now, what to do. The grief he'd battled earlier came rushing back, and he hurried down the stairs and out into the yard where he could be completely alone. He sank to his knees in a shadowed corner of the cold lawn, wrapped his arms around his middle and curled around them, sobbing without restraint. He was startled to feel a hand on his shoulder and realized he had no idea how long he'd been out here, but his legs and back ached, and he was freezing.

"Come inside," Alex said. "It's cold out here."

"I . . . don't want the kids to see me like this."

"They're all asleep. And it's a big house." He took hold of Wade's arm and helped him to his feet. "Come along, little brother." Wade's tears receded into shock as he leaned against Alex to walk. Alex guided him to a chair in the kitchen, left for a moment, and came back with a blanket that he threw around Wade's shoulders.

As Alex sat down, Wade glanced up to see that Jane was sitting across the table; a box of tissues and a pile of used ones were in front of her. He felt like he should offer her some kind of comfort, but he couldn't think of any. She sniffled, then tossed another wadded tissue onto the table as she said, "This is almost worse than when we lost Elena."

Wade felt stunned by the statement, but couldn't deny that it validated something inside of him. His emotion wasn't excessive or ridiculous; his heartache was not unfounded. Elena's death had been horrible, but at least he'd known exactly where he stood. Her death had separated them, but it had not marred their relationship. He'd had no ugly thoughts or memories to contend with beyond the death itself.

Feeling like he ought to say *something,* he cleared his throat and muttered, "Yeah, I know what you mean."

"So, now what?" Alex asked.

Wade took in a deep breath, then blew it out, as if to prove to himself that he still could. He pushed his hands through his hair. "Uh . . . they will . . . keep her . . . alive . . . until . . . she can . . . come around, I guess. In the meantime, I just . . . well . . . I just . . . move back in with you, make myself a burden once again, and try to remember why it is I'm trying to become a doctor."

"You are *not* a burden," Jane insisted, sounding perhaps more angry than he'd ever heard her. "I would be insulted if you even tried to get through something like this without allowing us to do all that we can."

"I echo that," Alex said. Then silence fell—heavy and eerie. Alex finally added, "I don't know what to say, Wade. It just feels so . . . unfair, so . . . *not right*. It feels like when I discovered Barrett had leukemia. How could such an innocent child be subjected to such a horrible disease? Not to mention how it affected us. I look at this and wonder how such an amazing woman could be reduced to such . . . I can't even think of a word."

Wade felt tears slide down his face as Alex expressed his sentiments exactly.

"Talk to us, little brother," Alex said. "You can't hold it all inside."

"I just . . . can't believe it. She *wants* to die. Can she not see how much I love her? How happy we were?"

"Obviously," Alex said, "she's not in her right mind, and if you try to reason this out according to *your* ability to reason, it will never make sense."

"Okay, so how do I cope with trying to understand her *wrong* mind?"

"You need a professional to answer that question," Alex said. "Dr. Hadley's a good man, and he knows what he's doing."

"Yes, I know," Wade admitted.

"Did you see him?"

Wade almost resented the memories that question evoked. He couldn't help sounding terse. "Yeah, I saw him."

"It didn't go well?"

"You could say that." He looked at Alex and Jane's expectant expressions and stood up, muttering, "You don't need to hear this."

Alex put a hand on his arm and urged him back to the chair. "Sit down and talk, Wade. Like it or not, I'm not going to let you carry this alone."

Wade didn't want to tell them what had happened, but he felt sure Alex was right. If he didn't say the words, they might eat him alive. He sighed and said, "Hadley, um . . . told me the . . . precautions they would take . . . to keep her alive."

"Such as?" Jane asked, as if she were genuinely worried.

He repeated what the doctor had said, while Alex and Jane both looked steadily more horrified by the evidence of how bad it really was.

"After we talked alone, he took me to say good-bye to Laura." He wiped at a new stream of tears. "She . . . pleaded with me not to leave her, begged me. Hadley had to practically pry her away and hold her back. Then I . . ." he sobbed and hung his head, "I . . . could hear her screaming at me until I got outside. She cursed me . . . said she hated me."

Now that he'd gotten the words out of his mouth, Wade checked their reactions. Jane was crumbling in tears. Alex had his arm around her, looking the same way he had at the ER when he had to accept that he'd lost a patient.

"You know what?" Wade said, erupting to his feet. "I appreciate your support more than I could ever say, but . . . I think we've all had more than enough trauma for one day. I'll see you tomorrow."

He hurried up the stairs, peeked in on Rebecca to find her sleeping peacefully, then he quickly got ready for bed and dragged himself between the covers, wondering how he could ever hope to sleep. Taking in the familiarity of his surroundings, he had trouble believing that it hadn't been that many weeks since he and Rebecca had been living here and he'd been alone and tired of it. Then he'd declared his love for Laura, and everything had been better. Now, everything felt worse than it ever had, and he hated the sick irony of regressing to such depths.

And oh, how his heart ached for Laura! What had gone wrong? He loved her so much, but he didn't even know her anymore. He'd almost *lost* her! Or had he lost her anyway? He kept seeing those pills on the counter, and hearing Alex's words in his mind. *Looks like you were just in time*. Well, he'd saved her physically, but the possibility of ever getting beyond this felt incomprehensible. He was staring wide-eyed at the ceiling when he heard a light knock at the door.

"Yeah," he called, and Alex appeared in the light reflecting from the hall.

"You need something to help you sleep?"

"Yes, actually. Another ten minutes, and I would have come begging."

"Here," he said, moving toward the bed with a glass of water in one hand and a pill in the other. Wade swallowed the pill and set the glass on the bedside table.

"Sleep as long as you can," Alex said. "We'll take care of Rebecca, and I've traded a shift so I don't have to work tomorrow, and that means you don't either."

Wade sighed loudly. "Oh, saying thank you feels so trite. Looks like God put you in my corner once again."

"It would seem so, but there's no other corner I'd rather be in. At least we don't have to plan a funeral tomorrow."

"Yeah," Wade said, "I'm more grateful for that than I could ever say, but . . . just knowing how close it came to that . . ."

"I know. Try not to think about it and get some sleep. I'll see you in the morning." He moved toward the door.

"Alex?"

"Yeah?" He turned back.

"Thanks for being my big brother."

"It's a pleasure, kid," he said and left, closing the door against the hall light.

The following morning Wade woke late and was grateful for a good night's sleep, free of dreams. Before he was even out of bed he took his cell phone from the bedside table and dialed the facility to see if he would be allowed to visit Laura. He hoped somehow to be able to smooth over their ugly parting the previous evening. But he was told that for the time being, Dr. Hadley had asked that she not have *any* visitors, not even her husband. When he asked why, he was simply told, "She's not in a good place right now."

"What does that mean?" Alex asked when Wade repeated it to him.

"One can only imagine," Wade said and forced himself to eat the breakfast Alex put in front of him. Once he'd eaten, he resisted the temptation to crawl back into bed and stay there, but maybe his lack of appetite and desire to hide in bed gave him the tiniest degree of empathy for what Laura was going through.

Instead of giving in to despair, Wade made an attempt at solving some problems. He called the clinic where Laura worked and told the receptionist that he needed to speak with the doctor on Laura's behalf. She told him a time to come in, and he was able to have a candid conversation with this man Laura worked for. He was kind and compassionate, but according to the regulations of the corporation that governed the clinic, Laura could only take a one-month medical leave before she would have to let go of her job. Wade prayed the problem could be solved within the few weeks she had left. But he felt doubtful.

Not wanting to be alone at all in the house without Laura, he went there and packed up a bunch of his and Rebecca's things. While he was there he made certain everything was in order, gathered the dirty laundry and put it in the car, and packed a few of Laura's things he thought she might appreciate once he was allowed to see her. He also gathered bills that needed to be paid, and took their wedding portrait—the one that had been taken on the temple steps—down from the living room wall. He hung it on the wall of the room where he would now be staying and stood back to ponder the day he'd married Laura. He hoped the picture could give him some positive visualization that might help block out all the negative images and thoughts.

Once he had officially moved back into their old rooms in Alex and Jane's home, Wade called the bishop to tell him what had happened and to inform him that Laura would not be able to teach her Sunday School class, and that he and Rebecca would be staying with his brother. The bishop offered to ask the ward for prayers and fasting on Laura's behalf, without saying anything specific about her illness. Wade told him that would be good, and he only felt compelled to call one other person in the ward other than the neighbor that he asked to keep an eye on the house.

"Sister Williams?" Wade said when he heard her answer.

"Yes?"

"This is Wade Morrison. Laura's husband."

"Oh, of course," she said, sounding immediately concerned. "How *is* Laura?"

"Not well, I'm afraid. She's been hospitalized, actually." He heard the woman gasp softly, but she waited for him to explain. "I felt like I should call you," he said. "I know your promptings on Laura's behalf were important, and the card you wrote meant a great deal. I feel that I can trust you to be discreet about the situation."

"Of course," she said. "Tell me what I can do to help."

"Well . . ." he found it difficult to say but just forced the words out, "she's staying at a crisis facility. She's being treated for severe depression and . . . suicide prevention."

Sister Williams gasped again, and Wade forged ahead. "You need to know that . . . you saved her life." He heard her sniffling and knew she was crying. "She waited to take the pills because she knew you were coming. I felt prompted to go home early, but without your call, and your determination to come and see her, she probably would have done it long before I ever could have gotten there. So . . . thank you . . . for being the kind of person who pays attention to such promptings, and acts on them. You will never know how grateful I am."

"I can't believe it," she said tearfully. "She's always been so . . . positive and . . . cheerful."

"Yes, I know. But she's had a lot of rough things in her life to overcome, and I'm afraid it's all kind of hit her at once."

"Tell me what I can do," Sister Williams repeated.

"Just more of the same. Whatever you feel is right. I was thinking . . . if maybe you could just . . . stick a note in the mail here and there, let her know somebody cares. I think it would help. That's all."

"I would be more than happy to do that. Is there anything else? Is your daughter needing—"

"We have a lot of family around, so Rebecca is well cared for, but thank you. Beyond that, prayer is the best thing anyone can do."

"Of course," she said. "I'll call and put her name in the temple."

"Thank you."

"Please call me if you think of something else."

"I will, thank you." He gave her the mailing address for the facility, then got off the phone and cried like a baby.

In the midst of his tears he heard the doorbell in the distance, and a minute later Jane knocked at his bedroom door. "There's someone here to see you," she said, but rushed away to answer the cry of a child before he could ask her who it was. He hurried downstairs, trying to appear composed. In the study he found Neil Keane, looking at the books on a high shelf, his hands in his pockets.

"Dad," Wade said, surprised. He hadn't called any family as of yet to let them know about the problem.

"Hi," Neil said, his brow furrowing as he took in Wade's countenance.

"What are you doing here?" Wade asked.

Neil sat down and crossed an ankle over his knee. "You know I talk to Alex every day. Today he mentioned that I should remember you and your family in my prayers, and that you and Rebecca would be at his house for the time being." In his typical forthright way he added, "I think my prayers might be more effective if I know what I'm praying for. And since you *are* my son, I thought that maybe you should be telling your father what's going on that would have you moving out of the house when you've been married less than two months. Is there some cause for this sudden separation?"

Wade hurried to sit down, his knees threatening to give way.

"It's not like that," Wade said, pushing both hands through his hair. "I had every intention of telling you everything, but . . . until yesterday I thought we could work it out, and there was no need to involve anyone else. And today . . . well . . . I've been busy . . . and a mess."

"Work *what* out, Wade?" Neil asked, his voice firm but kind. "Is your marriage in trouble?"

"No!" Wade snapped, then he noted his father's wide eyes and quickly added, "I'm sorry, Dad. I . . . I . . ." Tears crept into his voice. "I almost lost her yesterday, Dad." He sobbed. "She's . . . been depressed, and . . . I kept thinking she'd snap out of it, but . . . yesterday . . ." He sobbed again. "I found a letter . . . and the pills . . . were all . . . dumped on the counter, and . . . I almost lost her."

Wade found his father's arms around him, and again he cried like a baby. "I'm so sorry, son," he heard Neil say. Once he'd calmed down, Neil handed Wade the box of tissues from the end table and asked, "So, where is she now?"

"The same place I went to, but I couldn't stay in that house without her, and I need help with Rebecca anyway."

"Tell me what we can do, Wade; anything."

"I don't know, Dad. If I knew *what* to do, maybe I wouldn't feel so blasted helpless. Of course, the army of Rebecca-tenders is still in place, so that's not a problem. I just . . . have to keep putting my hours in at the hospital and . . . try to get through this."

"What about the finances?" Neil asked. "And don't get proud on me. Tell me where it stands. You still have life insurance money?"

"Yes, I do."

"But you need that to get you through your education so you won't have to work as well."

"All I can do is what has to be done now," Wade said. "I wrote a check for what the facility needed as a down payment. We're fine for the moment."

"Let me help pay for it," Neil said.

"Dad," he drawled, "it's really not necessary for you to rescue me financially every time a crisis comes up. You paid for the whole thing when *I* was in there."

"Wade, do I need to remind you that I'm your father, but not knowing of your existence I had no opportunity to contribute even a dime to your upbringing?"

"I never went without."

"I know that. And if I didn't have the money, it would be different. We'd have to explore other options. But I have it, and I want to help. I'm certain there are plenty of other places for your money to go. I don't want you to run out before you get that degree. Rebecca needs a father who can be home with her at least part of the time. If you have to work *and* go to school, that won't be possible."

"Okay, I hear you, but . . . we're okay for the moment. Actually, I found out today that Laura's insurance through her job will pay a percentage, and I have the option to keep up the premiums even if she can't work, and the coverage is pretty good."

"Okay, but it won't cover everything, and I want to help."

Wade shook his head. "I don't know, Dad. I can't think right now. I'm grateful for your offer; it means a lot—it really does, but . . . I just need some time. I promise I'll let you know if it becomes a problem."

"Okay. I'll be counting on it."

Neil stayed for a while, playing with Rebecca and the other children until it was time for them to go to bed. He hugged Wade tightly before he left and made him promise to call if he needed anything at all. After he left, Wade realized that he really needed to let his parents know what was going on. If a crisis happened in their lives and they didn't call him, he would be very unhappy with them. Their shock and concern were both validating and comforting. Brad and Marilyn offered to pray on Laura's behalf, and suggested a family fast. Wade knew that meant the entire family would be informed, but he figured that was inevitable anyway. He graciously accepted their offer to arrange it and, as always, was grateful for their love and support.

The following morning Wade and Alex had to be at the hospital very early to put in a shift. He called the facility on a break and was told the same thing—that Laura was not up to company. Dr. Hadley would contact him when he had something to go on.

He was grateful to find Alex standing by the counter at the central desk, doing paperwork.

Winona, one of the girls working there at the desk said, "Has anybody ever told you guys that you look like brothers?"

Wade turned to look at her, eyes wide, stunned into silence once again in a matter of seconds. Winona was one of the more colorful employees in the ER. She was efficient, and nothing rattled her. With the excess hardware she wore in her ears and her bizarre hairstyle, he felt sure she was more suited to a job back here where no one but other staff members ever saw her. But Wade liked her. What little their shifts had crossed, they'd chatted here and there. But this comment was something he was going to leave up to Alex.

Alex turned to look at Wade with mock astonishment. "We do not!" he said, just the way he'd said it the first time one of their sisters had made the same comment. And in truth, he was right. They technically shared no resemblance in facial features whatsoever, since Wade looked a great deal like their father, and Alex strongly favored his mother's side of the family. Alex added the next comment he'd also said to their sisters. "Wade's much better looking than I am."

"Oh, you're both adorable," Winona said and blew a bubble with her gum, then popped it. "But . . . well . . . okay, you don't really *look* alike, but you . . . act the same. There's something about the way you talk and stuff. And you're like . . . exactly the same height. I bet you could wear each other's clothes."

Alex just chuckled and said, "I'll tell you what, Wade. If you ever need to borrow something to wear, I'll let you know where I live."

"Great," Wade said and followed him to exam room three where a new patient was waiting.

That night Wade received an email from his brother, Brian, expressing his concern for Laura, since he'd just read an email from their mother, briefly explaining the situation. Brian committed to pray and fast on her behalf, and he told Wade to hold tightly to his faith, and all would be well. Wade appreciated the principle, but he couldn't deny that it was a challenge at the moment. Still, it was good to hear from Brian and to feel the love and support of family—even long distance.

Three days later, nothing had changed. Wade almost felt as if Laura were dying of some horrible disease, as surely as if she had cancer or Alzheimer's. He felt startled to realize how everything that had been so right had gone so wrong so quickly. All he could do was hope and pray and press forward. He couldn't bear to lose Laura, emotionally or otherwise. She was the center of his life in every respect, and he needed her. He felt helpless, believing that she needed him too, but he didn't know what to do to help her. He'd never felt so utterly helpless in his entire life. While he waited and wondered if she would ever fully recover, he did his best to keep up with the obligations of his education, and keep Rebecca cared for. As always, Jane and Alex were his towers of strength. He marveled that they could be so giving and genuine, and they actually seemed glad to have him and Rebecca back under their roof—in spite of the horrid circumstances.

Four days after Laura had been admitted, Wade called the facility as he did every day, and he got the same answers. He forced himself to stay busy by doing some laundry so that he and Rebecca would have something to wear. Between shifts with the washer and dryer he paid bills, did some errands, and picked up mail at the house. Around three o'clock, Hadley's assistant called him on his cell phone to set up an appointment for the following morning. She made it clear that he would not be seeing Laura, but the doctor wanted to discuss her condition.

When he arrived at the facility, Wade gave one of the attendants a bag of Laura's things that he felt sure she could use or enjoy. He knew it would be searched, but he'd been careful about what he'd put in there. She took the bag and thanked him, then she led him to Hadley's office. Once they were seated across from each other, Dr. Hadley said, "I thought you might like to know how we're progressing."

"Very much, yes," Wade said. "*Are* we progressing?"

"At this point I can only say that we're getting a better grasp on what's going on with her, and we're taking some steps in the right direction, but it's going to be slow. She's still very much preoccupied with the desire to end her life, so we're keeping her at the highest level of protection."

Wade felt stunned all over again to hear this reality. He squeezed his eyes closed, but that didn't hold back the tears. Hadley just passed him a box of tissues. He could only think of how he might have felt to find Laura dead, after what he'd been through with Elena. He couldn't fathom ever surviving it. While struggling for composure, he asked, "How . . . could it have gotten that bad? We were so . . . happy. Or so I thought."

"This is what I believe we're dealing with, Wade. Laura survived an extremely difficult upbringing. She came through brilliantly, as you well know. But at some level, there was a great deal that occurred through those years that she pushed away and never really came to terms with. And you know her more recent history. The incidents related to her friends have been extremely traumatic for her. Tina's suicide was horrid enough to send anyone into a tailspin of grief. But she didn't really grieve over it. She didn't have time. She couldn't afford to. She was all alone and had to take care of herself. But she also didn't grieve over Fiona's death in that car accident years ago for the same reason."

Wade had actually forgotten about that. Laura had been a part of four friends throughout most of her life, and she'd lost the first of them years earlier. Then Tina had gotten into an abusive marriage, which had eventually led to her complete downfall, and Rochelle had taken the path of least resistance.

Hadley went on. "She didn't grieve over the abuse in Tina's marriage, and Rochelle's spiritual suicide, if you will. And she didn't grieve for her own failed marriage. Her ex-husband's visit just triggered an entire lifetime of abuse, and hurt, and grief. She hit an emotional overload, and her spirit just . . . shut down. Emotionally she is reliving episodes in her life that were never addressed; they were just stuffed deep inside in order to keep living. Now it's as if those episodes are demanding to be acknowledged. It's going to take time to sift through those events and face them sufficiently to let them go."

Wade swallowed carefully and resisted the urge to demand to see her, to insist on knowing how long it would take, and to know that she would recover. He settled for quietly asking, "When can I see her?"

"I don't know, Wade. We need to take it one day at a time. Trust me when I tell you that your seeing her now would only make it harder for you."

"But . . . maybe she . . . needs me, and . . ."

"Wade, right now she will find no connection to you whatsoever."

"Why not?" he asked curtly, hating the dread that tightened his heart.

Dr. Hadley remained patient and compassionate. But his hesitance to answer implied that Wade wouldn't like the answer.

"I need to know," Wade added.

"Right now, emotionally, she is huddled in the back of a dark closet, hiding from her mother's drunken rage."

Wade hung his head, feeling nauseous. He looked back up when Hadley said, "Now, this is very important for you to understand." He leaned forward, and his eyes became intense. "I'm going out on a limb here and assuming how you must feel right now. If I'm off, you feel free to correct me." Wade could only nod. The knot in his throat was so tight that it threatened to choke him. "Her suicidal thoughts are not an indication that she was not happy with you, Wade. She simply doesn't want to feel the way she feels, and she can't see any other way out. *You* of all people know how that feels. If she were in a place where she could reason soundly, she would be able to know that's not the answer, and she would never want to hurt you. She feels like a burden to you, but I know that she loves you. Even if she can't grasp that right now, it's still readily evident."

Wade nodded again, wishing he could express his appreciation for the validation he'd just been given. Hadley had his concerns pegged accurately, and he was grateful for not having to ask questions that were difficult to voice.

Hadley went on to say, "Now, the other thing you need to understand, Wade, is that the timing of this breakdown is a compliment to you."

"What?" he squeaked.

Hadley's voice became tender. "For the first time in her life, she felt safe enough . . . cared for enough . . . loved enough . . .

that she could actually *feel* the injustice of all that had happened in her life prior to marrying you. You truly are the best thing that's ever happened to her, and if anything beyond the gospel can get her through this, it's your love for her."

Wade's hope and relief poured out of him in a rush of tears. Once he'd calmed down, Hadley said, "She's going to need to be here a while. It's going to take time. I've got her on a new antidepressant, one she hasn't tried before, but it will take time to see if it's going to make any difference. I've seen great things happen with the right medication, but it can be trial and error to match it to a person's body chemistry, and unfortunately there are side effects that require other medications to balance them out. In her case, I really believe the need for medication is only temporary—just to help even her brain chemistry out a little. But we'll just have to wait and see."

"How long before you can tell if it's helping?"

"I would expect some improvement in a month."

A month? Wade wanted to scream. *Some* improvement in a *month?*

Then Hadley added, "It will really take about three months to see significant progress."

"And if it doesn't work?" Wade asked, hating the edge in his own voice.

"We try something else."

Wade wanted to cry like a baby, but he didn't have time to focus on that thought before Hadley went on. "Eventually I want to have you present for some counseling sessions. Even though these problems have nothing to do with you, she needs to talk them out with you present. She needs to feel your love and support, and she needs you to help her get back to the real world. Does that make sense?"

"Absolutely," Wade said. "I'll do whatever it takes."

"I'll let you know when I think we're ready to take that step. In the meantime, I just ask you to be patient and trust that we are doing everything in our power to take good care of her and get her through this."

Hadley talked a while longer about some of the specifics he'd been addressing with Laura, and his plan for helping her climb out of the abyss she'd fallen into. When their meeting was finally over, Wade sat once again in his car for an undetermined length of time before he could even find the strength to drive home.

CHAPTER EIGHT

The following morning, Wade woke up to find his mind presented with a problem. He knew that Laura was not going to get through this before time ran out with her job. She was therefore unemployed. He needed to let the clinic know she wouldn't be coming back, and he needed to make arrangements to continue her insurance premiums so that the cost of her care would be covered to some degree. And if Laura wasn't contributing an income, he had to consider what changes would need to be made.

Right after breakfast he got on the phone and took care of the first two problems, but he couldn't think about the third one yet. He just couldn't. And he had to hurry and get ready for a shift that began at eleven A.M. Riding to the hospital with Alex, his thoughts rolled. Little had been said between them since he'd come home the previous evening. He'd made it clear that he didn't want to talk about it, and he'd kept close to Rebecca and the other children, finding comfort in their laughter and normalcy.

Pulling into the doctors' parking lot, Alex asked, "Are you going to be okay?"

"Do I have a choice?" Wade countered, sounding especially terse.

"Listen, kid, I can easily understand why you're angry. I know this is ugly, but don't shut me out the way she's shutting you out. If you need somebody to yell and scream at, I'm your man. But at least yell and scream something productive and get it out of your system."

He put the car in Park but didn't turn it off. A glance at the clock let Wade know they had a few minutes. "I'm sorry," he said. "You've been nothing but good to me. I guess I just . . . think you must be sick to death of hearing me gripe and complain about my life. It's been like that for as long as I've known you."

"Actually, there have been some really good times in there, and I've done my fair share of griping and complaining to you. Let's not forget that you saved my son's life."

"Oh, will you stop bringing that up!" Wade said, really sounding angry. "It was *nothing!"*

"It was his *life,* Wade. But that's not why I stick by you. We're brothers, and we're friends. But I will *never* forget how I was once believing that Barrett would die and all hope was gone, and you showed up and saved him. It's not the fact that you had matching bone marrow; it's the fact that you were so eager to give it. But you didn't just give it, you sat by his bedside and prayed for him, and you listened to me cry and vent while we waited and waited, and you visited other kids in the hospital, spreading hope around like jelly on a peanut butter sandwich."

Wade looked at him with wide eyes. If only to avoid the tension of the compliment he said, "That's probably the stupidest metaphor I've ever heard."

Alex chuckled. "Yeah, well . . . going into pediatrics as you are, you might get some mileage out of it. Obviously we need to get to work. But I'd like you to just tell me in one sentence how it went with Hadley so I don't feel like you're drowning in this all by yourself."

Wade looked out the window and took a deep breath. "In summary, it seems she is emotionally reliving the events in her life that caused her grief or pain that she's never dealt with, and if the medication they've put her on actually works, we might see some improvement in a month."

Alex let out a weighted sigh that fully expressed how Wade felt. He hurried to add the words Hadley had spoken that had haunted him the most. "He told me that emotionally she is huddled in a dark closet, hiding from her mother's drunken rage."

"Oh, help," Alex said, but Wade had to admit that it felt good not to be alone in knowing that—even before Alex turned and gave him one of those brotherly hugs that always managed to feed something good into his spirit, no matter how battered it might feel.

"Okay, let's face it," Wade said and got out of the car.

Wade was glad to settle into a busy shift at the ER, which kept his mind on accomplishing something besides grieving over Laura's condition and the effect it was having on his life. A couple of hours into the shift, Wade was watching Alex fill out the paperwork for a patient when Kay, a nurse, approached and handed him a chart. "Room five. Stat. You're not going to like it."

"I hate it when you say that," Alex said and grabbed the chart.

Wade followed him into room five while Alex walked slowly, reading from the chart as he went. "I hate this kind of stuff," he muttered.

"So she was right."

"Yes, blast her!" He hesitated at the door and gave Wade a hard stare. "I don't think you're going to like it either."

Wade had a hard time not gasping when he saw the woman's face. It needed stitches in two places. Her nose was clearly broken, and her cheeks were distorted by swelling and deep contusions.

"Hi, I'm Dr. Keane," Alex said as if he weren't horrified by what he saw. "This is Wade; he's assisting me." He rolled the stool close to the bedside and sat down. "Can you tell me what happened?"

"I fell," she said. "The stairs are outside . . . they're concrete. I hit pretty hard."

"Do you know why you fell?" he asked. "Did you lose consciousness? Faint or something?"

"No." She spoke timidly, or perhaps she was just consumed with the pain. "I just . . . slipped, I guess; lost my footing."

"Okay," Alex said, looking closely at her face. "How's your pain . . . on a scale of one to ten."

"Uh . . . seven or eight . . . I guess."

"Where else are you hurt?" Alex asked gently.

"My . . . back . . . mostly . . . I think."

Alex stood and helped her roll to her side. With the sheet up to her waist, he moved the hospital gown aside to reveal dark bruising on her back. He touched the woman's ribs, and she winced.

"I think you might have some broken ribs," Alex said gently. "And that could mean internal injuries. I'm ordering some scans and X-rays to see what exactly is going on inside. I'll check back. Is there anything you need right now besides something for the pain?"

"No . . . thank you."

"Okay, we'll get you feeling better right away," Alex said and left the room. He went straight to the desk and said to Sara, the woman currently in charge there, "I want a plastic surgeon, whoever's on call." Kay was also standing there. "Her face is going to need surgery, and right away." He then stated the other tests he wanted done, the pain medication he wanted given, and some jargon Wade didn't understand about bringing in a certain person to talk to the patient, and about some paperwork that needed to be done. Sara picked up the phone, and Kay left to do his bidding before Alex pulled Wade aside and said quietly, "When you fall, Wade, what hits the ground first . . . most often?"

Wade only thought a moment. "Your hands . . . arms . . . because a person instinctively tries to break the fall."

"Exactly," Alex said, and Wade felt his stomach tighten. "That's no fall. That looks more like a fist fight—with someone who has much bigger fists than she does."

"Good heavens," Wade muttered. "Domestic violence?"

"Yep," Alex said. "The real trick will be getting her to admit it, and to press charges."

Wade shook his head and made a frustrated noise. They were too busy to talk more than that at the moment, but Wade was present when Alex and a very kind woman on the staff spoke with this woman, gently explaining that the injuries were not consistent with the fall she'd described, and that evidence of previous cracks in her ribs and on her face had shown up on the X-rays. The victim became defensive, then terrified, then hysterical, while Wade's insides turned to knots. He was amazed at how Alex could say the right things in the right way, even though the woman who had come in with them did most of the talking, gently urging this woman to do the right thing and protect herself from any further abuse. She was told that such behavior was illegal and could not be tolerated. The woman finally agreed to press charges, but only if the police could guarantee that she would be protected. She was turned over to a social worker who would work out the details of seeing that she and her children remained safe.

At dinner Alex said, "What's wrong? You've hardly said a word. Is it Laura?"

"Well . . . yeah, it's always Laura, but . . ."

"The domestic violence?" He didn't wait for an answer. "It can really get to you, but—"

"I need to let it go; I know. I just . . . was thinking of . . ." He rubbed his eyes with his fingers as he realized he'd never told Alex about any of this. He didn't have to wonder if he *should* tell him. He knew that Alex would keep his every confidence, and he certainly needed someone to listen so he could vent these thoughts and emotions.

"What is it, Wade?" Alex asked gently.

"Um . . . Laura's first husband, he . . . slapped her a couple of times. That was it, as far as I know, but I know it left some deep emotional scars."

"No doubt," Alex said with compassion.

"But . . . Laura had a dear friend, who was in a violent marriage. She never said a word to anyone until she ended up in ICU. But apparently he was a very convincing talker. He had everyone duped into believing she was out of her mind, and she lost custody of their child to him." He sighed. "I was horrified when Laura told me, but . . . what I just saw makes the story more . . . real, I guess."

"I'd say," Alex muttered. "Where is this friend now?"

Wade straightened in his chair and looked away. He cleared his throat loudly. "She's, uh . . . she's dead."

"He *killed* her?"

"No, although that might have been better. At least he would have gone to prison or something. Actually, it was suicide. She overdosed, but someone found her, and she had her stomach pumped. She went home and called Laura to tell her everything was fine. Then she shot herself."

"Good heavens." Alex leaned back, looking stunned and upset. "You mentioned she had a friend who had committed suicide, but . . . that's horrible. When did this happen?"

"Not long before I first asked her out, actually. I don't think she ever really grieved over it. That on top of everything else, just . . . sent her over the edge, I guess."

"And no wonder! I'm so sorry, little brother."

"Yeah, well . . . so am I. But I don't know what to do about it."

The following morning Wade got a call from the facility to set up an appointment for a session with Laura, but he was disappointed to realize they were scheduling three days ahead.

They did, however, think it would be good if he came to see her for a few minutes in the next day or two. He set up a time that would work with his scheduled shifts, and he felt consumed with nervous anxiety as the appointed hour approached. While he wanted to see her so badly it hurt, he had to admit he was far more afraid than excited.

When it came time to meet his appointment, Wade was taken to a room with large windows between it and the hallway. Apparently privacy was not an option. He'd been there a couple of minutes when the door opened, but he turned to see a middle-aged Hispanic woman enter. She was pretty, and her smile was kind as she closed the door and said, "Hi, I'm Patty. Someone will bring Laura in just a minute. I wanted to meet you. I'm the psych tech who has been with Laura more than anyone during the hours she's awake."

Wade offered a kind greeting, pleased to see that Laura was spending time with someone who was apparently kind and amiable. He wanted to beg her to give him anything at all to go on, but didn't want to sound pushy or groveling. He was pleased to hear her say, "I want you to know that while she's not doing very well at the moment, I've seen people much worse off who have completely recovered."

Wade internalized that with definite hope and relief.

Patty went on. "I also think you should know that she loves you very much. She hasn't been in touch with reality much, but she's said your name over and over. It's like you're the only thing in her mind that gives her something good to hold onto; at least that's the way I see it. I thought you should know that." She touched his arm and echoed her concern with her eyes.

"Thank you," Wade said intently.

"Now, you need to realize you're not going to get much out of her. Don't try to convince her of anything, or get her to say anything. Just let her know you love her, and we'll see how it goes."

"Okay," he said.

"She knows you're coming, but that doesn't mean it will really register or . . ."

The door came open and Wade's heart quickened as a young man guided Laura into the room by holding to her arm. Just seeing her made him feel more concerned, more sick inside. She looked thinner, more pale, and that hollow look in her eyes was more defined.

"Look who's here," the young man said to Laura in a bright voice, but he said it as if she were a child and hard of hearing. Still, she looked dazed, and he wondered if it took some volume to reach past the barriers in her brain. "I think you've got a big date," he added. Laura looked up at him in question. He nodded toward Wade, and Laura turned to see him there. He wondered if she would show any acknowledgment or recognition at all. Her eyes widened with such surprise that he wondered if she had truly believed what she'd said when he brought her here, that he had left her here with the intention of never seeing her again.

"Hi," he said.

She didn't respond, but she was still looking at him. Patty touched Laura's shoulder and said close to her ear, "We're going to give you a few minutes with your husband. I'll be right outside the door if you need anything."

Patty winked at Wade as she and the young man left the room and closed the door, but Patty immediately showed up on the other side of the windows, and he knew she'd been assigned not to let Laura out of her sight.

"It's good to see you," he said, feeling as if he were lying.

She looked away as if she didn't believe him, and he wanted to scream. His mind went to frantic prayer, begging to know what to say, what to do—anything to give her some connection to him. He was startled by how quickly the answer came. *Dance with her*. And following the impression came a memory. It was when Alex and Jane had given Wade some dance lessons prior to his asking Laura on a date. But it was something Alex had said that felt significant now. *You know what's the greatest thing about dance, little brother? Eye contact. You don't have to say a word to let her know exactly how you feel.*

Wade hoped his instincts were serving him well as he took a step toward her, praying she wouldn't retract or protest. He glanced toward the windows and saw Patty talking with someone there. Tentatively he took Laura's left hand and put it on his shoulder. He was relieved when she left it there, but she didn't look at him; he couldn't make eye contact if she wouldn't look at him. He took her other hand into his and put a hand to her back. He knew it would take a little more participation on her part to even attempt a waltz, so he just gently swayed her back and forth, relieved beyond words when she began to move with him. He wanted her to look at him, but she put her head to his shoulder and eased a little closer, and he concluded that wasn't a bad thing. For several minutes they danced to silence. He didn't know if it was doing her any good, but he concluded that it wasn't hurting any. And just holding her close filled him with hope and helped him remember all the good that they'd shared. He closed his eyes to shut out their surroundings and the evidence that they were being observed. He pressed his lips carefully to her forehead, then wondered if he shouldn't have when she stopped moving and looked up at him. *Eye contact.* His heart responded when she lifted her hand from his shoulder to touch the new beard on his face, saying quietly, "You stopped shaving."

"Yeah," he said, wondering if she would catch the implication. He'd once told her that he and Alex had a running joke about not shaving when things in life got tough. Quite accidentally it had become significantly proportionate to the endurance of struggles, and the beards had come off when things got better. He'd not shaved since he'd brought Laura here, mostly because he'd felt no motivation to do much of anything. But maybe that wasn't the entire reason. Laura had once admitted to liking his beard, and he believed she'd actually been disappointed when he'd shaved it off prior to their marriage. Hoping to draw her attention to something positive he added, "I think you prefer me this way." She said nothing, and he couldn't resist adding, "I love you, Laura."

Something disbelieving came into her eyes, then in an instant the disbelief turned to sorrow, and just as quickly to fear. She backed away as if she'd just committed a carnal sin, and a split second later the door came open. Patty had obviously taken note of her change in behavior and was there to make sure it didn't get out of hand. The moment Patty touched Laura's arm she turned and hurried out of the room. Patty stuck to her like a magnet, tossing an apologetic glance over her shoulder toward Wade. He let out a heavy sigh and hurried from the building before he lost it.

In the car, Wade turned the music up intolerably loud and just drove to kill time until his shift started at the hospital. He forced himself to get something to eat and showed up a few minutes early to find Alex in a consult with another doctor. When Alex was finished he said to Wade, "How did it go?"

"It was good . . . for a couple of minutes . . . until I told her that I love her. Apparently that's not acceptable."

"She'll get it one of these days," Alex said with compassion. "So . . . tell me about the good minutes."

"We danced," he said, and Alex smiled before they were thrown into the chaos of a typical afternoon in the ER. After working there for weeks, Wade was beginning to think he could handle just about anything. Then a car-accident victim came in, presenting an experience that took him to a new edge. The call had come in from paramedics en route, giving them an idea of what to expect. Alex was the doctor available, and he was assigned to be ready. By the time the ambulance arrived they, along with four nurses, were all waiting, wearing sterile gloves, gowns, and masks. The medical team fell into step with the medics who gave a full report as they rushed into a trauma room. Their report included the fact that the patient's name was Joan. Within seconds Joan had been efficiently shifted to a trauma table, and Wade realized he'd reached a point where he could actively participate in this stuff without even thinking about it. But his confidence immediately waned as he got his first truly good look at the horror of this head-on collision. He'd never seen so much blood in his life, and somewhere beneath it was a middle-aged woman who had probably been on her way to the grocery store. He managed to follow Alex's orders, along with the others in the room, while several problems were addressed all at once. One of the nurses gasped when an artery sprayed Alex with blood, then she got her finger over it with an order to keep it there. Then the patient's heart stopped, and Alex's efforts took on an intensity that Wade had only seen when a situation became life and death.

"Don't you do this to me, Joan," Alex said, as if she could hear him and do something about it.

When the usual methods didn't work, Alex didn't hesitate even a moment before he cut her chest open, asked for a rib spreader, and started massaging her heart with his hand. His intensity increased as if holding this woman's heart had suddenly made it more personal.

"Don't you dare die on me!" he shouted softly, and Wade realized he'd never seen Alex like this, but the nurses all seemed to take it in stride, as if they had.

Minutes later it became evident that Joan was not going to respond to Alex's best efforts. While everyone in the room seemed to accept that, Alex kept working on her. Wade felt helpless, but realized he'd felt that way a lot lately. Laura's hollow eyes seemed startlingly similar to this woman's sudden and tragic death. The damage to Laura's spirit couldn't possibly be any less gory and horrific than the damage to Joan's body.

One of the nurses finally stopped the agony by putting a gentle hand on Alex's arm, saying quietly, "She's gone. Call it."

Alex looked angry, then he sighed. He squeezed his eyes closed for a long moment before he reluctantly eased his hand out of the patient's chest and stepped back. He sighed again, glanced at the clock, stated the time in a toneless voice, and stripped off the gloves and gown, tossing them in the trash, followed by the mask. Wade did the same and left the room right behind him, grateful they weren't the ones who had to clean up the mess, even though he was relatively certain he would be the one sent back in to close her up enough to send her to a mortuary. However, the damage to her face was bad enough that he felt sure it would be a closed-casket funeral.

Wade found Alex a few minutes later in the men's room, both hands pressed to the sink, his head hanging.

"You okay?" Wade asked.

"Not really," Alex said. "But sometime between now and the end of the shift I'll find a way to stuff it so I don't take it home with me—hopefully."

"I've never known you to bring your work home with you."

"Not that I let on, anyway," Alex said and sighed loudly. "Jane always asks me about 'the trauma of the day' as she calls it. She helps me decompress, and I'm grateful for that." He stood straight and looked at Wade. "But no one can really understand if they haven't seen it." He shook his head. "I just *hate* it when I can't stop it."

"It?"

"Death."

"Obviously that's out of your hands; you can only do what you can do."

"I know that, Wade. I do." He sounded angry. "I rehearse it to myself over and over. But it's still hard to watch someone die."

"So why did you stay so long? Why did you keep working on her when everyone else in the room knew it was hopeless?"

"Because I have to *know* I did everything I possibly could. I have to *know.*"

Alex hurried from the room, and Wade gave him a few minutes. He decided there were moments when it wasn't good to be too close of a shadow. He went back to the trauma room and put on fresh gloves in order to repair the body. A supervisor peeked in and said, "Oh good, you're already here. You're catching on." What she really meant was that being a medical student put you at the bottom of the totem pole, and you got the jobs no one else wanted. But he actually didn't mind. He imagined Joan's spirit hovering nearby, and he took extra care in trying to make her look as good as possible. He cleaned the blood off her face as much as he could and felt sure she'd been a beautiful woman before her head had gone through the windshield of a car.

He was just stripping off his gloves when Alex pushed open the door, saying, "Good, you're finished. I need you to come with me." With harsh sarcasm he added, "You're going to love this."

Wade followed Alex to a consultation room. Five adults were sitting in the room; one appeared to be the father of the others. They all stood as Alex closed the door.

"I'm Dr. Keane," he said, "and this is Wade; he's assisting me. Please, sit down," Alex said, and they did, but they all remained at the edge of their chairs, their expressions filled with hope and expectancy. Wade now realized what was coming, and his stomach tightened. Alex sat down and motioned for Wade to do the same. Alex leaned forward and made eye contact with each of the people in the room as he said gently, "I was with Joan the moment she came through the door. I want you to know we did everything we could." Wade saw the hope fading to fear in these people's faces. "I'm afraid she didn't make it,"

Alex concluded, and then Wade recognized the role of the doctor at this point. *Waiting for the reaction to sink in.* Alex sat, unmoving, his expression calm and compassionate. He shared a quick glance with Wade, then mostly looked at the floor. As Wade took in the reaction of a family to the death of a loved one, he could only think of those words from the scriptures. Weeping and wailing and gnashing of teeth. He'd never observed such anguish. It was the husband who calmed down enough to say to Alex, "Please . . . tell us what happened . . . what you did."

Alex gently explained the injuries, and gave a vague, appropriate description of what had been done, avoiding any words that might allude to just how gory and horrible it had been. Alex stood up as he finished his explanation, as if to indicate the conversation was ending.

"Thank you, Doctor," Joan's husband said, "for trying."

"I wish I could have done more," Alex said. "I'm truly sorry for your loss. Someone will come in and talk to you about arrangements."

"Thank you," he was told again, and Wade followed him out of the room.

As soon as the door was closed, Alex said to Wade, "*That* is why I have to *know* I truly did everything I could."

Wade could only nod.

"So, you still want to do pediatric oncology?"

"Do you think I can't handle it?" Wade countered.

"I think you can handle anything, Wade. For the record, I think you're doing great. I've seen medical students start puking when it gets that ugly."

"I felt more like puking in the consultation room."

"So, you think you can tell parents that their kids are going to die of cancer?"

"I might need some more practice first, but with any luck, I'll get to tell at least as many that their kids are going to live."

Alex just smiled at him, but Wade felt the bond between them deepen. Kids with cancer, and life-altering moments; the gut-wrenching realities of life and death; the brotherhood of two men who had stood side by side through it all. The whole spectrum came together in Alex's eyes, and Wade suddenly felt very much like his little brother. He felt overwhelmed with life, more scared for his wife than he was about the career ahead of him, and incomprehensibly grateful for this man who stood by him through every aspect of life. He was grateful to find no one around when he had to give in to the urge to just give his brother a hug. Alex returned the embrace with fervor, then they went back to work without another word being said. There was no need.

* * * * *

"Guess what?" Alex said to Wade, not long after the trauma over Joan's death had settled.

"What?" Wade asked without enthusiasm.

"It's time for our dinner break, and I hear a rumor that we don't have to eat in the cafeteria."

"Really?" Wade said and just followed Alex out to the waiting room, where their father was sitting. And in the chair next to him was a white plastic sack.

Neil smiled when he saw them. He stood and hugged Alex quickly, then he hugged Wade long and tight. As he pulled back, he said intently, "I've been worried about you, son. Are you okay?"

"I'm functioning," Wade said.

"Well, let's go function over some Chinese food, shall we?" Neil picked up the sack and they went to find a quiet place where they could eat and visit. He insisted that Wade give him an update on everything he knew about the situation with Laura. He couldn't deny that it felt good to be able to talk it through, but when Wade expressed his frustration and helplessness, Neil put a hand over his on the table and said, "Wade, we've talked about depression before. I've been through it. Your mother's been through it. Do you remember what we talked about when you were so worried about your mom not so many months ago?"

"I'm afraid it's eluding me," Wade said.

"You can't fix it, Wade. The best thing that you can do for her, beyond your prayers, is to let her know you love her and—"

"I don't think that's getting through," Wade said with an edge, losing what little appetite he felt.

"It will," Neil said. "You need to be patient with—"

"Well, I don't *feel* patient," Wade interrupted.

"I know it's rough, Wade," Neil said with nothing but compassion. "When I had my breakdown, after your mother left me, it took months for me to get through it. The point is that I *did* get through it. And she will too. When she starts to come around, she just needs to know that you love her and accept her no matter what her state of mind might be. She needs to know that you won't judge whatever she might be struggling with, because you simply cannot see life through her eyes."

Wade sighed and pondered his father's wisdom. "I know that; I do. I know that I can never fully understand what she's going through, and I . . . can never give up on her. It's just . . . hard."

"I know it is," Neil said gently. "But we're going to get through it together. We're family."

Wade had to admit, "For that I am deeply grateful."

As he and Alex went back to work, he kept trying to remind himself of his father's wisdom. He had no trouble with loving and accepting Laura, no matter what her mental state might be. But he felt terribly impatient and frustrated over the fact that she had no comprehension of his love and acceptance. He prayed that her healing would come quickly, and that they could get on with their lives.

The following morning, Wade went to the house to water the plants and pick up the mail from the neighbor. He checked the messages on the answering machine and found nothing significant except for one that sent his guts roiling.

"Hi, Laura, it's Randall. It was good to see you."

Wade listened to the recording, wondering if Randall had completely forgotten that their visit had been nothing more than an argument.

"Anyway, I'll be back in town next week and wondered if I could take you and your husband out to dinner, for old-time's sake. Who knows? It could be fun. Give me a call."

Wade deleted the message as if it were contaminated, then he grabbed a ceramic bowl from the kitchen counter and threw it at the wall, hating this man with his every cell. He forced himself to calm down and tried to remember that Randall was not responsible for the abuse in Laura's youth, or the tragedies related to her friends. But he'd treated her badly in their marriage, and his obnoxious visit had sent her over the edge. At the moment, Wade hated him for it. He looked around and felt suddenly terrified on Laura's behalf. How could he ever bring her back here with the possibility that this man could show up at any given moment? While a part of him hoped that she could eventually heal enough to be able to face her ex-husband and not crumble, he had difficulty comprehending that she could ever be anything but fragile over certain people and circumstances. He just wasn't sure what to do about it. After he'd cleaned up the mess he'd made with the broken bowl, he *still* didn't know what to do about it.

That evening Cole and his children came over for dinner. When Wade walked into the kitchen and saw him there, he realized that he'd forgotten all about his new friend and the struggles that *he* was going through. He wondered if Cole and the kids had come over last week and Wade had missed it. A moment's thought made him realize it would have been the evening he'd met with Dr. Hadley.

Cole's face was healing, but the loss was still evident in his eyes, and he still wore a leg brace. Wade was trying to think of something to say when Cole stepped forward and gave him a brotherly hug.

"Alex told me," he said as he stepped back. "I'm so sorry. If there's anything I can do . . ."

Wade forced a humorless chuckle. "I guess that puts us both in this stupid boat of being on our own."

"Well, I hope Laura comes around long before I ever think about getting married again."

Wade sighed. "We'll see, I guess. How are you, anyway?"

"I'm still breathing," Cole said, as if it were a great accomplishment. Wade knew exactly how he felt. But the evening turned out to be nice. The kids had fun together, and Wade really liked Cole. He enjoyed visiting with him and Alex while Jane eagerly offered to watch the children and give them some guy time. At moments they talked and laughed as if nothing in the world were wrong, and at others they shared each other's heartache for the losses and struggles in their lives. And then there were moments of raw silence when there was nothing to say, and they all knew that nothing could be said to make it better.

The next day Wade felt sick with dread as he approached his appointment with Laura and Dr. Hadley. When he arrived, he was taken to a room that he recognized from having spent time here himself. He tried to imagine having been here then and how it might have felt if he could have fast-forwarded to this day and all that had happened in his life through the time in between.

Dr. Hadley brought Laura in with him, saying lightly, "I believe the two of you know each other."

Laura appeared about the same as she had the last time, but she wouldn't look at him.

"Yeah, we've met," Wade said, trying to sound facetious, while he felt tightly knotted.

Hadley motioned them to a couple of chairs that were side by side. Wade reached for Laura's hand, grateful that she didn't resist his holding it, but she didn't respond when he gently squeezed her fingers. The session mostly consisted of Dr. Hadley asking Laura questions under the context of letting her husband know how she was doing, and where her thoughts were. But at least she was talking. He counted that as progress, even if the verbalization of her thoughts left him utterly and abjectly disturbed. As she described the thoughts and memories that consumed every cavern and crevice of her mind, he felt starkly educated on the crippling capacity of depression, and deeply compassionate toward what the world must look like through her eyes.

As the session was winding down, Dr. Hadley asked her, "What would you like to have happen now, Laura?"

Laura turned to look at Wade for the first time since the session had begun, but her eyes showed some level of guilt. She turned back to face the doctor and retracted her hand from Wade's. "That question is irrelevant when you already know the answer."

"So, the answer hasn't changed?" Hadley asked.

"You know it hasn't."

"Maybe your husband would like to hear the answer."

Again she looked at Wade, but only for a second. "I seriously doubt it," she said, sounding angry.

"Can you remember what it was like for you and Wade before this happened?"

"Yes, of course."

"Don't you believe it's possible to have that in your life again?"

"Do you?" she countered like a snotty teenager.

"Yes," Hadley said, unaffected by her mood.

"Well, I'm glad somebody does," she said. "If you figure out how to make that happen, you let me know. But with any luck, I'll be dead before you figure out that I'm a lost cause and you're all just wasting your time."

Wade felt stunned and a little nauseous. Hadley hurried to say, "Do you feel like you're wasting your time, Wade?"

"No," he answered quickly, but Laura looked at him as if he'd lost his mind.

"Well, I'm with Wade. I think we'll just stick it out and not get too impatient, and maybe some good things will happen."

She just glared at the doctor, then at Wade. Hadley graciously ended the session, and someone came to get Laura. The doctor talked to Wade for a few minutes about the normal stages of the process and how he believed that Laura was making progress in spite of appearances. But Wade still left feeling as if his world had ended. Even when Elena had died he'd never felt this alone, or lonely.

Chapter Nine

Over the next few days Wade felt increasingly uneasy about two particular points of concern; then it occurred to him that one solution could solve both problems. He talked to Alex about it, then he talked to Dr. Hadley, knowing the reality needed to be faced, and he couldn't face it alone. But he didn't want to upset Laura or make the situation worse. He was relieved when Hadley encouraged him to go ahead and discuss the situation with Laura, and he agreed to meet with them so that he could do it with some guidance.

"And what if she doesn't agree to this decision, Doctor?" Wade asked. "I'm not sure what I'll do."

"Wade," Hadley said, "as difficult as this sounds, you need to do what's best for you and your family." Wade opened his mouth to protest, but no sound came out as he began to grasp the implication. Hadley clinched it when he added, "You are legally entitled to make any necessary decision on her behalf."

As his meaning sank in fully, he felt somewhat horrified at the irony. This was Laura's house. He'd moved in with her when they'd married; it was in her name, and she'd worked hard to make the mortgage payments. And now, as her husband, he could legally do whatever he wanted with it. In his heart he knew that Laura's best interests were his greatest motives. But what if it had been Randall? Laura had owned the home before she'd married Randall. If this breakdown had occurred during that time, would he have been conscientious to what was moral and ethical, as opposed to what might be within his legal rights?

He couldn't resist sharing his thoughts with the doctor. "What if I was a jerk who just wanted to take everything she's got?"

He was appalled to hear the answer. "It happens." Hadley added, "But I know you'll do whatever is best for Laura. You need to at least try to talk to her first, and then you'll know what to do."

Wade wished he could feel so confident. He prayed very hard and even fasted prior to their meeting. As soon as the session began, the doctor said, "Wade needs to discuss something with you, Laura."

Laura turned toward him with wide, fearful eyes. Before he could utter a syllable she said, "You want a divorce, don't you."

Wade felt like he'd been slapped. "No! I do not want a divorce; not even close. Why would you think that?" She looked away, and he added, "Why, Laura? Have I done or said something that would make you believe that's what I want?"

"No," she admitted. "I just can't imagine why you're still here."

"Because I love you. Because the vows we exchanged did not have disclaimers. This marriage is forever, Laura, in sickness and in health. Okay?"

"Okay," she said meekly but with eyes that were mistrusting and disbelieving. "Forgive me," she said, but it felt forced. "What did you need to talk about?"

He took a deep breath. At least she was talking, and she didn't seem lost and oblivious. Perhaps his prayers were being heard. He cleared his throat and began the words he'd thought through carefully. "This situation has brought some changes into our lives, Laura, and you and I need to look at our options and make some decisions. In another week you will be officially unemployed, and we both know this isn't going to be over in a week. And that's okay. I want you to take the time you need to deal with this in the best possible way, but we need to make some decisions. We have family who are willing, even eager, to help us—which is no small blessing. But we need to do what's best for *you,* and for us as a family. Now, if you're not working, then we need to either find a way to pay the mortgage and utilities, or we need to sell the house." He didn't add that selling the house would leave her ex-husband with no way to ever find her. "You know I have enough life insurance money put away to cover a certain amount of expenses while I get through medical school, but if we start using that to make house payments, it will be gone very quickly. I can get a job. I really can. That is an option, and I'm willing to do it. Most people have to work while they get through medical school, and I can find a way to do it. But with the shift work of my rotations it would be very difficult, and you have to understand if I do that, it means leaving Rebecca in the care of others a great deal more. Eventually you will be able to take more of that responsibility." He hoped that his positive attitude might give her some seeds of hope at some level. He'd felt strongly impressed that he needed to approach this with an attitude of taking for granted that she would return to normal.

"So," he went on, "I could get a job and let family take care of Rebecca until you are able, and then you can help cover the bases with her. Or if we do decide to sell the house, Alex and Jane have invited us to stay with them for as long as we need. Space is not an issue, and you know Rebecca and I lived there comfortably for a long time. We're staying there now. But I don't know if *you* would be comfortable with that. I've given up trying to be prideful over their hospitality. They're good people, and they genuinely love having us in their home. I'm thankful for that, plain and simple. What I need to know is what *you* feel good about, and what *you* want to do. I know it's a lot to take in and think about, so if you need some time to mull it over, that's fine. You tell me what you can and can't live with, and we'll find a way to work it out. Okay?" He drew in a sharp breath, grateful to have all of that out.

"Okay," she said, not sounding upset or concerned. But he wondered if it had penetrated her ofttimes clouded brain.

Following a minute of silence, Hadley asked her, "So what do you think of what your husband just told you?"

Laura gave a humorless chuckle and spoke to Hadley as if Wade weren't there. "To tell the truth, I'm completely amazed that anyone could present a difficulty in such plain and simple terms, and not make a drama out of it like my parents would have."

Wade felt surprised by her coherency, but Dr. Hadley's expression implied that it was something akin to miraculous.

Laura went on. "And I'm amazed that he didn't say anything to make me feel the least bit guilty or ashamed, like Randall would have. I feel guilty and ashamed anyway."

"Why?" Hadley asked.

"This *difficulty* is my fault. If I were capable of solving these problems like any normal adult, then—"

"Laura," Wade said, moving his chair directly in front of her, taking both her hands into his. "If I was diagnosed with cancer next week and couldn't work, what would you do?" He didn't wait for her to answer. "If I were in an accident and became confined to a wheelchair, what would you do? Would you leave me? Write me off?"

"Of course not."

"Then why is it so difficult for you to understand that I do not resent or begrudge this? I *love* you. And we have a wonderful family, people who would do just about anything to help us through a crisis."

"They're *your* family, Wade."

"*Our* family," he corrected. "You exchanged vows with me; you took on my name. They're your family too. They love you; all of them."

Again she looked like she didn't believe him. In a voice that was almost cold, she said, "I think we should sell the house. I don't want to go back there."

Wade wanted to talk about how he knew she loved the house. He wanted to reminisce over the good times they'd spent there together. But he feared that would bring her to the tough memories she had there as well. She'd lived there with Randall; she'd gotten the news of Tina's death there. He wanted to suggest that a fresh start would be good for her when she was able to leave here, and to remind her that once he got his degree and started his residency they'd have to leave the state for a few years anyway. But he knew that such a conversation would be pointless. He sensed that her willingness to sell the house was more in the category of checking complications off of a list so that she could eventually end her life.

"Are you sure?" he asked.

"Yes, of course. I don't want it to be a burden to you."

Wade didn't like the implication, but he knew better than to try to clarify his purpose.

"Was there anything else?" she asked as she stood up.

Wade shook his head. "No . . . thank you. I'll keep you informed."

After leaving the facility, Wade went straight to the house and just wandered through it before he sat down and had a good cry. Then he tried to get a grip and watered the plants; they were looking almost as bad as Laura. He got the mail and checked the answering machine. He found several messages from Rochelle, and one from Randall. There was also one from her father, who said he was just calling to see how she was doing. He hurried to call her parents' house, hoping that this time of day would allow him to just leave a message. When the machine answered he simply said, "Hi, this is Wade. Laura is actually not feeling well, but it's nothing to worry about." He made his voice sound positive, and purposely left them ignorant. He knew the last thing he and Laura needed was any complication or dramatic intervention from her family. And since they rarely talked more often than every month or two, he doubted they'd even notice her not calling back. He almost left his cell phone number but said instead, "We'll keep you posted. Take care."

Rochelle's first two messages were simply telling Laura to call her. The third was a facetious comment, "You shouldn't ignore your friends just because you're a newlywed." The irony left Wade heartsick. Rochelle's next message said, "Did you go on vacation without telling me, or is something wrong?" He wanted to ignore the issue, knowing that Rochelle had warned Laura not to marry him, and her first assumptions over the situation would be the worst possible. But her most recent message made it clear he had to be courteous enough to call her.

"Laura? Where are you? After what happened with Tina you can't honestly expect me not to be worried. Call me."

Wade put himself in the right frame of mind to call her, hoping that she might feel some concern for Laura, as opposed to immediately blaming him for the problem. He nearly went in search of Laura's address book, then realized the number was on the caller ID log. He uttered a quick prayer and prepared himself for the barrage, determined to just give her the minimal information and get off the phone. He was hoping for a machine there as well so he could just leave a message, but she answered after two rings, saying, "It's about time you called me back."

"It's not Laura," he said.

"What's happened?" she demanded, sounding panicked.

"She's in the hospital," he said. "If you'll just give me a minute to explain, then you can ask me whatever you want."

"Okay," she said cautiously.

"There's no easy way to say it." He cleared his throat. "She hit a wall, Rochelle. It started when Randall showed up. She sank into depression hard and fast. It's a miracle she's alive."

"What do you mean?" Her panic increased.

"I'm saying she had the pile of pills on the counter, and she'd written the letter."

Rochelle cursed and started to cry, and Wade couldn't help thinking that she would have lost *two* friends to suicide if Laura had succeeded. The expected response then burst out of her, "I guess she wasn't as happy as she was letting on."

"You know what, Rochelle? I'm not going to try and convince you that I'm worthy of Laura's love and commitment, and I'm not going to tell you that this had nothing to do with me. My whole life has turned upside down and I'm really not in the mood to convince you of anything. I love Laura more than I could ever put into words, and I would do *anything* to see her whole and happy. But the truth is that I have no idea what's going on in her head, and I can't do anything to fix it. If you need any more answers than that, you'll have to call the facility. I'll call and give them permission to discuss her condition with you."

A moment of silence preceded her saying, "Okay. Thank you. I will."

He told her the phone number, and he also gave her his cell number, telling her that he was staying with his brother while Laura was in the hospital. She thanked him for calling. Before he could hang up, she said, "Wade?"

"Yeah?"

"For both our sakes, and especially for hers, I hope she comes through okay."

Wade couldn't keep his voice from cracking. "Yeah, me too."

The following day Wade put the house on the market. He walked through and took careful digital pictures of every room from every view, for his own memories as well as Laura's. He also took pictures of the back yard. Like the house, it was filled with Laura's love and care, creating an atmosphere that was warm and comfortable. Evidence of her personality and her life was everywhere he looked, but without her here he could only feel heartache. So he took the pictures and started packing.

For the next several days he spent every minute he wasn't at the hospital packing up the house. He kept Rebecca with him as much as possible, and was grateful for Alex and Jane coming over to help him more than once. Barrett was eager to help, and Wade appreciated the way he kept Rebecca safe by being her shadow while he tried to make progress.

In the tiny basement he found mostly storage that was already boxed up and neatly labeled, along with Laura's sewing machine, surrounded by evidence of her last project, which had been making Rebecca a pair of pajamas. He touched the things that she had touched and missed her so badly he wanted to scream. Instead he just forced the thoughts away and kept packing. When the basement was pretty much empty, he found a box oddly placed in a dark corner. It had a shipping label on top that had been cut through, and then taped closed again. He tipped it and turned it around, wondering what it might be, when Laura was so immaculate about having her things organized and labeled. Then he saw, written in marker on one side of the box: *Tina's Stuff.*

Wade let out a burdened sigh, recalling Laura's emotional explanation about going through Tina's things following her death, and the box she had sent home—and how she hadn't been able to do more than barely open it due to the smell. She'd obviously taped it back up and had left it separate from any of her other belongings, as if it might contaminate them. Wade took a deep breath and opened the box. There was no denying a disagreeable odor, and while the reasons for it were a little creepy, he didn't have the emotional disturbance over it that Laura did. He took out the items one at a time and laid them on the floor of the empty room. There were some books and CDs, a few framed photographs, and some odds and ends that obviously had sentimental value. Wade went upstairs and found some disinfectant cleaner and some deodorizing spray. He cleaned everything carefully, most worried about getting the smell out of the books. He left the stuff to air out, and before he went home he sprayed everything again. The following day he did it once more, then he put it all into a new box and took it home, where he took out a book and handed it to Jane, saying, "Does this smell weird to you?"

She sniffed it. "No, why?"

"Just wondered," he said and put the box in a secure place with his own things in the garage.

On Saturday when Alex didn't have to work, and consequently Wade didn't either, both sets of Wade's parents came to help finish up the packing and to clean out the house. He was grateful to put the women in charge of organizing and boxing up Laura's things with care and respect for her in her absence. As always it was a little strange to observe the deepening friendship between his mother and stepmother. Roxanne had befriended Marilyn during her simultaneous struggles with cancer and depression, and they'd had lunch together once a week ever since. But their relationship didn't feel nearly as bizarre as seeing his two fathers working together to move furniture out to the rented truck, talking and laughing as they did. Since Neil had had a lengthy affair at one time with Brad's wife, their tolerance of each other would have been a miracle. But the forgiveness between them was so deep and complete that there were no ill feelings whatsoever. It wasn't the first time they'd worked together to help get him through a crisis, but he never fully got used to the bizarre circumstances.

Alex picked up a box from the front room floor and nodded toward Brad and Neil taking a break on the lawn, sharing a bout of laughter. "I think your fathers like each other."

"Good thing," Wade said. "Someone who gets his life into as much trouble as I do *needs* two sets of parents."

Alex just smiled and carried the box outside, but Wade couldn't help recalling the trip that Neil and Alex had taken with him to go back east and pack up the contents of his apartment following Elena's death. There was a pattern here, and he didn't like it.

All of the furniture and many carefully labeled boxes went into a storage unit, and everything else went to the house. Cole showed up to help unload while Barrett watched the kids and Marilyn and Roxanne coddled the baby. The things Laura would use regularly were put into place in the room she would share with Wade once she was able to come home. He appreciated Jane's help in noticing the things that obviously had meaning for Laura, and putting them out in a way similar to how Laura had left them. She also suggested that one of the many empty rooms in the house could be used for Laura's sewing things, and she helped put those out as well. With all these special touches, Wade felt sure Laura could feel comfortable and at home here when the time came. He felt both comforted and disconcerted to see her clothes and things mixed with his own. He could only hope that it wasn't too long before she might actually be able to come around enough to share any kind of a life with him at all.

Once the house was empty it sold quickly, and Wade was able to take the papers to Laura to have her sign them. It was the first time he'd seen her since she'd agreed to this option, but they had little to say to each other, and he was actually relieved to have it over.

Wade couldn't deny feeling better once he'd settled more fully back into life in Alex and Jane's home. He'd been perfectly content in the house he'd shared with Laura, but once she'd left, it just hadn't felt right to even go there and pick up the mail. He felt more comfortable here; however, without Laura, everything felt all wrong.

* * * * *

When Dr. Hadley called to tell Wade that he wanted him to meet again with Laura, and that he wanted Wade to talk openly about how all of this had affected him, Wade felt both concerned and hopeful.

"Are you sure that's a good idea?" Wade asked. "I mean . . . I'm not questioning your judgment, but . . . if I get going, it could be ugly."

"I think you have the discernment and intuition to express your feelings appropriately, and I think she needs to start looking at the consequences of her actions."

"You've been telling me she wasn't in her right mind, that she was beyond controlling her behavior."

"You, of all people, Wade, should know that the reasons for making poor choices don't take away the consequences, and they still have to be faced."

Wade sighed. Since his very existence was the result of a poor choice, he could only say, "Okay, you got me there."

He understood Hadley's reasoning, but he still felt scared of what his own reaction might be once he allowed himself to express his feelings, especially in front of Laura while she was so fragile. When Laura was brought into the room, he noticed she sat farther away from him than last time, and he wondered if that was to avoid having to hold his hand. However, he could see her better from this angle, and it would be easier to gauge her reactions.

Hadley cut straight to the point and said, "I thought it would be good if Wade talked to you about how all of this has affected him." Silence followed until he added, "Go ahead, Wade."

Still more silence. "I'm sorry. I . . . don't know what to say; I don't know where to start."

"Let's start with one word," Hadley said. "Tell us one word that best describes how you feel about all of this."

"I have to choose one?" Wade asked, trying to sound light.

"For starters," Hadley said with a smile. "We can move up to more."

Wade took a deep breath and looked directly at Laura. "I feel betrayed," he said.

"Could you expound on that?" Hadley asked, and Wade hated being the one who was forced to talk. But perhaps it gave him some empathy for Laura. Without looking at his wife, Wade explained how Elena's death had affected him—things that he'd certainly told Laura before. He made it clear that nothing in life could be more difficult for him than to lose Laura to death as well, especially when it would have been her choice. He spoke of the peace he'd felt over Elena's death, and how he never could have felt that way over losing Laura to suicide. Having given his explanation, he looked at Laura's stunned face and said, "You knew all of that; you knew what I'd been through. I realize that the depression is affecting your thoughts, and this is not black and white here, but I can't deny that *I feel betrayed*. I have trouble believing that you would make a *choice* to do that to *me*. Forgive me if that sounds selfish, given what I know you must be going through. But that's how I feel. Nearly losing you like that has traumatized me, Laura. I feel sick to my stomach every time I think about it. And then I remember how you promised me . . . you *promised* me that you would talk to me, that you would let me help you so that depression wouldn't completely overtake you. We had that conversation the day before we were married. Do you remember that conversation, Laura?"

She didn't answer. She looked horrified, and he wondered why. He hung his head, saying, "That's all; that's all I have to say."

Wade was startled when Laura erupted to her feet and started pacing the room, wringing her hands, breathing frantically as if she were in some kind of danger. Wade looked to the doctor for some indication of what might be going on. Hadley looked calm as he observed her closely, apparently waiting to see what she might do or say. Then she rushed out of the room, and Hadley followed her.

Wade said to the empty room, "Well, that was fun."

About five minutes later, Hadley came back in to say that someone was with Laura.

"I should have kept it to myself," Wade said, almost angry with Hadley for prodding him into saying all those things.

"In spite of appearances, Wade, what you just saw was progress. She's got to face these things. I really believe she was ready to hear what you said. Just give her some time to let it soak in, and we'll keep you informed."

Wade knew what that meant. More waiting and wondering.

The following morning he got a call from Patty, who immediately said, "She wants to see you."

"Okay," Wade drawled, wishing he could feel more hopeful than skeptical. "Do you know why?"

"She just says there's something she needs to tell you."

"Okay," he said again. "Is there any remote possibility that we could have some privacy?"

Patty said lightly, "You want to kiss her, don't you?"

Wade felt almost guilty for being pegged so well. "The thought had crossed my mind, even though it's probably a long shot. Either way, I just . . . want a few minutes alone without feeling like we're a spectacle."

"I'll make sure I'm the only one in the observation hallway, and I'll keep my back turned. You just promise me you'll holler quick if something goes weird."

"I promise," Wade said. "Thank you."

Wade arrived at the appointed time that evening, and waited for several minutes before Patty brought Laura into the room. She gave him a thumbs up and a wink before she closed the door. A moment later he saw her at the window, leaning back against it as if she clearly intended to ward off anyone who might come near.

Wade turned his attention to Laura and found her wringing her hands, just as she'd been when she'd left their session. When she didn't talk he said, "Patty told me you wanted to see me."

"Yes," she said. "Thank you . . . for coming."

"It's not a problem. What do you need?"

She looked down, and he could see her trembling. He stepped closer and said gently, "Just tell me, Laura."

"I . . . I just wanted to say that . . . I'm so sorry for what I've put you through. When I think how it would have been for you . . . after losing Elena like that, I just . . . feel horrible. I can only say that I wasn't thinking clearly, but . . . I know that doesn't change how all of this is for you."

"It's okay, Laura."

"I . . . don't really expect you to forgive me . . . for what I've done to your life." She hugged herself tightly as if she were freezing, even though she was wearing two sweaters. "But I just wanted you to know . . . I truly am sorry."

Laura looked up at her husband while tension wrapped tightly around them. She couldn't think of anything more to say and wished that he would speak. But he didn't. In her heart, she truly believed that he would be better off without her and the sooner he realized that, the better. Still, she couldn't let him go without letting him know the regret she felt. She'd done that now and felt certain she should suggest that perhaps it would be better if they were to just separate officially so that he could move on. While she believed it was best, the very thought of being without him only encouraged this seemingly unquenchable desire she had to end all of this misery, once and for all.

Through a torturous silence, Wade struggled to find something to say, anything to bridge this horrible chasm between them. He wanted to tell her how much he loved her, how his deepest hope was to see her find her way back to the happiness they'd once shared. He ached to let her know that he truly believed there was nothing that couldn't be fixed if they both wanted it badly enough. He prayed for the right words to say, but nothing came, and the silence continued.

"Say something," she said tensely. "Tell me you can't live with this. Tell me it's too hard, that this isn't what you bargained for, and I'll understand. Truly I will. Tell me what you need to say, Wade. I don't want you to pretend for the sake of my feelings. I'm not going to try to manipulate you into staying with me simply because you feel sorry for me. Just say what you have to say and—"

Wade stepped abruptly toward her. In one lithe movement he took her face into his hands and pressed his mouth over hers. He sensed her stunned surprise, then felt her soften in response. He looked briefly into her eyes, then kissed her again, pressing his hands into her hair. For a moment he felt as if he were doing something he shouldn't, as if kissing her this way was somehow forbidden. Then his mind took hold of the reality that they were husband and wife, and he eased her completely into his arms, kissing her on and on. A once-familiar warmth and passion crept into their kiss, and for the first time in weeks he actually felt like she really was his wife. When the rigidity and nervousness had completely disappeared, he looked into her eyes and whispered, "I love you, Laura, and what I bargained for is a marriage commitment that is stronger than anything life throws at us. Are you hearing me?"

"But . . ." her chin quivered, "you said it yourself . . . I betrayed you . . . in the worst possible way."

"No, Laura, not in the worst possible way. But even if you had, I would still forgive you. Remember who you're talking to, Mrs. Morrison. I am the product of betrayal—physically, at least. Emotionally, spiritually, I am the product of forgiveness. I was raised with love, and the finest examples of respect, and of living the gospel because my father forgave the worst possible betrayal. Now, what makes you think that I would give you any less than that? When I knelt at that altar with you, Laura, the vows I made did not have conditions."

She looked stunned, then her eyes shifted guiltily away.

"What?" he demanded gently. "Tell me what you're thinking."

"Maybe they should have . . . for your sake."

"For *my* sake? I *want* to be married to you, Laura."

"You *want* to live like this?" she snapped.

"No, I don't want to live like *this!* I want us to work together to get beyond this so we can be together again, so that you can be free of whatever it is that's got hold of you."

"Maybe that's just not possible," she said, her voice resigned.

"I don't believe that. I *refuse* to believe that. I *love* you, Laura. What do I have to say to make you believe that?"

"I love you too, Wade. That's why I don't want to . . . hurt you any more than I already have. I'm afraid that . . . all I will ever do is . . . hurt you. Maybe it would be better if . . ."

"If what?" he demanded, feeling angry. Judging by her reaction, he had a pretty good idea what she was thinking, and it made him sick. At the risk of making the situation worse, he couldn't keep from venturing a guess. "What are you implying, Laura? If we end the marriage now, you think it will hurt me less when you *do* finally self-destruct and end your own life?"

The guilt in her eyes rose hard and fast. He'd hit the nail right on the head, and he knew it. He had to count to ten—then to twenty—before he could dig through his own anger and find beneath it some measure of compassion for her. But lurking beneath the anger he also found his own fears. His voice cracked when he said, "It's still there, isn't it? You're still wishing you were dead."

She turned her back to him abruptly, and once again his anger battled with his fear. Through the minute it took to find his composure, sadness overtook them both. "Laura," he said, his voice barely steady, "isn't what we shared enough to live for? Tell me what more I can do, Laura. Anything. Anything at all, and I'll do it."

"That's not it, and you know it," she said, keeping her back to him.

"I don't know anything anymore, Laura, because you won't *talk* to me. Help me understand this."

"How can I when I don't understand it myself? I only know it has nothing to do with you. You've never been anything but perfectly good to me. You're the best thing that ever happened to me. The problem, Wade, is that I am the worst thing that ever happened to you."

Wade grabbed her arm and turned her to face him. "No!" he shouted softly, close to her face. "This *depression* is the worst thing that's ever happened to *both* of us. I love *you,* Laura. Can you not understand the difference?"

She hung her head. "But . . . it's part of who I am, and . . . I don't know how . . . I can ever be free of it."

He took hold of her other arm as well and pulled her closer, forcing her to look at him. "We will find a way through this, but you've got to hold on. You've got to trust me, and trust these people who can help you. I love you more than life, Laura. Please . . . if you can't find anything else to hold on to, remember how much I love you."

He saw something soften in her eyes as she said, "I love you too, Wade. I do. I just . . ."

"Love me enough to live, Laura. I need you to live; I need you to be alive again. Please, I'm begging you. Do it for me. Do it for Rebecca. We *need* you."

The subtle glimmer of hope in her expression quickly melted into disbelief before she looked away and squeezed her eyes closed, as if she couldn't believe him. Wade let go of her and stepped back, suddenly too weary and scared to press it any further. His frustration threatened to take over, and he couldn't let that happen.

"I'll see you soon," he said and hurried from the room before he said something he regretted.

"Thank you, Patty," he said to let her know that he was leaving, and then he practically ran.

Wade sat in the car for nearly half an hour before he could even start it and drive home. He wanted to cry, hoping it might release the tight burning in his chest and head. But he felt numb, in shock, horrified. At home he sat for another ten minutes before he could go inside. Once inside the house, he found the main floor dark except for a light on the stairs. Even though it was early, he could tell from distant noises upstairs that the family was gathered up there. And that was fine. He had no desire to see or talk to anyone. He wished that he could get to his bedroom without being noticed, but knew it was impossible, especially since Rebecca would still be awake. Instead, he slipped into the study and sat at one end of the leather couch, but he didn't bother to turn on the light.

The noise upstairs quieted down as it became evident the children had been put to bed. Wade told himself he should go kiss his daughter goodnight, but he couldn't move. He felt as if he could barely breathe. More time slipped by, but he felt oblivious to it. He was startled to feel his cell phone vibrate where it was hooked onto his belt. He pulled it off and looked at it to see that the call was coming from the house he was sitting in.

"Yeah," he answered.

"Where are you?" Alex asked. "It's late. Forgive me for sounding like your big brother, but I was getting a little concerned."

"I'm in the study," Wade said.

"Okay," Alex drawled skeptically. "How long have you been there?"

"I have no idea. I'm home safe, so you can go to bed and . . ."

Alex flipped on the light and turned off the cordless phone in his hand. "And what?" he asked as Wade turned off his phone. He said nothing, and Alex added, "How long have you been sitting here, alone in the dark?"

"I have no idea," Wade repeated.

Alex sat down at the other end of the couch. "Talk to me, little brother."

Wade didn't know where to start; he couldn't even come up with a comment.

"You can't even tell me to shut up and leave you alone?"

Wade sighed and rubbed a hand over his face. "Maybe depression is contagious."

"I don't know how it couldn't be," Alex said with compassion. "I take it your visit didn't go well."

"Oh, it had its moments. There was a little serious kissing."

"Ooh. Maybe that's when you caught the bug."

"No, I think that came after." He sighed again and just said the words that he was having so much trouble accepting. "She doesn't want to live, Alex. All this time, and she still doesn't want to live." He shook his head. "I just feel so . . . helpless."

"I think I can understand that . . . to some degree. It seemed like forever when all we could do was wait and wonder if Barrett was going to die. Remember all that time when he just seemed . . . lost. It was like he just . . . wasn't with us, as if he had no will to live."

"I remember," Wade said.

"All we could do was put it in God's hands. We realized that while fasting and prayer and faith were vital, no amount of fasting or prayer or faith could alter God's will."

"I understand that, Alex, but there's a glitch in that as far as Laura is concerned. Even God's will cannot override a person's agency. If she *wants* to die, and she is too out of her mind to understand how *ludicrous* that is, what can I do? What can *God* do?"

"You can do everything in your power to keep her alive until she comes to herself enough to get beyond this, and you can trust in God to guide you and to help you do that."

"And what if it's not enough, Alex? What if she never comes to herself? What if, after all I can do, I still lose her?"

"You'll know you did everything you could. If you're concerned about her eternal salvation, then—"

"I am *not* concerned about her salvation! I am absolutely certain that such choices are judged in direct proportion to a person's ability to reason, and she has *no* ability to reason. What I am concerned about is living the rest of my life without her! I feel like . . . I'm losing her as surely as if she had . . . cancer, or something equally horrible."

"More like Alzheimer's," Alex said. "She's lost inside her mind while she's physically here."

"Yeah." Wade drew a ragged breath. "She's not dying, she's fading, disappearing right before my eyes."

"You've got to give it some time, Wade. I know it feels hopeless now, but there hasn't been enough time to know if the medication is working or—"

"You know what," Wade said, coming to his feet, "I appreciate your support. I really do. But I can't hear it any more, not right now. I'm going to bed."

"Okay," Wade heard Alex say as he left the room, resisting the urge to slam the door.

In his bedroom he slumped onto the edge of the bed and pressed his head into his hands. A part of him knew he needed to be patient, to give the matter some time. But he felt so thoroughly drained of hope that he couldn't fathom being able to muster any degree of patience. He knew he should pray, but the only words that could form in his mind were simply, *God help me*. It seemed a common request.

Wade heard a noise and looked up, surprised to see Barrett standing in the doorway.

"What are you doing up? It's way past your bedtime."

"I couldn't sleep," he said. "I was worried about Laura."

"Well, that makes two of us," Wade said.

Barrett moved closer, looking inquisitive and concerned. Wade struggled for an explanation of his mood that would appease the child and still be honest. "I feel helpless, Barrett. The only thing I can give Laura is my love, but she won't accept it."

"Isn't your love enough?" Barrett asked with wise innocence.

"Apparently not. It feels like . . . anything I can give her is like a very tiny little drop in a great big bucket."

Barrett looked deeply thoughtful for a long moment before he said, "As long as you keep giving love to her, eventually she's got to notice."

"I'm sure you're right," Wade said, forcing a smile if only to ease Barrett's concerns.

Barrett then added, "If the drop in the bucket is like blue food coloring, one drop might not turn the water in the bucket blue—but if you keep adding one drop after another, eventually the water will turn blue. Won't it?"

Wade felt stunned as he realized the theory had just gone straight to his heart, and with it came hope. He chuckled to avoid sobbing and opened his arms. Barrett stepped closer and hugged him tightly. "You know what?" Wade said. "You're absolutely right. I just need to keep loving her, no matter what."

Barrett stepped back and smiled. "Love is pretty powerful stuff," he said.

"Yes, it certainly is," Wade said. "Thank you for reminding me. You're the best friend a guy could ever ask for."

Barrett smiled again and left the room, as if he knew that he could now sleep just fine.

"Thank you, Father," Wade muttered into the empty room. The prompting given to a child to offer simple words of wisdom had given Wade the hope and perspective he'd needed to believe he could make it through another day.

Chapter Ten

The following day Wade drove to the hospital to begin a shift at two P.M. Alex was sitting in the passenger seat, talking to their father on his cell phone. Wade's phone rang, and he glanced at the caller ID. It was a wireless number he didn't recognize and wondered who it might be.

"Hi, it's Rochelle," she said after he'd said hello.

"Hi."

"I'm in town," she said, and he felt almost terrified of what she might stir up. "I talked to Dr. Hadley, and I saw Laura. And . . . I'd really like to talk to you . . . face-to-face, if I could."

"Okay," Wade drawled, "as long as we can meet in a public place."

She sounded insulted. "What exactly do you think I'm after?"

"I don't think you're after anything. It's the principle. I'm a married man, and that's the way it's going to be."

"Okay," she said, sounding more impressed than put off.

"Or you're welcome to come to my brother's home where I'm staying; his wife will be there. Except I won't be there until tomorrow morning. I'm on my way to work now and won't get off until two in the morning."

"Oh," she said, clearly disappointed.

"I'll have a dinner break around eight. You're welcome to meet me at the hospital."

"Hospital?"

"I'm doing a rotation in the ER at the U of U."

"The what?"

"University of Utah Medical Center," he said, noting that Alex had ended his own call and he was looking curious and entertained over listening to Wade's.

"Okay," she said. "I'll be there at eight, if you're alright with that."

"Sure, it's fine. If I'm late, be patient. Sometimes we get in a trauma and can't leave. Do you need directions?"

"If I take a cab, I assume they'll know the way."

"I should hope."

"Where should I meet you?"

"The waiting area at the emergency room."

"Okay, thanks. I'll be there."

"Who was that?" Alex asked when Wade turned off his phone.

"Laura's friend, Rochelle," he said with dismay. "She's in town and wants to talk to me. She sounds upset. She said she saw Laura and talked to Hadley." He shook his head. "I can't wait to hear her take on all of this. She tried to talk Laura out of marrying me. I don't think she's very fond of men." He gave an ironic chuckle. "No, let me rephrase that. She doesn't believe that any man is worth marrying or trusting. She's *very* fond of men as long as she can kick them out after she's slept with them."

"Oh, I see. *That* friend of Laura's. So she's meeting you for dinner."

"It looks that way; can't wait." His sarcasm was thick.

Wade was only a few minutes late getting out to the waiting room, then it took him a moment to recognize Rochelle, and that was only because she stood up when she saw him. He couldn't remember what color her hair had been the last time he'd seen her, but it hadn't been the dark brown that it was now. Beyond that, she wasn't the woman he remembered. When she'd come to town for the wedding, she'd had perfect hair, professional false fingernails, and excessive makeup. Those things were now starkly absent, but even more conspicuous was the emptiness in her eyes.

"I'm a mess, I know," she said as he approached her.

"It's very vogue around here," he said, already feeling more comfortable with her than he'd expected. At least she seemed real. Hoping to ease the tension further, he added, "You should have seen me a little while ago. I would have scared you to death."

"Why is that?" she asked.

"I don't think you really want to know," he said and motioned toward the long hall leading away from the ER. "Do you want to get something to eat?"

"I'm not hungry, but . . . I know you need to eat. I'll just come along."

He started walking, and she fell into step beside him.

Silence fell until she asked, "Really, why would you have scared me? You've roused my curiosity."

"Just . . . ER stuff. We had a guy come in who'd gotten his hand stuck in some machine where he worked."

"Ooh."

"Yeah, it was pretty ugly."

"Will he be okay?"

"In a manner of speaking. The hand was irreparable. He's in surgery now to have it removed."

"Oh, that's horrible."

"Yeah, um . . . I'm sure you didn't come here to talk about the ER."

"Well, I'm interested in what you're doing. I didn't realize you were going into emergency medicine."

"I'm not. I'm still in medical school. This is a student rotation. Once I get my degree, then I'll do my internship and residency in my chosen field."

"Which is?" she asked, and Wade realized that he obviously hadn't been a topic of conversation between her and Laura.

"Pediatric oncology."

"Cancer?"

"Yeah."

"That's brave."

"Maybe. I don't know. I've got a long way to go. What did you need to talk to me about, Rochelle?"

He slowed his pace when she did, even though they still had a long stretch to cover to get to the cafeteria. "I . . . um . . . I saw Laura." She started to cry and reached for a tissue from her purse. "I've never seen her like that."

"Yeah, I know what you mean."

Rochelle dabbed at her eyes with the tissue and sniffled.

"Did she have anything to say?"

"She was just . . . angry."

"Yeah, that's the emotion of the day," he said. As it came out of his mouth, an associated memory caught him off guard, and he abruptly stopped walking.

"What is it?" she asked. He just shook his head. "Come on, tell me. Is it something to do with Laura?"

"Yeah," he croaked and leaned against the wall. "Just . . . a memory, something I hadn't thought about since she . . ."

"Went over the edge?"

"Yeah. On our first date . . . she told me about her emotional eating."

Rochelle smiled. "Yeah, it was a running joke between us—what flavor of ice cream could solve any given problem."

Wade chuckled as the memory became more clear. "On our second date we were eating ice cream out of the carton with two spoons, and I asked her if this was emotional eating. She said the emotion of the day was . . . bliss." He chuckled tensely and looked down, wondering why he was telling her this, barely managing to keep from crying while people rushed back and forth in the hallway. "After that she'd often come up with the emotion of the day. Euphoria was one of her favorites. Now the emotion of the day . . . or the month . . . is usually . . . anger."

"Why is she so angry, Wade?" Rochelle asked. "I don't understand."

Wade looked right at her and just said it. "She's angry because I won't let her die." Rochelle gasped. "I came home early and saved her life, and I took her to this place where they won't leave her unattended for even a second, and the only thing she wants is to die."

Rochelle leaned against the wall beside him and pressed a hand over her mouth, whimpering behind it. "Yeah, I know what you mean," he said. "Come on. There's a ladies room up here."

He guided her to it, then waited outside for a few minutes until she came out looking a little more composed. As they began walking again she said, "I had a long visit with Dr. Hadley. I offered to pay him for his time. He told me that a certain amount of consultation for loved ones was included." She looked up at Wade. "It must be costing you a fortune to keep her in there."

"I'm keeping up the premiums on the insurance she had before she lost her job. We sold the house, and I've used some of the equity to help with the costs. I'm hoping to save the rest for her to do whatever she wants with it. It was her house, but we couldn't keep up the mortgage without her working. My dad's helping a little. Truthfully, we're doing fine."

"Are you sure? Because I would be glad to help if—"

"It's okay, Rochelle. We really are doing fine. But thank you." Attempting to keep the conversation on track, he added, "You talked to Dr. Hadley."

"Yeah, but . . . it can wait a minute."

They'd arrived at the cafeteria, and she waited for him to get something to eat. He asked her again if she wanted anything, and she declined. When they were seated and he had his food, she said, "Just . . . eat and I'll talk, if that's okay."

"Okay," he said. "What did Dr. Hadley have to say?"

"He explained it to me . . . how this breakdown is the result of . . . her feeling completely safe . . . for the first time in her life." She sniffled loudly and dabbed at her eyes. "And I just . . . want to thank you . . . for making her feel safe, and . . . I need to apologize . . . for my misjudgments."

Wade couldn't believe what he was hearing. He swallowed carefully and simply said, "Apology accepted."

She gave him a wan smile, then started rambling about her lengthy conversation with Hadley. He was stunned to realize how completely open she was being with him, and a little concerned to hear signs that she wasn't doing well at all. He knew she'd been living a deplorable lifestyle for a couple of years, and it was obviously catching up with her. She talked about Tina and Laura and the struggles they'd had, and how her heart was broken on their behalf. Laura's condition and her suicide attempt had frightened Rochelle so badly that her own recent struggles with depression had shocked her out of denial. He was glad to hear that she'd made another appointment to see Dr. Hadley for herself. Apparently her very successful career had given her a great deal of money in the bank, and a lot of time off with pay. She would be staying in Utah for a while with the hope of seeing Laura improve, and to find some answers for herself. Wade knew that if anybody could help her, it would be Hadley. He was a good man, and he knew what he was doing.

Wade finished eating and pushed his tray aside while Rochelle expressed her regret over the choices she'd made. He wondered why she was telling him all of this, then realized that she'd probably substituted him for Laura, because she'd been given evidence that Laura had trusted him completely. While he was thinking that it wouldn't be appropriate to encourage any further conversations like this between them, he felt a hand on his shoulder and looked up to see Alex.

"How was the chicken?" he asked.

"Not bad. What did you have?"

"The same. We need to get out more."

"Or stay home more," Wade said. He motioned toward Rochelle who had now discreetly dried her eyes, which he suspected was the biggest purpose for Alex's inquiry about the food. "This is Laura's friend, Rochelle."

"Hi," she said with a smile. "You look familiar."

"Hi." He held out a hand, and she shook it. "I was at the wedding. I'm Wade's brother, Alex. My son was the best man."

"Oh, of course," she said. "It's good to see you again."

"Are you in town for long?"

"Yes, actually . . . at least until Laura shows some improvement. I just want to be close, even if I can't do anything."

"Well, you should come over for dinner. We're off tomorrow. Dinner's at six."

"Okay, you talked me into it," Rochelle said.

"Good." Alex smiled, then said to Wade, "Maybe I could score some points with Jane, eh?" More to Rochelle he added, "She misses Laura so bad it hurts. She'll appreciate some female company. She swears there's way too much guy talk over the dinner table."

"Poor woman," Wade said.

Alex said to Rochelle, "We'll see you tomorrow then. Wade can tell you how to find the house." To Wade he added, "If you need a few minutes I'll cover for you."

"Thanks," Wade said. "I won't be long."

Alex left, and Rochelle said, "He'll cover for you?"

"He's an ER doctor; I'm working with him at the moment."

"Was that planned or—"

"It was one of those things where you have absolutely no doubt that God's hand is in your life. If I'd been working with anyone besides him these past weeks, I'd have lost my mind, and I could have moved into the facility with Laura. Maybe we could get a group rate."

Rochelle showed an unenthusiastic smile, then teared up again. "Do you think it's possible for someone like me to ever have God's hand in my life again?"

"Absolutely," he said without hesitation. "If His hand were not in your life, you wouldn't be sitting there wanting to make some positive changes. All you have to do is reach out to Him, and He'll reach right back and lead you."

"I hope you're right," she said and stood up. "I should let you get back to work. Thank you for listening to me ramble."

"It's okay," he said. "I think you're on the right track, Rochelle. I'll keep you posted if anything changes, and we'll see you tomorrow evening. Call my cell phone, and I'll give you directions."

"Okay, thanks," she said.

"You want to walk back with me so you don't get lost?" he asked.

"No . . . thanks. I'll ask someone if I need to. I'm okay."

Wade smiled and hurried away, wondering if a silver lining had just appeared in the clouds of Laura's situation. He said a little prayer for Rochelle as he traversed the long halls back to the ER, and as always, he prayed for Laura. It had become a habit. Every minute of every hour when his mind had nothing else to do, he was praying for Laura.

The following day Wade spent some significant time with Rebecca. Together they changed the sheets and did some laundry and errands, then they picked Barrett up after school and went to Wal-Mart, just for fun. Rochelle called his cell phone, and he gave her the address and directions to the house.

"What does it look like?" she asked.

"Like a bed and breakfast," he said.

"Is that a joke or something?"

"No. It's an old family home: early Victorian, three stories. You can't miss it."

"Okay," she said, sounding intrigued.

"See you at six," he said and got off the phone. Barrett was holding Rebecca's hand while they looked at shoes. Rebecca loved shoes; she always had. Laura loved shoes, too. There was now a very large box in Alex's garage marked: Laura's Shoes. He missed her. He missed seeing what pair of silly shoes she might wear to work as a conversation piece for the children who came into the clinic. He missed the scrubs she wore that were even sillier. She had pigs, and Care Bears, and the Wizard of Oz. There were Minnie Mouse scrubs and dragon scrubs, and scrubs for Valentine's Day, Halloween, and Christmas. And there were special shoes to go with each set.

Wade missed her brilliant laughter, and her emotional eating, and he missed dancing with her in the kitchen, and watching her play with Rebecca. He missed the way she would mess up his hair right after he'd combed it, just to make him laugh. And he missed the messages she would leave on his cell phone throughout the course of a day. He smiled to recall one in particular that had made him laugh out loud at the time, embarrassing himself in front of a couple of nurses who had been standing nearby while he'd checked his messages.

"Hi," she'd said, "this is Laura. I don't know if you remember me, but I'm the one who let you go down the slide first on the playground last week during recess. I was wondering if you want to come over and we could play house. I'll be the mommy and you can be the daddy, and I have this adorable friend named Rebecca, and she's very good at being the baby. You can pick up the groceries, and I'll cook dinner, and we'll live happily ever after. If you think your mom and dad will let you come over, call and let me know. And by the way, we need laundry soap."

Wade wished he'd never deleted that message, or the dozens of others she'd left for him. How he longed to hear her sounding so happy again! He just wanted to have her come home, to hold her close through the night, and eat meals at the same table. He wanted to tell her every hour that he loved her—and have her believe him.

"You okay?" Barrett asked, startling him.

"Yeah, just thinking," Wade said.

"How awesome is that?" Barrett asked, pointing at Rebecca's feet. She was proudly displaying the shoes that Barrett had tried on her.

"Those are boy shoes," Wade said with a little laugh.

"They're *Batman* shoes," Barrett corrected firmly. "Hello? They're awesome."

"Okay, whatever. Batman shoes it is."

"I wish they came in my size," Barrett said.

"Or mine," Wade added.

The minute Wade got home, he left Rebecca in Barrett's care and dug into the box full of Laura's shoes until he found a particular pair. He found a box, wrote a note, and let Alex know he needed to run an errand so he'd keep track of Rebecca.

* * * * *

Laura had no idea how long she'd been sitting with an open book on her lap, staring at the wall instead of reading.

"Laura," she heard and turned to see Rita, the usual evening psych tech who babysat her. Apparently Patty had gone home and she'd missed the changing of the guard while her mind had wandered. "Somebody brought you something." Rita handed her a nondescript shoe box. "It was left at the front office. Why don't you see what it is."

"It's not a cake with a file in it?" Laura asked, knowing it would have been closely inspected before coming into her hands.

"Sorry," Rita said.

Laura opened the box to see a snapshot of Wade and Rebecca that she'd taken herself with his digital camera. She touched the image of their faces and ached to a depth beyond description. Beneath the picture was a little note, written in Wade's hand. It simply said, "There's no place like home." She folded back the tissue paper and heard an emotional noise come out of her month. There she found her very own shoes, the red glittery ones with buckles. She always wore them with her Wizard of Oz scrubs. Her ruby slippers. She looked again at the note, then the picture. She wondered what Wade and Rebecca were doing right now. And for the first time since she'd come to this place, she wondered if it really might be possible to ever go home. Impulsively she put the shoes on and looked at her feet as if she'd never seen them before. And for just a moment, she smiled.

* * * * *

Wade returned home just a few minutes before six. He'd forgotten until he saw Cole's car that his family was coming over for dinner tonight as well. *With Rochelle coming, this could be interesting,* he thought. In the house he found Barrett setting the table while Jane stirred something at the stove. Cole was tearing lettuce for a green salad—and Alex was flat on his back on the kitchen floor while Rebecca and Ruthie were tickling him. Alex pretended to be hysterical with agony while the girls giggled.

"Oh, hi," Jane said when she saw him. "How did your errand go?"

"I have no idea. I left something for Laura. I'm not expecting a thank-you note or anything, but maybe she'll know I'm thinking about her."

"Can't hurt," Alex said, then resumed his performance for the girls.

"Is she doing any better?" Cole asked in lieu of a greeting.

"It's hard to say. I'm just trying to convince myself to be patient and . . ."

The doorbell rang, and Wade said, "I'll get it."

"Hi," Rochelle said when he pulled the door open. She looked better than she had the day before, and, in his opinion, significantly better than when he'd seen her at the wedding a few months ago when everything about her had appeared so false.

"Hi," he said. "You found the house okay."

"Yeah, it was easy." She looked around as she stepped inside. "It's beautiful."

"Yes, it's also lived-in, so be tolerant. I contribute a great deal to that." He moved down the hall, and she followed. "Everyone is in the kitchen."

When they entered, Cole was now slicing a cucumber, Barrett was stirring a gallon-sized pitcher of red Kool-Aid, and Jane was pulling something out of the oven. Alex was still on the floor, but now Preston was jumping up and down on his chest as if his father were a horse. Rebecca, Ruthie, and Cole's daughter, Natalie, were chasing each other around the table and squealing. Little Andrew was sitting in his baby seat, making happy—but very loud—noises. And Katharine was saying to her mother in a whiny voice, "Is it ready yet? I'm starving."

Wade chuckled and said quietly to Rochelle, "Would you like to reconsider? There's still time for a hasty escape. I could recommend a nearby Carl's Jr."

"Oh no," Rochelle said with a smile. "It all looks very . . . entertaining."

Wade added facetiously, "It's not just a home; it's an adventure." He then reached out to grab Rebecca as she ran past him. She squealed with laughter as he lifted her quickly, then Ruthie wanted equal treatment, and he picked her up as well, making an exaggerated groan as he said, "You girls are getting too big!"

All eyes turned toward them as Rochelle's presence became noticed. "Oh, hi," Jane said, setting the hot casserole dish on top of the stove. "Rochelle, right?"

"That's right," she said as Jane stepped forward, but instead of holding out a hand she gave Rochelle a hug.

"I'm Jane. We met at the wedding. It's good to see you again. Come in. Sit down. We can eat in just a minute."

"That's what you said ten minutes ago," Katharine snarled.

"Don't talk to your mother like that," Alex said, getting up from the floor. "Next time, you can cook dinner."

"Okay," Katharine said as if she liked that idea. Alex just gave her a comical glare.

"Hi," Alex said to Rochelle. "Make yourself at home. I'll let Wade make the introductions."

"I don't know if I can remember everybody's names," Wade said, as if he were genuinely nervous. He looked first at his daughter in his arms and said, "This is Rebecca. She belongs to me and Laura. And this is Ruthie. She's two weeks older than Rebecca and belongs to Alex and Jane." He set the girls down and pointed at the other children, "That's Preston. He's the king of kindergarten. Katharine is eight, and Barrett is ten."

"I remember you," Rochelle said, smiling at Barrett. "You were the best man at the wedding."

"That's me," Barrett said, looking pleased.

"You know Alex and Jane," Wade said. "That's Cole. He's—"

"Another brother?" Rochelle interrupted.

"No," Cole said with a chuckle.

"Well," Rochelle said as if to justify the assumption, "he *is* about the same height, same build as the two of you."

"Brother in spirit," Alex said, and put a cucumber slice into his mouth.

"Yeah, that's it," Wade said. "That's Natalie, Cole's daughter." He pointed her out where she was playing on the floor with

Ruthie and Rebecca. "And that," he pointed at the baby, "is Cole's son, Andrew."

"And Mrs. Cole?" Rochelle asked, then shot an apologetic glance toward Wade when it became immediately evident that her question had generated tension.

Cole became very focused on helping with the salad. Wade quietly said, "Megan passed away not so many weeks ago."

Rochelle looked astonished and upset. She turned toward Cole as she said, "Oh, I'm so sorry. Forgive me if—"

"It's okay," he said, giving her a quick smile. "You didn't know."

As the noise level of the kids suddenly went up, Rochelle said quietly to Wade, "And that's why you're brothers in spirit."

Wade nodded slightly, then motioned Rochelle toward the table. "Have a seat."

Two minutes later the food was all on the table, and everyone was seated. Alex said the blessing, praying that Cole and his children would be comforted and strengthened through this difficult time. As always he prayed that Laura would find healing and peace, and that Wade would be given comfort and strength as well. He also expressed appreciation to have Rochelle with them, and asked that God's blessings would be upon her. And of course, he asked for the food to be blessed. After the amen was spoken, Wade noticed Rochelle discreetly wiping tears with her napkin.

Wade thoroughly enjoyed the meal, as long as he didn't allow himself to think of Laura's absence. Even Cole seemed in better spirits than he'd ever seen him. The children were fairly well behaved and just silly enough to provoke frequent laughter. When they were finished eating, everyone pitched in to clean up the meal, then they all went to the family room to visit while the children went upstairs to play. Jane begged Cole to let her feed the baby when he got hungry. Watching Jane's tender expression while she fed the baby his bottle, Wade was reminded of the endless hours of mothering she had given Rebecca following Elena's death. She was an amazing woman. Not unlike Laura, he thought, and his heart ached. She had taken to mothering Rebecca like a bird to the sky. He missed her so much it hurt. Noting a somewhat dazed look on Cole's face, he felt certain they were feeling much the same way.

In the middle of the conversation, Rochelle stood up and moved toward a wall that was covered with framed photos of all sizes. He saw her surveying them closely while Alex asked Cole questions about the mission he'd served in the New England area.

"You have a beautiful family," Rochelle commented during a lull in the conversation.

"Yes, we do," Alex said proudly.

"Who is this?" Rochelle asked, pointing at a picture of two women.

"Our sisters," Alex said. "Charlotte and Becca. They both live out of state."

Jane handed the baby to Cole so that he could burp him. She stood beside Rochelle while Alex made silly noises at the baby and commented on how big he was getting.

"And who is this?" Rochelle asked, sounding genuinely interested.

Wade heard Jane say quietly, "That's Wade's first wife, Elena, right after Rebecca was born."

"Oh, I see the resemblance now. Rebecca looks just like her."

"Yes, she does."

Rochelle laughed softly. "Laura talked on and on about Rebecca. I've never seen any woman so excited to become an instant mother."

Wade sighed and found Alex looking at him, as if to gauge his reaction. He was glad when Jane went on to tell Rochelle about certain pictures of the kids and the events they represented. And there were pictures of Alex and Jane related to their lifetime pursuit of ballroom dancing. As Jane gave her a brief history, Rochelle turned toward Alex and said, "I'd like to see that."

"We'll dance if you will too," Alex said.

Rochelle gave him a comical scowl and turned to look at more pictures. "What's this?" she asked, sounding concerned.

"Oh, that's our little bald-headed Barrett. He had leukemia."

"No! That's awful."

"Yes, it was. But as you have seen, he's alive and well, and we're very grateful."

"Thanks to Wade," Alex said, and Wade wanted to slug him.

"Do you have to keep bringing that up?" he retorted, sounding only mildly angry.

"Yes," Alex said proudly, as if he only did it to get on Wade's nerves. To validate the theory he added, "What are brothers for if not to harass you and keep you humble?"

Wade let out a disgusted sigh, then found Rochelle looking at him, then at Alex, as if she expected an explanation. He simply said, "Wade donated the bone marrow that saved his life."

"I didn't know that," Cole said. "So . . . you have the same blood now, right?"

"It wasn't a big deal," Wade said. "How many times do I have to say it? God gave me the right kind of bone marrow. I had little to do with it." He stood up, feeling like he might scream if he didn't get out of here. And he wasn't certain why. "I'm . . . going for a drive. Can you watch Rebecca?"

"Of course," Alex said. Wade hurried from the room and out to his car, having no idea where he was going. But half an hour later he found himself in the parking lot of the facility where Laura was staying. He sat in the car for ten minutes before he could gather the courage to go in there, knowing he would likely be told he couldn't see her. And if he *did* see her it would probably end in disaster and leave him feeling more discouraged and lonely than he already felt.

"Please God," he muttered, opening the car door, "give me something to hold onto. Please."

At the front desk he was relieved to find someone there he'd encountered a number of times.

"Hi," Nola said with a smile. "What can we do for you?"

"Is there the remotest possibility that I could see my wife?"

Her eyes showed compassion. "Just a minute, and I'll see what's going on."

"Thank you," he said and paced the floor, praying and fighting the knots in his stomach. He prepared himself to be told that she wasn't up to it, or it wasn't a good idea.

His palms turned sweaty when Nola came back. He held his breath until she said, "Come on back. Rita's with her. She said it might be good."

Oh, thank you, God, Wade muttered internally as he followed Nola, not to the usual visitors' room, but to the room where Laura slept. There were two beds and two dressers, but only Laura and Rita were in the room. Rita sat in a chair with a book. Laura was sitting on the bed, her back against the wall, hugging her knees. And on her feet were the shoes he'd left here earlier. She had the side of her face pressed to her knees, looking in the other direction. Wade made eye contact with Rita, who smiled and motioned him toward Laura.

He moved quietly closer, but couldn't think of anything to say. He sat on the edge of the bed but she still didn't move. "Hi," he said. She lifted her head and turned slowly to look at him.

"Hi," she said, actually sounding pleased.

"So . . . what are you doing?" he asked.

"A whole lot of nothing," she said.

"Would it . . . be okay if I join you for a while? I can do nothing."

"Sure," she said, and he leaned his back against the wall so that he was sitting right next to her.

They sat in complete silence for more than ten minutes while he discreetly stole glances at her face and tried to just enjoy being with her. He didn't want her to feel like she had to talk or be on guard just because he was there. He sensed her relaxing but was surprised when she took his hand into hers. He watched as she threaded her fingers between his, then she unlaced them and pressed her palm to his as if to measure the length of her fingers against his. It was something she'd commonly done, and as simple as it was, it gave him comfort. But she continued to play with his hand longer than she ever had, as if boredom had become so intense for her that she was capable of finding entertainment in the simplest of things. Wade became fascinated with her little game, amazed that holding hands could be so intimate.

Wade had been there about forty minutes when she became bored with that and just relaxed her hand, keeping hold of his. Then she laid her head on his shoulder, and he soaked in her nearness with a long, slow breath.

"I like your shoes," he said, nodding toward them.

She lifted one of her feet, and then the other, as if to examine the glittery red texture. "I bought them on sale," she said. "Randall thought they were ugly; he was embarrassed when I wore them."

"What does he know? I think you should wear them to church, and I'll hold your hand. Maybe we should find some in Rebecca's size."

She said nothing, and he let the silence stand until he'd been there an hour. When she eased a little closer, he let go of her hand and put his arm around her shoulders, grateful beyond words just to have her so close, oblivious to Rita sitting on the other side of the room, reading near a lamp that cast a soft glow over the room. He feared the mood was shattered when someone brought Laura her medication, but she took it and resumed her comfortable position, where they remained in contented silence. He felt her relaxing more deeply, and a moment later she shifted her legs to her side and put her head in his lap. Wade took full advantage of the moment to just watch her while he ran his fingers lightly through her hair. He loved her so much!

Again he feared losing the mood when he felt his cell phone vibrate. He checked the caller ID, then answered it to hear Alex say, "You okay?"

"Yes, actually. I'm with Laura."

"Okay." Alex sounded pleased. "Stay as long as you can."

"Thank you, I will."

He hung up the phone, and Laura asked, "Who was that?"

"Alex."

"He takes good care of you," she said.

"Yes, he does."

A few minutes later he realized she was all but asleep, but she didn't look very comfortable, curled up with very little room for her legs. "Hey," he said, urging her away enough to guide her head to the pillow. "Now, that's better." He touched her face. "You look tired."

"I'm always tired," she said.

He started to unbuckle one of her shoes until she said, "No, I want to wear them."

"To bed?"

"Yes," she said and retracted her feet, tucking them beneath the covers.

"Okay," he said and pulled the sheet and blanket up over her.

"Don't leave," she said, and his heart quickened with the realization that she truly wanted to be with him.

He glanced toward Rita, who looked at her watch and said softly, "I think we can get away with a little while longer."

"I can stay a few more minutes," he said to Laura. She eased toward the wall, silently inviting him to lay down beside her. He did but stayed on top of the covers, longing to go back to the days when they had slept in the same bed and shared every aspect of their lives.

He relaxed his head on the pillow next to hers and looked closely at her face, only inches away. Her eyes looked sleepy, and he wondered if the medication was affecting her. She lifted a hand to touch his face, murmuring softly, "Such a nice beard."

Wade put his hand over hers to keep it against his face. She closed her eyes, and a few minutes later he knew she was asleep. He pressed a careful kiss to her brow, then her lips, and then he just watched her until Rita tapped him on the shoulder and whispered with apology that he needed to go. He kissed Laura's brow once more, touched her hair, and eased away. He thanked Rita and slipped away, silently thanking God for answering his prayers, for giving him something to hold onto, for giving him hope.

Chapter Eleven

In the car, Wade called the house, hoping Alex would still be awake. He answered after one ring, sounding alert.

"You're awake," Wade said.

"Are you kidding? I worked until two in the morning the last four days."

"You're not the only one. I hope Rebecca was a good girl."

"As always. How did it go?"

"Really well, actually," Wade said. "We held hands and they let me stay until she was asleep. It was nice just to be with her."

"I'm glad to hear it."

"How long did Rochelle stay?"

"She's still here," Alex said.

"Oh . . . I'm sorry," Wade said, knowing she was more his guest.

"It's not a problem. We told her she was welcome to stay as long as she wanted. Cole and the kids are spending the night. I could tell he was having one of those not wanting to go home nights. So the kids are all asleep. He and Rochelle have been in the study talking for more than an hour, actually."

"Really?" Wade said, more than a little surprised. "That's interesting."

"Yes, it certainly is," Alex chuckled.

"You don't think it's . . . romantic, do you?"

"How should I know?" Alex asked lightly. "I just live here. You sound worried."

"Maybe I am. I mean . . . I don't want to be judgmental or anything, but . . . Rochelle's lifestyle has been . . ."

"Yes, I know. You don't have to say it."

"And Cole is . . ."

"Lonely and vulnerable?" Alex guessed.

"Yeah."

"Well, he's a big boy, and his values are strong. I can't imagine him being ready to even have a romantic thought, anyway. I really don't think we need to baby-sit him."

"Okay, you're right," Wade said. "I'm almost home. Thanks for everything."

"I'll get even one day, since I'm so much older than you. I'll become old and decrepit, and you'll have to take care of me."

"I'm your man," Wade said, and ended the call.

At the house, Wade knocked lightly on the open study door just before he leaned around the corner to see Cole and Rochelle sitting at opposite ends of the leather couch with a box of tissues and several used ones on the couch between them.

"Sorry to interrupt," Wade said.

"You're not interrupting," Cole said. "Come in."

Wade said to Rochelle, "Sorry to abandon you like that. I just . . . needed to see Laura."

"How is she?" Rochelle asked.

"She seemed a little better, but we'll see what tomorrow brings." Nothing more was said, and he added, "Well, I'm going to bed. Stay as long as you like. I'm sure Cole can show you out when you're ready to go."

"Yeah, no problem," Cole said. "And I'll lock up."

"Thanks," Wade said. To Rochelle he added, "I'll let you know if anything changes, and you keep in touch, okay?"

"Okay," she said. "Thanks for everything."

Wade went up to bed, peeking first at his little sleeping princess. Crawling into bed he ached to have Laura there beside him, but for the first time since she'd gone over the edge, he almost felt as if she really were his wife. He grabbed onto that glimmer of hope and held it tightly as he drifted to sleep with a prayer in his heart that this torturous waiting would soon be over.

The following morning, Wade was glad that he and Alex had another day off. At breakfast he said to Cole, "So, apparently you had a good visit with Rochelle." Everyone else had already eaten, so it was just the two of them.

"I did, yes."

"You like her?" Wade asked.

"I do, actually. Maybe it's too soon, but . . ."

"I don't think there's any required time frame. If you feel ready, then you're ready."

"Well . . . I'm ready to have a long talk with a woman. That's all. I like her, though."

"I understand," Wade said. "I actually met Laura about six weeks out, and I think I felt attracted to her, but it was a long time after that before I was *ready*. You'll know."

"Is there a difference between being lonely and being ready?"

"Yes," Wade said, and repeated, "You'll know." He wanted to say something to discreetly alert Cole to Rochelle's lack of values. But he knew she was on the verge of making some changes, and he didn't want to say anything inappropriate. Her past was none of Cole's business, unless Rochelle chose to make it that way. Still, in a day when diseases were as rampant as the promiscuity that caused them, he found it difficult not to be concerned about someone like Cole considering a relationship with someone like Rochelle, even though she had repeatedly assured Laura that she had taken every precaution to protect herself from such things.

Cole went on to say, "It was good to talk to a woman who knows what it's like to be alone."

"She's going through some pretty rough things herself right now. I'm sure she appreciated a listening ear."

"Yeah, she talked about that. She asked for my advice, and I told her what I thought. She said that what I told her just validated the things she'd been thinking she should do. So, she's going to do them."

"Okay," Wade said, impressed with the theory but lost on what exactly she intended to do.

Cole chuckled as if he found Wade's ignorance amusing. He went on to say, "She's going back to Chicago long enough to quit her job and arrange for her things to be moved. She's got enough money put away to live on for a while until she can deal with some issues and find a job. She wants to make a clean break from the social life she has out there. I'm going to help her look for an apartment this afternoon. Once she finds a place to live, she's going to get her membership records transferred as quickly as possible so she can start the process."

"The process?" Wade echoed.

Cole looked a little hesitant. "Maybe I'm saying too much."

"She's already poured her heart out to me, Cole. And she had no qualms about telling Laura everything. I'm well aware of the kind of life she's been living."

"Then you know that she'll probably be excommunicated. But she wants to get it over with so she can start working her way back."

"Wow," Wade said. "You must be a good influence on her."

"Not me," Cole insisted. "She'd already come to that on her own. She just needed someone to reassure her that it was the right course."

"So you were the right person at the right time," Wade said, and Cole just shrugged.

Later that day, Wade walked into the kitchen to see the table and counters covered with ribbon and fabric, glue and wire, and a variety of Christmas garlands and lights.

"Oh, boy," Wade said, "it's that time of year." As he said it, he felt a little unsettled to realize that the holidays were approaching. And in this household, the first sign came when Jane started putting together her homemade decorations for the Festival of Trees. The festival was for the purpose of raising funds for Primary Children's Medical Center, and since Barrett's life had been saved there, Jane had quickly made it a tradition to donate a custom-decorated tree that would be auctioned to help meet the charity needs of the hospital.

"Yes, and I'm already behind," Jane said.

"What's the theme this year?" he asked, fingering the gold shimmery fabric on the table.

"Angels," she said. "I learned how to make these really adorable angels." She held up the prototype to show him, pointing out the intricate wings, halo, and delicate golden dress. "And I'm making garlands out of the same fabric by sewing it into long tubes and scrunching it up."

"Wow," he said. "Looks like a lot of work."

"Yeah," she said with chagrin. "Don't be surprised if you get enlisted before it's over."

"I'll look forward to it," he said facetiously.

A few days later Wade left in the middle of the night with Alex to do a shift, well aware that Jane was feeling frustrated and overwhelmed with the project. Apparently the angel ornament she intended to recreate dozens of times was much more intricate and time-consuming than she'd anticipated. He'd overheard Alex telling her that he'd take care of the meals when he wasn't working until the project was done, and they could all pitch in to help. But he felt sure that Jane knew men and children weren't very adept at doing the detailed work that needed to be done.

When their shift ended in the middle of the afternoon, Wade noticed that Alex was driving in the wrong direction.

"Where are we going?" he asked.

"Jane called and left a message. She wants us to meet her; said it was a surprise."

"Okay," Wade said, then didn't pay much attention until Alex turned into the parking lot of the facility where Laura was staying.

"A surprise?"

"That's what she said."

When they walked through the front door, Nola smiled and said, "Good, you're here. I think they're expecting you."

Alex and Wade exchanged a cautious glance as they followed Nola down the hall and into a room Wade had never seen before, even though he'd actually spent some time here himself years earlier. The familiar items related to Jane's craft project were spread out over a couple of large tables. Jane, Laura, a couple of other patients, and a few staff members, including Patty, were all working on the intricate ornaments, while Christmas music played softly from a CD player in the room.

"Unbelievable," Alex muttered and chuckled softly.

Jane noticed them near the door and came over, kissing Alex quickly before she said, "I think I was inspired. After I prayed for help this morning to get through this, I had the idea to just call here and ask if I could get Laura involved. They said I couldn't bring anything sharp or potentially dangerous, and they did a thorough search of what I brought in. But I had all the cutting and sewing done anyway. It's all that turning and fluffing that takes forever." She smiled at Wade and said, "I think there's an empty chair right across from your wife, little brother." Jane glanced over her shoulder. "She seems to be enjoying it; she's been working very hard."

"You're a genius," Wade said and kissed Jane's cheek.

"I was inspired," she said and shrugged.

"You *are* a genius," Alex said to her as Wade moved away to sit across from Laura.

"Hi," he said, and she looked up, showing little reaction beyond a smile that barely lasted an instant. He watched her face while she meticulously concentrated on the work her hands were doing.

"Will you show me what to do?" he asked.

As if she were talking to a stranger, she handed him a long, narrow piece of fabric that had been folded and sewn so that it could be turned to make a tube that would be scrunched and wrapped around the tree as a fabric garland. "Just . . . use the tongue depressor to push the fabric through until it's right side out," she said.

"Okay," Wade said, looking at the tongue depressor she handed to him. "I wonder where Jane got these."

"Her husband's a doctor," Laura said. "I think he has connections."

"No kidding," Wade said, wondering for a moment if she'd honestly forgotten who she was talking to. But the barest hint of a smile touched her lips, and he realized she was teasing him.

Almost no conversation took place between Wade and Laura during the next couple of hours while Alex and Wade helped with the project. The completed ornaments and fabric garlands began to pile into boxes while a warm spirit hovered in the room. Alex ordered pizza for everyone, and everything was cleaned up and put away just before the pizza arrived. Wade realized it was the first meal he'd eaten with his wife in weeks, but she didn't eat much, and she said nothing. And Patty stuck to her like glue; clearly they were still concerned about her personal safety. In the middle of the pizza party, Rita came to take Patty's place as Laura's bodyguard. The whole thing just felt so sick and wrong to Wade, but he tried to look on the positive side of the situation and appreciate the time he'd just spent with her, however strained it had been. When he left, he kissed Laura's cheek and got little reaction, but again he tried to keep perspective. Hope and patience, he reminded himself. Without one, he could never hold on to the other.

The day that Jane went to the Expo Center to set up the tree was a huge family project. And the day after that, Wade was at the hospital when he got a message to call Jane. Since he was standing next to Alex when the message came, he turned to his brother expecting him to know what this was about. Alex just shrugged, obviously ignorant as well.

"Hi," Jane said when Wade called home. "I hope you'll be okay with this. If you're not, say so. I went to see Laura this morning. I just felt like I should. She said she'd really like to see the tree now that it's finished. I spoke with Dr. Hadley, and he's approved an outing so that she can go to the festival with us, as long as Patty comes with her. But he has a couple of stipulations, and he wants to talk to you first. Something about making sure you understand exactly where her frame of mind is. So what do you think?"

"It sounds wonderful," he said. "Sometimes I think that never seeing the outside world's got to make it hard to keep perspective."

"I'm sure you're right, but when she's still on high-level suicide watch, that's tough to do."

"They said that?" he asked.

"Yes, but I think you need to talk with Dr. Hadley, and then you can decide if you feel good about this. Okay?"

"Okay," he said. "Thank you."

"I hope it works out."

Wade called Dr. Hadley's office and left a message for him to call back. They played phone tag a few times before they finally connected. He got right to the point. "I think having Laura get out for a few hours could be a good thing, as long as Patty stays with her, but I think you need to know where her thoughts are, so you're prepared to handle whatever she might say or do. And I don't want your expectations to leave you disappointed."

"Okay," Wade drawled skeptically.

"I'm not worried about her trying to escape Patty's care or doing something impulsive to harm herself. If I did I wouldn't be letting her go. She respects Patty and doesn't want to do anything that would get Patty into trouble, so to speak, and she knows that it's Patty's job to keep her alive."

"So, you're saying she's still very much suicidal."

"That's exactly what I'm saying. She will not view an outing like this as progression toward returning to a normal life. She has no comprehension of that possibility to any degree. She will see this as one more thing to check off of a list before she dies. She helped make the decorations for the tree; she wants to see the tree, and while she's at it she can enjoy the other trees and displays at the festival. It's as simple as that. I would suggest that you don't try to talk about the future. Just be in the moment with her, and you're less likely to get her aggravated or argumentative. I would also suggest that you don't talk about your feelings for her. She feels completely unlovable right now, and hearing someone say that they love her only makes her feel like she's being lied to. Just be with her and enjoy the moment. Am I making sense?"

"Yes," Wade said. He hated it, but he understood.

"There are a couple of other stipulations I'm putting on this, and I have my reasons. I've already discussed this with your sister-in-law. I think it would be better if the children in the family are not present. Alex and Jane are going with you; Laura wants to share this experience with Jane. But they will take the children another time. The children will likely create confusion for her, rather than any kind of grounding. More importantly, it's not good for children who know and love her to see her this way. Her behavior toward them may be too disconcerting and difficult to explain. When she's come a little further, Rebecca may be able to help her connect to her maternal instincts. Right now, I believe Rebecca might only spur more guilt for not being a good mother to her, and that will heighten the need in Laura to end her own life."

Wade listened with repulsion, hating that word *need* associated with ending her own life. How could she *need* to die? He just didn't understand, and he hated it.

"If you're okay with all of that, then this can be arranged," the doctor said.

"Yeah . . . of course. I trust your judgment."

"Okay. Patty and James will meet you there."

"James too?" Wade asked, knowing he was an LPN who worked at the facility.

"I'll just feel better with him there as well. I know it sounds ridiculous, but try to have a good time."

"I'm sure going to try," Wade said, but he cried when he got off the phone, recalling how simple it had once been to just get in the car with Laura and Rebecca and go to the mall or the zoo.

That evening, Wade discussed the stipulations with Alex and Jane, so that they could be as prepared as possible. He was grateful for the positive spin they put on this outing, which helped draw his mind away from the negative aspects.

The following day, Wade waited in the huge front lobby of the Expo Center for Laura to arrive. She came through the door like some rock star or dignitary, flanked by her bodyguards, who both looked discreetly alert.

"Hi," Wade said, kissing Laura's cheek.

"Hi," was all she said.

The rest of them all exchanged greetings and introductions, then they went in to see the endless rows of beautifully decorated trees, gingerbread houses, and other displays. All proceeds went to Primary Children's, and the atmosphere had a marvelous warmth of giving to it.

Wade held Laura's hand as they ambled slowly up and down the rows. She said nothing, and he said little, but he enjoyed watching her take in all of the magic there was to see. When they finally arrived at the tree they had specifically come to see, Wade almost felt moved to tears to see the framed picture of Barrett in front of the tree, with a notation that read, *In honor of Barrett Keane, who bravely survived leukemia and two bone marrow transplants.* Elsewhere a card read, *Donated by the Keane and Morrison families, in appreciation for the kindness and care shown by the staff at Primary Children's Medical Center.* There was also a card posted that said the tree had been sold for a significant price, which made their efforts—chiefly Jane's—especially gratifying.

Laura examined the tree closely and said, "Oh, it's beautiful, Jane."

"I never could have done it without you," Jane said, taking Laura's hand.

Wade observed the tenderness between them and felt hard-pressed not to cry. Being with Laura physically was nice, but it didn't fill the ache inside of him due to her emotional absence. In some ways it was almost harder to be with her under these circumstances as opposed to not seeing her at all. He wanted life to go back to the way it had been before. But he was learning more and more that life rarely gave him what he wanted.

The remainder of their excursion through the festival went without incident. Wade bought lunch for everybody before they completed their tour, then he once again kissed Laura's cheek, saying, "I'll see you in the next day or two, if that's okay."

She nodded. He thanked Patty and James for going the extra mile, and watched them walk away, hating the loneliness he felt.

That evening, Wade felt especially down. The waiting felt torturous, while Laura's lack of progress was agonizing. He perked up a little when he got a lengthy email from Brian. He wrote of a couple of recent and touching experiences with investigators, and he expressed his profound love for the gospel and reiterated how much he was enjoying his mission. He said that he was remembering Laura in his prayers, and Wade as well, and he finished with a stirring testimony of the Savior that moved Wade to tears. He almost wrote back but knew Brian wouldn't get to a computer for nearly a week, and Wade could write a more thoughtful letter when he felt less distracted.

Wade was surprised when Brad, the father who had raised him, stopped by to see how he was doing.

"Not very well, to be truthful," Wade said once they were seated in the study. He rehearsed the day's events, Laura's apparent state of mind, and his own deepening frustration.

"Would you like a father's blessing?" Brad asked, and the very suggestion soothed something in Wade's spirit.

"Yeah," he said, "I would. Thank you."

In the blessing Wade was told that Laura had the potential to heal and be whole, and he needed to be patient and trust in the Lord's timing and the Lord's methods. He was also told that as new difficulties arose in his life, the power of the Atonement would sustain him. The underlying message was both comforting and somewhat disturbing. Wade almost felt that he was being warned to be prepared to face something new. How could he face anything more on top of this? He reminded himself that he'd been told how. His knowledge of the gospel and how it worked would sustain him. And yes, he needed to be more patient. He had no doubt of that. And if he had anything to learn through all of this, perhaps that was it—to be patient and trust in the Lord.

When the blessing was completed, Wade thanked his father and embraced him. Then Brad said, "How long has it been since Laura received a blessing?"

Wade took a deep breath. "Just before she went to this place."

Brad said, "It can't hurt, can it?"

"No, I'm sure it can't. Truthfully, I've been so strung out, and . . . my opportunities to see her have been very few and . . . strained. But . . . you're right. Maybe it would be a good idea, if she's not opposed to it."

"I'd be happy to help you if that's what you want."

"Let me call and see what's going on," Wade said.

He called the facility and talked to Nola, who was LDS. She felt certain it wouldn't be a problem to arrange a few minutes for Laura to be given a blessing.

During the drive, Wade appreciated talking with his father about the challenges of Laura's condition and how it had affected him. And he admitted aloud that he knew he needed to be more patient, and made a commitment to work on that.

At the facility, Laura was evidently surprised to see Wade and his father. Brad hugged her in greeting, and she seemed pleased, so Wade hugged her too, wishing it wasn't so brief and passive. She was apparently indifferent to receiving a blessing, but at least she wasn't opposed to it. Wade asked his father to speak the majority of it, fearing that his own desires, and even his challenge with impatience, might influence his words. But Brad said quietly, "No, I think you need to do it, son. If you open your mind to the Spirit, it will guide your words no matter what your own feelings might be."

Wade felt taken aback, but in his heart he believed that was true. "Okay," he said, and they proceeded. Wade uttered a silent prayer and tried to feel the influence that he knew was necessary to do this. He felt comforted and strengthened when the words came to his mind with clarity, and he had no question about what needed to be said.

In the blessing, Laura was told, as she had been in the last one he'd given her, that there were children waiting to be born to her. But now she was also told that she had the capacity to raise them with love and a sound mind and a strong spirit. She was told that with time, and by trusting in the Lord, all would be well. Wade didn't know if the blessing had any effect on Laura, but it made him feel better. He just hoped that Laura could reach past her own pain enough to trust in the Lord and find the capacity to lead a normal life.

During the drive home, Wade expressed his appreciation to his father for his visit, his insight, and the blessings. But a few hours later, while he was staring at the ceiling, attempting to get some sleep, Wade couldn't deny that this patience thing wasn't going to be easy for him. He missed Laura, he hurt for her, and he yearned to be with her. And he hated this, plain and simple.

* * * * *

Wade walked into the ER and felt dismayed to see, even there, evidence of Christmas approaching. He'd not seen Laura or heard of any changes in her condition for days, and he wondered if this nightmare would continue through the holidays and leave him feeling, once again, on the outside of normalcy. He ached for Laura, both on her behalf and out of his desire to have her with him. On both counts he felt helpless and lost and confused, and just plain weary. And while he kept telling himself he needed to be patient, he knew he wasn't handling this well at all.

A few hours into the shift, Wade followed Alex out of an exam room after finishing with an antagonistic patient. Alex made him do the paperwork while he watched, then Alex signed it off so the patient could be admitted to the cardiac unit. While Alex was signing his name, Wade noticed a handful of staff members gathered in the doorway of a vacant exam room, apparently watching a news story on the TV there.

"What's going on?" Alex asked Winona, who was working the desk and apparently too busy to join the others.

"Oh, it's horrible," she said. "There was a terrorist bombing in London."

Wade's heart felt like a car that went from zero to sixty in a split second. He turned to look at Alex, who said with mild alarm, "Is Brian still in London?"

"Yes," Wade said, glad they were speaking quietly enough not to be overheard.

"Okay, but . . . there's a gazillion people there, right?"

"Right," Wade said.

Winona handed a patient's chart to Alex. "Difficulty breathing in room four."

"Tell you what," Alex said lightly to her. "Let's trade places today. *You* be the doctor, and *I'll* sit there and boss people around."

"I didn't avoid all those years of school for nothing," Winona said with a smile.

"What was I thinking?" Alex said facetiously, and Wade followed him to room four.

Observing the usual assessment, Wade's mind wandered to the tragedy in London. He told himself he was being paranoid, and that this uneasy feeling was nothing more nor less than that. When they came out of the room, even Winona was watching the TV, but Wade preferred to avoid it. He went to the men's room while Alex checked on another patient. They both came back to the central desk at the same time, and Winona was back in her chair. She looked toward them and said, "You're a Mormon, aren't you?"

Wade wasn't sure if she meant him or Alex. They both said, "Yes," at the same time, then Alex asked, "Why?"

"There're four Mormon missionaries unaccounted for in London. It's horrible, just horrible." Wade met Alex's eyes, grateful to see his own concerns reflected there without a word being spoken. Winona went on to say, "I don't understand all of this Mormon stuff, but you'd think that some kid out there doing God's work would be protected."

"You'd think," Wade said tersely enough that Winona looked alarmed.

"Did I say something wrong?" she asked, concerned.

Wade just walked away as he heard Alex say, "His brother's on a mission in London."

"Oh, my gosh!" Winona said way too loudly just before Wade closed the door of the staff lounge.

It wasn't a surprise to have Alex enter right behind him. "You okay?" he asked, leaning back against the door.

"Something doesn't feel right," he said, startled by the anxiety in his own voice. "But maybe I've just become a paranoid man, given the pattern of my life." He sighed loudly. "Seven thousand miles feels awfully far when I'd prefer to be digging through the rubble and treating the injured there, as opposed to sitting around here . . . wondering."

"I hear you," Alex said. "But I don't think you'll have to wonder long. The Church keeps pretty close track of their missionaries. No news is good news."

"Yeah," Wade said with sarcasm.

Before Alex could respond, he was told they were both needed. A fifty-two-year-old male was coming in on Life Flight after a significant fall at a construction site. Over the next two and half hours, patients kept coming, and the staff remained busy—but every little while one of them got a glimpse of the TV and reported the progress. Two of the missing elders had been located; they'd been nowhere near the bombing. Eleven bodies had been found, dozens of injuries were being treated, and rescue crews were still digging.

When it came time for a lunch break, Wade was at first dismayed to find the news on in the cafeteria where he and Alex went to eat, then he felt drawn to it. He wondered if he should be calling his parents to see how they were doing, but he couldn't bring himself to do it. He had nothing inside of him to offer any encouragement or hope.

Less than an hour after they'd returned to the ER, breaking news came in. The missing elders had been found. They *had* been at the bombing site. One was in critical condition, the other was dead. The names were not being released until their families could be notified. Wade felt all eyes turn toward him, and he knew that Winona had been talking. He hurried to the men's room, grateful to find it empty. But of course, Alex came right behind him.

"Who is shadowing whom?" Wade asked tersely.

"If you want to be alone just say so," Alex said with compassion. Wade said nothing, and Alex added, "You don't really think it's him, do you?" Still, Wade was silent. "You can't just assume the worst until you have something to go on."

Wade swallowed hard and willed his heart to slow down. "No news is good news, right?"

"Right."

Their eyes met, and they heard over the intercom, "Wade Morrison, line three."

Wade squeezed his eyes closed briefly then opened them and turned toward the door, as if it might give him the answer to what he could expect when he picked up the phone. He realized he was trembling and wondered if this was instinct or paranoia. He was trying to come up with words to ask Alex to stick close by when he heard his brother say, "I'm right behind you, kid."

Alex watched Wade walk out of the men's room as if he were facing the guillotine. He'd been trying to convince himself that Wade's mood over this was normal, and given some time they would know that Brian was fine. Now he was wondering if his own instincts had been put on alert, or if Wade's fear was simply contagious. He was grateful that the ER was quiet, and he hoped it lasted. He saw Wade move stealthily toward the phone on the counter at the central desk. He looked at it, then looked alarmed. He glanced at Alex, as if to be assured he was there, then he said to Winona, "I thought I had a call on line three."

"You do," she said.

"There's no call on any line. There are no lights on." He picked up the phone and pushed the button, saying more to Alex, "Dial tone."

"I don't know what happened," she said. "It was there, and I know I pushed the right button."

"Do you know who it was?"

"I'm sorry. I don't." Her expression turned tender. "Are you okay?"

"Not really, but thanks for asking," he said, and began pacing and wringing his hands.

Alex discreetly pulled Winona aside, saying quietly, "Could you make some calls and see if you can get someone to cover the rest of my shift? Call it a family emergency."

"Family?" she echoed.

He sighed and added more softly, "Wade is my half-brother."

She looked astonished. "Really?" She chuckled. "Wow. I *did* say you looked like brothers."

"Yes, you did, and so we are."

She seemed pleased. "And you got assigned to him by . . ."

"Some call it coincidence; but being a Mormon, I call it God knowing he might need me to hold him up if something tough were coming. I don't know if that phone call is what he's afraid it's going to be, but . . ."

"I'm all over it," she said.

"And Winona, people don't need to know that. We're not trying to keep a secret or anything. I just don't want anyone to think I'm giving him any favoritism or . . ." He motioned with his hand and could see by her eyes that she understood his implication to the political undertones that were present here, just like in most workplaces.

"You don't have to explain it to *me,"* she said. "My lips are sealed."

"Thank you," Alex said, and Winona went to the phone to find a fill-in physician. Thankfully there were several phone lines coming in. Alex started pacing with Wade, hoping that whoever had called wouldn't be too slow calling back.

The phone rang. Wade jumped. Winona was on the other line. Everybody else was gathered around the TV or with a patient. Alex grabbed the phone. "ER," he said. "This is Dr. Keane."

"Alex?" he heard a man say.

"Yes."

"It's Brad." Alex's heart quickened, and his stomach tightened. Alex knew Brad well; he was the father who had raised

Wade, and he was Brian's father. Could he just be calling to check on Wade, or to assure him that everything was okay? He didn't dare even ponder beyond that.

"I called a few minutes ago and they put me on hold, but another call beeped in, and I had to get it." His voice was steady, but strained. "I need to talk to Wade."

"He's right here," Alex said, and turned to see Wade staring at him, making no effort to mask the trepidation he was feeling.

"It's your father," Alex said, holding the phone toward him.

Wade looked at Alex's face and the phone in his hand. He knew it was Brad; if it was Neil he would have said *our* father. He took the phone and told himself to stop fearing the worst.

"Hello," he said.

"Hello, son," Brad said with a tenderness that was typical, along with an underlying apprehension.

"Hi, Dad," he said.

"You've heard the news? About London?"

"Uh . . . yeah."

"There's no easy way to say this, Wade," Brad said, and Wade felt his chest tighten.

Alex saw Wade press a hand over the center of his chest and squeeze his eyes shut. He took hold of Wade's arm and found it trembling. *Heaven help us,* he thought. Could it really be possible?

Wade held his breath and waited for the axe to fall. "It was Brian," Brad said, his voice breaking. "He's the one who died."

Wade gasped, then staggered, and then found Alex holding him up. He took hold of his brother with his free hand and wondered how to say anything to his father when he could feel the floor sucking him down. He realized that Winona was staring at him, horrified. Her expression snapped him back to the realization of where he was. Surely he could hold it together another minute, long enough to find a place to be alone.

"Wade?" he heard his father say. "Are you there?"

"Yeah," he croaked, while his mind tumbled through a hundred thoughts. "Uh . . . how's Mom?" he asked.

"Not as bad as I'd expected," Brad said.

"Expected?" Wade echoed, wondering how long it had been since they'd been informed.

"I need to call the others, Wade. Are you going to be okay?" Wade couldn't answer. "Wade, is Alex still there?"

"He wants to talk to you," Wade muttered, and he almost dropped the phone as he handed it to Alex before he turned like a frightened animal looking for refuge. The staff lounge was too popular. The men's room the same. Outside too open. But that empty exam room called to him, and he hurried that way, closing the door behind him as if it could keep the news from catching up to him.

"Brad?" Alex said into the phone.

"Is Wade okay?" Brad asked.

"I don't think so."

"You'll stay with him?"

"I will," Alex promised; he didn't even have to ask what Wade had been told. He couldn't believe it, and couldn't imagine how Wade must be feeling. Alex knew Brian, but it had been a cursory relationship at best, meeting him in passing at family gatherings, exchanging light chitchat at most. But Wade was closer to Brian than to any of his other siblings on that side of the family.

There was a moment of silence before Alex said, "Brad, I'm . . . so sorry."

"Thank you, Alex. You just . . . watch out for Wade."

"Of course," Alex said, and ended the call.

He found Winona staring at him, looking horrified. Thankfully, everyone else was busy elsewhere. "It was him?" she squeaked. Alex just nodded. "Your brother's . . . dead?"

"No, *Wade's* brother."

"But you said that . . ."

"Wade and I are half-brothers; we share the same father. He and Brian share the same mother."

"Oh," was all she said. He started to walk away, and she added, "Baker's on his way. You can go. I already told the super, so you're set."

"Thank you. I owe you one."

"No," she shook her head. "Just . . ." She waved her hand as if she couldn't finish, and Alex hurried to the room where Wade had gone.

Chapter Twelve

Alex found Wade gasping for breath, holding on to the exam table, his head hanging. Surely this on top of the ongoing situation with Laura was simply too much. Alex felt stunned and shocked and horrified. He couldn't even imagine how Wade must be feeling. Attempting to simply offer some silent support, Alex put his hands on Wade's shoulders. As if the contact had given him permission to let loose, Wade's heaving for breath turned to heaving sobs. Alex guided him to a chair and sat close beside him, while he cried and expressed his disbelief over and over.

Wade finally calmed down enough to say, "I've got to get out of here. I can't stay here and—"

"It's all covered. Why don't you take a few minutes to get a grip while I make a quick call, then I'll make sure the coast is clear, and we'll get to the car."

"Okay, thank you," Wade said. He looked hard at Alex. "How is it that you're always right beside me when I need you?"

"I think God has something to do with that."

Alex left and closed the door. He hurried to call Jane and tell her what was happening. She hadn't even had the news on and was completely shocked. He quickly told her he would be with Wade for a while and would see her later. Once off the phone, he spoke for a few minutes with Dr. Baker, who had arrived to fill in for him. They'd been friends as well as colleagues for many years, and he was grateful now for Baker's compassion as well as his willingness to cover the shift.

Alex found Wade unemotional but pacing frantically. "Come on, let's go," Alex said, and guided him quickly out of the ER to where the car had been parked.

Once in the car, Wade said, "I need to go to my parents' place."

"I figured as much. We're on our way."

Wade watched out the window as Alex drove, startled by the fact that life was going on normally around him. It felt to him as if the world had stopped turning. How could people be buying groceries and putting gas in their cars and walking down streets when lives had been violently stolen? The shock and horror felt eerily familiar, and in the course of a long moment his mind recounted four previous events that had taken him to these depths. Each had been time-stopping and debilitating. The first had been the discovery that he didn't have the same DNA as the father who had raised him, consequently bringing him to the moment when he'd attempted to end his own life. Thanks to Alex he had come to terms with that tragedy in his life, and all had been well until Elena's death. Finding his wife cold in their bed had been one of the most horrible moments of his existence, and almost as bad had been the moment when he'd realized how close Laura had come to taking her own life and leaving him alone once again. And through it all, Alex had been by his side. There had been other challenges and heartaches, but these moments rose above the rest, mingling now with the new reality that his little brother was gone, taken tragically through means that felt too dramatic to be real. And there was Alex: his rock, his shoulder, his big brother in every sense. And Wade wondered what he had ever done without him. While he was tempted to feel somehow abandoned or betrayed by God, to have his brother taken while in God's service, Wade only had to turn and look at Alex to know beyond any doubt that God loved and cared for him. He had counted it a blessing many times to be working with Alex through the course of Laura's illness. And this present tragedy left him convinced that his being paired up with Alex at the hospital was nothing less than a miracle, one of those tender mercies that left no doubt of God's hand in his life. Still, the pain was intense, unbelievable, confusing at best. He pressed a hand over the center of his chest as if he could counteract the tightness there that threatened to constrict his breathing and impede the beating of his heart. In the time it would take a pendulum to swing from one extreme to the other, Wade was overwhelmed with the reality of his life, now compounded with this implausible tragedy. He couldn't fathom facing his parents and the grief that was surely consuming them. He couldn't accept that he would never see his little brother again in this life. How could he possibly go on? How could he ever hope to keep putting one foot in front of the other?

Following many minutes of silence, Alex asked, "You okay?"

Wade just said the first thing that came to mind. "Give me a reason to keep going, Alex."

"I can give you several," Alex said easily.

"Name one," Wade challenged.

"Rebecca," he said without hesitation.

Wade sighed. "Okay, you got me there. How could I forget about Rebecca?"

"Because your mind has just been engulfed by something truly horrible," Alex said with compassion. "I don't know if you can appreciate this at the moment, and if you can't, that's okay, but . . . I just need to say that . . . in those moments when you can't think of any good reason to keep believing, it's most crucial that you keep believing. If Rebecca's need for you is the only thing that can keep you getting out of bed in the morning, then consider her your guiding star until you can find something else to hold onto." He took a deep breath. "Maybe that's one of the reasons God put her into your life before He took Elena."

Wade let out an acrid chuckle. "Yeah, because He knew it was all downhill from there."

"It's not over yet, Wade. No one—especially not me—would ever dispute that this just feels like too much for one man to bear, but you're not in it alone, and trust me, things will get better."

"You sound like you have experience," Wade said with subtle sarcasm, knowing well that he did. But he wasn't prepared for the impact of Alex's comeback.

"You mean like the moment when Barrett was in the ICU, and we thought he would die, and I found you bleeding all over the floor from slitting your own wrist?"

Wade sighed and pushed a hand through his hair. "I've brought a lot of grief into your life and—"

"No, you have not! You have brought a great deal of good into my life; you have blessed my life more than you could ever know. I didn't say that to add to your burden. I was simply trying to illustrate that I have some empathy. I may not know *exactly* how you feel right now. Our challenges certainly have their differences. But I do know what it's like to have to stand back and watch people you love suffer and struggle while you are incapable of doing much more than pray and ache and try to hold onto some hope. But I'm still here, and so are you. You've survived a great deal, and you've come through brilliantly. You will get through this as well."

"I'm glad somebody believes that," Wade said with an edge of cynicism.

"Well, I'll just keep believing for you until you can believe it yourself."

Alex pulled the car up in front of the Morrison home. Wade took a rough breath and said, "Looks like I'm the first one here." There was a car parked near the house that he didn't recognize, but he suspected it belonged to the bishop. It didn't belong to any of his siblings.

"The others all live farther away. But then, your parents always call you first anyway."

Wade felt a little startled by the comment. He'd never really thought about it, but Alex was right. His mother had admitted many times to feeling closer to him than the others in the respect that they had more similar personalities, they understood each other—they were friends. For that reason his father often called him first when difficulties arose.

"Well, here goes," Wade said, his heart pounding as he considered what his parents must surely be facing right now. He opened the door, then realized that the car was still running and Alex hadn't moved. He looked at his brother questioningly, silently demanding to know why he would send Wade in there alone.

Alex answered quietly, "They need you, not me. Call me whenever, and I'll come and get you."

"They *love* you."

"And I love them, but . . . I think it would be better if I offer my condolences another time."

Wade closed the car door and looked to Alex for an explanation. He felt disconcerted when he realized that Alex was struggling with his emotions. Without looking at Wade he said, "This is not my family, Wade. I care very much for your parents, and they've been very good to me. I cared for Brian, but I barely knew him. And whether we like it or not, we both know that some of your siblings are not comfortable with my presence in your life. When it comes to family functions directly related to you, you have the right for both of your families to be there. But this isn't one of those occasions. The last thing you need today is any tension or friction among your siblings because I'm there and they don't think I should be."

Wade felt so angry he hit the door with his fist. "Everybody else is going to have a spouse by their side through this. You're my best friend, Alex. I need *somebody* at my side."

"They will only see me as the *scandalous* half-brother, Wade, and we both know it. At other times it might be okay to just let them think what they want and go with it, but not today. I have to go with my gut on this, little brother, as hard as it is."

Wade blew out a harsh breath and rubbed a hand over his face, attempting to keep perspective, struggling to accept that what Alex had said was true. He respected Alex's insight, and appreciated his consideration for the family, even though he hated it.

"Okay," he said and looked toward the house as if it represented certain doom and he was being forced to face it alone. "I understand. I hate it, but I understand."

"I'll be back at a moment's notice, no matter how late."

"Okay," Wade said again. "Thank you."

They shared a long, tight hug before Wade got out of the car.

Alex watched him walk to the door, glancing over his shoulder with obvious hesitation in his countenance. It felt like leaving Barrett at school on a day when he'd had to face a difficult encounter. Alex wanted to jump out of the car and run and fix everything. He wanted to stand between the harsh reality of life and this person he cared for so deeply. But he couldn't. He realized then that he'd found great fulfillment in being Wade's big brother. It had become a large portion of his identity. But being a brother, just like being a father, meant knowing that there were times when the right thing was the hardest. And he knew it just wouldn't be appropriate for him to be with Wade right now. Still, he couldn't hold back tears as he drove away. And as the reality of Brian's death settled into him, his tears turned to sobbing until he had to pull over and take a few minutes to get a grip.

Instead of going home, Alex drove to his father's house, praying that he would be home. He didn't even want to call on his cell phone and ask. He was afraid he'd start crying again if he even heard his father's voice. So he just drove the half hour it took to get there and unlocked the front door with his key. He knew it always remained locked whether they were home or not, and their vehicles would be out of sight in the garage even if they were home.

"Dad?" he called. "Are you here?"

"In the study," Neil called back. Alex stepped into the room and found his father half-reclined on the couch with a thick novel in his hands. "What's up?" Neil asked.

Alex couldn't form the words and asked instead, "Have you seen the news today?"

"No, I've been reading. Roxanne's shopping with a friend. Why?"

Alex recalled Jane being oblivious as well and grumbled, "Doesn't anyone in this family watch TV during the day?"

"Probably not," Neil said as Alex flipped on the TV, not surprised to find the story still running live on whatever channel the set had been left on. Neil sat up to pay attention. Alex sat down beside him, feeling too emotional to speak and more than willing to let the television take over as far as it was possible. They watched footage of exploded wreckage, rescue crews working, and the injured being treated, while a commentator recounted numbers related to deaths and injuries.

"Where is this?" Neil asked, horrified.

"London," Alex stated tonelessly. Neil shot him a concerned glance, then looked back at the TV.

Alex realized this was national news, and he grabbed the remote to flip it to a different channel with a local report. A summary of the event was being given, which led right into the biggest topic of local news, something that was surely being repeated over and over on local channels. The commentator stated, "The two LDS missionaries caught in the terrorist attack were located by rescue workers more than an hour after the bombing occurred. One has been verified dead, the other is in critical condition and being treated at a nearby hospital. The families have been notified, but the names have not yet been released. At this point, the only information we have is that one of the missionaries is European, and the other is said to be from the Salt Lake City area." Neil glanced at Alex again, looking mildly alarmed but saying nothing. Alex just stared at the TV, not wanting to say it, hoping and praying his father would figure it out. He recalled being the one who'd made all the calls to tell family members that Elena was dead. He just didn't want to be that person again.

Their attention turned back to the TV as the report continued. "Stay tuned for an official statement from a representative of the LDS Church. According to the rescue workers who located the elders, it appears that the one still alive was saved only because his companion's body blocked him from the full impact of the explosion."

The report continued with a more general update of the incident and the rescue work in progress. Neil asked without moving his eyes from the screen, "Is there something you came here to tell me, son?"

Alex let out a weighted sigh and pushed a hand through his hair. "Yes, but . . . I don't want to say it."

Neil turned abruptly, eyes wide with enlightenment and trepidation. "Brian is in London." He glanced at the TV, then back to Alex. "It can't possibly be . . ."

"I'm afraid it is," Alex said, and new tears came.

"Which one?" Neil demanded. "Is he injured or . . ."

"He's dead," Alex stated, and wiped a hand over his wet cheeks. He heard his father suck in a harsh breath, but he said nothing. For a few minutes the shock settled in, then Alex said, "He's my brother's brother. It's like some kind of sick riddle. Who is my brother's brother? Well, it should be me, but it's not. It's someone else in some other family, and I have to stand back and do *nothing* because it's not *my* family, but it's *my* brother who is suffering with this right now."

"And my son," Neil said sadly.

"Yes, well . . . that puts you and me in the same boat, because . . . your son's brother . . . just died."

Neil cried silent tears while he said, "And that's why we will be there for Wade whenever he needs us, and we will stand on the outside of his life when it's appropriate. That's the way it's always been, and the way it will always be. And that's my fault. I'm only sorry that, in this respect, you have to be in that boat with me."

"I'm grateful to know that Wade is my brother, and to have him in my life. I just wish that . . ." his voice broke, "there was something . . . more I could do."

"Where is he now?"

"With his family, of course. I dropped him off. The news came while we were at the hospital. I told him I'd come and get him whenever he was ready."

"Then we should go to your house and wait. It's much closer."

"Okay," Alex said, and they both stood up, exchanging a long embrace. Alex picked up the remote to turn the TV off just as the news stated that the identity of the missionaries had been released. There it was, leaving no opportunity for question or doubt. Elder Brian Morrison of Salt Lake City, Utah, had been killed.

Neil followed Alex home in his own car. Jane was waiting for him with all the love and compassion that she always gave, but her tears were a stark reminder that Wade was going to need a great deal of support to get through this.

* * * * *

Wade walked through the front door of his parents' home to realize that four men in suits were there. He recognized the bishop and was introduced to the stake president, one of his counselors, and a representative from the Church. His parents looked surprisingly calm and composed, but he felt certain that was mostly due to being in the presence of company. Wade sat close to his mother and held her hand while the conversation he'd interrupted was finished. Then they all stood up when the brethren left, and Wade expected his parents, his mother especially, to fall apart. But she put a hand to his face and asked gently, "How are you?"

"How should I be?" he growled, feeling more angry than anything at the moment. He knew grief well enough to know this was normal, but he still hated it.

"Wade, look at me," Marilyn said, holding his face in her hands. Her eyes turned moist, but she almost smiled. He felt disoriented and perhaps troubled by what the evidence told him. This was a woman who had struggled with depression off and on over the last couple of years. He would have expected her to be debilitated by this. But there was peace in her eyes. A peace so intense that it radiated into Wade's aching heart even before she said, "It was his time. *This* is his mission. His death was foreordained to happen at this time, in this way." Her voice broke. "And Brian knew that."

Wade took a step back as if he'd been struck in the chest. "He *knew?*" Wade croaked, looking at his father as if to verify this. Brad's expression was firm, his eyes serene.

"Yes, he did," Brad said. "And so did we."

"You *knew?*" Wade countered, feeling his anger rise without bothering to analyze why. He looked at his mother again, then his father. "Why . . . didn't you say something?"

"You, of all people, should not need an explanation," Brad said. "You knew Elena was going to die, but you told practically no one."

Wade staggered backwards a couple of steps and sank onto the couch. "You got me there," he said, pressing a hand over his chest, while his breathing became ragged.

Brad and Marilyn sat down as well. He looked to them with questions he couldn't voice. He was grateful to hear some explanation. "Brian didn't want us to say anything to anyone," Marilyn said. "He didn't want his leaving to be weighed down by grief and speculation."

"His leaving for his mission, or dying?" Wade asked.

"Both," Brad said.

"But . . . he told the two of you . . . before he left."

"He didn't have to," Brad said. "We both felt it . . . in the temple."

"But . . ." Wade protested as if doing so might bring Brian back to life, "his patriarchal blessing talks about . . . marriage . . . and children."

"Clearly those are promises that will come to pass in the next life. Those blessings are for our eternal lives, not just the ones we live here."

Wade shook his head, unable to accept what he was hearing. He squeezed his eyes closed as he recalled the day Brian had left to go to the MTC in England—the last time Wade had seen him. Brian had been especially emotional, and so had his parents. Now Wade understood why. Considering what he'd just learned, he couldn't deny the comfort it gave him, but it also contributed to a certain surreal quality related to this event. And just like when he'd lost Elena, knowing it had been her time to go had not eliminated the heartache of separation.

Following a few minutes of silence, Wade said to his mother, "And I expected you to be curled up in bed over this."

Marilyn took Brad's hand and squeezed it before she looked at Wade and said, "I can tell you now, Wade, that a portion of my depression was related to this. You know I was struggling with other things, on top of the cancer. But knowing I would never see Brian again made everything just feel too heavy." Wade took in her words as the confusion he'd felt then suddenly made sense. "Truthfully, now that it's over, I don't have to dread it any more. It's hard." She began to cry. "We will miss him dreadfully, but . . . I have felt him closer to me today than I have since he left, nearly two years ago."

Wade joined his mother in having a good cry, and before he got his emotions under control, a couple of his siblings arrived with their spouses. He went into the other room to get some grief out of his system and find some composure. He came back to find that all the others had arrived. They all shared embraces, and his younger sister, Robin, motioned to his attire and said, "Scrubs? Did I miss something?"

"I don't think so. I'm going to medical school. You didn't miss that, did you?"

"No, but . . ."

"I'm doing a student rotation in a hospital."

"Oh." She nodded. "Are you enjoying it?"

"Yes and no," he said, feeling a little awkward having casual conversation when their brother had just been killed.

"How's Laura?" she asked, and Wade wished she hadn't.

"The same," was all he said, and he was grateful when Brad asked everyone to sit down. As they repeated what they'd been told by Church officials, the tears started to flow with everyone in the room. They'd been warned that the local media would be giving this a great deal of attention, and had been advised on the best way to handle it. With that discussion over, Brad and Marilyn repeated everything they'd told Wade, which brought on a variety of reactions. Wade just sat and listened, feeling numb. He realized this was one of those moments when he felt out of place and uncomfortable in his own family. He'd always felt that way at times, long before he'd ever known he didn't have the same biological father as the others. But having different fathers had nothing to do with their differences. They all just thought differently than he did, had different preferences, different ways of dealing with things. Of all of them, Brian was the one he'd related to the most, even though they had many different tastes. And now he was gone. But Wade's discomfort was deepened now in being the only one here without a spouse. He'd endured this feeling throughout the time following Elena's death until he'd married Laura. And now, here he was again—the loner, the fifth wheel. His mind wandered to Laura, and he felt sick. He knew he should let her know this had happened, but he couldn't imagine even having the strength to call the facility and leave a message. He felt afraid somehow of what this might do to her. Or perhaps even more afraid that she would be indifferent. Either way, he couldn't even think about Laura right now. It was just too much. He could only think of how alone he felt while his siblings each had a hand to hold, a shoulder to cry on.

Wade had expected that this meeting would entail some funeral planning, but apparently Brian had that all written down, and other arrangements needed to be made before details could be taken care of. His older brother, David, would be flying to England in a few hours to take care of some things from that end. He was the only family member with a passport and visa, since travel was occasionally required for his job. When Wade realized that nothing of any significance was going to happen from here on out, he slipped away to call Alex for a ride.

"I'm on my way," Alex said, and Wade returned to the front room where everyone was still sitting, crying, and sharing memories that to Wade were only hurtful at this point. Perhaps if he'd not been alone, it might have been different.

Marilyn noticed him standing and said, "Are you leaving?"

"In a few minutes, yes. I need to be with Rebecca." He didn't tell her *why* he needed time with his daughter. "I was dropped off, but Alex is on his way to pick me up."

"There's something you need before you go," she said and hurried out of the room. He wasn't sure if she meant for him to follow her, but he did. He watched her kneel in front of her cedar chest, carefully remove a couple of things that were on top of it, then open the lid. She shifted a couple of things inside to reveal a large manila envelope. Written in black marker, in Brian's hand, it read: *Just in case.* And there was a silly cartoon drawing that Brian often doodled just about anywhere. Wade's heart began to pound as his mother stood up while opening the envelope. She pulled out a stack of business-sized white envelopes and thumbed through them until his name appeared, also written in Brian's hand. "Read it when you're alone," she said, giving it to him.

Wade could only swallow carefully and nod. He hurried back to the front room and hugged everyone once more, lingering over long embraces with his parents, who whispered reassurance and comfort to him. He marveled at their strength, their faith, their example—and he prayed that it might rub off. He could use some strength and faith right now, but he felt neither strong nor faithful.

Wade stepped outside, unable to drag the good-byes out any longer, not caring if Alex was here yet or not. It was dark and cold, but Alex's SUV was parked across the street, and leaning against it, waiting, were Alex and their father. He breathed in a cold breath of fresh air and hurried to meet them. The hug he got from Alex, and then Neil, filled him with something sustaining and rejuvenating, and he was grateful. It wasn't that he didn't appreciate the family he'd grown up in, and he certainly loved them. He loved and respected Brad and Marilyn beyond words. But there was something he found with Alex and their father that went unexplainably deeper. They understood him without even trying.

"Let's go home," Alex said, and guided him into the front passenger seat of the car. Neil got in the backseat, and Alex drove while Wade held tightly to the unopened letter in his hand and tearfully repeated everything that had been said, and how it had made him feel. At the house, Jane greeted him with a tight hug, warm tears, and hot soup that she'd made. He didn't feel like eating, but Alex insisted, and he and Neil both stayed close by while he did. Rebecca came in and out of the room, offering him the balance for his life that was so evident in her happiness and vibrancy. But she was too busy to sit still for long and wanted to be playing with her cousins.

When it was time to get the children ready for bed, Wade spent some time with Rebecca, giving her a bath and reading her some stories. After he had put her down with a prayer and a kiss, he talked for a while longer with Alex and Neil before Neil went home, then Wade asked, "Where's Barrett?"

"He's at a sleepover birthday party," Jane explained. "He went right after school. He's been looking forward to it, and I didn't want to tell him the news before he left and spoil the party for him. We'll have to tell him when he gets home in the morning."

"His letters from Brian meant a lot to him," Alex said, shaking his head. "This could be rough."

Wade just let out a heavy sigh and insisted that he needed some time alone. Sitting on the edge of his bed, he held the unopened letter in his hands and felt terrified. He glanced at the picture of himself and Laura on the bedside table, wishing with all his heart that he had someone to hold his hand while he did this. His thoughts went more to Laura, and the pain on her behalf struck him so deeply that he had to set the letter aside and sob, pressing his head into his hands. Then suddenly something felt different. He looked up, certain he'd see that the door had opened, that Alex had come to check on him. But it was closed. He was alone. *But he wasn't!* He drew in his breath and held it, closing his eyes if only to focus more on what he felt, even though he knew he could not see it.

"Elena," he breathed and knew she was there. He couldn't believe it! His fears were soothed, his pain comforted, his heartache calmed. Just to know that she would be allowed to spend even a moment so close to him in spirit gave him a perfect certainty of life after death, of the tender mercies of God, and of the reality that his faith was not unfounded. For a long minute he just sat, absorbing the sensation of her presence, in awe of the miracle and of the fact that he could not deny its reality. Then he felt impressed that he needed to read the letter—that she had been sent to be with him while he did. He opened it carefully, but he hesitated before pulling it out of the envelope as another impression came over him, several thoughts all at once. He knew that Brian was happy and at peace. He knew that Elena was the same. He knew that Elena was mindful of him and Rebecca, but more profoundly, he knew that she was also mindful of Laura. He could feel the closeness between Elena and Laura, and then he felt his first wife whisper to him that all would be well with his second, that the ministering of angels would guide them through this valley. It took Wade minutes to absorb what his spirit had just been taught and the comfort he'd been given, while tears ran steadily over his face. Everything felt different. *Everything!* He pulled out Brian's letter to read it through new eyes, with new hope and understanding.

Dear Wade, If you're reading this, then you know that my mission didn't turn out as most do. I have wondered sometimes if my feelings were just a test, to see if I would serve a mission anyway, even if I was led to believe that I wouldn't survive it. But in my heart I don't believe that's the case, and I'm pretty sure that once we say good-bye at the airport I won't see you again in this life. I want you to know that it's okay. I know that the message I am leaving home to share is true, and even though I have to admit to being scared in a way, I also feel honored and privileged. I've read a lot about the followers of Christ in the New Testament who gave their lives for their testimony, and then there's Joseph and Hyrum. How could I not be honored to have the privilege of being given the same opportunity to give my life in His service? I want you to know that you have been the most amazing example to me. I know what we discovered about our family a few years back was tough for all of us and shook the family up pretty badly, but you came through it like a champion. It was your example of forgiveness and following the Savior that changed the way I looked at everything in life. You need to know that you are the reason I chose to serve a mission, and I will always love you for that. I'm sorry that I didn't tell you how I felt before I left, but I think you'll understand. I knew you would understand better than anyone, but after the way you lost Elena, you were the last person I wanted to be burdened with this. You need to know how much it meant to me to know that someone I love has already been through this. Your experience with Elena's death and the way you knew it was coming has given me courage and strength. I don't believe it's a coincidence that it's happened twice in the same family. I think God put me in this family to be your brother so that I could learn from you and your experiences and your example. I love you, and I look forward to keeping track of you from the other side. Remember, I'm not really gone or lost. My mission will just be longer than yours, or maybe just different. Keep the faith, brother, and be good. I'll see you in heaven. Love, Brian.

Wade read the letter twice, then he curled up on the bed and wept without control while a combination of peace and sorrow swirled inside of him. He was vaguely aware of Elena's presence and turned his thoughts to the gratitude he felt in knowing that his prayers had been heard and answered. At least for these brief minutes, he had not been left alone to face the reality of his brother's death.

Wade fell asleep crying and woke up with the light still on, still wearing his scrubs, and freezing. He hurried to change into pajamas, spent a few minutes in the bathroom, then climbed beneath the covers. Staring into the darkness, he pondered the miracle he'd been given, imagining that Elena had stayed with him until he'd slept, then she might have kissed his brow and slipped back through the veil between her world and his, perhaps to come back again to check on their daughter, or to be with Laura and give her comfort. He slept again with that image in his mind, and a prayer in his heart.

The following morning, Wade woke up to the familiar noises of Rebecca coming awake that he could hear on the monitor that was always nearby. While he could hear her playing happily in her room, since she'd learned to climb out of her crib, he picked up the letter from Brian and read it again. He felt a little chilled as his mind went to the letter Laura had written him that had been intended to be read following her death. The contrast was troubling, but he reminded himself to be grateful that she'd been spared from doing herself harm that day, and that he'd been given a promise that all would be well.

He was still sitting on the edge of his bed when Alex knocked on the door, then immediately opened it, saying, "I need your help. It can't wait. Katharine's watching the girls."

Without further explanation, Wade followed Alex down the hall, soon becoming aware of Barrett screaming. He entered Barrett's room right behind Alex and found Jane kneeling on the floor in front of the child, holding his shoulders while Barrett cried and screamed indeterminable words. Wade immediately urged her aside and took her place. He wrapped Barrett tightly in his arms, ignoring the way he squirmed and screamed.

"It's okay, Barrett," Wade said close to his ear. "It's okay. We need to talk about this. You've got to calm down so we can talk about this. Are you hearing me?" His behavior didn't change. "Barrett!" Wade shouted softly. "I know it hurts. I know it's hard. He's my brother, Barrett, so I know. But you have got to calm down so we can talk. Calm down." Barrett began to respond, and Wade softened his voice. "Calm down. Take a deep breath."

Barrett struggled to catch his breath while he made a visible effort to gain control of his emotions. Wade looked at Alex and Jane, sitting on the edge of Barrett's bed. Jane had a hand pressed over her mouth, tears streaming down her face. Alex just looked nauseous. Wade mouthed the words to his brother, "What have you told him?"

Alex responded the same way. “Nothing; just that Brian died in the bombing.”

“Barrett,” Wade said gently as he sat on the floor and eased the boy onto his lap. Barrett was small for his age, due to the leukemia temporarily stunting his growth, and it was no problem for Wade to cradle the boy against him. “Do you remember when Elena died . . . and you told me about the place she’d gone to? How it was more beautiful and happy than it is here? Do you remember?”

Barrett nodded, then said, “But . . . Brian was a missionary, and . . . he . . . he . . .”

The child started to get upset again, and Wade made a soothing noise before he said, “I have something very important to tell you, Barrett. It’s something that I know Brian would have wanted you to know. Actually, he wrote it to me in a letter—a letter he left before he went to the MTC. He gave it to my mother to give to me, and I just read it last night. Would you like to read it?”

Barrett nodded, and Wade stood up, carrying the child to his room. He motioned with his head for Jane and Alex to follow. He set Barrett on his bed and handed him a tissue before he took the letter from the bedside table where he’d left it. Alex and Jane sat together in a little love seat on the other side of the room.

He sat to face Barrett directly and began to read aloud. After the first few sentences, he stopped and gauged the child’s reaction. He looked wide-eyed, stunned. “What do you think that means, Barrett?” Wade asked.

“He . . . knew?” Barrett squeaked.

“That’s right, Barrett. He knew. He wrote this letter before he left. Now listen to the rest.”

Wade continued to read, aware of Alex and Jane both crying. And Barrett cried too, but there was a different feeling to these tears. He was calm and receptive to what he was hearing. When the letter was finished, Wade took both of Barrett's shoulders into his hands and said, "I know that your letters meant a great deal to Brian, and his letters meant a great deal to you. You'll always have them to remember him by. And when you're old enough to go on a mission, I want you to remember Brian's example. Do you think you can do that?"

Barrett nodded and wrapped his arms around Wade, crying harder. Wade just held him, crying as well, until Barrett calmed down and said quietly, "It's not fair . . . that you had to lose Elena, and now your brother, and Laura's sick too."

Wade felt hard-pressed not to crumble as his own inner child echoed the sentiment exactly. But he reached deep down for any measure of faith he could find and said what needed to be said. "No, it's not fair, Barrett. And it's hard. But we have to trust in God, and we're very blessed to have the gospel and to understand things that make it easier to find peace. You understand those things, Barrett. You're the one who helped me when Elena died, to understand that this is not the end. Brian is with her now, and I know that everything is alright." He hugged Barrett tightly and muttered tearfully, "I know it hurts, Barrett. It hurts so badly that . . . I sometimes . . . don't know how I'm going to get through it. But we will. We'll get through it together. Do you hear me?" He felt Barrett nodding as the child clutched onto him tightly, and together they cried.

Alex watched Wade grieving with his son while he kept his arm tightly around Jane, well aware that she was crying even more than he was. While nothing was spoken amidst the shedding of many tears, the moment became almost surreal, detached from their human existence. In the space of a heartbeat Alex saw in his mind the history shared by his brother and his son. How could God's existence be questioned or remotely doubted in consideration of the single fact that Wade had come into Alex's life while Barrett had been barely clinging to life, and Wade's bone marrow had saved him? And from the moment that a part of Wade had gone through the IV tubes into Barrett's little body, Wade had been drawn to the child in ways that defied logic or explanation. It was as if Wade could never be too disconnected from the bone marrow he'd donated, and the fact that they shared the same blood made them as close as twins of the same womb could ever be, in spite of their dramatic age difference. The years since had brought many experiences of joy and heartache, and Alex had seen his young son grieve on behalf of Wade's losses at a depth that most children could never reach. But Alex had never seen Barrett so upset or traumatized. Even through his fight with leukemia, he had been the brave one who had rarely cried or complained. It was he and Jane who had fallen apart. And when Elena had died, Barrett had cried and grieved in his own way, but if anything, he had been a strength to Wade by his simple faith and extraordinary insight. His outburst upon learning of Brian's death had taken both of his parents completely off guard. Barrett had exchanged letters with Brian, and he'd shown a great interest in the specifics of his mission. But Alex suspected that the real source of anguish for Barrett was on Wade's behalf. Over the past several weeks he'd told both Jane and Alex a number of times that he was worried about Laura, and Wade as well. He'd commented more than once that after Wade had lost Elena, it wasn't fair for Laura to be so sick. While Barrett didn't understand the full ramifications of Laura's illness, and he didn't know she'd come close to taking her own life, he was especially sensitive to Wade's moods and challenges. And Alex felt certain that Barrett's greatest source of grief now was on Wade's behalf. It would be the evidence of Wade's peace and understanding that would get Barrett through this.

The tears finally faded into an eerie silence. Alex saw Wade glance toward him over the top of Barrett's head, then he closed his eyes and tightened his hold on the child, as if he drew great comfort from the grief they were sharing. Another few minutes passed before Wade said to Barrett, "Hey, buddy, why don't we get some breakfast, and then we can read some of Brian's letters . . . only if you want to."

"Okay," Barrett said sadly before he slid down from Wade's lap. On his way to the door he added, "I just need to be alone for a little while first."

"Okay," Wade said, and Barrett left the room.

Wade watched him leave and turned to see Alex and Jane, looking somber and concerned. Wade could only say, "I'm so sorry."

"For what?" Alex demanded.

"For bringing so much grief into your home . . . your family."

"We *are* family, Wade. And there is no amount of grief that could ever outweigh the joy you have brought into our home."

Wade looked away, not certain he could believe him.

Alex added quietly, "These things will make him stronger, Wade."

"Yeah," Wade said cynically, "what doesn't kill us makes us stronger." He resisted adding a comment about preferring death over any more strengthening activities. Laura's desire to die just didn't mix well with such a thought, even if he only meant it as some kind of sick wisecrack. He focused more on his most prominent concern. "It's one thing for *me* to be knocked over by life's struggles, but when Barrett . . ." He couldn't finish as emotion overtook him.

Wade found Alex beside him, and then he was wrapped in an all-too-familiar brotherly embrace. "He'll be okay, Wade," Alex murmured. "And so will you. We've survived much together, and we'll keep surviving. Do you hear me?"

Wade just nodded and cried. He cried for Brian's loss, for Laura's pain, for Barrett's grief, and for his own place in the tragedy his life had become.

Later, Wade sat with Barrett for more than an hour, reading through the letters Brian had written to the child. He had averaged about one a month. They were brief but tender, and were written with specific interest in Barrett, and in response to the questions Barrett had asked in his letters to Brian. They both cried a little, but they talked about all the good that Brian had done on his mission, and about the peace they could find in knowing that all was well for him.

Barrett seemed better as he went off to do his Saturday chores. Wade went back to his own room and dug out the handwritten letters he had received from Brian. Again he wept as he read them through, but he felt grateful to have them, as opposed to the little stack of printed emails from Brian, which were full of information, but lacked the personal touch of his handwriting. It was Brian's last letter that struck Wade most deeply.

So, you're married again. Wow! That's great. I sure wish I could meet her. She must be amazing to have snagged a guy like you. I'm certain you'll be deliriously happy.

How could Wade forget the day it had arrived? He *had* been deliriously happy. The irony was difficult to swallow. But what stood out even more to Wade was the way Brian had worded his sentiment. *I sure wish I could meet her.* He realized now that if Brian had expected to come home, he would have been more likely to say that he couldn't wait to meet her. He'd known. There was no doubt about it. He'd really known he wouldn't live to come home.

Farther down in the letter Wade was struck even more deeply with Brian's request on behalf of their mother. *I want you to tell her something for me. It's very important. I've told her myself, but I want it to come from you as well. You tell her that I know beyond any doubt that whatever trial might come into our lives, no matter how difficult or unfair it might seem, that God is mindful of us, that He holds us in the hollow of His hands. I know it, Wade. Tell her that no matter what happens, I will always love her and admire her for what a good woman she is, and all that she has taught me. Promise me that you'll tell her.*

Wade remembered calling his mother and reading the letter to her, and how she had cried. *She* had known! But neither of them had said anything. Wade understood; he truly did. But it was still tough to swallow. He called his mother right then, glad when she answered the phone and that she wasn't busy. She told him they'd had a great many visitors and much to work out, but the arrangements were all coming along as well as could be expected, and the Church support was beyond belief.

After she'd caught him up on all that was happening, he said, "Do you remember when I read you the last letter I got from Brian in the mail?"

"Yes," she said.

"I just read it again. I think he would want me to repeat this part to you now. Is that okay?"

"Of course," she said, her voice expressing a balance of grief and serenity.

Wade read the paragraph, then expressed how it made him feel while they cried together over the phone. They talked for a long while, then she told him what time he should be there the following day in order to help with the final plans for the funeral. He told her he loved her, and she returned the sentiment with fervor before he ended the call. Then he sat on the edge of his bed and stared at the floor until he felt a hand on his shoulder, and Alex sat down beside him.

"How are you?" Alex asked.

Wade sighed. "All things considered, I'm still in one piece. I guess that's something. How's Barrett?"

"He's fine. He's helping Jane make cookies for your parents. It was his idea."

Wade felt choked up. "Wow. What a kid."

"Well, I'm sure his doing something for them will be healing for him, even if cookies don't really do a whole lot to ease grief."

"I don't know," Wade chuckled through new tears. "I think cookies from Barrett could be pretty powerful."

"What've you got there?" Alex asked, motioning toward the letter in Wade's hands.

"It's the last one he sent in the mail. I've received some emails since then, but . . . this one has his handwriting."

He pointed out the wording that had stood out as significant, and they talked for a long while, allowing Wade to take another step toward accepting that this was real, while at the same time being able to cry freely and vent his grief. Once again, Alex proved how very good he was at mourning with those that mourn.

Alex commented, "That letter Brian left with your parents for you is pretty amazing."

"Yes, it is," Wade said. "It's a miracle, really. And . . ." he hesitated only a moment but felt good about sharing his experience with Alex, "speaking of miracles . . . Elena was . . ." He became too emotional to speak for a full minute, but Alex just waited. Wade actually smiled at his brother as he wiped his tears and said, "She was . . . here . . . with me . . . last night when I read the letter."

Alex got tears in his eyes and smiled as well. "You see, little brother, you're not going to be left alone. We'll get through this."

Wade just nodded and hugged his brother, grateful for the millionth time to have Alex by his side. He was truly blessed.

Chapter Thirteen

Throughout the following days, Wade had to fight to hold onto the peace he'd been given through miraculous means. The comfort he felt over Brian's death was no small thing, but he couldn't deny the heartache of the loss. He spent a great deal of time with his family in preparation for the funeral, and he found it difficult to try to comfort his siblings when some of them seemed to find it especially difficult to grasp the concept that this was meant to be. His parents held up pretty well, even though they had some moments that were difficult. He knew those moments well. And as always, his heart was with Laura. Several times he considered stopping by to see her, or at least leaving a message, but he just couldn't bring himself to do it. If he wasn't afraid of adding to her emotional burdens, he was afraid that seeing her condition would just be too much at the moment. He finally did leave a message that simply said he loved her and something had come up so he wouldn't be seeing her for a few days. Then he tried to focus on getting through the funeral. As always, he was immeasurably grateful to have Alex around, and, as an added bonus, he was grateful to be working with him. Alex helped smooth out Wade's schedule by making shift exchanges for his own. They did have to fill one shift prior to the funeral, but then they had a few days off, which would get Wade past the worst of this ordeal.

In the middle of their shift, Winona came to fill her own shift at the desk. She took one look at Wade and started to cry.

"What?" he asked.

"I just . . . can't stop thinking about your brother. It's so horrible."

"Yes, it's quite a shock," Wade said while he was watching Alex fill out some paperwork.

"Why are you so . . . okay?" Winona asked, as if his calm demeanor was a felony.

Wade exchanged a glance with Alex, then said to Winona, "I don't think I can answer that in fifty words or less."

"But if you can finagle getting all of us a break at the same time," Alex said, "Wade would love to answer that question."

"Okay," Winona said eagerly.

Later in the day, the three of them sat at a table in the Starbucks that was situated near the ER. Winona had a cappuccino. Alex and Wade had a soft drink. Wade gave her a ten-minute explanation of the reasons many LDS young men and women serve missions, and a short discussion about Brian's feelings prior to leaving. He included the brief version of the plan of salvation, and bore his testimony that he knew it was true. Winona just stared at him as if he'd turned purple.

"So," she said, "you're not upset over your brother's death?"

"Of course I'm upset," Wade said. "I've cried buckets, and I'm sure I'll cry more. I miss him, and it's hard, but I absolutely know it was his time to go, and he is in a better place. His spirit lives on, and I have a great deal of peace that helps buffer the grief. That's why I can actually be here today and not in the fetal position with the covers over my head."

"Wow," Winona said. "That's amazing. I mean . . . when my dad died, my mom lost it. She completely lost it. It took years for her to even get close to normal. And look at you. This isn't like . . . denial or something, is it?"

"No, it's not denial," Wade said.

"I've got some stuff you can read if you're interested," Alex interjected.

Winona was quick to say, "Okay, that would be great." She glanced at her watch. "I need to get back."

After she left, Alex smiled at Wade and said, "It would seem Brian is still very much a missionary."

"It would seem so," Wade said. "We'd better get back too, Dr. Keane. And I sure hope you've got some of those Mormon pamphlets and a spare Book of Mormon kicking around at home."

"At home? They're in my locker. Always keep some stuff on hand."

Later Wade noticed Winona at her desk, thumbing through a Book of Mormon between phone calls. "It's great stuff," he said in passing and said a silent prayer that she might be truly drawn to it and feel its truth. A while later he found her looking at it again, and he asked, "May I show you something?"

"Sure."

He turned to Moroni, chapter ten, and pointed out a particular verse as he said, "The man who finished up this ancient record and buried it, ended with this challenge. See here, it says if you read the book with a sincere heart and real intent, and if you ask God if it's true, He'll let you know that it is."

"How?" she asked, incredulous.

"See, it says by the power of the Holy Ghost. 'And by the power of the Holy Ghost ye may know the truth of all things.' Every person is entitled to know the truth for themselves. You don't have to take my word for it. Just read it and pray, and you'll know. You'll feel it."

"Okay," she said, sounding apprehensive but intrigued.

"Don't hesitate to let us know if you have any questions, and if you'd like, we can arrange to have some missionaries come and visit you, and they can explain everything."

"Missionaries like your brother?" she asked.

"Yes."

"Okay," she said. "I'll let you know."

* * * * *

The day prior to the funeral, Wade was once again struck with the enormity and surreal experience of his brother's death. He was stunned by the media attention, but not surprised by the outpouring of love and support from the neighborhood, the ward, and the community. He realized that while not many people would have a family member die while serving a mission, most members would at one time love someone who would serve a mission, and therefore a missionary's tragic death became personal for millions of people.

While discussing the topic, Alex commented, "A Christian cannot be unaffected when someone dies tragically while in the service of Christ. Perhaps for that reason, the impact of his death will reach much further than any of us will ever know."

"Perhaps," Wade said. He was often brought back to Brian's words in his letter, that he considered his dying this way an honor and a privilege.

The viewing that evening was tough for Wade to get through. Losing Brian was difficult in itself, but he couldn't help recalling Elena's funeral, when Rebecca had been an infant in his arms. Alex and Jane brought Rebecca for a short while, then Jane took her home to be with the other children. Neil and Roxanne came through the line, and Wade couldn't help noticing how all of his parents exchanged hugs and tears. It was all so weird and so wonderful at the same time. Elena's parents also came, and that too felt a little weird. But they had remained close, helping care for Rebecca on the average of once a week, and he'd told them a very brief version of Laura's challenges. He'd feared that they might show some concern over their granddaughter's stepmother having such difficulties, but they had been nothing but loving and supportive.

Cole came to the viewing, and Wade was grateful for the compassion and encouragement of this man he'd come to feel so close to. He knew from experience that attending such functions was difficult at best when recovering from the death of loved one. Cole's coming was a sacrifice, and he knew it. Cole mentioned that Rochelle had gone to Chicago to get ready to move, but he'd been in touch with her, and she sent her condolences. Wade expressed his appreciation, and they promised to see each other soon.

Wade was grateful to note that Alex hovered nearby during the entire evening. He remained discreetly aloof, but Wade could almost always see him somewhere in the room. On the way home he didn't hesitate to mention how much he appreciated it.

"I miss Laura so bad it hurts," he said. "Just knowing there was someone in the room who was there just for me means more than I could ever tell you."

"What are brothers for?" Alex said as if it were nothing.

Wade had to take something mild to help him sleep that night as images of terrorist explosions mingled with finding Elena dead and the nightmares he'd had of finding Laura in the same condition. And then he would remember Laura cursing him and telling him she hated him for leaving her in that facility. If one thing didn't make him cry, another did.

The following morning they were all up early in order to get to the chapel for another viewing prior to the funeral. Alex and Jane were in the building but kept some distance. Neil and Roxanne were there as well. The children were all home with a sitter except for Barrett, who was with his parents. After the funeral Alex and Jane were going to pick up Rebecca and bring her to the meetinghouse for the luncheon, since all of the other children would be there, and relatives would want to see her. Like a million times before, he wondered what he'd do without Jane and Alex. He couldn't even recount all they had done for him.

Just as on the previous evening, Wade was amazed at the endless line of people who came to pay their respects. There were many who didn't know Brian or the family, but they came anyway. A general authority of the Church was scheduled to speak at the funeral, and the entire thing still felt like some kind of strange dream.

Standing in the receiving line near his mother, Wade was struck once again with feeling like the odd one. Each of his siblings was there also, each with a spouse nearby. He reminded himself of the miracle he'd been given of feeling Elena's presence close by when he'd needed her most. But it was Laura he truly missed. He'd come to terms with Elena's death, but Laura's absence felt all wrong, and he hated it. He had to tell himself she was still very much alive and he had good reason to believe that all would be well with her in time. But at the moment she felt dead to him, and for that reason more than any other, he felt his heart breaking.

* * * * *

Laura stared out the window and wrapped her arms tightly around herself. She didn't have to wonder why Wade hadn't shown up for several days when he'd told her he would see her soon. She'd expected it all along. He'd finally come to his senses. She wasn't surprised at the heartache she felt, but she hadn't been prepared for how the thought of truly losing him made her wonder for the first time since she'd come here if it might actually be possible to find herself again, to be the wife he deserved, to go back to the life they'd lived. She *wanted* to be that woman again, for his sake as well as her own. But maybe it was just too late.

"Hey there, girl," she heard, and turned to see Patty. "I missed you."

"I heard you were sick," Laura said, and turned back to the window. "I missed you too. Dr. Hadley's sick as well. It's been pretty quiet around her. I take it you're feeling better."

"Much, thank you. So, how are you?" Patty asked. Laura didn't answer. "Oh, come on. You could at least say, 'the same.'"

"I'm not the same," Laura said. "Wade has only been here once since we saw him at the festival. He said he'd see me in a day or two."

"Oh, I see," Patty said. "Well, there's got to be a logical explanation."

"We both know why."

"You haven't heard from him at all?"

"He left a message . . . apologizing for not being able to make it. He's just trying to let me down easy."

Patty said nothing more, and Laura felt sure she had nothing to counter what was obvious. They went to breakfast while Patty rambled with typical chitchat that Laura barely heard, until Patty said, "Oh, I meant to ask you. Are you related to the Elder Morrison that was killed?"

"What?" Laura asked, looking up abruptly.

"Haven't you had the TV on, girl?"

"You know I don't watch TV."

"There was a terrorist bombing in London," Patty said, and Laura gasped. "One missionary was hurt but he's going to be okay; the other one is dead." Laura's chest constricted before Patty finished, "An Elder Morrison from this area. I just wondered if . . ."

"Oh, help," Laura said, feeling lightheaded and sick to her stomach—more than the usual effect of the medication.

"Laura, what is it?"

"No, no," Laura muttered, shaking her head.

"You *are* related?"

"Wade's . . . brother . . . is serving . . . in London."

"Good heavens!" Patty said, and their eyes met, as if Laura might find some measure of comfort or explanation from this woman. She simply added, "It would seem Wade might have a good reason for not showing up, after all."

Laura stood up and started pacing. "I . . . I can't . . . believe it. Why wouldn't he tell me?"

"He probably didn't want to upset you," Patty said.

Laura started to cry. "I should be with him. How could I . . . leave him . . . alone to face something like this?"

"The funeral's today," Patty said. "You'll probably see him again tomorrow."

Laura sank into a chair, her heart breaking on Wade's behalf. She'd betrayed and abandoned him once again.

* * * * *

Wade felt as if the viewing would never end, while at the same time he deeply dreaded having that casket closed. He felt so utterly disheartened that he wanted to curl up and bawl like a baby. He recalled the peace and hope he'd felt the night he'd read Brian's letter, and wondered where it had gone. He prayed silently for the strength to endure this, for some measure of hope that might keep him going. He had a moment of thinking he might be losing his sanity when he heard a gentle voice say just behind him, "Hello, Rebecca's father."

Wade turned abruptly and knew that miracles had not ceased. A joyful noise came out of his mouth before he breathed Laura's name and wrapped her in his arms. He felt response in her embrace for the first time in weeks, and the joy inside him deepened. He took her face into his hands and found tears in her eyes. "What are you doing here?" he demanded quietly, slipping out of the line, bringing her with him.

"I wanted to be here for you," she said, and he couldn't hold back a little laugh. She motioned toward Patty who was standing nearby. "Patty pulled a few strings."

Marilyn appeared beside them, saying to Laura, "It *is* you." She hugged Laura tightly. "Oh, my dear," she said. "I've missed you so much." She looked at her closely. "Are you feeling better?"

"A little, I think," she said with a forced smile.

While Laura was distracted, he heard Patty whisper in his ear, "Hadley will have my hide if I let her out of my sight for a second. I'm going to leave her with you, but I won't be far. Don't even let her go to the ladies room without me."

"Okay," Wade said and looked at her. "Thank you . . . for bringing her, for everything."

"Glad to help," she said. "And I'm sorry about your brother."

"Thank you," he said, and she eased away, giving him a little wave to indicate she'd be close by.

Wade turned back toward Laura to see her looking up at him. His mother gave him a little smile and a wink. He glanced around, scanning the long line of people waiting to pass by the casket and speak with the family. He didn't see a single face he recognized. He didn't hesitate a moment before he took Laura's hand and eased her out of the room, saying to Patty as he passed by, "I'll take good care of her." Once past the crowd, he hurried down a long hall of the church building and into an empty classroom, quickly closing the door. He didn't even pause to consider whether or not she wanted to be kissed; he just kissed her. She made no resistance, so he kissed her again, taking her face into his hands as if he could keep her from ever being away from him again. He looked into her eyes to gauge her reaction and saw nothing that could keep him from kissing her again, and again. She took hold of his face as he was holding hers, silently beckoning for more. He kissed her the way a husband should kiss his wife after being separated for weeks. He kissed her with all of the desperation and fear he'd been feeling. He pushed his hands into her hair, and she pushed her hands into his. Never in his life had he known a kiss like this! He was thirst, and Laura was water. He couldn't get enough of her, and she could never give him enough. But the quest was heart-pounding. Surely there *was* opposition in *all* things—even in a kiss. He could think of no other reason why the pain and agony of this horrific situation could create such a perfectly blissful moment. With their kiss came the memories of all they had shared, and the hope that they would yet share a lifetime. Then suddenly it *was* enough. At least enough for that moment. He slowly severed his lips from hers, looking into her eyes as if he could find the answer there to every question in the universe, and she returned his gaze with awe and veneration.

"Oh, Laura," he whispered and kissed her brow, her cheek, her eyelids.

Laura absorbed the wondrous evidence of his affection for her and felt a spark of life glimmering somewhere inside. She looked into his eyes, and no level of denial could overpower what she saw there. He *loved* her. He really, *really* loved her. After all she had put him through, he *still* loved her.

"It would have been a shame," he whispered with reverence in his voice, "if you had died before today. We both would have missed this kiss."

She sighed, and Wade saw tears pool in her eyes. He prayed that she wouldn't revert to the shell of darkness where she'd been existing, that she could find something to hold onto in the ethereal experience they'd just shared.

"Now I know how Snow White felt," she said and touched his lips. "The kiss of life."

The implication sent Wade's heart pounding anew. He found it difficult to set his hopes too high too soon, but any glimmer of hope, any sign of life, was a step in the right direction.

"Wade," she said, and the tears fell. He'd not actually seen her cry since she'd entered the facility. "I'm so sorry . . . about Brian. I . . . didn't know until a while ago. I can't believe it's real."

Wade took in the undeniable evidence of her concern. She seemed more like herself than he'd seen her in weeks. She was thinking about something besides her own pain.

"Yeah," he said, his voice breaking, but he felt more emotional over being with her than he did about their topic of conversation, "but it's okay. It's hard, but . . . I know it was his time to go. I never imagined it could be possible to feel such peace over something so hard, but I do."

She gave a subtle smile. "That's good then."

"Still, this is . . . a tough day to get through." His voice cracked. "Having you here means more to me than I could ever tell you."

Her chin quivered, and she bit her lip. "I should have been here for you long before now."

"You're here now," he said, and kissed her. "We should get back out there, I think. Although, now I think I can actually face it."

She gave him a sad smile. He kissed her once more and took her hand, leading her back to the receiving line, where he took his place between his mother and his older brother. Laura stayed beside him through the remainder of the viewing, while Patty sat on the other side of the room, occasionally glancing in their direction. Wade tried not to think of the reasons for her presence, and to just enjoy having Laura's hand in his. It had been several days since Wade had heard any official report of Laura's progress, but he knew that Patty would not be on such strict orders to shadow Laura if there wasn't still a high level of concern for her safety. Glancing at his brother in the casket, he pondered the peace he felt in knowing it had been his time, and that the matter was in God's hands. Then he turned to look at his wife, trying to imagine how he would cope with losing her if she made the choice to leave this world before her time. But he didn't just want her to live, her wanted her to be alive. Forcing his thoughts elsewhere, he squeezed her hand and told himself to enjoy the moment—if being at his brother's funeral could be considered something worthy of enjoying.

Wade had been asked to give the family prayer, and he was grateful to feel the guidance and strength of the Comforter as the words flowed out of him, his voice steady. But his own tears flowed as the casket was closed, and the grief of his parents and siblings all seemed to culminate in this moment where the reality of separation became stark, however temporary it might be. Peace and understanding were unmistakable among all those who loved Brian. Still, there was no denying the fact that Brian's time on this earth had ended, and the rest of them were left to face his absence.

Once they were all seated in the chapel and the service began, that blanket of peace returned fully for Wade. He sat with his right hand holding his mother's, and his left holding Laura's. He looked at his wife sitting beside him and tried to comprehend the roller coaster of emotion he'd experienced since she'd come into his life. The weeks they'd shared as husband and wife had truly been the happiest of his life. And then she had slid into this internal abyss, drowning within herself, sending him into his own downward spiral. There were only two other experiences in his life that were comparable: one was Elena's death, and the other his own dalliance with depression that had lured him to that suicidal moment. He believed that he understood her desperation, but for him the brush with death had scared him into wanting to live, and the road back to finding happiness and peace hadn't taken very many days. He knew there were many differences between himself and Laura, between their backgrounds, their experiences, and their perspectives. He respected that, and he had compassion for her struggle, but oh how he ached to see her happy again, to be living a normal life together!

Wade watched while she toyed with the fingers of his left hand in a way that had once been so familiar. He wondered where her thoughts were, or if she had read his own when she turned his hand over and slid the cuff of his shirt up enough to reveal the scar from his own suicide attempt. She touched it almost reverently, and he wondered if she found empathy in it—or longing for what it represented.

Wade rode to the cemetery in Alex's car, with Alex driving and Jane and Barrett in the front seat. He sat in the back seat with Laura beside him and Patty next to her. A few minutes into the drive, in the middle of the procession following the hearse, Laura leaned her head against Wade's shoulder, and he put his arm around her, relishing her nearness, praying that this was a sign of progress and not just a temporary reprieve.

At the cemetery, Laura kept her arm tightly around Wade's waist while she struggled with tears and kept wiping at her eyes and nose with a supply of tissues from her coat pocket. The dedication of the grave was beautiful, as were the flowers spread over and around the casket. Wade had a hard time leaving in spite of the bitter cold. Once he stepped away from the grave, the separation from Brian felt somehow more absolute. And now that the funeral was over, Laura would be returning to her home away from home, and he would be alone again. He found some hope in the signs of something softening in her, but he wanted to keep her by his side and take her home with him and never be apart from her again.

Wade was one of the last to leave the graveside, and once inside the car he had a bout of tears to contend with. Laura handed him a clean tissue but said nothing. Wade was grateful to hear Alex asking Patty if she and Laura would be able to stay for the luncheon. Patty said that would be nice, and Wade wanted to shout for joy. Maybe he'd get one more hour with his wife.

Back at the church, the atmosphere was more relaxed than it had been through the viewings and funeral. Family and close friends were visiting and mingling while the Relief Society set out a lovely buffet. Wade's parents and siblings all spoke with Laura and told her how good it was to see her. When she was asked how she was doing, she simply said, "Fine, thank you." And that was about all she said. The brief conversation they'd had earlier seemed to be all she had to say. Any questions he asked her for the sake of making small talk were given succinct, cursory answers. He recognized that look on her face. She was lost inside of her own internal darkness, and while it seemed she'd come up for air long enough to connect with him briefly, she'd quickly receded to the place where she was apparently most comfortable. But she clung to Wade as if he'd become her life preserver. If she didn't have her arm around him, she held tightly to his hand. She left once with Patty to go to the ladies room, then was quickly back by his side. He loved feeling her need for him. He wanted her to need him, ached for her to need him. He prayed that it might last, that he could have her back, that things could be the way they used to be.

Wade noticed that Laura didn't eat much, but he'd been told that the medication had affected her appetite. When they were finished eating, Patty took their disposable dishes to throw them away just before Wade heard a familiar little voice say, "Daddy! Daddy!" He turned to see Rebecca running toward him and Jane coming behind her. She'd obviously just arrived after going home to get the child. He didn't see Barrett with her and felt sure he'd gone home and stayed. Wade opened his arms, and Rebecca jumped into them before he situated her on his lap. He motioned toward Jane to let her know that he had her and she could get some lunch.

"Oh, you look so pretty," he said, spreading out the skirt of her dress, then holding up her feet that were decked in shiny black shoes.

"I pwitty," Rebecca said proudly.

Wade turned to see Laura watching Rebecca as if she'd never seen her before. He felt suddenly nervous as he recalled Hadley once telling him, *Rebecca might only spur more guilt for not being a good mother to her, and that will heighten the need in Laura to end her own life.*

And then Rebecca turned as if to see what he was looking at. She stared at Laura for a long moment, then said exuberantly,

"Mommy!" She reached for Laura, scrambling to get from his lap to hers while Wade recalled Hadley saying, *Children will likely create confusion for her . . . It's not good for children who know and love her to see her this way. Her behavior toward them may be too disconcerting and difficult to explain.*

Wade held his breath, praying silently that this might help and not hinder the situation. Surely there was some maternal instinct somewhere inside of Laura that would respond well to Rebecca's love for her.

"Mommy," Rebecca said again, wrapping her arms around Laura's neck. Laura hesitated only a moment before she hugged the child tightly, closing her eyes as if the moment were precious. He glanced at Patty, perhaps hoping for a cue on whether or not this was good. She was smiling as she observed the reunion. That was a good sign.

For another twenty minutes Rebecca sat surprisingly still on Laura's lap while some degree of the real Laura showed itself. They played patty-cake and the five little piggies and the itsy bitsy spider while Wade's heart overflowed to observe something so sweet and simple, and, in this case, miraculous. Rebecca finally became impatient and slithered down, running off. Wade saw her run to his mother, who signaled to Wade that she would look out for her. He turned to see Laura watching Rebecca across the room, then she looked at Wade with something dark and shameful in her eyes before she abruptly turned away and said to Patty, "When are we supposed to be back?"

"About half an hour ago," Patty said, and Wade's heart fell.

Wade stood up, saying to Patty, "Just give us a few minutes. I'll take good care of her."

He took Laura's hand and led her again into a vacant classroom where he closed the door and kissed her long and hard. Her response was evident, but not anything like it had been earlier. He tried to appreciate that he'd had her with him, if only briefly, when he'd needed her most. But he could only feel the heartache in knowing that she had once again become emotionally absent, and that this was far from over. He reminded himself to be patient, to hold onto hope, to find a way to keep going. The only positive aspect he could see in that moment was that letting her go back to the facility was easier than being with her physically when her emotional distance resulted in so little joy.

"I love you, Laura," he said, then stopped himself from babbling all of the words rolling around in his head. He wanted to pledge his eternal love and commitment, to plead with her to come back to him, to find herself again. But he just kissed her brow and led her back into the hall. It was empty except for Patty standing at the far end, talking on a cell phone. He moved slowly toward Patty with Laura's hand in his, while his mind wandered to the last time he'd seen Brian at the airport. He told himself that he *would* see Laura again. She would remain safe and protected until she could find herself in the midst of her inner turmoil. But he found it difficult to feel convinced. Perhaps the losses in his life had created a certain amount of paranoia. Whatever it was, he felt his insides turning to knots.

Patty hung up the phone and smiled at Laura, holding out her hand. "We need to go, honey."

Laura looked up at Wade and gave him a tiny measure of hope when she asked, "Will I see you soon?"

"Of course," he said, holding tightly to this indication that she actually *wanted* him to visit her.

He kissed her quickly, then became distracted by noise at the other end of the long hall. He turned to see his mother holding Rebecca. "Just wondering where you were," she called. "I'll just take her to the—"

"Mommy!" Rebecca squealed and squirmed out of her grandmother's arms with such zeal that Marilyn almost dropped her before she could get the child's feet on the floor. Rebecca ran the long hallway as fast as her short little legs would carry her.

Laura went to her knees and opened her arms, hugging Rebecca tightly as she came into them.

Please come home to us, Wade muttered silently, afraid to say it aloud. When Rebecca wouldn't let go, Laura looked up at Wade, saying with apology, "I need to go."

"Come on, princess," Wade said, taking Rebecca into his arms as Laura stood.

"Mommy!" Rebecca repeated, reaching for Laura.

"Good-bye, baby," Laura said as she stepped back, blew a kiss, and waved. "Mommy loves you."

"Mommy!" Rebecca squealed and tried to wiggle out of Wade's grasp.

"Mommy needs to go," Wade said in a soothing voice.

Laura turned and walked away with Patty as Wade called, "Thank you for coming."

Patty turned back with a wave and a smile. Laura just kept walking.

"Mommy!" Rebecca screamed as loudly and horribly as any two-year-old could be capable of. "Mommy! Mommy!" Wade knew exactly how she felt, and actually found some comfort in having his daughter express what he had to be too gracious to let out.

Patty and Laura turned the corner, and he heard the outside door open and close, while Rebecca took on a full-fledged tantrum, screaming and crying, squirming to get out of his arms. He turned around and found his mother looking upset and concerned. She started to say, "I'm sorry if—"

"It's okay," he said. "She's mostly tired, and . . . maybe Laura needs to know she's missed."

"Would you like me to take her and—"

"No, it's fine, Mother. Thank you. I'll take her. Go be with your family. I'll be in when I get her settled down."

Marilyn forced a smile and did as he'd asked. He went back into the classroom where he had just kissed Laura and closed the door. He walked back and forth with Rebecca, holding her tightly, whispering soothing words, and trying to explain in terms she might understand that Mommy wasn't feeling well and needed to be at the hospital. After ten minutes Rebecca finally calmed down, and five minutes later she was asleep against Wade's shoulder. It was rare that he actually got to hold her while she slept, and he found pleasure soaking up her closeness without all the wiggling and energy that came with her when she was awake.

When he knew she was sleeping soundly, he returned to the cultural hall where the luncheon had been held. The Relief Society sisters were cleaning up the mess while family members were still scattered around the room, visiting and even laughing as if this gathering had nothing to do with death. He chalked that up as evidence of the peace the gospel could bring. He took a vacant chair near his brothers, David and Lance, who were chatting. After listening for a minute he wondered why he'd chosen to sit here. Their animated conversation regarding professional sports simply didn't appeal to him, and he had no interest in it. He glanced around the room and tallied every other member of his immediate family, but realized that his *other* family had all left. He was beginning to think he should just use his sleeping daughter as an excuse to go home, when his brothers turned and made an attempt to include him in the conversation. He appreciated their efforts, but was anything but pleased when Lance said, "It was good to see Laura. I take it she's doing better." He simply didn't want to talk about it.

Wade knew that his siblings were aware of the basics related to Laura's condition. They knew she was being treated for severe depression, and that she'd been suicidal. And that was all. He felt that family should be made aware of big family problems, mostly because he was a big believer in the power of family prayer and fasting. But only his parents knew the details, and that was fine.

"It's hard to say," Wade said, hoping the subject would drop and they'd go back to sports. "She has her ups and downs." Trying to be positive he added, "It was nice to have her here."

"So, who was the friend with her?" David asked as if he were trying to be polite and show some interest in Wade's life. But Wade just didn't have the patience for it.

Wade forced a calm voice as he said, "That was not a friend, even though she's been very friendly to Laura. Patty is required to make certain that Laura is never left alone for even a moment."

David and Lance both looked stunned, disbelieving. Lance chuckled uncomfortably and said, "Not even in the ladies room?"

Wade sighed, unable to avoid the fact that he was in a bad mood. Still he kept his voice even. "In the ladies room she will wait just outside the stall. Since you're both obviously baffled over the reasons for something so apparently absurd, I'll just cut to the chase and tell you. My wife has been diagnosed with such an overpowering urge to die that her level of care requires constant one-on-one supervision."

Again they looked dumbfounded. "Is she going to get better?" David asked.

"I don't know," Wade said, wanting this conversation to end.

David shook his head as if it were pathetic—which it certainly was. He stood and put a hand briefly on Wade's shoulder. "I'm so sorry. We'll keep her in our prayers."

"Thank you," Wade said.

After David was gone, Lance asked, "Forgive me if this sounds blunt, but . . . can you really stay married to her when it's that bad?"

Wade counted to ten while he reminded himself that Lance had always been the abrasive one in the family. His lack of tact did not make him a bad person, and his intentions were likely good. He swallowed hard and said evenly, "My vows were for better or worse. Barring the possibility that she decides she doesn't want *me* in *her* life, it's forever. With our father's example of commitment through the worst of circumstances, I don't know how you could think I would do anything less."

"Well, you're a better man than I am," Lance said, coming to his feet. Somewhat facetiously he added, "Given that he's not really your father, I wouldn't feel any strong obligation to follow his example."

"Is that supposed to be funny?" Wade asked loudly enough for Lance to hear as he walked away. While Lance had shown moments of compassion and understanding regarding the circumstances of Wade's birth, it was apparent he really wasn't comfortable with it.

Lance turned to look at him, but so did several other people—including their parents. "Take it however you want," he said and walked away.

Chapter Fourteen

Wade had to squeeze his eyes closed and count to twenty while he willed himself not to react emotionally to such a petty comment. He heard someone sitting down in the chair Lance had just left and opened his eyes to see Brad watching him closely, looking concerned.

"What was that all about?" he asked gently.

Wade looked away, searching for words to smooth it over or brush it off without being dishonest. But he couldn't find any.

"You look as if you'd like to give your brother a fat lip. I haven't seen that look on your face in a very long time. What did he say?"

"It's not important. I'll just . . . chalk it up to the strain of a death in the family."

"And just . . . let it roll around in your head? What did he say?" Wade said nothing. Brad pressed, "Did it have to do with Laura?"

Wade sighed. "Some of it." He sighed more loudly as he realized he wasn't going to get out of this. His father had a way of pushing until the air was cleared. He never had tolerated unspoken feelings. "He asked if I could really stay married to Laura when the situation is so bad."

"Now, that sounds like a 'Lance is in a bad mood' kind of question if I've ever heard one."

"Well, he is dealing with a death in the family."

"Yes, and so are you . . . on top of other very heavy challenges. What did you tell him?"

Wade couldn't keep the terseness out of his voice. "I told him my vows were for better or worse. I said that with our father's example of commitment through the worst of challenges, I didn't know how he would expect anything else."

Brad's eyes softened with the indirect compliment, but he was quick to say, "That's not what made you angry."

"No, I got angry after he pointed out that since you're not my real father . . ." his voice cracked, "I shouldn't feel obligated to follow your example."

Brad's countenance showed immediate anger, but he was not a man to fly off the handle or behave impulsively. He took a deep breath and blew it out slowly while his expression softened, and his eyes revealed that his mind was weighing and measuring. Before Brad could speak, Wade felt compelled to add something that had bothered him off and on for years. "It would seem," he said, "in spite of certain moments where all seems well, there are still some underlying issues in this family. Obviously not everyone has come to terms with our *unique* situation."

"Obviously not," Brad said. "No one can force him or anyone else in the family to be happy about the circumstances. You once told them if they were uncomfortable with the situation, that they were entitled to their feelings."

"I also asked that we have tolerance for each other's differences."

"Maybe that's his version of tolerance."

"Maybe," Wade said, reminding *himself* to be tolerant.

"He just has trouble understanding that a parent does not have the same relationship with each child. He hasn't been a parent long enough to figure that out."

Wade detected an underlying implication and demanded quietly, "What has he said to you?"

Brad was typically calm and matter-of-fact as he said, "He thinks your mother and I show you favoritism. He can be rather obnoxious, you know."

"Yes, I've noticed," Wade said satirically.

"Maybe I'm more tolerant of such behavior in some of my children because it reminds me a little of myself . . . many years ago, before your mother left me."

Wade thought about that a moment. "Okay, but . . . they weren't raised the way you were. They were raised with the right examples of how to treat other people, and how to be kind and appropriate."

"Well, we sure tried to teach them that. But every person comes to this world with their own personalities already intact—and with their free agency. To some degree we just have to accept that some people tend to be a little abrasive. Your brother was bold enough to say that our behavior toward you is some perverse effort on our part to make up for your being illegitimate, although the word he used was less favorable than that."

Wade's heart felt pain while his mind attempted to block it with anger. "He called me a —?"

"Don't you dare say it!" Brad interrupted firmly. More softly he added, "Don't you ever say it, because it's not true. You were born with *my* name, and my complete acceptance."

"I know that," Wade said, "and I'm grateful, but . . ." He didn't like the path his thoughts were taking. He had to ask, "Is it true?"

"What?"

"Do you show me favoritism?" Brad hesitated, and Wade added, "I *feel* favoritism."

"Do you?"

"Yes. I mean . . . you're both very careful and diplomatic about it, but yes, I do. *Is* it some effort to make up for my being the . . . misbegotten brat?"

Brad looked a little taken aback, then said in that subtly disciplinarian voice of his, "I'll chalk that up to the strain of a death in the family." Wade looked away, and he added, "It's ludicrous to think that the relationships your mother and I share with each of you could ever be measured and compared. You all have different personalities, different strengths and weaknesses. Your mother has always felt closer to you than the others in the respect that she can talk to you like a friend; it's been like that since you were a kid. You always had a way of understanding her; you're of the same mind. However, we've always taken the attitude that our children's needs should be met according to their circumstances, not according to some abstract form of comparison. If one kid needs new shoes, you don't go out and buy six pairs of news shoes just to be fair. Would I be treating my children equally if I'd bought you the same sports equipment I'd gotten for your brothers? You didn't want it; you wanted books, and a telescope, and science kits—things that would have bored your brothers to tears. As adults, I've actually expended more time and money on some of your siblings than I have on you, because you've been a more independent adult. You've had struggles, but in different ways. We pray for you, we have long conversations with you, we watch Rebecca occasionally, but you haven't needed a basement finished, a roof replaced, a kitchen remodeled. Stuff like that. But from the outside looking in, different people perceive things differently. Some of my children understand that it all comes out in the wash and they let the little stuff roll off, but there are others who have noticed the relationship you share with your mother, and they have it all distorted. You should know that more than one of your siblings believes the reasons for that are mostly due to the fact that you are the spitting image of the man she once had an affair with."

"They *said* that?"

"They did."

"Who?"

"It doesn't matter," Brad said, but Wade already knew, just because he knew them all so well.

"To Mom?"

"Yes. And to me."

"Why are you telling me all of this?"

"Because I think you need to know the reasons for less than favorable behavior. I believe it's easier to deal with a problem when you know what it is. But all things considered, I think our family has survived the crisis rather well. I'm certain it could be much worse. I apologize if the timing is poor, but I really think we need to have this conversation before you go home and start stewing about what Lance said. I've had more than one of my children call me a fool for not seeing the truth in the way your mother favors you. I told them that I was well aware of the truth, and my relationship with my wife—and you—was none of their concern. I assured them they were not excluded in my will." A hint of a smile touched Brad's lips, but Wade didn't feel amused. More seriously he added, "I told them what you are well aware of. I know that my wife once loved another man, and I would not expect her to look at you and not be reminded of him, because I certainly am. But I am absolutely certain that she has not felt inappropriately about him since before you were born. Her emotional connection to you is due to your personality, and nothing else. Your resemblance to your father is a positive thing for us, Wade. Your existence has healed many broken hearts. Unfortunately, some of your siblings will never fully understand that . . . but it doesn't matter." Brad leaned forward. "You are my son, Wade, and I love you. I couldn't be more pleased or proud to be your father."

Wade couldn't keep from saying, "Neil Keane is my father, too."

"Yes, he is, and under the circumstances I am honored to share that title with him. He's a good man. Our differences are long past and forgiven. We've had that conversation before."

"I know."

"I'm trying to get to a point, Wade. In the Bible, Joseph is shown favoritism by his father. His brothers were so angered by it that they sold Joseph into slavery. But when you look deeper into the story, you realize that Joseph *earned* his father's trust. I believe Jacob loved all of his sons, but he trusted Joseph. Why? Because his other sons were guilty of deplorable behavior. Jacob rewarded Joseph for his loyalty and his righteousness; at least that's how I see it. I make a sincere effort to have a good relationship with every one of my children. I love them, each and every one, and I have never treated any one of them with anything less than the respect they have earned by their behavior. If that's favoritism, so be it." He put a hand on Wade's shoulder. "I'd give you a coat of many colors if I thought you'd wear it."

Wade found it difficult to fully accept the implication. He couldn't keep himself from saying, "But I'm not even your son."

He was startled by the anger that flared in Brad's eyes. Or was it hurt? He said curtly, "And should I chalk *that* up to the strain of a death in the family?"

Wade sighed and looked down. "Yeah, I guess you'd better."

"I thought this was perfectly clear, but apparently it's not, so I'm going to say it. You *are* my son, Wade. That was clear inside of *me* before you were born. I know you have a good relationship with your biological father, and I respect that. He has made a great contribution to your life. I know the two of you are close, and I don't begrudge that. Not even a little. I'm all for anything that can make your life the best it can possibly be. Neil is a good man, and he shares your blood. However, a man's biological contribution to the creation of a child has little to do with fathering. I'm grateful for the privilege I had to be the one who got to see you grow up. I was there every day of your life, Wade. I *earned* the right to be your father, not because of duty or obligation or some sense of guilt in trying to make up for the way I'd treated your mother so badly. I did it because I loved your mother, and because I loved you. I still do; I always will. And I have something that Neil Keane will never have. You may have his DNA and *look* like him, but you have my name, and you are sealed to me, because you were born within my marriage, and within the covenants I made with your mother. They were pretty shaky for a while, but that has all long been in order, and we are a forever family. DNA has nothing to do with it."

Wade felt this declaration sink into his heart with a validation and comfort that he now realized he'd needed. And he'd needed to hear the negative aspects of the situation in order to appreciate the positive. He'd certainly had no cause to question Brad's love or commitment to him, but there were times when his own value felt shaky for reasons that were difficult to define. He glanced around to realize that people were still cleaning up the meal and putting tables and chairs away, and others were visiting. But no one seemed to be paying any attention to them.

Brad leaned closer and added intently, "It doesn't matter what anyone else says, or does, or thinks, Wade. Not even your siblings. You are my son. I love you, and I'm proud of you for the way you live your life, for the kind of person that you are, for the way you handle the challenges you've had to face that would have broken many men."

Wade's mind went from his appreciation and respect for this wonderful man to the reality that his life was deep in challenge. "I don't know," he said. "I feel pretty broken right now."

"You're stronger than you think you are."

"I don't feel strong at all. I feel like . . ." He couldn't finish without emotion overtaking him.

"Wade," Brad said, putting a hand on his shoulder, "maybe it's time you let go."

Wade met his eyes, astonished and appalled. "I will *not* let go. You, of all people, should know that I could never give up on her. It took Mom two years to come back to you."

"Wade," Brad said, "that's not what I meant at all. Maybe it's time you let go of believing that you can fix this. In my case, I was very much to blame and had a lot of fixing to do. But I still had to accept that I could not take away her free agency, or her own challenges. And you have to do that too. In your case, however, you have no responsibility in this problem, Wade, and you can't fix it. Give it to God."

Wade closed his eyes and felt tears leak out. He forced his voice to the question that had haunted him, "And what if . . . it's God's will that . . . I lose her . . . like I lost Elena . . . and Brian?" He sniffled and wiped a hand over his face. "If . . . it's just not possible for . . . her to heal . . . even God cannot take away her agency. And I can't keep her alive under these circumstances indefinitely. The bottom line is that I have to accept God's will, and I don't know if I can."

"Do you *know* God's will for Laura's future?"

"No."

"Oh, but you do, son," Brad said, and Wade felt startled. "I think you're losing perspective here. I was there when you put your hands on her head and spoke on His behalf, and you stated His will very clearly. As I recall, she was told that there were children waiting to come to her, and she would be capable of raising them with love and . . . what was it? A sound mind and a strong spirit, I believe."

Wade had honestly forgotten. And it really hadn't been so long ago. But he had to ask, "What if those were just my words, my desires?"

Brad smiled. "They weren't your words, Wade. I had my hands on her head too. I felt the truth of those words when you spoke them. Now, some people may never recover from emotional illness. Some people will be faced with chronic depression throughout the course of their lives, just as some people are plagued with other illnesses and diseases. If that were the case, I believe the Spirit would guide you on the choices you would have to make, and how to cope with the problem in the best possible way. But I don't believe that's the case with Laura. I believe it's only a matter of time before she is able to work through this and find herself again. You just need to keep loving her, and give the rest to God."

Wade felt hope and peace rush into him so quickly that it took his breath away, forcing him to his feet while Rebecca continued to sleep against his shoulder. Brad stood to face him. Wade wrapped his free arm tightly around his father, as if he could draw more of that hope into himself and at the same time somehow express his gratitude to Brad for saying everything that he'd needed to hear. Brad returned the embrace with fervor, and Wade could feel this man's love soaking into him, filling the aching holes.

"I love you, Dad," he murmured.

"I love you too, son," he replied. "And it's going to be okay."

That evening Wade felt immensely relieved to have the funeral behind him, but the stark reality of Brian's death was still only settling in. He was profoundly grateful for the undeniable peace he felt that eased his grief, but he was not naive enough to think that grief didn't have to be felt and acknowledged. The fact that he hadn't seen Brian for nearly two years made his death feel less real, and he knew it would take time to adjust.

Wade pondered his time with Laura and the mixed emotions it had induced. He was grateful for the blessing of having her with him, and knew that the positive far outweighed the negative in just being with her. His fears and concerns were still there, but he held to the words of comfort his father had given him, and prayed that, if nothing else, Laura's maternal instincts toward Rebecca might leave an impression on her.

Attempting to sleep, Wade's mind wandered through the events of the day but kept being drawn to the conversation he'd had with his father. A certain phrase stuck in his head, feeling vaguely familiar somehow. He recalled his biological father once saying something similar, but its familiarity seemed more meaningful while he couldn't discern why. He suddenly had the urge to look at his patriarchal blessing and flipped on the light to search for it. He knew it was among papers that went with him no matter where he lived. He'd seen it not so long ago, but he honestly couldn't recall the last time he'd read it. He found it and got back in bed as he unfolded the paper it was typed on. The words felt familiar as he began to read. He'd read the blessing dozens of times—but not in recent years, he concluded with some self-recrimination. An almost eerie sensation rushed over him as he came upon a phrase that pricked his heart, especially considering how close it was to the words his father had spoken earlier. *Your very existence will heal many broken hearts and bring great joy into the lives of all who love you.* Wade took a deep breath and reread it three times. He'd received the blessing at the age of fifteen. He hadn't known the truth about his paternity, but God had known. He thought through everything he'd learned about his parents' past lives and the lives they were living now. He recalled his mother once telling him that the true healing in her marriage to Brad had taken place when he'd been born. And Brad had told him more than once that he considered his existence a gift. He thought of the way Alex and their father had always treated him, the love and support they'd given him through these difficult years, and he felt suddenly more blessed than he could comprehend as he contemplated the spectrum of life and the evidence that nothing was truly happenstance. God was mindful of him in every large and small way, and somehow he would get through whatever lay ahead.

Reading on, Wade found his thoughts wandering, as they always did, to Laura. He wondered if he was capable of bringing joy into *her* life. And then he read the phrase, *You have been given special gifts that will bring about great healing, both in your home, and in your life's work.* Again he felt an outpouring of peace and hope. Somehow he just *knew* that his choice of profession was not coincidence, and neither was his marriage to Laura. They *would* get through this.

The following day Wade and Alex had to start a shift at six in the morning. He was glad to be at work and busy. Winona wasn't working that day, and he wondered if she had put any effort into reading the Book of Mormon and the other materials Alex had given her. He hoped so.

On his afternoon break, Wade called the facility and asked if he could see Laura that evening. He was startled to be told, "I'm sorry, Mr. Morrison, but she isn't doing well, and she simply isn't up to visitors . . . at least until she's calmed down."

"What do you mean 'calmed down?'" he demanded, wishing it hadn't sounded so harsh.

"She hasn't stopped crying since she got back from her outing with Patty yesterday. We can barely get her to eat. She just sleeps and cries. Check back tomorrow. Maybe she just needs to get it out of her system."

Wade hung up, wondering what *it* might be. He felt angry and frustrated with this indication that she was getting worse, not better. The following day he got the same answer and asked to talk to Dr. Hadley.

"He's with a patient right now, but I can have him call you."

"Thank you. As soon as possible, please."

Hours later Wade finally got a call from the facility, but it wasn't Dr. Hadley. Instead it was someone calling to set up an appointment with him to meet with the doctor, but he wasn't available until the day after tomorrow. When Wade repeated the situation to Alex, reiterating his frustration, Alex just said, "Patience, little brother. Patience."

Wade just cursed under his breath and walked away before he gave Alex a fat lip and proved just how impatient he was feeling—even though he knew Alex was right. He really needed to work on this patience issue.

When the time for his appointment finally arrived, Dr. Hadley began by saying, "I know this has been very difficult for you, and you've been very worried about Laura."

"You got that right," Wade said firmly.

"I know you're aware that since she attended your brother's funeral, she's been extremely upset. She hasn't been willing to talk; she's just wanted to be left alone, but I was finally able to visit with her earlier today, and I believe I've gotten some idea of where her head is at. She's grieving, Wade, plain and simple. I haven't seen her shed a tear since she came here, and now she can't stop. I think something has finally opened up inside of her, and she's actually feeling all that's happened to her, and all that she's lost. But that's a lot of grief to contend with, and we just need to give her some time and see how she comes through."

More waiting, Wade thought, certain that God would teach him patience through this experience if it killed him. The doctor went on to ask Wade how he was doing with his brother's death, and the rest of their time together turned out to be more grief counseling on Wade's behalf. But he couldn't deny being grateful. Dr. Hadley was a good man with sound advice and a gift of offering perspective. But Wade still had to go home alone, without even seeing Laura, while his heart ached on behalf of what she must be feeling. If everything she had stuffed down inside herself all these years was now demanding to be felt, he couldn't even fathom the intensity of what she was facing. That night in bed he cried for her, and for himself, and then for everyone who loved Brian and had lost him. And then he just cried.

* * * * *

Laura came awake to the light of early morning and found herself curled up on top of the bedspread, with a blanket thrown over her. She was still wearing the clothes she'd had on the day before—even her shoes. And sitting in a chair on the other side of the room was Lacy, the psych tech who worked part-time, odd shifts, filling in on weekends and between Patty and Rita. She was sweet but not as talkative as the other women. Considering her own mood, Laura preferred silence.

Laura rolled over and looked toward the ceiling, attempting to gauge her own state of mind and where her thoughts might take her—usually against her will. Memories swirled and roiled in a familiar torturous mix, and with them came tears. More tears. How could there possibly be any more tears? For seemingly endless weeks she had felt mostly numb and in shock, not caring about anything but the desire to end all of this misery once and for all. Occasionally she had drifted into anger or fear, but never into grief or sorrow. Now that's all she could feel. Grief and sorrow chased each other through her thoughts and memories, provoking a steady flow of tears that refused to stop. Dr. Hadley had suggested that she was likely crying a lifetime of tears, and she would do well to let them come. But her eyes hurt, and her head ached, and she felt sure that for these women who had to watch her constantly, the only thing worse than keeping her alive had to be watching her cry during every waking minute.

Dr. Hadley had told her she was doing better, making progress. Previously, their sessions had consisted of him coaxing answers out of her that felt detached and unimportant. Now it took little effort on his behalf to send her into a tirade of ranting and screaming—and crying. How he figured that was good she couldn't begin to imagine. She only knew that she'd felt little at all for weeks, and now she was feeling everything. And it hurt so bad she couldn't imagine ever coping, ever getting beyond it. It was no wonder she'd been stuffing her emotions all these years. But later that day the tears suddenly stopped, and a startling revelation came to her mind. Somewhere back on the other side of this valley of grief she'd been traversing, there had been nothing but darkness. Everything around her and inside of her had been in shades of gray. But now it was different, as if a glimmer of light had trickled into her shadowed spirit, showing her that color truly did exist in the world around her. She first noticed the pictures hanging on the wall of her room. Had they always been so colorful and bright? Then she looked at Lacy's face and had to say, "Your eyes are the most beautiful brown."

Lacy smiled as if she heard the meaning behind the words. "And yours are a bit brighter, I believe."

That evening Laura actually felt like eating her supper, and she asked Rita if they could go to the rec room and see what was going on. Rita looked at Laura as if she'd sprouted wings. "You want to be around the others?" she asked.

"Is that a problem?"

"Not for me, it's not," Rita said, and they went to the rec room for a while where Laura just sat with a bizarre fascination, taking in the activities and conversations of the other patients. When it was time for bed, Laura realized that she couldn't remember the last time she'd ended a day without wishing that she'd never wake up. Lying in the darkness, well aware of Rita in the room with her, Laura silently thanked God for giving her a glimmer of hope that there might actually be a reason to go on living. The very fact that she felt capable of making any effort to pray seemed in itself a miracle. She fell asleep and woke up in the dark feeling uneasy. And then the pain began. It started out subtle, then abruptly became unbearable—a physical pain unlike anything she'd ever experienced. She was grateful for Rita's help and her insistence that something needed to be done. Funny, Laura thought, as Rita drove her to the hospital, that she would actually feel afraid something might be wrong, and that her deepest hope was that whatever the problem might be, she would survive it.

* * * * *

Wade heard his cell phone ring in the middle of the night, and he reached for it, heart pounding. When he saw that it was the facility where Laura was staying, he prayed that he would hear her voice, but it was a staff member, who hurried to say, "Laura's been taken to the hospital."

"What's wrong?" he demanded.

"We're not sure. She was in a lot of pain; that's all we know."

"Which hospital?" he asked, already pulling on his jeans. And he was disappointed by the answer. It wasn't the U of U, and he would have preferred going to familiar territory.

"Okay, thank you," he said. "I'm on my way."

Wade pulled on a shirt as he hurried down the hall, rapping lightly on the door to Alex and Jane's bedroom. A moment later Alex pulled it open. "What's wrong?" he asked, his eyes barely open.

"Laura's been taken to the hospital. They don't know what's wrong. Just . . . take care of Rebecca and I'll call if—"

"I'm coming with you," Alex said, and five minutes later they were en route with Alex driving.

Wade felt inexplicably grateful for Alex's confident nature in an ER when they walked through the door, and he immediately said to the woman behind the desk, "I believe my brother's wife was brought in here. Laura Morrison."

It only took her a few seconds to tell them, "She's been admitted. They just took her upstairs." She told them a room number, and Alex asked, "Can you tell me what the diagnosis was?"

"Sorry," she said. "You'll have to talk to the doctor."

"Okay, thanks," Alex said, and they hurried out of the ER, going toward the elevator.

Wade let out a weighted sigh, feeling scared out of his mind. Just what they needed—some physical challenge to complicate matters. Whatever it was, he prayed it wasn't serious.

Wade followed Alex to the nurses' station nearest the room number they'd been told. He motioned for Wade to do the talking, "I was told my wife was brought here; Laura Morrison."

"Just a minute," she said, then moved a few steps away to say to a different nurse, "Mrs. Morrison's husband is here."

"Hi," the other nurse said to Wade. Her ID badge identified her as Judith. "Dr. Lewis told me you would probably be coming. He had to go deliver a baby and asked me to catch you up to speed."

"Is she okay?" Wade asked.

"Oh, she's fine," Judith said. "I'm afraid she miscarried, and she lost quite a bit of blood. The doctor just wanted to keep her overnight for observation, and that will give us time to give her a transfusion and make up for some of what she lost. You're welcome to go in."

"Thank you," Wade said, and moved down the hall to where he could talk privately with Alex.

"She was pregnant?" Alex asked.

"Apparently," Wade said, trembling. "I . . . had no idea. Why would she keep something like that from me?"

"Well . . . I think you'd better talk to her before you jump to any conclusions."

"Okay, you're right. Thank you."

"I'll go make good use of that couch by the elevators. You let me know if you need me."

"Thanks," Wade said, and drew a deep breath before he went into the room. He entered quietly and found Laura laying on her side in the hospital bed, her eyes closed. And Rita was sitting in a chair reading a magazine.

"Hi," she whispered when she saw him. "I'll let you keep an eye on her. Let me know when you're leaving."

"Okay, thank you," he said, and she left him alone with Laura. For a long moment he just had to absorb her presence. He'd missed her so much! She was *so* beautiful. Not wanting to disturb her, he quietly moved a chair closer to the bed and sat down where he could just watch her. For the moment, unanswered questions didn't matter. He just wanted to be with her. The little snatches of time he'd spent with her at the facility hardly counted for much, especially when most of them had been strained and difficult. And the time she'd spent with him at the funeral just hadn't been enough. Since then he'd been worried and aching for her while the distance between them had felt unbearable. But now she looked so peaceful, so beautiful. And he loved her.

She stirred and grimaced slightly, and he wondered if she was in pain. Hair fell over her face, and he carefully eased it away. She opened her eyes, looking surprised. Then she gave a weak smile.

"Hi," he said, and kissed her brow. "Are you in pain?"

"Not much," she said.

"I came as soon as they called."

"Oh, Wade." She took his hand, squeezing it tightly, and her eyes brimmed with tears. "We were going to have a baby, but . . ." she sobbed softly, "it's gone now."

"You didn't know?" he asked, pressing a hand over her face.

She shook her head and closed her eyes. "I'd . . . lost track . . . of my cycles . . . with everything else going on. I didn't even think about it. I've been feeling nauseous, and . . . tired, but I just thought it was the medication." Tears flowed into the pillow. "By the time I knew . . . it was already gone." She sobbed again and reached for him. He eased closer and wrapped her in his arms. "Oh, Wade," she muttered, "I wanted to die, and I didn't even know there was another life growing inside of me." She held to him more tightly, and her tears increased. "I don't want to die, Wade. I want to live. I want to be the kind of wife you deserve, and a mother . . . to your children; all of your children. I just don't know if I can do it."

Wade had trouble believing what he was hearing. Could it be true? Had she really and finally found some reason to live?

He felt as if he would melt into the floor with relief as he sensed this change in her.

"Of course you can do it," Wade said, wiping at her tears. "You're the most amazing woman I've ever met."

"How can you say that . . . after what I've put you through?"

"Oh, Laura," he murmured, "I love you; I love you more than life. You and I are meant to be together. How can I ever be whole without you? It was all so perfect between us, and it can be that way again. I know it; I know it beyond any doubt. Just trust me, Laura. Share your heart with me, your fears, your grief. Let me carry them for you."

Wade watched his wife closely as her brow furrowed while she searched his eyes deeply. Then something marvelous happened. For the first time since Randall had walked through the front door of their home, Laura was *there*. "You really mean that," she said.

"I really do."

"Oh, Wade," she pressed a hand to his face, "can you ever forgive me?"

"There's nothing to forgive," he said.

"But I . . . I *did* break my promises to you. And I almost left you alone."

"You weren't in your right mind, Laura. We both know that. I don't understand the power depression has to take a person out of their senses and beyond reason, but I know that it happens. It wasn't you, Laura." He smiled. "But you're back." She smiled as well, and he couldn't resist pressing his lips over hers. The affirmation of her return deepened when her response was immediate and filled with the love he'd once felt from her in such abundance.

Wade realized he was crying the same moment he heard her sob in the midst of their kiss, then they both laughed through their tears, and he kissed her again.

"I want to come home, Wade," she said. "I need to be with you and Rebecca. I promise to never let it get that bad again. If I ever go even a day being depressed and not talking to you, promise me that you'll do whatever it takes to shake some sense into me."

Wade laughed softly. "I promise. But I think we'd better let Dr. Hadley decide whether or not you're ready to come home."

"Okay," she said, and he kissed her again.

They talked until she was too sleepy to keep her eyes open. He waited until she was sleeping before he left her in Rita's care and found Alex dozing on a waiting-room couch.

"Hey, big brother," he said, nudging him. "How can you sleep in a place like this?"

"It's a hospital," Alex said, sitting up, surprisingly alert. "I've had a lot of experience getting snatches of sleep in hospitals." He looked up at Wade. "How is she?"

Wade couldn't hold back a surge of tears, and Alex stood beside him. "What's wrong?"

"Nothing's wrong," Wade said, wiping at his face. "That's just it. She's back, Alex. She wants to come home. She wants to live."

Alex laughed and hugged him tightly.

Chapter Fifteen

The following morning Wade hurried to the hospital to see Laura before she was taken back to the facility. He found Patty with her, and she was dressed in her own clothes, nearly ready to leave.

"Hi," he said, pleased to see her smile at him when their eyes met.

"Hi," she said, and held out a hand from where she was sitting on the bed.

"I'll just be in the hall," Patty said, winking at Wade before she left the room.

"How are you?" he asked, sitting on the bed beside her. He kissed her in greeting, and she touched his face.

"I'm fine," Laura said. "I wasn't far enough along for the miscarriage to cause any trauma. The doctor said I should be back to normal in just a few days."

"And emotionally?" he asked, hoping he wasn't pressing too hard. "How do you feel?"

"I'm coming along, I think," she said, but she looked down and seemed mildly uneasy. She put her head on his shoulder and added, "I want to go home."

"We'll work on that," he said and pressed a kiss into her hair, holding her close.

The doctor who had taken care of Laura when she'd come to the hospital came to check on her and sign her release. When he left the room Wade followed him into the hall, saying, "Could I ask you something?"

"Sure," he said.

Wade gave him a one-minute summary of Laura's present situation, and the many medications she'd been on for depression and to deal with the side effects of the anti-depressant. He then asked, "Could that have caused the miscarriage?"

The doctor said straightly, "The cause for miscarriages can often be difficult to put a finger on. Overall, it's generally just an indication that something wasn't right with the fetus. Whether or not the medications contributed to that is hard to say."

Wade felt compelled to discuss another concern. "She was pregnant and didn't know it when she went on the drugs. What if she *hadn't* miscarried? Would there have been problems with the baby?"

"Again, that's hard to tell," he said. "Obviously we don't want women taking anything that might interfere with a baby's normal growth. If she'd discovered her pregnancy under these circumstances, we would have just weighed the options and hoped for the best. Sometimes the health of the baby has to be weighed against the health of the mother. Having a suicidal mother obviously isn't a good thing. I would, however, suggest that she get past this and get off the medications before she tries to get pregnant again."

Wade nodded and had to ask, "And what if she *always* needs the medication, Doctor?"

"Then options would need to be weighed and discussed. I believe some antidepressants are less of a concern than others, and she just may have to go off of them, with a doctor's guidance, long enough to get through a pregnancy, while other precautions are taken."

"Okay, thank you," Wade said.

"Glad to help. Just call the office and leave a message if you have any other questions."

“Thank you,” Wade said again, and the doctor hurried away.

Wade took a deep breath and let the information settle for a minute, realizing they needed to cross one bridge at a time. He had to assume that losing a baby was better than bringing one into the world that might have severe problems. But he knew that Laura’s maternal instincts were strong, and this couldn’t be easy for her.

Putting himself in the moment, he went back into her room just before a nurse came with a wheelchair to take Laura downstairs, where Patty was waiting with her car. Wade walked out with her and helped her into the car before he kissed her again and told her he’d see her soon. He hated seeing her leave in someone else’s care, but unlike the last time he’d had to stand and watch her go, he had some real hope that they were making significant progress.

Later that day he spoke with Dr. Hadley on the phone and told him of the changes he’d seen in Laura. Hadley said he’d spend some time with her in order to evaluate where she was at, and he would keep him posted. In the meantime, Wade wanted to see Laura, but his work schedule conflicted with the hours that she could have visitors. He was able to talk with her on the phone for just a few minutes, but the conversation felt trivial and flat, and he really couldn’t tell how she was doing.

Wade’s tutelage in patience continued when Dr. Hadley didn’t call back until late the next evening. Near the end of his shift at the hospital he got a message to call Hadley, but it was another hour before the shift ended and he was able to do so. While Alex drove home, Wade called the doctor on his cell phone.

“Sorry to call so late,” Wade said, noting it was just past ten o’clock. “I just got off.”

“It’s not a problem,” Hadley said. “I apologize for not getting back to you sooner, but I was unable to schedule some time with Laura until earlier this evening. You should be pleased to know that she is doing much better.”

Wade resisted the urge to laugh out loud. Instead he just listened.

"She still has a ways to go, but figuratively speaking, I think the Red Sea has parted, which might explain all of her intense emotion over the last several days."

"I don't understand," Wade said.

"This is an analogy that I've gotten a lot of mileage out of," Hadley said, "in psychology as well as spiritual matters." Like many times before, Wade was grateful to know this man was also a stake president, and he understood these struggles from a spiritual perspective. "Many people don't realize that in the scriptural account of the parting of the Red Sea, it states that the wind blew all through the night to part the water. The point being, that sometimes the worst turmoil comes just before the miracle. Laura has just gone through a stage of feeling a great deal of the grief and pain that she's been stuffing down inside all through her life. I think a combination of things have come together to make a difference. For one thing, it seems the medication is kicking in. That, combined with the timing of your brother's funeral and a few other events have spurred her past the worst of this. As I said, we have a ways to go, but we're on the right track, Wade."

"Okay," Wade said, wiping tears from his face, aware of Alex's concern when he obviously had no idea what the doctor was saying. "So, what now?"

"Well, for one thing, I'm taking her off of suicide watch."

"Really?" Wade asked, sounding more stunned than he'd intended. "I mean . . . I trust your judgment, but . . . are you sure?"

"I understand your trepidation. What happened before you brought her in was terrifying for you, and her state of mind has been extreme. But I have seen absolute evidence that she is past that. She *wants* to live, Wade, and she is horrified to realize what almost happened. We're still going to keep close track of her for a while, and she has some issues to work through before she can ease toward coming home, but we're making some immense headway."

"Okay," Wade said, and more tears came, although he managed to keep his voice steady. "Thank you. Thank you for everything."

"She's going to be alright, Wade," he added with compassion.

"Thanks to you, I actually believe that."

"I know your shifts are conflicting with her visiting schedule, but we'll work out a time for you to see her in the next few days. She's still adjusting, and we're doing some pretty intense counseling right now, but I think it would be good for her to start seeing you more often."

"It changes after tomorrow anyway," he said. "I'll call and set up a time. And thank you again."

"I'm glad to help," Hadley said, and ended the call.

Wade turned off the phone, and the emotion rushed out of him. He was aware of Alex's hand on his shoulder as he demanded, "Wade, what is it? What's happened?"

Wade couldn't speak as the joy and relief took hold of him with every bit as much power as the grief and fear had overtaken him in the past. He wrapped his arms around his middle and curled around them as far as it was possible while wearing a seatbelt. Alex pulled over to the curb and put the car in Park.

"Wade, talk to me," he insisted.

"I'm sorry," Wade said and shook his head, sitting up straight, pressing a hand over his chest. "I didn't expect to . . . react like that. I just . . ."

"What?"

"She's doing better," he managed to say. "She's been taken off suicide watch." A burst of laughter leapt through his tears, and he turned to look at Alex. "She's going to be okay."

Alex laughed as well and hugged Wade tightly. "I knew she would be," he said, then laughed again before he started driving while Wade repeated everything the doctor had said. They sat in the driveway to finish their conversation, and before they could get in the house Alex's pager beeped. Wade just waited while he called the ER. He talked for half a minute, then put his hand over the phone and said to Wade, "Lakes wants to trade a shift with me. Can you handle starting in the morning at six? Or do you want to work with Dr. Lakes tomorrow?"

"I can handle six," Wade said, and Alex said into the phone that he would do it.

On the way into the house, Alex said, "I guess we'd better get some sleep while we can."

"I'm all over it. But I'd give up a lot more than sleep to avoid working with Lakes. I say a prayer of thanks every day that they gave me to Dr. Keane."

Alex chuckled. "The super did say you were my baby now. If she only knew."

Six o'clock came too soon, but once they were at the hospital and working, Wade was glad to know that after the shift ended he would have the evening off, and they didn't have to work for three days. On a break, he called the facility and set up an appointment to see Laura at eight, and he spent the day looking forward to it, feeling a jittery excitement that he'd not felt since this nightmare had begun.

When he and Alex arrived home about six-thirty, they entered the kitchen to find Jane just pulling something out of the oven that smelled heavenly. The kids were all there as well, and Rebecca ran to greet him. "Hi," Jane said more to him, then she wrapped her arms around Alex and gave him a typical greeting that usually left Wade aching for Laura, but at the same time admiring the example of a good marriage he'd had the opportunity to observe during all the time he'd lived under their roof. Their hellos and good-byes were never treated as meaningless or trivial. Their seeing each other after any span of separation was always a moment of purposeful connection and tenderness. It wasn't just the way they asked each other how their days had gone, or the brief kiss they exchanged, but the way they looked at each other, and the sincerity behind their words. It was as if everything else they might have done was rooted in being together. Wade had thought more than once of the security their children surely felt in the way Alex and Jane so clearly loved each other. He longed to have that again with Laura, and prayed that her progress might be firm and steady.

Wade set Rebecca loose and teased Barrett for a minute before he turned to leave the room. "Hey," Jane said, "there's a surprise for you up in your room, little brother. Something you should probably take care of right away."

"Okay," he drawled skeptically. "What is it?"

Alex looked puzzled, so Wade knew he wasn't in on the *surprise,* whatever it may be. Jane smiled and said, "Once you get to your room, you'll know. We'll keep an eye on Rebecca, and you can heat up dinner whenever you're ready. We'll go ahead."

"Fine," he said and hurried up the stairs, stopping abruptly in the doorway to his room, certain he had to be dreaming. There she stood, like manna from heaven, looking contemplatively at their wedding portrait that was hanging on the wall. For a long moment he just watched her, silently thanking God for whatever had made such a moment as this possible.

Needing to alert her to his presence, he said, "Perhaps this is how Joseph Smith must have felt."

She turned toward him, her eyes full of intrigue, and more importantly, reflecting her spirit as opposed to being hollow and lifeless.

"And how is that?" she asked.

"He must have been amazed and in awe to find an angel in his bedroom." She comically looked over her shoulder and around herself as if to search out this angel. He added, "Yes, I mean you."

"No angel," she said. "Just me."

"One and the same," he said, then comically looked behind the open door and added, "Where's Rita? Or is it Patty's shift?"

"Patty dropped me off on her way home from work. I told her you'd be happy to take me back and see that I checked in before ten."

"Well, I'm certainly willing to do it, but it's a stretch to say that I'd be happy to take you back. I'll be much happier when you can stay here with me."

"All in good time," she said with an intensity in her eyes that made his heart pound. And then she looked inquisitive, searching, perhaps surprised.

"What?" he asked.

"You really *do* want me to come back?" she asked with a tremor in her voice.

"With all my heart and soul, Laura," he said, and his voice trembled as well.

He saw her chest rise and fall with a deep sigh before she said, "In that case, I think we have a lot to talk about." She stepped toward him and closed the door, then she locked it. Wade felt his breath quicken. Beyond a few minutes in a church classroom the day of his brother's funeral, he hadn't been alone in a room with his wife for more weeks than he cared to count. It felt like forever. She took his hand, and he was thinking the little love seat by the window looked like a good place to talk, but she lifted her lips to his with a kiss that was warm and inviting. She looked up at him with tears glistening in her eyes and whispered, "Hello, Wade."

"Hello, Laura," he said and kissed her again while she eased closer and wrapped her arms around him. "I thought you wanted to talk," he said, and kissed her still again.

"Later," she said, and he took her fully into his arms, savoring a moment in time where time itself seemed caught in a point so completely perfect that it could neither move forward nor back. He felt lifted from the earth in a timeless state that took them back to a place where they had been newlyweds, desperately in love and deliriously happy, where depression and death and despair didn't exist and had no place in the love they shared. For this moment in time, everything was perfect.

* * * * *

Wade sank back against the pillows beneath his head, feeling more content and relaxed than he had since Laura's ex-husband had walked back into her life. While what they'd just shared had lacked the intensity that had once been present in their relationship, it was good just to be close to her, to share any intimacy at all, to feel the evidence of her affection for him. Laura settled her head against his shoulder and held to him as if he were her reason to live. He loved her so much! He watched with fascination as she lifted his hand into hers, then pressed her palm flat against his, as if to compare the size of their hands. He'd seen her do it a hundred times, but in that moment it connected the life they'd lived before to the one that lay ahead.

"I love your hands," she said. "A doctor's hands."

"Not yet."

"I daresay you've already helped save at least a few lives."

"Yes, I suppose I have, but that doesn't make me a doctor."

"It makes you a hero," she said and shifted to look at his face. "You're my hero. You saved *my* life, Wade."

He looked into her eyes, absorbing gratitude in contrast to the resentment that had been there when he'd stopped her from taking her own life. He said the only thing he could say, "God just prompted me to be in the right place at the right time, Laura. It wasn't your time to go."

"But it's not just that, Wade. You've stood by me ever since that day, even when I gave you no good reason to." She shifted her head and focused again on their hands pressed together. She threaded her fingers between his and toyed with his wedding ring. "You didn't give up on me. I've struggled my whole life to find evidence that God loves me. Instinctively I believed that He did, but I often had trouble feeling it; maybe I still do. But I realized the other day . . . or maybe I just remembered . . . because I felt it that first time you took me out to dinner, and I feel it now. I know God loves me because He gave me you."

"It's the other way around, Laura," he said, pressing a kiss into her hair.

"There you go again," she said lightly. "You just . . . keep saying things that make me feel so . . . loved . . . when I feel so unlovable."

Wade leaned up on one elbow and looked down at her. "Why, Laura? Why would you feel unlovable? You're the most amazing woman I've ever known."

Tears rose into her eyes. "I don't know, Wade. I don't understand it. I only know how I feel, and it . . . scares me."

"Why?" he asked gently but earnestly.

Her emotion heightened. "I don't understand how . . . something inside of me . . . something so intangible . . . can completely take over everything I think . . . and feel."

"What does Hadley say about that?"

She sniffled, and he wiped his fingers over her temples where the tears were running into her hair. "He says we need to talk about it some more, that I *do* need to understand it so that I can heal, and not allow it to control my thoughts and feelings. But . . . what if it's not possible, Wade?" She sobbed softly. "I don't ever want to feel that way again." She wrapped her arms around him and pressed her face to his shoulder. "I don't ever want to lose you."

"It's going to be okay," he murmured, kissing her brow. "We'll work through it together, Laura. We'll do whatever it takes."

She held to him and cried while he rejoiced in her need for him and the newfound evidence that she loved him and wanted to be a part of his life. Then he kissed her, and kissed her, and kissed her, longing to make up for those weeks of being newly married and living separate lives.

When Laura's stomach growled, Wade insisted that she needed something to eat before she went back. They walked down the stairs holding hands and into the kitchen to find it vacant, with a note from Jane to let them know where to find what they needed. Together they heated up enchiladas in the microwave and ate them with green salad, then they fed each other ice cream.

"I love ice cream," she said, and he laughed.

"Is this emotional eating?" he asked.

Her eyes took on a faraway look as if she were remembering another time, then she smiled. "Yes," she said, "the emotion of the day is . . ." She hesitated, and he waited with anticipation to see what word she might find to define this moment. Her eyes brimmed with moisture as she touched his face and whispered, "Hope."

"Amen," he said and kissed her. A glance at the clock made him aware of their time together passing, and he hated it. Not wanting to have to be conscious of the time, he hurried and set an alarm on his cell phone for five minutes prior to when he'd need to leave to get her there on time. He clipped it to the belt on his jeans and tried to forget about it, but he didn't want to push the rules and ruin his chance for more such visits.

They were just finishing up their ice cream when loud music came from elsewhere in the house. Wade laughed and said, "Uh oh. I know what that means."

"What does it mean?"

"They're in one of those moods," he said and took her hand, leading her down the hall. They paused at the doorway to the family room, where the furniture had been pushed back and everyone was dancing. Jane and Alex were engaged in a comical version of some kind of tango while the kids just jumped and wiggled and laughed. It was a typical scene in this household, but Wade couldn't help being pleased to have a partner besides Rebecca for a change—even though Jane humored him once in a while and danced with him. But he wasn't about to attempt the tango.

Rebecca noticed them standing there and squealed, "Mommy!" as she ran to Laura. Everyone's attention turned their way as Laura bent down and scooped Rebecca into her arms. And Laura actually laughed before she said to Wade, "She was busy with the other children when I got here earlier. She's as precious as ever."

"Yes, she is," Wade said proudly.

Alex stopped the music to find a different song. In the silence he said, "Well hello, Mrs. Morrison. How nice it is to see you here!"

"It's nice to be here," she said, and seemed to mean it.

Rebecca squirmed to get away, and Laura set her down, only to be overwhelmed with a hug from Barrett. She laughed softly and hugged him back. "I've missed you, Aunt Laura," he said.

"I've missed you too, Barrett."

He looked up at her. "Are you feeling better?"

"Yes, thank you," she said, and he gave her a sheepish smile before he returned to hover among the other children.

Rebecca then took Laura's hand, saying in her high little voice, "Mommy dance."

Alex put on some loud, lively music, and there was an immediate dance free-for-all. Laura laughed while she held Rebecca and danced with her, then she set her free, and Wade took her hands, leading her into a haphazard version of the swing, not unlike the way they'd danced on their second date. He'd learned to dance because he knew she loved it, and he had quickly learned to love it as well—especially when he was dancing with Laura. He revelled in the experience, finding inexplicable joy in the simple pleasure of hearing her laugh and just being with her. After a couple of upbeat songs, Alex put on a waltz, which made the children immediately bored, but Wade certainly enjoyed it. Looking into Laura's eyes, carefully guiding her through a simple waltz step, he had that sense of time stopping again. This moment became connected to the day they'd been married, and all the times they'd waltzed together in the kitchen for no reason at all, giving him real hope that their lives could be that way again.

When the waltz was finished Alex said, "Okay, now we just need a good old-fashioned slow dance. I'm getting old and worn out."

He put in a different CD and found the right track. As soon as the music started, Wade recognized it as one of his favorites—"Unchained Melody," an old classic by the Righteous Brothers. He gracefully guided Laura into a simple, slow dance, swaying her back and forth with one arm around her waist, the other holding her hand. She put her hand to his shoulder and looked into his eyes, while the lyrics added to that time-stopping quality of the experience.

Oh, my love, my darlin', I've hungered for your touch a long, lonely time. And time goes by so slowly. And time can do so much. Are you still mine? I need your love. I need your love. Godspeed your love to me. Lonely rivers flow to the sea, to the sea, to the open arms of the sea. Lonely rivers sigh, wait for me, wait for me. I'll be coming home. Pray for me.

Wade felt inexplicably relieved when the same song began to play again. Alex had obviously set the CD player to repeat this track. Then he realized that he and Laura were the only ones in the room. Somewhere in the midst of gazing into Laura's eyes, he'd missed Alex and Jane herding the children upstairs to get them ready for bed.

He saw something in Laura's eyes that looked surprised, as if she'd remembered something.

"What?" he asked, tightening his arm around her waist.

"We danced . . . like this . . . but there was no music."

"That's right," he said, recalling one of his visits to the facility when dancing was the only thing he could think to do while there had been nothing to say.

"There are spaces of time that I don't even remember. Time became so meaningless. But I remember dancing with you."

"I remember it too," he said.

She gave a contented sigh and put her head to his shoulder. The song played through so many times that Wade lost count, while time seemed to stand still around them, and the need to take her back felt forever away. At moments they looked into each other's eyes, at others she laid her head against his shoulder, while they never lost the gentle rhythm of swaying gently back and forth to the music. He cursed inwardly when he felt his cell phone vibrate, and he stopped to look at it, hoping it was a call he could ignore. But it was the alarm going off, and he had to say, "I need to get you back."

"Okay," she said in a voice that reflected his own sadness.

He forced a smile and touched her face. "It's alright. I'm glad we had this time together. We'll have more, and before we know it, we'll actually be living under the same roof again."

She smiled, and he saw hope again in her eyes. He reluctantly turned off the stereo and kept his arm around her as they went outside and got into the car. Once he was driving, he called the house just to tell Alex where he'd gone so they wouldn't wonder. Little was said between him and Laura as he drove, but he kept her hand in his and occasionally pressed it to his lips. He sighed loudly as he pulled into the parking lot of the facility and turned off the engine. With chagrin he said, "I feel like I'm in high school, bringing you home from a date . . . like you'll turn into a pumpkin at ten o'clock or something."

"It was a pretty amazing date," she said. "Better than any prom I ever went to."

"Amen," he said lightly.

She looked out the window. "I'm sorry it has to be this way. I'm sorry this has been so hard for you."

Wade touched her chin to turn her face toward him. "Don't apologize, Laura. All I ask is that you do everything in your power to get beyond this and come home to me."

Tears rose in her eyes. "What if I can't fix it, Wade? I've felt better today than I have in such a long time, but . . . I know it's not fixed; it's not over. I feel like it's still hovering inside of me somewhere. What if this will always be a part of me, of our lives?"

"Then we'll take it on the best we can," he said firmly. "If we have a lifetime of medication, and counseling appointments, and highs and lows, so be it. We'll keep learning; we'll navigate through it. We just need to learn to manage it better, Laura. We need to be able to work it through before you reach such lows, because I cannot live without you. Do you understand?"

"I do," she said. "And that's why . . . as badly as I want to be with you and Rebecca, I have to see this through. I have to do everything they ask of me, and talk it out and understand what's going on inside of me, no matter how ugly, no matter how hard. I don't ever want it to get this bad again, for your sake as well as mine. I have to understand myself and this . . . illness I have . . . enough to feel confident that I can lead a normal life and not ever be sucked into this vacuum again." She touched his face. "Be patient with me."

"Of course," he said, and kissed her.

"I should go in," she said.

Wade got out and opened the car door for her. He kept his arm around her as they walked inside. Going through the front door he said facetiously, "It was a pretty scandalous date. Don't tell anyone we ended up in bed together."

She turned to face him. "I *am* your wife."

Wade lifted her left hand to look at her wedding ring. "So you are. I guess it wasn't so scandalous after all."

"I love you, Wade," she said, and kissed him. "Thank you."

"We'll have to do it again some time. And I'll look forward to the day when we can sleep in the same bed again."

"I'll look forward to that too," she said, kissed him once more, and left him standing at the door. He took a deep breath, as if he could pull the time he'd had with her closer to his heart. Then he forced himself to return home, reminding himself of the emotion of the day. *Hope.*

* * * * *

The following day Wade talked to Laura on the phone longer than any previous call they'd shared during her stay there. Every bit of evidence that she was more like herself increased his hope that they could yet share a full and happy life together. She told him about the group therapy she'd been attending that she mostly hated, but if nothing else it had helped give her some perspective on her own problems. She'd heard tales of abuse and dysfunction that were more than horrid, and her gratitude for the gospel had deepened in seeing how completely lost people became as they tried to solve their problems in all the wrong ways.

Two days later an appointment was arranged for him to meet with Dr. Hadley alone, and then he could spend some time with Laura. Once there, Hadley told him that in working toward having Laura return to a normal life, Wade needed to understand depression as much as possible and know how to handle it. He reviewed some of the basics, reminding him that for some people depression was completely chemical—with no events behind it, or the events might be insignificant. He was told that these people experience a great deal of guilt for their depression, often comparing themselves to people who have suffered abuse, wondering what they might have to be depressed about.

"While Laura has the events in her life that might *justify* depression, if you will," Hadley said, "she's still had some of this kind of guilt, because she does feel that she's been very blessed in many ways. It's important for people on the outside to understand that whether depression is situational or chemical, it is beyond a person's ability to control, and reasoning on a normal level will not ever solve the problem."

He went on to suggest some articles on dealing with depression that he could access through the Church's web site, lds.org, which might offer him more insight and some practical guidelines for handling the ups and downs.

Dr. Hadley then reviewed briefly the events in Laura's life that she had been struggling to overcome throughout the course of healing from her breakdown. He had to admit that he was coming to understand more fully the time bomb that had been ticking inside of her. With all she'd gone through in her life, some moment of reckoning had been inevitable. Randall's visit had just goaded it to the surface. And perhaps the timing wasn't so bad. When Wade looked at it that way, he was grateful to be the one in her life to help her get through this. He could also see that he was navigating through this himself, and he felt hope in being able to put it behind them. He knew that Laura might always be vulnerable to episodes of depression, that it was likely a combination of her chemical makeup and the circumstances she'd endured. But if she could only get beyond the mental state she was in now, he believed that with the extensive work she was going through, they would both be able to take those episodes on with knowledge and the ability to handle them. Challenges in life were inevitable, and someone susceptible to depression could take those challenges more harshly than others. But Hadley felt confident that Laura's will to be happy, and her strength of character, would guide her through whatever the future might bring. And he told Wade that his love and commitment to Laura, as well as the education he was getting in being able to help his wife through this, left him confident that if anyone could handle it, they could.

When their session was over, Wade was taken to Laura's room, where the door was open. He found her there alone, sitting on the bed, reading something in a folder, with a highlighting marker in her hand. For a long moment he just stood in the doorway while she was unaware of his presence. She looked different; there was an aura around her that was more like the woman he'd fallen in love with. His eye was drawn to the nightstand near her bed, where a little angel was sitting—one of the ornaments she'd helped Jane make for the festival tree. He stepped into the room, and she looked up, smiling at him as he picked up the angel.

"Hi," she said eagerly.

"Hello," he replied, bending to kiss her while he held on to the angel.

"It's beautiful, isn't it," she said.

"An interesting souvenir of a memorable time of life," he said, setting it back where he'd found it.

She gave a sardonic chuckle. "I'm not sure I really want to remember this time of my life."

"Only enough to remind us how not to get here again."

"Okay, I can agree with that," she said, and he sat on the bed beside her, kissing her again.

"What've you got there?" he asked, nodding toward the folder.

"Reading assignments from Hadley. Sometimes I think he's trying to turn *me* into a psychiatrist."

"Only enough to take care of yourself, I'm sure. He's suggested I do some reading myself."

She sighed. "I'm sorry this has been such a burden for you."

"No apologies," he said, touching her face. "I would do *anything* for you. And one day I may get even." He chuckled. "Wait until I'm doing my residency and we have seven kids, then we'll see who feels burdened."

Laura actually laughed. "I don't think it's physically possible for us to have seven kids before you finish your residency."

He kissed her and smiled. "We could try."

She looked down in that way he had come to recognize as feeling uncomfortable with something he'd said. Or perhaps more accurately, with something she was thinking or feeling that had been triggered by what he'd said.

"What?" he asked gently, tilting her chin toward him. "Talk to me."

Tears pooled in her eyes before she closed them. "Sometimes I . . . I . . . fear that . . ."

"What?" he pressed.

"That . . . I'm not capable of being . . . a good mother."

"I don't agree, Laura," he said firmly. "I don't believe this stage of your life is indicative to what's going to be the norm of your life. There may bc some difficult times, but that doesn't mean you can't be a good mother." She looked like she didn't believe him, and he added, "You've been told in priesthood blessings that there are children waiting to be born to you, and that you have the capacity to raise them with a strong spirit and a sound mind."

Her eyes widened. "I was really told that?"

"You really were," he said with a smile. "So . . . if you believe the power of the priesthood is real, then you have to believe that's not an empty promise."

Laura sighed and laid her head on his shoulder. A moment later she said, "I love children, Wade. No one knows that more than you. All I ever wanted was to be a good wife and mother."

"And so you are and will be," he said.

She put her arms around him, and he could tell she was crying. He just held her until she got it out of her system. When she'd settled her emotions she said, "You know why I love that little angel?"

"Why?" he asked, realizing how good it felt just to be with her and have normal conversation.

"It makes me think of Elena," she said, and his heart quickened. "It probably sounds crazy, but I've found a great deal of comfort in imagining that she might be with me."

Wade wasn't prepared for a sudden rush of tears as the Spirit verified the truth of what she'd said, and his mind was taken back to the moment when he had known beyond any doubt that Elena *would* help watch over Laura. When he sniffled, Laura lifted her head to look at him, surprised by the evidence of his emotion.

"What is it?" she asked, wiping at his tears.

"It doesn't sound crazy, Laura, because I know it's true. I felt her with me . . . after Brian died, and . . ." He chuckled tensely. "I . . . don't know how to say it, but . . . well . . . she let me know that she was mindful of you, and . . . I just felt that she would help you through this."

Laura said nothing, but her expression reflected the awe she felt. Wade hoped she would realize the evidence of God's love for her in the feelings she'd had, and also that the Spirit was closer to her than perhaps she might have believed. She settled her head against his shoulder, then she took his hand and did the standard ritual of threading their fingers together, then pressing her palm flat against his. They sat in silence for several minutes before she asked how Rebecca was doing, and he started telling her about the child's silly antics, which made her laugh. Then she started to cry and admitted, "I miss her so much. I miss *you* so much."

"It won't be long now," he murmured gently and kissed her brow.

Again they sat in silence until he noticed on the nightstand, near the angel, a stack of what appeared to be cards and letters. "What's that?" he asked. She looked up, and he pointed toward them.

She moved away from him to pick up the stack, which she handed to him, saying, "Remember Sister Williams? That dear woman who called me the day that . . ."

"I remember," he said when she obviously didn't want to finish the sentence.

"I've gotten something in the mail from her every few days. I never imagined such diligence from a visiting teacher—and since you sold the house we don't even live in her ward anymore."

"Well," Wade smiled, looking through the stack of cards and letters, all from the same return address, "I don't think true compassionate service has ward boundaries."

"She's been so sweet," Laura said. "When I get out of here, do you think we could go visit her?"

"I think that would be delightful," he said.

A minute later Rita appeared in the doorway and said, "How's it going here?"

"Great," Laura said, and sounded like she meant it.

"Hadley said you could have a little outing if you're up to it. Maybe you could talk your husband into taking you out for dessert or something . . . as long as you're back by ten."

"What an excellent idea," Wade said, coming to his feet with Laura's hand in his.

Twenty minutes later they were seated across from each other in an old-fashioned ice cream parlor, sharing a huge banana split. "I love ice cream," she said.

"Yes, I know," he chuckled. "I love eating ice cream with *you.*" He put a spoonful in her mouth and watched her closely, absorbing every moment into himself. She smiled with thoughtful eyes, and he said, "What are you thinking?"

"When you look at me like that . . . it's as if . . ."

"As if what?" he pressed when she hesitated.

"As if . . . I'm falling in love with you all over again."

Wade laughed and reached across the table to give her a quick kiss. "How delightful," he said. "So, the emotion of the day would be . . ."

She made a contemplative noise. "Delirium," she said decisively, and he laughed again.

Chapter Sixteen

That night when Wade came home, feeling almost elated from his time with Laura, he went straight to the computer to get on lds.org and search out any information he could find that might help him help Laura. He was pleased with the *Ensign* articles that came up from the archives. He found some that looked especially appropriate, printed them off, and took them to his room to do what he'd seen Laura doing. He found a highlighting marker and started reading until he was too tired to read any more. But as he lay in bed, the concept he'd just read about counteracting severe depression rehearsed itself in his mind.

At the *first* sign of negative thoughts or feelings, trace them back to their source. If something needs to be done to rectify a problem, do it. If something needs to be discussed, discuss it. If something is amiss in your life, fix it. Compare those feelings with reality. Are they in alignment with what's true and right? Or are those thoughts distorted and false? If so, talk back to them. Learn the difference between the Spirit guiding you through your conscience, and Satan trying to disguise his voice as conscience, attempting to weigh you down with thoughts and feelings that have no purpose beyond discouragement.

Wade repeated the concept until it felt deeply ingrained, and he intended to discuss it thoroughly with Laura. Like the article he'd read had stated, it could take a lot of time and effort to retrain your mind after a lifetime of negative thinking, but it was possible. Wade had come to believe that through correct psychology and gospel principles, *anything* was possible—even if that was simply finding the strength and tools to navigate through problems that were just a part of the human existence.

Wade finally slept but woke up early with the same concept going through his mind. As soon as it was a reasonable time, he called the facility and was glad to be able to talk to Laura and share his thoughts with her. She became emotional as she agreed to always acknowledge the *first* sign of any negative thoughts or feelings.

"I should have done it before," she cried. "You made me promise this very thing before we were married. If I had kept that promise to you, it never would have come to this."

"Laura," Wade said gently, "I think in this case . . . too much came at you too quickly. I don't think we ever could have gotten through this without some help. My only regret is that I didn't get some help before you sank so low. If anything ever hits anywhere near that hard again, we're going to get you some help—the same way we would if you had heart problems and started having chest pains. Does that make sense?"

"Yes," she said and sniffled loudly.

They talked for a while longer, then Wade did some laundry and paid some bills before he started a typical twelve-hour shift at one P.M. that began a four-day stretch of the same. During those days he phoned Laura each morning and talked to her for a while, but her therapy schedule made seeing her impossible. He looked forward to the three days he would have off once this stretch was finished, so that he could spend some time with her. Then he got a call from Dr. Hadley's assistant at the facility to find out when his next day off would be, and Wade told her. She set up a lengthy appointment for the day after tomorrow, telling him it would work perfectly with the doctor's plans for Laura.

"Dr. Hadley wants to set aside a significant portion of the day to guide Laura through some crucial steps, and he wants you to be a part of it. So, do you have any conflicts that day?"

"No, it should be fine. I can come in whenever it's good, and stay as long as I'm needed."

"Great," she said. "Ideally, if you could come about 11:30, and plan on having lunch here with Laura, then we'll just see how it goes. The lunch break is actually part of the project."

"Okay," Wade said, both curious and nervous. "I'll be there."

Sensing that this was a big deal in Laura's healing process, Wade took the liberty of calling some loved ones he trusted and asking for extra prayers on Laura's behalf. Some of them offered to fast as well, so Wade did the same, deciding to break the fast when he had lunch with Laura.

When it came time for the appointment, Wade's nervousness was definitely overriding his curiosity. Dr. Hadley met him in the front office, and they walked together down a long hallway while the doctor said, "Today we're working on a theory that I've discussed with Laura many times. She's known that this was coming, and I've asked her to give it a great deal of thought so that the exercise can be honest and thorough."

Wade nodded and listened while his palms turned sweaty.

The doctor continued, pausing in the hall to finish their conversation. "Imagine, if you will, that when a child is born, its mind is like a blank white screen. Or it can be a blank piece of paper. For some people, different visuals are easier to grasp than others. In this case, we're using a whiteboard for the sake of effect, and it's an easy tool to work with."

"Okay," Wade said, trying to fully absorb this.

"So, if a child's mind is a blank whiteboard, right from the beginning of its life, messages are written there, and gradually the board is filled with messages that are scattered all over the mind. If the messages are true and good, then a person functions on a relatively healthy level. You are an example of someone who has that board filled with healthy, positive messages. When you were faced with the challenges that once brought you to stay here for a few days, you came to terms with them quickly because your core beliefs, or the words on your board, were good. Is this making sense?"

"I think so."

"Well, in many cases, the messages are *not* good, and what we hope to accomplish is to erase the lies and false beliefs that are written in a person's mind, and replace them with the truth, and with beliefs they can hold to when life gets tough. If Laura can do this effectively, I feel confident that she'll never reach such depths of despair again."

Wade liked the sound of that and listened more eagerly.

"The problem in this theory is that sometimes the negative messages become so deeply ingrained that it's more like needing sandpaper to rub them out, as opposed to just an eraser—figuratively speaking, of course. However, I've found that giving a patient something visual to represent the process makes it stick more readily." He reached into his pocket and handed Wade a little block of wood. Turning it over in his hands, he could see and feel that it was smooth on all sides.

Dr. Hadley explained, "A few days ago, once we were not concerned about Laura wanting to do harm to herself, we gave her this and asked her to think of the most prominent words that came to her mind to describe herself. Then she carved them into this piece of wood. They were ugly words, and she carved them deep." Wade's stomach knotted at the implication, then Hadley added, "She has now spent many hours sanding them away until the surface has become smooth and clean, like new. It's time to put new words in her mind, new messages."

Hadley took the block of wood back and returned it to his pocket before he opened the door they were standing closest to as he said, "Laura has spent most of the morning with the assignment of transferring the core beliefs about herself that are in her brain to the whiteboard. According to the average, she should be just about finished."

They stepped into a small room that Wade immediately realized was an observation room with a one-way mirror. And on the other side, Laura had her back turned to the glass, writing vigorously on a huge whiteboard that was already slathered with a spattering of words in different colors of ink. He noticed there were markers of every color available, but she'd chosen black, blue, and red. The other markers were left unused.

"Does she know she's being watched?" Wade asked.

"Yes, and she has no problem with the observation. But she's had a difficult time with exposing other people to the contents of her mind. She's concerned about not wanting to offend anyone, most especially you. But we've talked it through repeatedly, and she understands that it's better to free her mind of what's there, as opposed to letting it roll around in there indefinitely, and she knows she can't do this alone. She gave me permission long ago to share with you any information that I felt was appropriate, and to even show you videotapes of our sessions if I felt it was necessary—which it hasn't been."

"Okay," Wade said, feeling better about observing her this way.

"I would like to ask the same of you, that I be at liberty to share with Laura anything that you and I talk about, and that she be allowed to observe our interaction if it would be helpful to her."

"That sounds fair. I don't have a problem with it."

"Your role in this is especially crucial. You've expressed a genuine desire to do whatever it takes to help her through this. You can do that more effectively by understanding why living inside of her head has been such a challenge."

Hearing it put that way, Wade focused more on what exactly she had written. And that's when his stomach turned to knots and his chest tightened. As he watched, she was writing the word *worthless* in red block letters over the top of other words that were layered and crisscrossed to the point that it was difficult to make out where one word ended and another began in the mass of confusion and chaos. There was practically no white left on the board whatsoever, but in spite of the bedlam, there was no mistaking the words written there, some of them over and over. *Worthless. Ugly. Stupid. Lazy. Selfish. Cruel. Wicked. Psycho. Evil child. Crazy. Unlovable. Tramp.* And then there were the words that crossed over into profanity and vulgarity.

Wade pressed a hand over his mouth, almost fearing he'd throw up. As if Hadley had expected this, he said gently, "I thought it would be better if you observed this where she couldn't see your reaction."

Wade swallowed carefully and cleared his throat. "I can understand that." His voiced croaked as he asked, "So is this . . . from . . . what? Her mother? Is this the kind of stuff she said when she was drunk?"

"It's mostly her mother; some from her father. And much of it was spoken sober."

"Oh, help," Wade said, silently thanking God for putting him into a home where love and respect and harmony were so prominent.

"Some of it wasn't spoken but implied by the way she was treated. Then a child goes out into the world with those beliefs in place and unconsciously invites others to treat them the same way, so the messages were reiterated by many people in her life. Most especially her ex-husband."

Wade just shook his head and watched Laura write the word *unlovable* several times over the top of other horrible and degrading words.

"Now, there's something you need to understand, Wade," Hadley said, and Wade looked directly at him. "What you're seeing is tough to swallow, but we're working on getting Laura to let it go. You have to do the same. She understands that to truly let these messages go, she has to forgive the messengers, whatever their intentions may have been." Hadley's voice tightened firmly. "And you need to do the same."

Wade sighed. "I could swear sometimes that you read minds."

"I just know anger in a person's eyes when I see it. The people in Laura's life who have scarred and injured her spirit will eventually face God with their accountability, and they will be judged according to their own ability to act in proportion to their own personal experiences. It's not our burden to carry, and accepting that one fact is the greatest factor in this kind of healing. Laura's wounds are distinctly defined as emotional and verbal abuse. When this kind of thing is accompanied by violence, or spiritual or sexual abuse, the process of undoing the damage is much more complicated and sometimes takes a lifetime to overcome. But people do it. They do it because they desire to be whole, and their willingness to forgive overrides all else."

Wade nodded and felt the message surround his heart. He knew the power of forgiveness. He'd seen and felt its blessings in his own life, and he knew Hadley was right. He also knew it was going to take some time. He felt grateful to know that Randall would likely never be able to find Laura again. He didn't know her last name, and she would never be living or working in the same places she had before. He also felt grateful that her parents lived out of state, and their contact would likely be very minimal. He understood that, just like his own parents, behavior was often a result of a person's circumstances. Perhaps these people had abuse or dysfunction in their own history, and he could never judge or understand that. Still, at this moment, he felt deeply hurt and angry on Laura's behalf. It was going to take some time.

"There's something else you need to understand," Dr. Hadley continued while Wade watched Laura through the glass. "Some people suffer from chronic depression for no logical reason at all.

They have no horribly negative experiences or abuse. It's simply a matter of brain chemistry. Sometimes those people write their own negative messages in their mind. They come to believe they are crazy, worthless, unlovable, because they can't be happy in spite of being richly blessed. These people struggle with a great deal of guilt, wondering why they would feel the way they do when there's no apparent cause. Medication and therapy can make a big difference in such situations as well. I'm telling you this because as of now, we really don't know how much of Laura's problem is chemical. She's obviously got the negative experiences that warrant depression. The need for chemical balance may be temporary for her, or it may be permanent. If she comes to terms with the abuse and challenges of her life and continues to struggle, she needs to understand that it's not something to feel guilty for, or ashamed of. It needs to be treated like other chronic illnesses. If we can help frame it for her in the same respect as having diabetes or MS, for instance, then she can press forward with a stronger self-esteem and have a stronger ability to battle it in a positive way. Is that making sense?"

"Absolutely, yes," Wade said.

"I believe for her the need for medication is temporary," Hadley said. "But only time will tell for sure."

While Wade listened, contending with the churning of his stomach, Laura stood back to admire her work as if it were rare art. Hadley hurried out of the room as if he'd been cued, saying over his shoulder, "We'll meet you in the hall. You'll know when to go out."

Wade watched through the glass as Hadley entered the room and said to Laura, "All finished?"

"I think so," she said, her voice sounding a little like Wade was feeling. She glanced toward the glass, which would be a mirror from her side, and asked, "Were you watching me?"

"Off and on."

She looked again at the mirror. "Is Wade here?"

His heart quickened. He didn't want her to be told anything that wasn't true, but he wasn't sure he wanted her to know he was watching her now. Hadley said casually, "You said it was okay for him to see what you wrote."

"Has he?"

"Yes. He'll be meeting us for lunch in a few minutes," Hadley said. "Now that you've gotten this far, how do you feel about the results?" he asked, leaning against a table and folding his arms.

"It's horrible," she said, looking again at her work. "It makes me *sick!*"

"Amen," Wade muttered to himself and realized that Laura was crying. Hadley handed her a box of tissues, and for several minutes Laura sobbed and ranted an emotional version of what she'd written on the board. Hadley listened, offered compassion, and waited for her to calm down.

"Do you think now that you've gotten all of that out of yourself, it might be easier to let it go?" the doctor asked.

"I don't know, but I want to," she said. "I don't want to live this way anymore."

"Okay, well . . . I think your husband is waiting in the hall." Wade knew that was his cue and he hurried out the door, hearing Hadley say before it closed, "Why don't we get something to eat, and then we'll talk some more."

Wade leaned casually against the wall, as if he'd been waiting there for ten minutes. She smiled when she saw him, but she looked disconcerted, perhaps afraid. Did she fear what his reaction might be since she'd been told that he'd seen what she'd written?

"Hi," he said and hugged her tightly, kissing her brow. "I've missed you."

"Oh, I've missed you too," she said, holding to him tightly.

Hadley led the way to the cafeteria while they shared small talk. When they were seated over their meal, he asked Wade how he was doing with his brother's death, and how the other members of his family were doing. He asked about Rebecca, and about Alex and his family. Laura questioned how Hadley knew Alex, and together they filled in more details of Wade's own experience in this place, and how much Alex had been involved.

While Laura went to the ladies room, Hadley briefly told Wade some questions he wanted him to ask Laura once they returned to the room with the whiteboard. Wade uttered a silent prayer that he could say it right and respond appropriately and help her get through this in the best way possible.

As they walked together back to their destination, Wade sensed Laura becoming nervous. He felt a little that way himself. They all entered the room, and Hadley took a chair as if he intended to have a friendly chat. Laura sat as well, facing the board directly. Wade took a chair and glanced casually at the board, then looked straight at Laura. "That's pretty pathetic, Mrs. Morrison. Do you think that stuff is true?"

She looked down, but not before he caught shame in her eyes. "Sometimes I can make myself believe it's not true, but . . . there are other times when it's the only truth that feels real."

"So . . . when I say things to you that contradict what you've written here, do you believe them?" She hesitated, and he added, "Do you think I would lie to you?"

"No, of course not."

"Okay, then . . . I want to say what I've said many times before, but this time I want you to hear it with your heart, with your spirit. Are you ready?" She nodded, and he leaned toward her. "I love you, Laura Morrison. You are the most amazing woman I have ever met, and I consider it an honor and a privilege to have you as my wife, and the mother of my children."

Laura watched him in awe while tears slid down her cheeks. Following a full minute of silence, Hadley said, "Are you ready, Laura?"

"For what?"

He held out an eraser. She actually looked frightened as she glanced at the board, then at the eraser, then at the board again. Hadley asked, "As ugly as it is, these are thoughts you've become very comfortable with. Do you think you can let them go?"

"I want to," she said.

"Now, you understand," Hadley said, "this is just an exercise to give you a tangible representation of what's going on in your head. Erasing that board isn't going to automatically keep these words from ever coming up again. It's up to you to hear the thought when it enters, stop it, and correct it with the truth until you can reprogram your brain to hear the truth all the time. Does that make sense?"

"Yes."

"Do you feel capable of doing that?"

"Yes," she said, and grabbed the eraser with firm determination. She stood, then hesitated. She lifted her arm, then hesitated. Then she drew a deep breath and started erasing—and crying at the same time. She got the board about two-thirds clean when she stopped and hung her head, crying uncontrollably. Wade stood behind her, putting one hand around her waist. He just stood there until she calmed down, then he took her hand into his, helping her hold the eraser. He held her tightly against him, her back to his chest, while he helped her erase the remainder of the ink from the board. When it was done she dropped the eraser to the floor and turned abruptly, taking hold of Wade and crying against his chest. Wade looked at the doctor over the top of Laura's head and found his expression pleased and confident. Apparently they were on the right track.

When Laura had once again calmed down, Hadley invited them both to be seated. Wade kept Laura's hand in his. Hadley said gently, "Look at the board, Laura. What do you see? Look closely."

Wade almost felt nervous when he realized that the images were still there. Laura noticed it too and looked at Hadley in alarm.

"Residue," he said easily, then he leaned closer to Laura and spoke intently. "Emotional residue is something you may have to contend with for the rest of your life, Laura. It might creep in when you're vulnerable and take you off guard when you least expect it. We just talked about how you can reprogram your thoughts, and your husband can help you do that. When you have false or negative thoughts, talk to him about them right away. Let him help you keep perspective." He sighed. "Now, it wouldn't be appropriate for me to share my religious beliefs with you when our relationship is purely professional. But I already know that you and I share the same beliefs, so I'm going to share with you what I know beyond any doubt to be the strongest and truest key to complete healing and peace over any matter. Nothing can help you combat the emotional residue, or the ongoing challenges in your life, better than this one remedy." From behind his chair he reached for a squirt bottle of some kind of cleaner, and a white rag. He handed them to Laura and said firmly, "The Atonement." He smiled gently and added, "It's been given to you. But it's up to you to use it."

Wade watched Laura while she studied the objects in her hands as if she were trying to accept the metaphor into the deepest part of herself. Her eyes became moist once again just before she shot to her feet with zealous determination and sprayed the stuff abundantly all over the board, then wiped it meticulously clean, not seeming in any hurry, occasionally tilting her head and looking at it from a different angle to make certain she'd missed nothing. When she was apparently satisfied with her work, she stood back and said, "Perfect." And it was. The board was completely white, without a flaw.

"Yes," Hadley said. "Now, if that board represents your life, do you think it's going to stay that clean?"

"Not likely."

"We hope to put positive messages there to replace the negative ones, but experiences and memories will always bring up negative thoughts and feelings. That's why you take the Atonement with you every day. It makes all the difference where we fall short. It's not there for a one-time use. It's there for life. Forever." He paused for emphasis. "Do you believe that's true, Laura?"

"I do," she said without hesitation. "I've had trouble believing that it would apply to me, but I think I'm making progress with that."

"Good, we can keep working on it. And we've talked about ways that *you* can keep working on it. At some other time you can discuss those things with your husband, and the two of you can work together to strengthen those beliefs. Your testimony of the Atonement is the most powerful tool you can use in your life."

Laura nodded and wiped away tears while she squeezed Wade's hand tightly.

"Now," Hadley said, motioning toward the board, "what kind of messages would you like to see written there?" She looked at it contemplatively but said nothing. "It's your life, your mind. From this day forward you don't have to allow anything to be put there that you don't want." He paused to give her the opportunity to speak, but she didn't. "Is there something you'd like to put up there for starters?"

"I . . . don't know . . . where to start." She seemed hesitant and nervous.

"That's okay," Hadley said. "Something like this takes time and thought, and you're probably overwhelmed right now. Before the end of the day, I have something I want to give to you. I know you're a journal keeper, but you haven't wanted to write anything since you came here. What I have for you is a journal. The pages are blank and white, just like this board.

They don't even have lines, and I chose it that way for a reason. These pages are not required to have any structure to them. You can glue or tape pictures in there that inspire you, or doodle or draw if you want. This is not a journal for you to record personal experiences, but rather a place for you to record positive thoughts and feelings. The words you put in this book will always represent what you *want* to have inside of yourself, what you desire to believe and achieve. When you hear quotes or thoughts that make you feel good, or affirm those positive beliefs, this is the place to put them." He smiled. "And I'm including a bottle of whiteout, because you just might slip and write something that shouldn't be there, but you're capable of blocking it out and replacing it. Which brings up something else we've talked about that I want to remind you of. Are you up to talking about this some more right now?"

"Yes, I'm fine," she said, squeezing Wade's hand.

"You've made some good choices in your life, Laura, and you've surrounded yourself with good people who love you, most especially your husband. He can help you replace the bad in your life with good. But he's not perfect, you know." He winked at Wade. "As much as we would all like to be perfect and be on our best behavior all the time, it's just not possible. It's good for you to listen to the good things he says to you, and to believe them, and to trust him. But I want you to consider what might happen if you rely too heavily on his words and his opinions to build up your own value. What if he comes home from a really horrible day at work, in a bad mood that has nothing to do with you, and he says something that triggers an old memory and makes you feel worthless or unloved. What are you going to do?"

"After I cuff him upside the head, you mean?" she said, and Wade turned toward her, startled. Then she chuckled and smiled at him. "Just kidding. I would never cuff you."

"I know," he said. "Not literally anyway, but if I ever need it figuratively, don't hesitate to straighten me out."

"And vice versa," she said, then turned to Hadley. "If that happens, I will remind myself that I can't expect people around me to always speak and behave the way I want them to, and I will separate his words and actions from my own beliefs about myself."

"You get an A-plus," Hadley said with a proud smile, then he added, "Why don't you tell Wade the only source of perfect love that will never fail you."

"God's love," she said with a tremor in her voice. "I have a Heavenly Father who lives and loves me. He is the literal Father of my spirit, and He knows and loves me intimately. He hears and answers every prayer. Even when it doesn't feel like He's there, I know that He is, and that I need to be patient and trust in Him and understand that He knows what He's doing in trying to help me grow and become a better, stronger person." New tears began to flow. "I have a Savior who atoned not only for my sins and weaknesses, but also for my suffering and pain. The Atonement was personal and intimate. I know that because I have felt the evidence of it in my life." She sniffled and reached for a tissue. Wade reached for one himself, touched beyond words by what he was hearing. "And I have the Holy Ghost," she went on, "available to me as a constant guide, comforter, and companion. From them I will always know that I am loved, that I have value."

"That is one of the most beautiful and incredible things I have ever heard in this place, Laura." Dr. Hadley sounded a little emotional himself.

"It's what you taught me," she said, wiping at ongoing tears.

"But few if any have ever received it into their spirit so fully. If others here could follow your example of trusting in God's love, there would be a lot more healing." He sighed and added, "I'm giving you the assignment to write down what you just said in that book I'm going to give you. It needs to be the first thing you put there, on the very first page. Okay?"

"Okay," she said.

"And beyond that, you can start filling it up with good things. This book then becomes one of the places you can turn when your thoughts and feelings become negative. Alright?"

"Okay," she said. "That sounds nice. Thank you."

"Do you know where else you can turn to overcome negative thoughts and feelings?"

It felt like Sunday School for a minute as she said, "I need to keep the channels of prayer open all the time, and not keep myself from praying because I don't feel worthy. I need to remember that God loves me and that He will always be there for me. I need to study the scriptures every day, and go to the temple often, even when I feel depressed—or *especially* when I feel depressed."

"That's right; however, I want to remind you of something important. And Wade needs to know this, too. It's important to look at these things through the proper lenses. For a person who is depressed, all of the scripture study and temple attendance in the world will not take away those depressed feelings. Some people who don't understand depression believe that it will. However, it's still highly important to do the things that keep the Spirit close in spite of depression. If you actively do these things, even when you don't feel like it, you're more likely to feel the comfort and guidance of the Spirit to get you through the lows. When people withdraw from those spiritual things, they're more likely to make the wrong choices and start down negative paths that will only make the problems in their lives worse. You understand that, don't you, Laura."

"Yes, I do . . . thanks to you."

Dr. Hadley stood up, saying, "Wade, I would like to talk with you privately for a little while. But I think Laura's had enough for the moment, and she likely could use some rest. You can see her again before you leave."

"Okay," Wade said and stood to give Laura a quick kiss before she was ushered out of the room.

Hadley said over his shoulder, "Sit tight. I'll be right back."

"Okay," Wade said again and sat back down, contemplating the blank whiteboard.

In the hall, Dr. Hadley took hold of Laura's shoulders and looked into her eyes. "This has been a difficult day. How are you holding up?"

"I'm okay, really. Maybe some of this will sink in later. I don't know."

"If you want to rest right now you can, but I have a choice to offer you. You're aware that the room we were just in has an observation window."

"Yes," she said.

"I'm going to go back in there and talk to Wade about your situation. I wanted him to believe you were going to rest so that he would be completely candid as we talk. If you want to observe our conversation you can. He's let me know that's okay, even though he probably won't suspect it at the moment. But I have to warn you. If he doesn't suspect you're watching, he may say things that could be difficult for you to hear. You tell me what you want to do."

"I want to know how he really feels," she said. "You can put me back together later if it doesn't go well."

"Fair enough," Hadley said and showed her into the observation room.

Laura sat down and watched her husband through the glass, in awe that he would be so good to her. But she couldn't deny some fear in wondering what he *really* thought and felt about all of this. Still, she preferred to know the truth, even if it meant more therapy to recover from it.

She took a deep breath as Hadley walked into the room with Wade and sat down.

"So," Hadley said, "how are you feeling about what just happened?"

"Right now?" Wade said. "I'm feeling a great deal of hope. She's come a long way, and I'm grateful."

"I would agree with that," Hadley said. "How did you feel about what she had written on the board?"

"It made me sick. I never imagined . . . but I'm still glad I saw it. Maybe it gave me some understanding of what life has been like through her eyes. It makes me grateful for my own upbringing, in spite of certain challenges that you are well aware of. I want to just . . ." he became teary, "take her home and surround her with all the love that I've been given throughout my life."

"What a marvelous idea," Hadley said with a smile. The doctor leaned more toward Wade and said earnestly, "You understand how important it is through this kind of therapy to be completely honest. If you cover up feelings or issues you have about any of this, then they could likely surface later on and create challenges."

"I understand, yes."

"So . . . if there's anything going on with you related to all of this that you want to talk about, we should do that. Is there anything you want to say that you would be hesitant to share with Laura?"

"No," he said immediately. "I've already told her how this has affected me. You were there."

"Let's do a quick recap of that. How did you feel when you discovered her intention to leave you and let you find her dead?"

Laura sucked in her breath, then had trouble letting it out. Her regret over this issue was too deep to even fathom. She still didn't understand why Wade hadn't washed his hands of her long ago. Her heart pounded painfully as Wade's expression made it clear he was taken aback by the question.

"Initially I was furious," he said. "But I understand that anger is tied into other emotions. I was terrified, horrified. I felt hurt, deeply hurt—betrayed. I couldn't believe she would leave me to suffer such a loss, especially after losing Elena the way I did."

Laura put a hand over her mouth and was grateful to be alone when it didn't hold back her sharp whimpering.

"But," Wade went on, "I've come to realize that she was crippled by the depression. She really didn't know what she was doing. I believe she loves me and that she regrets what happened. I believe she would never want to hurt me that way."

"So you've forgiven her."

"Absolutely."

"Do you trust her?"

"With what?" Wade asked, almost sounding insulted.

"Your heart, your future, your children?"

"Yes, I do," he said firmly. "I know her heart, and I've felt the progress she's made. I have also been given a frank education on depression, and I am now wise enough to recognize the signs of something serious. I am more than willing to stand by her side and help her see that it never gets that bad again. I have no regrets, Doctor. If I could go back to the day I asked her to marry me, knowing what I know now, I would still do it. Marrying her is the best thing I could have possibly done with my life, and I haven't changed my mind about that."

They talked for a few minutes about the warning signs of suicidal tendencies, and how to manage them. Laura listened, while her grief and regret melted into awe and wonder. When they seemed done with that, Dr. Hadley motioned to the whiteboard and said, "If you had the opportunity to put new messages into Laura's mind, what would they be?"

Wade smiled at the doctor, then pointed at the board. "May I?"

"Of course," Hadley said and leaned back in his chair.

Wade chose the purple marker first and wrote the word *amazing* three times across the top. He went back to widen the letters and make them more prominent while he said, "Do you know why she's so amazing?"

"Tell me," Hadley said.

"It's not so tough for someone who is raised in a loving home to grow up and be a decent human being. But when someone has the will to rise above what she's had to deal with, and still be all that she is, that is so amazing!" A little burst of laughter came through Laura's ongoing tears.

"I agree," Hadley said.

Wade then picked up a green marker and wrote a series of words with large exclamation points. *Beautiful! Wise! Tender! Sensitive! Good mother! Great wife! Compassionate! Good cook! Tidy! Clean! Organized!* He wrote *beautiful* again, and after it he wrote, *stunningly beautiful, takes my breath away.* He traded green for red and wrote more words. *Great kisser! Funny! Spiritual! Kind! Loving!* And in huge capital letters he wrote, *Lovable! Lovable! Lovable!* He picked up a blue marker and wrote, *She wears funny shoes and makes children smile, and she has a passion for life that leaves me in awe, and she laughs deeper and cries harder and loves more truly than any woman I've ever known. Laura Morrison is charming and unpredictable and full of so much life that she makes my life more alive.*

He picked up the purple marker again and began filling in every space of white by repeating words he'd already written, over and over. He changed colors and kept filling it in while Dr. Hadley just watched him, and Laura just cried. Wade filled every bit of available space, but unlike when Laura had written on the board, he didn't write words over the top of each other. He just filled them in with great care and enthusiasm. As he stood back to admire his work, he asked, "Is she going to see this?"

Hadley said, "You told me it was okay to share anything we talked about with her."

Wade looked at the doctor abruptly, then at the mirror, as if he could see Laura, but she knew he could only see his own reflection. His surprise was so evident that she had no problem believing he'd spoken candidly and from the heart, that the words he'd written and spoken were sincere.

"Is she in there?" Wade asked.

"Unless she left," Hadley said. "I thought it might be good for her to hear what you had to say and not have to wonder if you were saying what she wanted to hear."

Wade looked again at the mirror, then he hurried from the room without hesitation or permission. Laura struggled to get her tears under control, but an instant later he had opened the door and was standing there looking at her. She came to her feet and held her breath.

"I love you, Laura Morrison," he said and wrapped his arms around her, almost crushing her with the force of his embrace.

"I love you too," she murmured and clung to him, unable to stop crying.

Chapter Seventeen

Dr. Hadley gave them a few minutes alone, then he invited them to join him in a different room with a more comfortable atmosphere. While Laura kept her hand firmly in Wade's, the doctor talked them through a summary of what Laura had been through since she'd taken a sudden spiral into this depression, bringing her to this point. And they talked about where they would go from here, but no time frame was mentioned on when she might be able to come home.

Wade found it difficult to leave when the time came, but he couldn't deny the progress that had been made, and the hope he felt that kept growing bigger inside of him. He felt inexplicably grateful for Dr. Hadley. Not only for his expertise, but for the way he coupled it with his spiritual wisdom. And he felt grateful for the healing power of the Atonement and how it covered all the broken pieces that were left behind when things like this happened in people's lives. And he felt grateful for Laura. He loved her, and he had no regrets.

* * * * *

Laura spent the evening, at Dr. Hadley's suggestion, just pondering the day's events and allowing them to catch up with her. Just before bedtime, Rita came to her room and handed her a flat white box. "Hadley asked me to give this to you," she said, then she smiled. "It's good to see you doing better."

"Yes, I do feel better," Laura said, "but I know I have a long way to go. I still feel . . . confused, and . . . down, I guess."

"It will take time," Rita said. "Be patient with yourself."

Laura nodded and hugged her, grateful for her and other people who worked here that went the extra mile in their assignments.

After Rita left, Laura opened the box, not surprised to find a beautiful, leather-bound journal with blank, white pages. There was also a package of high-quality pens in a variety of colors, and a bottle of whiteout. She *was* surprised to find glued inside the front cover a photograph of the whiteboard, just as it had looked after Wade had finished with it. She laughed and cried as she read every word written there, even though some of them had become rather tiny now. Still, she could make out every letter, and his words filled her with hope and joy. She wondered if she could find it in herself to go on living and find happiness if she didn't have someone like Wade in her life, and she was surprised to realize that she could. She was grateful for Wade, grateful beyond words. But the things she had learned about herself through this experience had given her a perspective that made life worth living, with or without anyone to share her life with. Wade was just the frosting on the cake.

She thought of cake and laughed to herself. Before she went to sleep she called Wade and said, "You know that German bakery on South Temple?"

"Yes," he said with humorous suspicion.

"Well, I was thinking . . . that maybe life is like cake . . . and maybe you in my life is like frosting on the cake, and . . . I thought that the perfect piece of cake might be a great opportunity for some emotional eating. So, maybe I can get out of here for a few hours soon and we could get a couple of those delectable little cakes with too much frosting—except that in this case, the frosting is so good that you have to eat every bit of it."

"It sounds wonderful," he said, recalling how Alex had once told him that dancing was like frosting on the cake of life. The comparison made him smile. "So, a little cake for emotional eating. It sounds like a marvelous date. And the emotion of the day would be . . ."

"Gratitude," she said, then neither of them spoke for at least a minute.

"I should go," she finally said. "I love you."

"I love you too, and I'll see you soon."

"I'll look forward to it."

The following day Wade was grateful to have another day off. He caught up some things that needed to be done before he went to the German bakery that Laura loved. He picked out a variety of delectable little cakes, and later that evening he went to the facility carrying a pink box and a couple of plastic forks. Laura laughed when he opened the box to show her half a dozen different varieties, when eating one would be a stretch.

"I didn't know what you'd be in the mood for," he said. "So you can eat some of every one and save the rest for . . . breakfast or something."

She hugged him tightly, then they sat close together and fed each other cake while Laura told him about the day's therapy. She admitted that her mind still felt more cloudy than clear much of the time; the medications were giving her side effects that were annoying, and she was struggling some with fear in facing the outside world. But still, she was making progress. She could admit it, and he could feel it. And the emotion of the day, once again, was gratitude.

The next day Alex's cousin Susan and her husband, Donald, arrived home from an eighteen-month mission. Susan was actually his mother's cousin, but they were very close, and Alex had purchased the house from Susan with the agreement that Donald and Susan would live there when needed between missions and spending time with their grown children, who were scattered all over the country. Wade didn't know them well, but well enough to know that they were wonderful people, and they'd always been immensely kind and gracious to him. The household dynamics felt different with them there, but they stayed fewer than twenty-four hours before they were on a flight back east to begin an extended vacation of staying a significant amount of time with each of their children.

A couple of days later, Wade and Alex began a three-day stretch of shifts that began at four A.M. Wade's gratitude continued as he developed a habit of either seeing Laura every day, or at the very least having a lengthy phone visit. But as Christmas drew closer, he couldn't avoid a certain heartache over the thought of not having her there to share it with him and Rebecca. Dr. Hadley had said she could probably have a home visit for some hours on the holiday, but it just wasn't the same. He thought of his last two Christmases and how dreadfully alone he'd felt, even though he'd been surrounded by family and had found great joy in seeing his little daughter taking in the glory of Christmas. He wanted nothing more than to just have Laura by his side for every big and little aspect of the celebration. Alex even had no shifts Christmas Eve or Christmas day, which he'd said hadn't happened for as long as he'd been a doctor. Wade tried to keep perspective and remind himself to be patient and grateful for the progress, but he couldn't help feeling some disappointment as the time eased closer and he'd been given no reason to believe that Dr. Hadley had any intention of letting Laura come home before then.

Wade felt a glimmer of hope on that count when he received a call from Dr. Hadley's assistant. He wanted to meet with him and Laura together, and he wanted Jane and Alex to be there. She said it was important for all of the adults in the household where Laura would be living to be fully prepared for, and understand, Laura's challenges. Wade spoke with Alex and Jane, then called back and set up an appointment for the following afternoon, since he and Alex would be off at four P.M.

Through Wade's regular contact with Laura, he believed that she was doing well. But he still felt concerned with her mood swings and her expressions of fear and confusion over merging the past into the future. All things considered, Wade was grateful to have her in the care of competent counselors under the direction of Dr. Hadley. While he desperately wanted her to come home, he wanted her to be ready. He wanted her healing to be as deep and complete as possible. Laura expressed concern over the appointment that included Alex and Jane. Wade assured her that they were happy to do all they could to help, but she didn't seem convinced.

Later that day, Wade got a call from Rochelle. She had officially moved into an apartment in the Salt Lake area, she was going to church, and she was meeting with her bishop. A disciplinary council had been set, and while she was dreading it, she admitted readily to looking forward to a fresh start.

"I realize you didn't need to know all that," she said, "but . . . I know you're well aware of the way I've been living, and it seems only right that you know what I'm doing about it. Obviously, I can't talk to Laura right now, but—"

"Have you seen her since you got back?" he asked.

"No. I just . . . can't right now. I'm afraid I'll only make it harder for her. I'm kind of a mess. But when you feel like it's right . . . you tell her what's going on with me, and maybe she can call me when she feels ready."

"Okay," Wade said.

"I've been seeing Dr. Hadley," she added. "He's amazing."

"Yes, he certainly has a gift," Wade said, and they agreed to keep in touch.

Wade wasn't surprised to get a call from Cole the following day. They kept track of each other regularly. He *was* surprised, however, to hear that Cole had helped Rochelle move into her apartment and that they were seeing each other frequently.

"It's nothing romantic," he said, "but . . ."

"But it could be eventually?" Wade guessed.

"Maybe. We'll see," Cole said, then he asked about Laura, as he always did, and Wade gave him an update. Cole signed off as he usually did, saying that he would remember Wade and Laura in his prayers.

"And vice versa," Wade said, a bit disconcerted to think of how dramatically life had changed for both him and Cole since their paths had crossed. Much of what had happened felt disjointed and surreal, and he longed for this bad dream to be over.

When it came time for the appointment with Laura, she appeared visibly nervous and withdrawn when she was brought into the room. Alex and Jane each hugged her, telling her how good it was to see her. She simply said, "Hi." Wade greeted her with a kiss on the cheek and held her hand as they were seated.

As always, Wade was relieved by Hadley's straightforward, clearing-the-air attitude. "So," he began, "you seem a little uneasy, Laura. What's up?"

She looked hesitant, but said, "I just . . . hate having such a fuss made about all of this. I really would prefer not to disrupt Alex and Jane's lives over my problems. They've been very good to me. I know that it was necessary for Wade and Rebecca to move back in with them, and that's where I'll be going when I leave here, but . . . I feel like a burden. Surely they have better things to do with their time than baby-sit me."

"Do you think you'll require baby-sitting?" Hadley asked.

"I don't know what I'll require," she said, sounding almost angry. "You tell me."

As always, Hadley remained calm and composed. "I think it's a blessing to go home to a situation where you won't be alone during the hours when your husband needs to be gone, but I wouldn't be sending you home if I thought you needed constant supervision. You've come far beyond that. We've simply asked Jane and Alex here to discuss the situation openly so that you can feel completely comfortable with the adults in your home while you work to stay on top of this."

Wade wasn't surprised to hear Alex and Jane each express a sincere eagerness to have Laura in their home. They discussed the dynamics of the household, and how it had long been established that Wade and Rebecca had their own living space with two bedrooms and their own bathroom. Wade's bedroom that Laura would share was large enough to have a love seat and a TV, and she could be there and have her privacy. The house was very big, and it would be up to Laura how much she chose to interact with the family. Jane said that she loved Laura dearly and was looking forward to her company, that she would never consider her a burden. Wade was pleased with the way Jane said that she would appreciate Laura's help in the household, but she put it in a way that would make Laura feel needed more than pressured.

Dr. Hadley prompted some conversation about the probable ups and downs Laura might be going through for some time yet, and how it was best to handle them. Laura agreed that she would never be afraid to tell Wade—or Alex or Jane if he wasn't there—that she was struggling and needed to talk, or cry, or be alone, or get out, or whatever she might need. As the session drew to a close, Laura admitted that she felt better. She expressed appreciation for Alex and Jane, and for Wade, but she still said, "I feel like a burden. I'm certain when Wade brought me into his family, they didn't expect to have to take care of me or—"

"Laura," Alex interrupted and leaned his forearms on his thighs to look at her more closely, "not so many years ago, I didn't even know I had a brother. Wade and I have both been through some tough times together since that discovery was made. He helped me get through Barrett's illness, and we've had the opportunity to help him get through the struggles he's had since Elena died. But we have never considered him, or his family, any degree of a burden. He has always contributed far more to the household than he's ever taken, but that's not really the point. The point is that the biggest reason we're here on this earth is to help each other through. This is a tough time for you, but we're family. We all made covenants to mourn with those that mourn, and comfort those that stand in need of comfort. We consider it a privilege to share the home we've been blessed with, and to help you and Wade through this season of life. Who knows what's around the corner? There may come a day when the tables will turn and we will need *your* help. But it really doesn't matter. We *want* to have you in our home, and we will all work together to do whatever it takes to get through this. If problems arise, we'll talk about them and work them out. We promise we're not going to let this disrupt our household or create problems. We promise to be completely honest, as long as you're willing to do the same. Okay?"

"Okay," Laura said, squeezing Wade's hand.

Wade smiled at Alex, then said facetiously to Laura, "That's my brother."

Later that evening Wade talked to Laura on the phone. There was one point that wouldn't leave his mind, a question he needed to ask her. "Laura," he said, "I need you to be honest with me. I mean . . . we can't go back and change it, but . . . I still have to know . . ."

"Just say it," she said.

"Do you regret selling the house?" he asked.

"No, Wade, I don't," she said without hesitation. "Now that I can think clearly and put it all together, I have to admit that . . . even before you brought it up, I'd felt like I could never go back there. Right now I'm grateful that . . . well . . . it probably sounds silly, but . . . I don't know that I could ever be alone in that house again, and now I don't ever have to worry about Randall finding me. He doesn't know my married name, and I know he would never call my parents or Rochelle. So, for that reason I'm relieved as well. If we didn't have any options, then I'd have to find a way to deal with it, I suppose, but . . . given the situation, I'm relieved that you sold it. And . . . I'm grateful that you didn't have to go to work, Wade. You need to have time with Rebecca, and I would feel even more horrible about all of this than I already do if I were the reason you couldn't do that."

Wade felt indescribably relieved, but simply said, "Well, I'm glad it worked out okay."

She was quiet a moment, then said, "Wade . . . now I need you to be honest with me and tell me . . . how all of this has affected us financially. I'm afraid to hear the answer, but I need to ask. I know it must have cost a fortune." She started to cry. "I can't even fathom how much it must have cost, and I seriously doubt the equity in the house was enough to cover it, and I feel sick when I think what this must have done to you in that regard, and—"

"Laura," he interrupted gently, "before you get carried away, just let me answer the question. But before I do, I want you to know that there is no price tag on keeping you alive and safe, and helping you heal. However, we've been very blessed. The insurance you had through your job was actually very good, and they've paid a significant portion. I kept up the premiums. I did use some of the equity from the house, but there's still some left. It's in the bank. My father has helped a little. He gets very insistent about such things. We still have enough of the life insurance money put away to cover our living expenses until I get my degree. We're fine, Laura. I'm sure we got through it much better than most people would, but even if we hadn't, I wouldn't begrudge it."

"You really are so good to me," she said, and he could tell she was still crying. "I can't believe how blessed I am. If this had happened when I'd been married to Randall . . . I shudder to think."

"Well, we're glad it didn't," he said.

Laura continued to cry as she expressed her gratitude for Alex and Jane, and the way they were so gracious about all of this. Then he heard her saying again that she felt like a burden, and then the words *useless* and *nuisance* came out of her mouth.

"Whoa," he said. "Back up. Erase that and repeat after me. 'I am not a burden to the people who love me.'" She said nothing, and he pressed, "Come on. Say it."

"I am not a burden to the people who love me."

"Very good," he drawled, even though she'd said it with no enthusiasm. "Now say this. 'I am valuable and lovable and I have much to give to the people who love me.'" Again she hesitated, and he insisted, "Say it."

She cleared her throat carefully. "I am . . . valuable and . . ." her voice cracked, "lovable, and I . . . have much to give . . . to the people who love me."

"There, that wasn't so hard."

"Actually, it was."

"It's going to take some practice."

"You're too good to me, Wade."

"No, I'm not too good to you, Laura. I love you. Just say, 'Thank you, Wade, for helping me remember that I am worth the love people give to me.'"

Laura couldn't speak. The words she heard her husband saying made perfect, logical sense with everything she'd learned, but at the moment she felt disoriented and confused. Was she so thoroughly accustomed to believing the opposite of what she'd just said that she couldn't comprehend truly believing anything else? She struggled for composure enough to say, "I need to go. I love you." Then she hung up and cried for nearly an hour, while the ugliness of her past battled with the hope of her future for power over her sanity. She fell asleep praying and woke up doing the same, and with her prayers the hope became more dominant—at least for the moment.

* * * * *

Wade was walking out of an exam room at the ER when he heard over the intercom, "Wade Morrison, line two."

He'd left more than one message with a doctor that Alex needed to consult with and felt sure that was the reason for the call. Since the previous evening's conversation with Laura had ended on a sour note, his concern for Laura had been weighing on him heavily, and he didn't feel at all like talking to anybody, especially not some arrogant cardiologist. The fact that Christmas Eve was the day after tomorrow didn't help any.

He picked up the phone and pushed the button, saying, "This is Wade Morrison."

"This is Wade Morrison's wife," he heard Laura say.

"How delightful," he said. Just hearing her voice made his day better already—especially when she sounded cheerful. "To what do I owe this unexpected pleasure?"

"I was wondering if you could come over as soon as you get off."

"If I get to see you, it might actually make the day worth getting through."

"Good. I'll see you this afternoon then."

"Okay," he said.

"I love you, Wade."

"I love you too, Laura," he said, and ended the call.

As he hung up, he noticed Winona watching him. "Your wife?" she asked.

"Yeah," he said.

"Forgive me if I'm being nosy, but . . . is she the reason you get calls from a crisis facility?" He looked at her sharply, and she added, "I'm not trying to be obnoxious, Wade. I was just wondering if there's anything I can do. You've been very sweet to me. I'd like to know if I can help, and I'm not going to go blabbing anything."

"Thank you, Winona, but there's not much anybody can do . . . except pray."

"I can do that," she said. "In fact, I've met with your missionaries a couple of times."

"Really?" he said.

"They've been teaching me how to pray and stuff like that. It's all good. I'm nearly finished reading that book Alex gave me. I never thought I could like reading scriptures, but I do."

"That's great," Wade said, and couldn't hold back a smile. "Keep me posted on that."

"Okay," she said. "And . . . I'll pray for your wife. It's Laura, right?"

"Right."

"Is she going to be okay?"

"She's doing much better, actually. Thank you. But it's still rough." He sensed her curiosity, but also her desire to be polite and not push too hard. He just hurried to say, "I'm not trying to keep it a secret, Winona. It's just not pleasant to talk about. She had a pretty ugly upbringing, and she struggles with severe depression. When she got serious about wanting to die, I had to get serious about getting her some help. That's all."

"But she's doing better?"

"Yes."

"So . . . Mormons have problems too, eh?"

"They certainly do," he said. "In fact, my life feels like a soap opera sometimes. We're not excluded from life's challenges, by any means. Sometimes I think we might have more challenges, or at least different ones. But I think we know more about getting through them in the best possible way."

Winona smiled, then the phone rang, and she had to answer it. Wade found Alex and told him about Laura's request. A short while later Alex told him that Jane had some errands to run, and she would pick him up after work so that Wade could go see Laura without having to take him home first, since it was in the opposite direction.

"Are you okay?" Alex asked, as he often did.

"Yeah," Wade said without enthusiasm. "I'll just be glad to get my wife back."

"But we're making progress," Alex said. Wade appreciated the way he said *we.*

"Yes," Wade said, "and I'm grateful. But I realized earlier today that we have been separated longer than we were married before this happened." He gave a sardonic chuckle. "So much for being newlyweds."

"Life really stinks sometimes, doesn't it," Alex said, and again Wade was grateful that his brother didn't try to talk him out of his feelings. "But hey, it gives you something to look forward to, right? One of these days the two of you can live like newlyweds all over again."

"Now, that's a pleasant thought," Wade said, and forced himself back to work.

Later that day as Wade drove to the facility, he wondered if this visit would leave him feeling hopeful and positive, or discouraged and weighed down. It was always a gamble, and he couldn't deny being terribly weary of the routine. He thought of the endless weeks that Alex and Jane had practically lived at the hospital while Barrett had been struggling to live. Perhaps that's why they were so eager to help, and so compassionate. In spite of the drastic difference in circumstances, they likely understood how he felt more than most people would.

When he arrived, Wade was told he could go to Laura's room, and he knew the path well. He found her sitting on the bed with her new journal open on her lap, writing in it with a purple pen.

"Hi," she said, and stood up.

"Hi," he said, and watched her put the journal into a suitcase and zip it closed.

His heart quickened before she said, "There are some papers you need to sign before we can go."

"Go?" he echoed, unable to believe it could be true.

She picked up the suitcase and handed it to him as she said, "It looks like I'm out on parole. They're putting me into your care. I hope you know what you're in for."

Wade set the suitcase down and wrapped her in his arms, lifting her off the ground as he let out a burst of laughter and turned in a circle. She laughed as well and said, "You appear to be happy about this."

"I think we need ice cream," he said. "And Chinese food."

"In that order?"

"Maybe. It qualifies more as emotional eating that way." He set her down but didn't let go of her.

"And the emotion of the day would be . . ."

"Just plain happy," he said, and kissed her. "Come on. Let's get out of here."

It only took a few minutes to take care of the paperwork, then Wade laughed again as they walked outside. He held her suitcase in one hand, and her hand in the other. In the car she said, "You know this isn't over, Wade, just because I'm coming home."

"I know," he said. "Hadley has been very clear about that. But we'll work on it together." He kissed her hand and drove to Baskin Robbins, where they picked up a couple of cartons to go, then he called the house to tell Jane not to cook dinner.

"Why not?" she asked.

"We're picking up Chinese for everybody. We're celebrating."

"We are?" She laughed. "Is Laura with you?"

"She is," he said and laughed as well. "She is now officially an outpatient." Wade saw Laura smile.

"Wow, that *is* cause for a celebration. Chinese sounds great. You know what we like. But buy a lot. Cole and the kids are coming over."

"Okay," he said, then a thought occurred to him that left him disconcerted. He'd said nothing to Laura about what was going on with Rochelle. He didn't want to take her home to a situation that might feel bizarre and leave her disoriented. He knew she cared a great deal for Rochelle, but they'd also had some negative encounters in the past. "Is he bringing a date?"

"Yes, I believe he is," Jane said. "He assures me it's not romantic, but I'm not so sure."

"Well, he's a big boy," Wade said. "I'll get plenty. We'll see you in a while."

Wade immediately hit the speed dial on his phone for their favorite Chinese place and made an order for takeout.

"Is who bringing a date?" Laura asked when he'd ended the call.

"Cole will be there with the kids," he said, silently praying for the right words, wishing he didn't feel afraid of shattering Laura's fragile emotional state.

"He's dating?" she asked. "How long has it been? I've lost track."

"A couple of months, I think. But hey," he smiled at her, "I fell in love with you when Elena had been gone six weeks. If he's ready, he's ready. But then . . . he assures us it's not romantic."

"You sound doubtful."

"I think he's in love. I just think he knows that they both need some time. She's going through some pretty traumatic stuff right now herself. So, my bet is they'll be friends until they reach a point where they're ready to move forward, and then . . . I guess we'll see."

Wade didn't know whether to curse or bless her perception when she said, "So, what's wrong? You seem . . . tense. Is there something about this with Cole that makes you uneasy? Or is it something else?"

Wade glanced at Laura, grateful at least for the evidence that she was becoming more like herself. She had once been very perceptive and straightforward, but he'd become accustomed to her being mostly oblivious to what was going on around her. They *were* making progress.

"Okay, you got me," he said. "There's something I need to tell you that's going to seem weird. Something pretty big happened while you were . . . away." He pulled into the parking lot near the Chinese restaurant, but knowing it would be at least another fifteen minutes before the food was ready, he just put the car in Park and turned to face her.

"Something bad?" she asked warily.

"Much more good than bad, I believe. But . . . strange."

"Okay."

"Do you remember when Rochelle came to see you at the facility?"

"Vaguely," she said, her brow furrowed. This obviously wasn't what she'd expected.

"Well, you were pretty bad off at the time. She had left messages for you at the house and was worried, so I called and told her what had happened. She was pretty upset. I suggested she call and talk to Dr. Hadley if she had questions. Well, she just came out here and talked to him face-to-face, and saw you at the same time. She called and wanted to talk to *me.* I met her at the hospital on a break, and we had a good visit, I believe."

"Wait a minute," Laura said, holding up a hand. "Rochelle and you . . . had a good visit? I thought she didn't like you. She certainly made it clear to me that she didn't trust you."

"Yeah, I know," he said, trying to sound light. "But apparently Hadley convinced her that I was a half-decent human being." Laura smiled slightly. So far so good. "Anyway, she told me she hadn't been doing very well. I guess her lifestyle caught up with her."

"I'm not surprised," Laura said.

"And . . . when she found out what was going on with you, it kind of pushed her over the edge."

"What did she do?" Laura demanded, so panicked that Wade had to take her shoulders into his hands and look hard into her eyes.

"She's fine, Laura. Take a deep breath. She's fine."

Laura did as he ordered, fighting to breathe normally. "Okay," she said.

"She did, however, make some pretty drastic changes in her life. I'm sure she can fill you in on the details, but she asked me to catch you up when it was a good time. She hasn't come to see you because . . . well, she said she was afraid she'd only make it harder for you right now, because she's been struggling herself."

"She's still here?"

"She went back to Chicago to make some arrangements. Now she's back. She's moved here."

"Here?" Laura echoed dubiously. "Salt Lake City? The capital of Mormondom? She's scoffed at the very idea of living *here."*

"Well, she's obviously changed her tune. She has an apartment. She's living on some savings for a while. She's seeing Dr. Hadley. And she's going to church. She's also taking steps to work toward getting her membership back in good standing."

Laura stared at Wade for more than a minute, her mouth open, her eyes wide, and he just allowed her to let it sink in. She finally said, "I can't believe it." She let out a sharp chuckle. "I can't believe it." Tears came to her eyes. "I've prayed so hard for her, but . . . I never really dreamed she would . . . come around like this."

"Miracles do happen," Wade said. "Anyway," he added, needing to get to the point, "Alex and Jane invited her over to dinner when she first came here. That's when she met Cole."

Laura let out a noise of disbelief, staring at Wade as if she might find some evidence that he was joking. "Cole is . . . *dating* . . . Rochelle?"

"He tells me they're just friends," Wade said.

"Okay, but . . ."

"But what?" he urged. She hesitated still, and he added, "Just say what you're thinking."

"I don't trust her."

"I think that's understandable. Her history and . . . some of the things she's said to you, are . . . well . . . I've had my concerns, too, but . . . I really think she's sincere, Laura. And Cole needs to take care of himself."

"But does he have any idea the kind of life that she—"

"Actually, he knows everything."

"Everything?"

"That's what he tells me."

Laura sighed loudly. "So . . . Rochelle is going to be there this evening."

"It sounds likely. If you prefer, we could go elsewhere for the evening and—"

"No, it's okay. I want to go home." She took his hand. "She was once one of my best friends. It's just that . . . I haven't felt comfortable with her for a long time. If she really has changed, then . . . I owe her the opportunity for a fresh start."

"I would agree with that," he said. "But if she's said and done things to hurt you, then the trust between you is something that will take time. And that's okay. You can be kind to her, as you always have been, but you don't need to have any deep, personal conversation with her."

"Okay," she said with obvious relief. "While she's there . . . will you stay with me?"

"Every minute if that's what you want," he said, then he smiled. "Like I'd want to be anywhere but with you. We have a lot of time to make up for."

She smiled in return. He kissed her hand, then they went inside and picked up their order.

Chapter Eighteen

Wade laughed out of nowhere as he pulled the car up in front of the house.

"What's funny?"

"Not funny," he said, and kissed Laura quickly. "Just happy." He touched her face. "You have no idea how happy I am just to have you coming home with me . . . to stay. And I pray to God that we never have to be separated again." He kissed her once more and saw tears in her eyes, but he'd come to realize that was the norm lately. Her emotions were fragile and tender, and that was fine. She desperately wanted to live and become healthy. How could he not be grateful?

Wade carried Laura's suitcase and the ice cream into the house, while Laura carried the two sacks of Chinese food. Since there were no other vehicles parked outside, Wade knew Cole hadn't arrived yet. Inside the door they were met immediately by Barrett, who was full of smiles as he first hugged Laura tightly, saying, "Mom said you were coming home. I'm so glad you get to be home for Christmas."

"Me too," Laura said, and smiled at him.

Barrett then hugged Wade as well and said, "You look pretty happy."

"You noticed," Wade chuckled, then he took the sacks from Laura and handed them to Barrett, along with the ice cream. "Would you please take these to the kitchen? We can heat the food up when Cole gets here."

"Sure thing," Barrett said eagerly and walked away.

Wade took Laura by the hand and led her upstairs to the room they would share. He set her suitcase down, then they went to the next room and found Rebecca and Ruthie sitting in the midst of a variety of scattered toys. "Hey there, baby," Wade said, and they both looked up. "Mommy's home," he added, and Rebecca jumped up and ran to Laura.

"Hello, princess," Laura said and knelt down to hug Rebecca tightly. Ruthie followed right behind, wanting in on the action, and Laura hugged her as well. "Oh, they're so sweet," Laura said as they went back to their playing, apparently not interested in too much social interaction at the moment.

"Yes, they are," Wade said, and kissed Laura. "And so are you."

"No, you're the sweet one," she said, and kissed him again. He smiled, and she added, "Maybe I should unpack a bit. I've got to take some medication with dinner and . . ."

"What?" he asked when she hesitated.

"I . . . have some prescriptions we should get filled."

"You need them tonight?" he asked.

"No, tomorrow will be fine, but . . ."

"It's not a problem, Laura. I need to do some errands anyway. We can make an outing of it."

"Okay," she said, and gave a subtle smile.

They went back to their bedroom where Wade sat and watched her unpack, relishing the simple pleasure of watching her put her things away among his own. He recalled the moment when he had haphazardly packed her things to take her to the facility. He'd been scared out of his mind and worried sick, and life since then had been some of the toughest he'd ever lived. But Laura was back with him now, and things were looking up. There was a hovering sense of melancholy around her that occasionally receded with a smile or a little laugh, and he knew she was far from back to normal. But the progress was miraculous, and he was glad to be where they were now, and to have these difficult weeks behind them. He was a little taken aback by the handful of prescription bottles she carried into their private bathroom, but he reminded himself that she was taking them under the supervision of an excellent psychiatrist, and the drugs were helping her. He needed to separate that from the image of the pills she'd once intended to take to end her life. He had to let go of his own fears and remember that both he and Laura were well prepared to never let it get that bad again.

When Laura had her things put away, including the book Hadley had given her, which she set on the bedside table, she sat beside Wade and put her hand into his. "It's nice to be home," she said, "even though . . . it feels a little strange since I've never actually lived here."

"Well, if you can get past the noise of the kids, it's a great place to live."

"Oh, I love kids," she said.

Wade chuckled. "I love kids too, but they're still noisy. I hope you'll be comfortable here."

"I'm sure I'll be fine," she said, and looked carefully around. "What a beautiful room."

"Yes, it is."

"Is this where you always stayed while living here?"

"No, Elena and I shared a different room. After she died, the family moved my things here, and I've pretty much monopolized it ever since."

"We're very blessed," she said, "to have such a good family."

Wade smiled at her, loving the way she'd included herself in that remark. "Yes, we are," he said, and kissed her.

A moment later Barrett appeared in the open doorway and said, "Cole is here, and Mom says we're eating in five minutes."

"Okay, we're coming. Thank you," Wade said.

"I'll get Rebecca and Ruthie," Barrett added, and he left to go get the girls.

"He's such a good kid," Wade said.

Laura put her head on his shoulder. "Remember when you were writing me emails and I only knew you as Barrett's Uncle?"

"But you didn't know I was the same guy you'd met at the clinic."

"Yeah. Romantic, isn't it."

"Yes, I believe it is."

Laura laughed softly. "I was thinking about Barrett the other day, and how sweet he is. And I remembered the letter you wrote that started out with . . . what did you say? Something like . . . you'd resisted the urge to address the letter to Barrett's Aunt. And then I thought, wow, I *am* Barrett's aunt, and I just felt . . . privileged, I guess."

"Yeah, I know what you mean."

"Well, you're related by blood."

"Boy, am I," he chuckled, thinking of the bone marrow they shared.

She smiled and said, "You know what I mean."

"Yes, I know what you mean."

"But . . . I'm related to him by marriage, and I'm just . . . grateful to have married into such a wonderful family."

"Amen," he said. "I mean . . . I'm grateful to be part of such a wonderful family, and even more grateful that you married into it." He stood up with her hand in his, and they started down the stairs. "You okay?" he asked.

"Yeah," she said. "Just a little . . . foggy sometimes."

"You let me know if anything is too much, okay? You don't have to be involved any more than you want to be, okay?"

"Okay," she said. "Thank you."

Laura wondered why she felt so nervous as she approached the kitchen with Wade's hand in hers. Of course, she'd felt much the same way on the one home visit she'd had before, but being with Wade had quickly put her at ease. She heard Cole's voice among others, making it clear that everyone was gathered. Just before they came to the kitchen doorway, she remembered that Rochelle might be with him. She'd honestly forgotten. The same moment she thought of it, Rochelle came into view, and Laura held back, tugging at Wade's hand. "Just . . . give me a minute," she whispered, grateful that she could see Rochelle, but no one had noticed them in the hallway. She couldn't believe what her eyes were telling her! She and Rochelle had grown up together, had been close in one way or another for most of their lives, but the last couple of years she'd become a stranger in many respects, even though they'd stayed in close touch. She'd become false and shallow, wearing too much makeup and jewelry, expensive clothes, and focusing on everything worldly. But there she was, her hair closer to its natural color than Laura had seen on their last several encounters. Her fingernails were her own, and she had very little, if any, makeup on at all. She was wearing jeans and a lavender turtleneck sweater, and no jewelry whatsoever. But equally peculiar was the fact that she was holding little Andrew, Cole's infant son, feeding him a bottle. And she did it so naturally that it was evident this was far from the first time she'd fed the baby. As far as Laura had known, any maternal instincts of Rochelle's had flown out the window along with her values. And Laura was stunned. She stepped back farther into the hall and urged Wade with her.

"You okay?"

"Yes, I just . . . she looks so different. I can't believe it."

"Miracles *do* happen," Wade said with a smile.

"That's the only possible answer. I mean . . . what you told me earlier, I wasn't sure if I could believe it, but . . . just seeing the *visible* changes . . . wow." She shook her head. "I can't believe it," she said again.

"Why don't you go say hello to her?" Wade urged. "She's been very worried about you."

Laura looked up at Wade and found in his eyes all the courage and perspective she needed to turn around and go into the kitchen, after taking a deep breath. Before anyone became aware of their presence, she saw Rochelle handing the baby to Jane, who was insisting that she hadn't seen him for a week and she wanted to burp him.

Barrett noticed Wade and Laura in the doorway and said, "Oh good, we can eat now."

All eyes turned toward them, but it was Rochelle that Laura was watching. As their eyes met, the affirmation deepened. *Her friend was back!* That hard, angry cynicism, that indefinable darkness that had been there for years was now gone. It *was* a miracle.

"Laura!" Rochelle said breathlessly and came to her feet. "You're here." She rushed to meet her, wrapping her in a tight hug, and Laura returned it firmly, starting to cry just before she realized Rochelle was crying too.

"Oh," Rochelle said with an embarrassed chuckle, taking Laura's face into her hands, "you look so much better."

"So do you," Laura said, and laughed softly before they hugged again.

"I didn't know you were going to be here," Rochelle said. "Are you . . ."

"I'm officially released now," she said.

"Which makes this a celebration dinner," Wade interjected.

"Oh, that's so amazing!" Rochelle said. "Come on, let's eat. We can talk later."

"Okay," Laura said, but before she could sit down, she got a hug from everyone in the family, including another one from Barrett. When Cole hugged her she said, "You're looking much better as well."

"I'm coming along," he said. "It's so good to see you."

"And you," she replied.

They were all seated around the table once the girls were put into their high chairs, then Alex offered a beautiful blessing on the food, where he also expressed gratitude for the privilege of being gathered as family and friends, for the healing power of the gospel, and, more specifically, for the joy of having Laura home. She felt so touched and humbled that she had trouble keeping her tears under control as the meal began. Then she focused on how wonderful the Chinese food tasted. She mostly just sat back and took in the conversations and interactions, reminded of how she'd grown to love Alex and Jane and their children very quickly prior to marrying Wade. She loved the atmosphere in their home, and she shouldn't have been surprised to realize how comfortable she felt there already, even if her brain still felt relatively foggy. Laura watched Cole and marveled at how well he seemed to be doing after losing Megan only a couple of months earlier. She had seen the evidence of his grief after it had happened, and she felt so grateful on his behalf to see that he was finding peace. The last time she'd seen him, he'd been wearing a leg brace, and his face had shown stark evidence of the accident he'd been in. Now he had no sign of the trauma, and even his eyes showed hope more than sorrow. And then there was Rochelle. Laura still couldn't believe it. She didn't feel at all uncomfortable with her as she'd expected to. In truth, this was more the Rochelle she had known through most of her life. She felt as if she were with an old friend again, instead of the woman who had seemed to be impersonating her for the last couple of years.

When they were finished eating and the children had all run off to play, Laura stood when Jane did to clear the table. Wade then stood and said, "You relax. I can do this."

"So can I," she said, not realizing how curt it had sounded until she noticed the stunned look on Wade's face. She was grateful the others were talking and hadn't noticed. In a gentler tone, she added, "It's okay. I want to help."

"Okay," he said, and she carried some dishes to the sink where she started rinsing them to go in the dishwasher. Once the kitchen was cleaned up, all of the adults moved to the family room to visit. Again Laura mostly just absorbed it, feeling a little lost in her surroundings, almost as if she were in a dream. She left for a few minutes to take her evening medication and returned to sit close to Wade.

Barrett came to report that he'd gotten Rebecca and Ruthie to bed. After he'd left the room Alex said, "He's trying to chalk up points with Santa Claus, I believe." And the conversation continued. Laura continued to feel amazed with seeing Rochelle this way, and also with the way Cole kept holding her hand and looking at her with a certain warmth in his eyes.

Gradually Laura started feeling sleepy and realized that her body clock was used to going to sleep early, aided by the medication she'd taken. "I need to go to bed," she whispered to Wade.

"Okay," he said and immediately stood up, urging her along. "Laura needs to get some sleep. She's had a big day. We'll see you guys around, I'm sure."

The others all stood up to say goodnight. Cole and Rochelle each hugged Laura again, and Rochelle said, "We'll talk soon."

"Okay," Laura said, and was grateful for the way that Wade efficiently navigated her out of the room and up the stairs. She felt so sleepy that she wasn't sure she could have made it without leaning on him.

"Are you alright?" he asked once they were alone in the bedroom.

"Just . . . sleepy; the medication. Bedtime came early in that place, and . . ."

"It's okay," he said. "Do you need anything?"

"No, I'm fine. If you want to go back down and—"

"I'd rather be with you," he said, "sleepy or not."

Laura found her pajamas, then she felt the need to say, "I'm sorry, Wade, if I . . ."

"What?" he urged.

"In the kitchen. I didn't mean to snap at you. I just . . . I don't want you to treat me like I'm sick or something. I'm perfectly capable of helping in the kitchen, and of taking care of myself."

"I'm sure you are," he said. "I also know the medications make you tired, and . . . I just want you to relax and—"

"I'm fine, Wade," she said, and went into the bathroom.

Wade let out a long sigh and reminded himself that this was not over yet. But she was here, and he was grateful. While he heard water running he recalled Brad once telling him how difficult it had been after his mother had come back after her lengthy affair with his biological father. He'd been so grateful to have her back that he'd called it the parting of the Red Sea in his life, but he said that the weeks, even months, following her return had been immensely difficult. Wade just needed to mark the progress they'd made and be patient. That patience thing again, he thought with chagrin. But all things considered, they were doing relatively well.

He went to check on Rebecca and found her sleeping. When he returned he found the light turned out and Laura in bed. He spent a few minutes in the bathroom, then crawled into bed beside her, breathing in the opportunity to just sleep next to his wife again.

"I love you," he said, and kissed her. "It's so good to have you home."

"I love you too," she replied, her voice slurred with sleep.

He put his arm around her and urged her head to his shoulder where she quickly slept. Wade just held her, listening to her even breathing, and counting his blessings until he finally drifted to sleep himself. He woke up to daylight and distant sounds of Rebecca giggling. He usually came awake to hearing her on the monitor that he kept on the bedside table, but it had been turned off. He hurried into Rebecca's room and just leaned in the doorway to watch Laura sitting on the floor, playing the five little piggies with Rebecca's bare toes. The child was dressed except for her shoes and socks, and her hair had been put into pigtails. Laura was still in her pajamas. Rebecca giggled again, Laura laughed, and Wade said, "Isn't it fun to have Mommy home?"

Laura smiled up at him as Rebecca said, "Mommy do piggy."

"Mommy is very talented," he said firmly, and Laura laughed again as he sat down beside her and kissed her. "Good morning, Mommy."

"Good morning, Daddy," she said warmly.

"How did you sleep?"

"Not bad . . . but I woke up early. I'm either too sleepy to sit up, or I have insomnia. It's never in between."

"I'm sorry," he said.

"I just hope I can eventually get off these drugs and be a normal person again."

"Patience," he chuckled.

"What's funny?"

"I'm just being a hypocrite. I've come to learn through all of this that I am *not* a very patient person, especially when it comes to living without you."

"I'd like to take that as a compliment," she said, and put Rebecca's socks on her little chubby feet.

Laura urged Rebecca to her lap to put on her shoes, and Wade asked, "Do you think you're up to going out with me today? I can bring you home if you get tired."

"Where are you going?" she asked, sounding eager.

"Well, I have a few stupid errands, but . . . the truth is . . . I've been a terrible procrastinator this year." He whispered, "I need to go Christmas shopping. Tomorrow is Christmas Eve, you know?"

"It is?" She actually gasped. "Really?"

"Really," he said.

"I'd completely lost track. Wow. Well, I certainly haven't done any Christmas shopping."

"Great. We're in it together. Do you think you're up to it?"

"It sounds marvelous."

"Barrett's already agreed to tend the little lady, so as soon as we have some breakfast we can be off." He stood up and helped her to her feet, then he pulled her into his arms and kissed her. "Ooh," he muttered, "it's nice to be able to kiss you good morning." He kissed her again, "and goodnight."

"Yes, it is," she agreed.

Wade enjoyed every minute of errands and shopping with Laura. He could easily see signs of a lack of enthusiasm that had once been her trademark, but she still smiled and showed glimmers of excitement as they picked out Christmas gifts for Rebecca, as well as other family members. Wade had done *some* shopping previously, but now he was glad he'd waited so that Laura could be with him. They shared a nice lunch together before they were finished, and he loved just looking at her across the table. When he asked if there was anything else she wanted to get, she said, "I'd like to get something for Sister Williams."

"What an excellent idea," he said, and they found a lovely gift basket that Laura liked very much. When everything else was done, he drove into their old neighborhood, but avoided going past the home they had once lived in. He pulled into Sister Williams' driveway just as Laura said, "How much did you tell her?"

Wade hesitated, hoping his answer wouldn't cause her any grief, but he knew he couldn't be anything but honest. "I told her she saved your life."

Laura sighed loudly and looked the other way. "So . . . she knows where I've been . . . and why."

"She's been writing to you, Laura. Obviously she knows where you've been."

"Of course, but . . . she knows why."

"Yes. I felt like I should tell her. I thought she needed to know that her efforts on your behalf were not meaningless." He took her hand and leaned toward her. "She saved your life, Laura."

Laura turned to look at him, and for a moment he feared that she might be angry with him, or just become upset. She only said with a cracking voice, "She did, didn't she."

Wade lowered his voice and said gently, "It's evident God didn't want you to die that day, Laura, but what if Sister Williams were the kind of woman to brush off promptings? Or what if she had been too timid to act on it, or to be vigilant when you tried to talk her out of coming over?"

Tears spilled down Laura's face before she put her arms tightly around Wade. "I'm so sorry," she whimpered, "for what I did to you that day. I'm . . . I'm . . ." She was crying too hard to speak.

"Just take a deep breath," he murmured. "It's okay."

She took three deep breaths and wiped her face with her hands as she muttered, "I'm so grateful I didn't die, Wade. I have so much to live for."

He smiled and helped dry her tears. "We both do," he said, and kissed her. "How about if we deliver this gift and go home? I hear Jane's got the kids making sugar cookies a little later."

"How marvelous," she said, and laughed softly as she glanced in the mirror to check her appearance. "Okay," she said, "I can't guarantee I won't cry again, but I'm ready."

"Crying's good for you," he said, and got out of the car. He opened Laura's door and helped her out, but she insisted that he carry the gift.

Laura was visibly nervous as they stood on the porch whle he rang the bell. He wondered for a moment if this was a good idea, but he felt sure it was good for her to be facing up to what had happened, as opposed to hiding from people who knew the truth. He reminded himself that it *had* been Laura's idea.

The door came open, and Laura squeezed Wade's hand more tightly.

"Hello," he said as Sister Williams looked at them with astonishment.

"Hello," she said eagerly. "What a wonderful surprise!" Before Wade could say anything more she hugged Laura and said with unabashed pleasure, "Oh, it's *so* good to see you, my dear! How *are* you? I've worried and prayed."

"Yes, I know you have," Laura said. "I wanted to thank you . . . for everything. You've been so kind and . . ." She took the gift basket from Wade and handed it to Sister Williams, who looked stunned, as if she'd not even noticed him holding it. "We just wanted to wish you a merry Christmas."

"Oh, there's no need for gifts," she said, "but . . . oh, it is lovely. Thank you. Won't you come in for a few minutes?"

"Just for a few minutes," Laura said, and they followed her inside. Her home was clean and cozy, and during their brief visit, they learned more about each other, and Sister Williams was thrilled to hear that Laura was doing so well. Laura thanked her again for all of the cards and letters, assuring this sweet woman that they truly had made a difference. Sister Williams got tears in her eyes and insisted it was nothing, and they promised to keep in touch.

They returned to the house to find it filled with the magic of Christmas. A CD playing carols serenaded the making of cookies in the kitchen, while the children chattered excitedly. Wade was pleased to see Laura quickly get into the middle of the project, and she occasionally smiled toward him, warming his heart.

It seemed like it took forever to get the children to bed that evening due to their excitement over tomorrow being Christmas Eve. Alex said facetiously, "Just think how fun it will be *tomorrow* night."

When the house was finally quiet, Wade found Laura in bed but not asleep. He sat on the edge of the bed and pushed her hair back off her face. "How are you?"

"I'm fine," she said. "It's good to be home. I mean . . . I still kind of feel like I'm just visiting, but . . . my home is with you, so I guess I'm home."

"Yes, you certainly are," he said, and kissed her. "Sleep well."

"I love you, Wade."

"I love you too," he whispered, and kissed her again.

The next day was Christmas Eve, and the Christmas festivities were full of fun and anticipation. Together with Laura, Wade wrapped gifts, helped with more baking and cooking projects in the kitchen, and helped keep the kids under control with other fun activities. While Laura was clearly not herself and lacked enthusiasm, she was involved and pleasant, and Wade was simply grateful to just have her with him, living under the same roof.

Christmas morning was a delightful experience, mostly in just watching the children. At one point Wade caught Laura crying, and he asked her quietly what was wrong. She just put her head on his shoulder and murmured, "I'm so grateful that I lived to see this moment."

Wade held her tightly and whispered, "So am I."

Wade was touched by the gift that Jane gave to Laura, which was a scripture that had been written out in beautiful calligraphy and framed. It read, *For God hath not given us the spirit of fear; but of power, and of love, and of a sound mind. 2 Timothy 1:7.*

Laura was clearly pleased with the gift, and equally pleased with the little block of wood that Wade gave to her. Dr. Hadley had given it to him; it was the one she'd carved negative words in, and had then sanded them out. Now Wade had written with a wood burner the words that he hoped she would cling to as she tried to replace those thoughts and images, words he had written on the white board, words that he wanted her to believe. She smiled with tears in her eyes when she realized what it was, and then she hugged him.

That night before they went to bed, he noticed the little block of wood placed strategically on the dresser that they shared. He hoped it would remind her every day of how he saw her and felt about her.

The day after Christmas, Wade decided he would rather have a root canal than go back to work. He couldn't decide if he just didn't *want* to be away from Laura, or if he felt afraid to leave her on her own. Since his shift didn't begin until eleven, he had much of the morning to dread leaving.

While he was helping Rebecca with her breakfast, Alex asked, "What's wrong, little brother? We're not going to a funeral today, you know. It's just work."

Wade sighed and resisted the urge to glare at his brother. It was one of those moments when he both blessed and cursed his perception. While he was grateful to have someone share his burdens, he wasn't necessarily in the mood to talk about it.

When he said nothing, Alex added, "Are you worried about her?"

"I guess I am," he admitted.

"She'll be fine," Jane said, and he realized she was in the room as well.

"You're not *really* concerned that something will go wrong, are you?" Alex asked.

Wade had to ponder that question, and felt some relief in being able to say, "No, I'm not. I just . . ."

"What?" Alex pressed.

Wade sat down now that Rebecca was happily eating a waffle. "I don't know," he said, pushing his hands through his hair. Perhaps talking it out would help him understand what he was feeling and why. "Maybe I'm just . . . thinking too much about the last time I left her alone and went to the hospital."

Alex pulled out a chair and sat to face him. "Okay, well . . . that was a pretty traumatic day. But I think you need to separate the memories from the present situation. She's not despondent and curled up in bed like she was then. She's doing pretty well, all things considered, right?"

"Right," Wade said, and took a deep breath. "Okay."

"And," Alex drawled, "you have to remember that both you and someone else were prompted that day to intervene. If you pray for her protection and stay close to the Spirit—which you do—you have every reason to believe that she'll be fine. Put some trust in the Lord, little brother."

Wade took another deep breath. "Okay, I know you're right. Thank you. I guess I just needed some perspective."

"And I'll keep an eye on her without being too nosy, I promise," Jane said.

"Okay," Wade said again. "And you'll call if—"

"Wade, it's alright," Alex said. "Eat some breakfast."

A few minutes later Laura came to the kitchen. He greeted her with a kiss, and they ate together. She seemed her usual self, mildly melancholy and quiet. While they were the only ones in the room, he asked, "Are you going to be okay today?"

"Of course," she said with a smile, but it seemed slightly forced.

"Don't be afraid to talk to Jane if you need something," he said.

She took his hand and squeezed it, saying with reassurance, "We've been over all of this several times, Wade. I know what to do. I'll be fine."

"Okay," he said, and kissed her. "I'm going to miss you."

"I'm going to miss you too, but you know what? When you get home, I'll be here."

"What a pleasant thought," he said, and kissed her again.

The shift at the ER was busy, but it kept Wade from thinking too much about what Laura might be doing. He called her on his break, and she sounded fine, and Alex reported after he'd talked to Jane that their day at home was going well. He said that Laura had taken complete charge of Rebecca, and had helped with Ruthie some as well. She'd done some laundry, and some reading and writing in her journal, and she had taken a nap when Rebecca did. Jane reported that they'd visited some, even though Laura didn't have much to say. But she didn't seem necessarily down.

When Wade made it home just past eleven-thirty, he truly felt grateful to crawl into bed and find his wife there. She rolled over and greeted him with a kiss, and asked how his day had gone. They talked for a few minutes, then she drifted back to sleep, and Wade did the same.

For the next several weeks, life went on with little change, but thankfully very little drama. Laura seemed to be managing as well as could be expected. She had regular appointments with Dr. Hadley, and occasionally Wade was asked to be present. She completely took charge of caring for Rebecca while Wade was working, and she helped with the child when Wade was home. She took care of their laundry, kept their living space clean and in order, and helped Jane just a little in the kitchen. According to Jane, Laura was pleasant and would do anything Jane asked her to, but she was quiet and reserved, and often just seemed distant or melancholy. She was also tired much of the time, taking naps every day and going to bed early. Wade knew the medications were partially to blame for both her behavior and her fatigue, but it was difficult to tell where the effects of the drugs ended and her own ongoing depression began. The doctor had told Wade that Laura could also be emotionally exhausted, and he said more than once that given some time they would be able to judge more fully how much good the medications were doing and at what rate to continue them. They had evidence that the drugs were working, because she had shown significant improvement in getting beyond her suicidal obsession. Again, Wade felt sure he was being tutored in patience. He kept holding onto the hope that with time Laura would become the woman he'd fallen in love with, but truthfully he missed her. She was present physically, and for all intents and purposes everything was going fine. But how could he not recall those blissful weeks of their early marriage when she had been so full of life, so passionate about everything she did? Now she was passionate about nothing—not even him. The medication and depression had crept into the intimate relationship they shared as well—something that Hadley made clear was also normal and would get better with time. And again Wade was resigned to patience. In some ways he sensed gradual improvement, but for the most part it was too gradual to notice. But he was grateful to have her living under the same roof, sleeping in the same bed, and being an active part of his life, even though he sensed that her own confidence was still very fragile and that she continued to struggle with keeping her thoughts and feelings in a positive vein. But Hadley continued working with her, and Wade and Laura talked about it regularly. She was open with him regarding those thoughts and feelings, and if nothing else, he felt a strong bonding with her in navigating through this, and the emotional connection they'd once shared was ever so slowly becoming stronger.

Chapter Nineteen

A happy note appeared in their lives when Winona let Wade and Alex know that she was being baptized. They all attended the baptism, and Wade felt certain that Brian was also present. He couldn't help feeling grateful to see something so good come out of the tragedy of Brian's death, and he felt sure there were many other good things that had occurred elsewhere and with other people, even if he might never know about them. While he occasionally struggled with grief over losing his brother, the sorrow never lasted long before peace replaced it.

A difficult juncture occurred when Wade's rotation at the ER came to an end. He'd apparently passed with flying colors and was now being assigned to work with a pediatrician who specialized in childhood diseases. This doctor worked with nearly everything *except* cancer, but he spent a lot of time at Primary Children's Medical Center, and the opportunity to work with children felt heaven-sent. Once again Wade couldn't deny divine guidance as he prepared for his career. There were many possibilities he could have ended up with in a rotation assignment, but this one would be closer to his chosen field than anything so far. And he hoped that spending some time at Primary Children's would allow him to meet Alex occasionally for a break and perhaps help wean him from their working together continually. It was difficult for both of them to see such an opportunity come to an end, but Wade felt deeply grateful for all he had learned from Alex as a doctor, and for the months they'd been able to work together, which had also given Wade the blessing of having Alex by his side through some of the most difficult moments of his life.

Cole and his children continued to come around regularly, and Rochelle was often with him. He'd confided to Wade that while he'd not so much as kissed her, he believed more every day she was the woman who could fill the hole Megan had left in his life. They often held hands and sat close together, and Rochelle had become very comfortable with Cole's children. Whenever they were around, she looked out for them every bit as much as Cole did.

The passing of time was clearly healing Cole's broken heart over losing his wife, and the changes in Rochelle were even more evident. Even though she had been excommunicated and could not presently participate actively in certain aspects of Church membership, it was evident that living the gospel had become a priority in her life. And it showed. She had found a new job, which she declared to be in a much better environment than what she'd left in Chicago. And she had a warmth and glow about her that had been absent when Wade had met her.

Rochelle had made a habit of taking Laura to lunch once a week, and Wade was almost as pleased as Laura to see how their friendship was healing. He felt sure that Rochelle's own desire to put her life in order was helping contribute to Laura's desire to be whole again.

It was evident that Jane and Laura were also becoming close. One day, out of the blue, Wade came home to hear from his wife that she'd spent the afternoon pouring her heart out to Jane in a way that she had with very few people in her life. After that day Wade sensed a closeness between them that eased some of his own concerns about Laura. He knew well enough that it was good for a woman to have another woman to confide in that she could trust. And while Laura had renewed her friendship with

Rochelle, they had minimal contact, and Rochelle was involved with a career and her own life. But Jane lived under the same roof, and it was easy to see they had a great deal in common—even beyond being married to brothers. They both loved children and enjoyed sewing and craft projects, among many other things. Laura began spending a great deal of time in the room where her sewing machine had been put, working on a variety of projects that kept her busy and seemed to give her some fulfillment.

Laura hit a rough spot when she was struck with a new layer of grief over Tina's death. Wade knew well enough from personal experience that grief came in phases, and it could hit you out of nowhere. For a couple of days Laura was especially weepy and just needed to talk over and over about Tina's death and how it had affected her. Wade just listened, offered compassion, and prayed that she would find peace.

All the crying and talking seemed to help, and he was grateful. Then it occurred to him that maybe something else might help as well. He went to the garage and dug out the box of Tina's things that he'd found in Laura's basement when he'd cleaned the house out. When he opened the box, he found no hint of a negative aroma. He took out a couple of framed photographs of Laura and Tina, and a little porcelain angel that had been carefully wrapped, which seemed to have significance. He closed up the box and went into the house where he found Laura in the bedroom reading.

"Hi," he said, leaning in the doorway, keeping his hands behind his back.

"Hi," she said back.

"I have something for you, but if you don't like it I can take it back. Or maybe I should say I could *put* it back where I got it."

"Okay," she said warily.

Wade sat on the bed and showed her what he had. She gasped and touched them reverently, then she held them close. "Where did you find these?"

"In a box in your basement," he said. He saw her mind working through the memories, and her expression became distasteful. He briefly told her what he'd done with the contents, and assured her that they no longer had any aroma that would bring back difficult memories. He told her where the *new* box of Tina's belongings was in the garage, and that she could get into it anytime she liked. She hugged him tightly and thanked him, then she set the things out on the dresser and smiled as she gazed at them with nostalgia.

With the passing of time, Wade began to see evidence of Laura's slow and steady progress. She reached a point where she told him she felt a strong desire to get off the medications. He gave her a husband's blessing and felt the same impression, so they met with Dr. Hadley and discussed it. He suggested waiting a few more weeks, and then they would begin a slow tapering off and watch her closely to see how she did. Wade prayed night and day that she *would* be able to live without the medications, or at least manage well enough without them to be able to have a baby without enduring horrible depression in the meantime. She said little about the baby she'd lost, but he saw the way she looked at Cole's baby, or babies they would see at church. And she didn't have to say anything for him to know that her maternal instincts were strong. He thought of how she'd held Rebecca the first time he'd met her, there in the pediatric clinic where she'd chosen to work just so she could work with children and hold babies. And Wade couldn't deny his own desire to have a baby with Laura. Rebecca was easing toward the age of three, and life was moving on. But as always, he reminded himself to be grateful for how far they'd come, to keep perspective, and to be patient. Sometimes he really hated that patience thing.

While Wade found great comfort in Laura's overt desire to be alive—and she'd come so far in dealing with the grief and pain that had been bottled up inside of her—it was evident she continued to struggle with her own confidence in battling the negative messages that were still etched into her mind and spirit. She often made comments that indicated she didn't feel worthy of Wade's love, or that she felt like a burden or useless. Wade would talk her through it and remind her of what was true and right, but he felt concerned for her lack of enthusiasm and her apparent disbelief. Again, he knew it would take time—and patience. But he loved her, and she loved him, and in his heart he knew that between God and the two of them, they would be able to endure whatever this struggle might entail. God had never let him down so far. Wade had no reason to believe that He ever would.

* * * * *

Laura came awake in the dark, orienting herself to the soft sounds of Wade getting ready for work. He'd been leaving very early lately, doing hospital rounds with the doctor on his present rotation. The thought of facing the hours without him felt heavy and terribly unpleasant. He was so easy to be around, and so quick to remind her of what was important, and true, and right. Within herself she knew she needed to have the self-confidence and strength to be whole entirely on her own, that it wasn't healthy to be dependent on anyone else for her strength. But how to accomplish that seemed the overriding question. No matter how hard she tried to will herself to believe that all of the wonderful things he said about her were true, her deepest self stubbornly resisted accepting it. She'd worked hard to fill the book Hadley had given her with positive thoughts and other things that reminded her of her own value and the things she had in her life that were worth living for. But she often looked through the book, feeling as if it belonged to someone else, some kind of alter ego to herself that was radiant and positive and confident. She simply didn't feel capable of being everything that Wade deserved, and everything she secretly longed to be. And while she prayed diligently to be that person, and intellectually she understood the need to replace her negative thoughts and feelings with positive ones, emotionally she kept coming up against a wall.

Wade distracted her from her thoughts when he sat on the edge of the bed and bent to kiss her, as he always did before he left. "I love you," he murmured. "You try to have a good day."

"You too," she said, and touched his face.

"Is there anything you need before I go?" he asked.

"No, I'm fine. Thank you."

He kissed her once more, then headed out of the room.

"Wade," she said, and he hesitated at the door, "I love you too."

He smiled in the glow of the hall light. "Have a great day," he said.

"You too," she said, and he left the room, closing the door behind him.

Laura drifted back to sleep and came awake to the sounds of Rebecca on the monitor that was sitting on the bedside table. While she hated getting out of her comfortable bed, and the temptation to just curl up there for the day was strong, she felt grateful for the incentive to get up, and she loved the way Rebecca could make her smile. Before Laura could get out of bed, Rebecca burst into the room, now having learned how to open doors, one arm loaded with a stack of storybooks.

"Good morning, Your Majesty," Laura said, and Rebecca climbed onto the bed.

"Mommy wead towy," she said, handing one of the books to her.

"Okay, Mommy read story," Laura said, and they snuggled up close together. Watching Rebecca's chubby little hands turning to the first page, she recalled how she'd fallen in love with the child—and her father—through their visits to the clinic where she'd worked. She remembered fantasizing about being involved in their lives; she'd even written about it in her journal. But never had she believed that it would actually come to pass. She reminded herself of how blessed she was, absolutely certain that were it not for Wade she *would* have eventually reached a breaking point in her life and likely would have ended it. Tears came to her eyes as she hugged Rebecca tightly, grateful to be alive, if only to enjoy such a moment as this.

"Mommy wead," Rebecca said impatiently. Laura swallowed her tears and began to read the simple story that was one of the child's favorites.

A few minutes later Ruthie came into the room, seeking out Rebecca. The girls were often searching for each other, very much like twins as they'd been dubbed. Laura had quickly grown to love Alex and Jane's children as well, and she loved seeing the girls together. She was surprised, however, to find that Ruthie was still in her pajamas and wearing her nighttime diaper. They were working on potty training both of the girls, and they were doing very well during the days, but they still wore a diaper at night. But Jane usually would have had Ruthie changed and dressed long before now, and Laura wondered if she was having a bad morning.

While she read stories to the girls, Laura was aware of the sounds of the other children getting ready for school, then the house became quiet and she knew they were off for the day. Still not having seen Jane, she got both of the girls changed and dressed, then they followed her down the stairs for breakfast. Laura opted to stay in her pajamas, as she often did, but she was surprised when she entered the kitchen to see Jane in *her* pajamas. Her sister-in-law was a morning person, generally up and dressed early, and there were now two clues that something wasn't right. Then, before Laura could even get into the kitchen, holding the girls' hands in hers, Jane rushed to the sink and threw up. Laura held back, not wanting to embarrass her, grateful that the girls were quiet. She discreetly saw Jane rinse the sink with the sprayer and run the garbage disposal, then she squirted the sink with a nearby bottle of disinfectant cleaner and rinsed it again, as if it were a well-practiced ritual. The girls became noisy but it was lost in the sound of the disposal and water running.

When the process was apparently done, Jane moved unsteadily to a chair and put her head down, as if she might be lightheaded. Laura stepped into the kitchen and felt compelled to ask, "Are you okay?"

Jane shot her head up, startled as the girls ran into the kitchen. "Oh, you got Ruthie dressed," she said as the child climbed onto her lap. "Thank you."

"It's not a problem," Laura said, and asked again, "are you okay?"

"I'm fine," she said, but Laura thought she looked a little green. A moment later she was at the sink, throwing up again.

"Liar, liar," Laura said, mocking a snotty child.

"Okay, you got me," Jane said as she repeated the ritual of cleaning the sink.

"What's wrong?" Laura repeated as Jane sat down again, this time looking even more ill.

Jane got teary as she admitted, "I've been hoping to keep it a secret."

"What?" Laura asked, alarmed.

"I'm pregnant," Jane said.

"Oh, I see," Laura said. "Well, your secret is safe with me."

"It really doesn't matter," she said. "I mean . . . it's okay if you and Wade know. But . . . we haven't told the kids . . . or anyone else yet."

"So, Alex knows . . . obviously."

"Yes, of course." Jane pushed a hand through her matted hair, and Laura couldn't recall ever seeing her look so unkempt. She was usually so well put together. Now that Laura knew what was going on, she realized that Jane had seemed more tired and less than perky lately, but until now she'd done a great job of disguising her condition.

Laura set to work getting the girls some breakfast. Jane stood up to help, and Laura said, "It's okay, I can do it. Maybe you should go back to bed."

"I'm fine, really. Just . . . a little slow."

Jane opened the fridge to get the milk out, and Laura took her by the arm, guiding her back to the chair, repeating gently, "I can do it. Heaven knows you've done a great deal to take care of *me.*"

"I've done practically nothing to take care of *you*. You take care of yourself just fine."

"Okay, but . . . you took care of Rebecca while I was in the hospital, and . . . you do most of the cooking, and . . . just let me help."

"Okay, you talked me into it," Jane said, and pressed her face to the table. "Not because you owe me anything, because I love cooking and taking care of Rebecca, but because I admit it. I feel horrible. I've never been this sick with a pregnancy before, and for some reason it's really hit me hard today. Maybe I'm getting old."

"Maybe you're just worn out. Maybe you do too much for too many people."

Jane made a scoffing noise but said nothing. She stayed as she was while Laura got the girls situated with some cereal and juice, then Laura insisted, "Go back to bed, Jane. I can handle the girls. I know where to find you if I have a question."

"Okay," Jane said, standing up, "you talked me into it." Then she threw up again in the sink. She did the cleaning ritual, then headed for the door, and Laura added, "You have your cell phone?"

"Yes."

"Take it with you, and you can call the house line if you need anything. I'll keep a cordless set with me."

Jane smiled at her but still looked nauseated. "Thank you. You're a gem."

"Just . . . get some rest. Let me know if you feel like eating anything."

Jane just waved and headed toward the stairs. Laura actually enjoyed her time with the girls, and she cleaned out the fridge and got all the dishes washed and put away as well. She checked on Jane once and found her sleeping, and later she took her some chicken soup she'd made from a can, and crackers, and apple juice.

"Maybe this stuff will go down easy," Laura said, setting the tray on the bed.

"Oh, you're so sweet," Jane said. "I know I need to eat something, but I didn't have the energy to get to the kitchen."

"That's what the phone is for," Laura said, lightly scolding.

Jane just smiled and said, "Thank you. Are the girls—"

"They're being their delightful two-year-old selves. Don't worry; just rest." Jane smiled again, and Laura left the room, adding, "Call me!"

Laura rested herself for a short while during the girls' naps, then she started mixing some cookies, timing it so the other children could help her finish them when they came in from school. She told them their mother wasn't feeling well and to let her rest, and they didn't question the reason. While cookies were baking she checked the children's backpacks and helped them with their schoolwork and reading. After the homework was done and the cookies were baked, Laura assessed the available ingredients and made a large batch of potato cheese soup according to the recipe in Jane's recipe box, along with a green salad. She asked Katharine to set the table and Barrett to watch the little ones while she cleaned up the kitchen, loaded the dishwasher, and washed the items that were too large to fit. When dinner was ready, she sent Barrett up to his mother's room with a tray, and an admonition for her to stay in bed and not worry about a thing. She only hoped that Jane or Alex wouldn't feel that she'd overstepped her bounds in the household with what she'd done. She knew that Wade would be home soon, and then they could all sit down to eat—except for Alex, who wouldn't be home until about seven-thirty.

Wade walked in the door to pleasant aromas and the usual peaceful atmosphere. The distant sounds of children playing indicated contentment and laughter. He stepped into the kitchen, where he usually found Jane working on dinner. Instead he found Laura, towel drying a baking sheet, which she then slid into a cupboard before she noticed him.

"Well, hello, Mrs. Morrison," he said, and she turned to see him.

"Oh, hi," she said, and smiled so brightly that his heart quickened. He hadn't seen her countenance that cheerful since before her ex-husband had triggered the nightmare that had ensued.

"What are you doing?" he asked as he crossed the room to kiss her in greeting.

"I was drying a pan," she said. "Jane's lying down. Dinner's ready. Will you call the kids?"

"Sure," he said, and did just that.

Wade felt intrigued with his wife as they all gathered around the table for supper. It wasn't unusual for her to help with the little ones, and in Jane's absence she was obviously taking more of an active role in seeing that all of the children had what they needed. But there was something different. After the children had all eaten and left the table, he commented, "You seem . . . dare I say . . . happy?"

"Do I?" she asked and let out a little laugh. "I guess I am," she said, and stood up to clear the table.

He helped rinse dishes and put them in the dishwasher, saying, "Is there a reason for that?"

"I don't know," she said. "I hadn't really thought about it till you mentioned it. Maybe something is finally kicking in."

"Maybe," he said, and couldn't resist pausing in his work to kiss her. He impulsively decided to press beyond what had become the normal quick kiss they exchanged several times a day, and instead kissed her in a way that he hoped would express how very much he loved her. She drew back, looking surprised, and he wondered if she would just smile and step away, which also fell into what had become normal. But she smiled and kissed him again while a hint of passion crept into her response. He drew her into his arms and allowed it to go on, relishing her active participation and the tangible evidence that she was not only living, but coming back to life.

"I love you, Laura," he murmured, his lips close to hers.

"I love you too," she said, and touched his bearded face. "You aren't going to start shaving when I go off my medication, are you?" she asked as if she'd be sorely disappointed.

"Do you think I should?" he asked.

"No," she said quickly, then she laughed for no apparent reason. "But I'll still love you if you do."

"Well, that's something," he said, and was prevented from kissing her again when Jane came into the room, wearing her pajamas, looking perhaps worse than he'd ever seen her.

"Thank you *so* much," Jane said, setting a tray of dishes on the table. "For *everything*. Dinner tasted wonderful and I actually kept it down."

"Good, I'm glad," Laura said, "but maybe you should still be in bed. I could have gotten the—"

"I'm fine," Jane said. "I needed to move around."

"What's wrong?" Wade asked, realizing he'd forgotten to ask Laura amidst his pondering over the change in her mood.

He was met with nothing more than quiet. Laura resumed her chore as if she would leave the answer up to Jane. Wade looked at her, and she said quietly, "I'm pregnant, actually. But the kids don't know yet."

"Wow," Wade said, "that's great." He made his enthusiasm sound convincing—and he *was* happy for Jane and Alex. But he couldn't help wondering when he and Laura would be able to have a baby, and he also wondered if Laura had the same thought. "But you don't look so good," he added.

"I've felt terrible, to be truthful. I've been managing . . . but it really hit me hard today. I've never been this sick with a pregnancy. But Laura saved me." Wade glanced toward his wife, noting that she worked more vigorously at rinsing dishes and loading the dishwasher. He looked back to Jane, silently asking for more explanation, and she was eager to give it. "She got Ruthie dressed this morning, watched her all day, made cookies with the kids, waited on me, and cooked supper."

"I'm glad to help," Laura said without looking up. "Whatever you need, just let me know."

"Well, right now I feel pampered and well rested, so I think I'll help the kids with their homework and—"

"Um . . ." Laura stopped and looked toward Jane, perhaps sheepishly, "it's already done. Their backpacks are ready to go for tomorrow."

"Their reading too?" Jane asked, her eyes wide.

"Yeah, we did the reading," Laura said nonchalantly and kept busy while Wade just leaned against the counter, watching her, full of pleasant disbelief. He discreetly met Jane's eyes and knew she shared his sentiment, and he was sure she sensed Laura's need for her not to make too much fuss over it.

"Well, thank you," Jane said. "Since you did all that, you need to let me finish the dishes."

"No, we can manage just fine," Laura insisted. "Wade will help me. Won't you, Wade." It wasn't a question.

"Of course," he said eagerly. "And we'll see that Alex gets some dinner when he comes in."

"Okay," Jane drawled. "Well . . . I guess I'll just go . . . play with the kids or something . . . frivolous."

"What a marvelous idea," Laura said, and Jane left the room.

"Wow," Wade said once they were alone. "Look how amazing you are." She only made a scoffing noise and cleared more dishes off the table.

"It was nothing," she said. "I'm glad to help." Wade sensed that he should follow Jane's example and not make too big a deal of it, so he just took her hand and kissed her again.

Laura smiled, then said, "Are you going to help or not?"

"Yes, I'm helping," he said.

"Good. Put that soup in a bowl that can go in the fridge, and wash the pan."

"Yes, ma'am," he said, and he laughed, reminded of their working together in the kitchen during those early days of their marriage.

When the kitchen was cleaned up they sat together at the table, and he told her about his day while they ate cookies and ice cream. As he talked about working with children, both at the clinic and at Primary Children's, she admitted that she missed working at the pediatric clinic, but she also said that she loved being with Rebecca all day.

"Well, maybe when you get feeling better," he said, "you can do a little of both."

"Maybe," she said, then changed the subject.

They were still sitting there when Alex came in, and Laura stood up to put some soup in the microwave to heat it for him.

"Hey, I can do this," he said once they'd shared greetings and he realized what she was doing. "Thank you, anyway. Where's Jane?"

"With the kids, I believe," Wade said.

"She called and told me that Laura was taking very good care of her; even cooked dinner, I hear."

"That's the rumor," Wade said.

"I'll be right back," Alex said, and went in search of his wife. Wade knew he would never be home more than a minute or two without giving Jane a proper greeting. When he returned, Laura had his meal set out nicely on the table. He thanked her again, and they visited with him while he ate. They heard Ruthie starting to fuss, and Laura stood up to go and check on her. After she'd left the room Alex said, "Wow. Jane said she's covered all the bases today."

"Yeah, and she's *cheerful,"* Wade added.

"Perhaps the timing's good, eh?"

"Perhaps," Wade said. "And you've been holding out on me. Jane let the cat out of the bag." Alex looked alarmed, and Wade added, "She told us why she's not feeling well."

"Yeah, well," Alex said, "needless to say, we're excited to have another baby, but she's never been this sick before. She wanted to hold out telling the kids because they get so anxious, and the waiting seems so long for them, but with her being this sick I don't know that we can keep it a secret. She's been doing pretty well at keeping things up, but when I left this morning I was concerned. Please thank Laura for me."

"I'll do that," Wade said.

After Rebecca had been put down for the night and Laura was sitting in bed, rubbing hand cream carefully into every knuckle of her fingers, Wade passed along Alex's appreciation. She just changed the subject, then kissed him goodnight and went to sleep.

Over the next few days, Jane continued to struggle, and Laura kept the bases covered. She did a major grocery shopping trip, caught up all the laundry, and kept up with the meals and the homework until Alex had some days off and could take over. But the day that Alex started back to work with twelve-hour shifts beginning at two A.M., Jane became especially ill. While Laura got the children off to school and looked after the little ones, she periodically checked on Jane and found her miserable and frequently throwing up. When Alex got home before the children arrived from school, he came to the bedroom where Laura was sitting on the edge of Jane's bed, feeling concerned. Jane looked horrible, but she was also unusually lethargic. When Laura reported how much she'd been throwing up, Alex took one look at his wife and said, "I'm taking her to the hospital.

She's dehydrated, and I'm not messing around with it." He looked at Laura. "Will you be okay with watching the kids?"

"Of course, but . . ."

"But what?" Alex asked, carefully helping Jane to her feet.

Laura just had to say what she was thinking. "Alone?"

"You've been doing it alone quite a lot lately."

"But . . . Jane was *here.*"

"Physically perhaps," Alex said, helping Jane into a bathrobe, then he looked hard at Laura and said, "If something's wrong, just say so."

"I just . . . didn't know if you'd . . . trust me."

"With what?"

"Your children," Laura said, and Alex chuckled.

"You're kidding, right?"

"No," Laura said, reminding herself of the agreement they had to always be completely honest with each other.

"Laura," Alex said firmly, "I am absolutely certain that my home and family are in the best of hands in my absence. I really appreciate everything that you do. I'll call if there's any news."

"Okay," she said, and he helped Jane toward the door. When her weakness and fatigue became alarmingly evident, he just picked her up and carried her down the stairs and out to the garage. Laura stood where she was for a few minutes, wondering why Alex's trust felt so surprising. Then she told herself it was a silly issue and just got busy, knowing the kids would be home soon.

When Wade came home at the usual time, she told him that Alex had taken Jane to the hospital.

Wade said, "I'm sure once they get some IV fluids in her, she'll be fine."

"Yes, I'm sure she will," Laura said.

"So, what's wrong?" he asked.

Laura repeated her conversation with Alex, but Wade looked confused. "Why is this a problem?"

"I don't know," she said. "I was just . . . surprised."

"That he trusts you? Why wouldn't he? *I* do."

She sighed and said, "I guess . . . the problem would be . . . why do I not feel trustworthy?"

"That's a good question," Wade said. "Talk to me," he added, which he always said when he knew she was struggling with negative thoughts and feelings. "Is there a reason you would think you're not trustworthy with the children, or anything else?"

"No," she said. "I'd never do anything to hurt them, or even neglect them. I think that . . . even if I were severely depressed, I believe I could admit that I wasn't up to being in charge before I would ever leave them unattended."

"Okay, so where are the negative feelings coming from?" he asked, much like Dr. Hadley would.

"Habit, probably."

"Okay, so habit is telling you something that's not true. What's the truth?"

"I don't know," she admitted.

"Laura, you are amazing. You've been running a household and taking care of five children."

"Jane does it," she said, as if it were nothing.

"Jane's amazing too. But other than Rebecca, she took the kids on one at a time."

"They're good kids," she said. "Barrett and Katharine are very helpful, and they hardly ever fight and—"

"Laura," he interrupted, "just admit that what you're doing is a good thing, and it's amazing."

She looked doubtful and said, "It's not a big deal, Wade."

"It's a big deal to Alex and Jane. What would they have done? And it's a big deal to me. Do you have any idea what it means to me to have an opportunity to give back to them just a little of what they've done for me and Rebecca? But I'm gone most of the time. *You're* the one who's giving back to them, on my behalf."

"And mine," she said. "They've been very good to me, as well."

"Yes, and it feels good to help them, doesn't it? Admit it. You've been in better spirits than I've seen in a *very* long time."

"Yes, it does feel good. It's nice to feel needed . . . and useful."

"Maybe a while back you might not have been up to this, but clearly you are now, and I think it's a good thing. It's okay for you to admit that you're doing a good thing."

She took a deep breath. "Yes, I suppose it is."

"So, I think you should go write a few thoughts in that little book of yours about all that you've been doing for Jane and how good it's made you feel."

"Okay, I think I will," she said, and smiled.

Jane stayed in the hospital for two days while they attempted to calm down her nausea with medication and get some nutrition into her through an IV line. Alex and Wade both had to work long shifts, and Laura continued to keep the household functioning in their absence. They both pitched in to help when they were around, but Wade continued to be amazed at all she accomplished and how smoothly everything was running. Managing a household was more than a full-time job, but she was handling it well and remaining mostly cheerful, although her exhaustion at night was clearly evident.

After Jane came home she was still down most of the time. The medication that kept the nausea under control made her sleepy, but Alex insisted that was good and that she needed to rest. He formally asked Laura if she was okay with keeping things under control when he had to work. She assured him that she was happy to do it, and he expressed sincere appreciation.

"It's nothing," she insisted. "You know what they say. What goes around, comes around. Where would we be without you?" Before he could answer she informed him that Preston needed a permission slip signed for a school field trip, and the others needed a check for lunch money. Then she hurried away to put in a load of laundry.

While Jane continued to struggle with the effects of her pregnancy, Dr. Hadley started working Laura slowly off of her medication. By the time Jane started feeling better, Laura was medication-free and seemed more like herself than she had since the ordeal had begun. In every logical way she behaved normally, and interacted with others as if nothing in the world were wrong. The personal relationship they shared as husband and wife had regained much of what it had lost. But instinctively Wade knew something wasn't right. He just couldn't quite put a finger on it. He often asked her if something was troubling her, and she insisted that she was fine. He didn't believe she was lying to him; he believed that she wasn't conscious of the problem.

The next time they had a joint session with Dr. Hadley, Wade brought up the issue. The doctor looked hard at Laura and asked, "Could you tell us what you've come to believe about yourself through all of this, Laura?" She hesitated, and he added, "If you stop and really listen to what your thoughts are telling you, what do you hear?" He allowed her some time to contemplate the answer, then her eyes watered and tears spilled. "What is it, Laura?" Hadley asked with all the tenderness of a concerned parent.

"I . . . I . . . look around at my life, and . . . I see how blessed I am, and . . . I just feel . . . so unworthy."

"Unworthy?" the doctor echoed, as if to be sure he'd heard her correctly. "Is there some grievous sin or crime you've committed that we've not discussed? Is there some underlying guilt that's weighing you down that we haven't dealt with?"

Laura thought for a moment. "No, of course not."

"Then . . . let's try to understand why you would feel unworthy. Unworthy of what exactly, Laura?"

"Of . . . everything," she said, her tears continuing.

Dr. Hadley gently reminded Laura of all she had learned about overcoming the false beliefs of her upbringing, about replacing them with the truth. He talked about driving the darkness out of her spirit and replacing it with light. He reminded her of the gospel principle that all good things come from Christ, and that the thoughts and feelings that induced her discouragement and this sense of unworthiness were not from that source. He also reminded her that she had the power within herself to make these changes, but it was up to her to do it. Laura listened, nodded a great deal, and agreed to keep trying. But Wade took her home feeling terribly uneasy about the outcome of the session, and praying very hard that she *would* find the power within herself to overcome this. He was hoping to talk more about it later, but once Rebecca was down for the night, Laura declared exhaustion and went straight to bed and slept quickly. He knew she wasn't on any medications, and he wondered if this was what Dr. Hadley had called emotional exhaustion.

The following morning Wade was glad that he didn't have to go into the clinic until mid-morning since the doctor he was working with had a personal matter to take care of and had no appointments scheduled until then, and another doctor would be seeing to his hospital rounds. Wade had no question that the timing was a blessing when it became evident that Laura had no desire to get out of bed. He had Rebecca dressed and breakfast taken care of while she remained beneath the covers. He repressed the urge to give in to the fear that was immediately triggered, and instead went in the other room to do some serious praying. He pondered what he'd learned, asked for guidance, and felt compelled to call Dr. Hadley. He went down to the study to do it so he wouldn't be overheard, even though he knew he'd probably just have to leave a message. He chalked it up to a small miracle when Hadley was available and Wade was put right through.

"I don't know what else to do," Wade admitted. "Tell me what more I can do to help her know that she *is* worthy of the good things in her life."

"You can't fix it, Wade," Hadley reminded him. "You know what you *can* do; we've discussed it many times. But you can't take responsibility for what's going on inside of her. She's a free agent. You're doing all the right things, but you have to allow her the choice of whether or not she'll take hold of what she's learned and apply it in her life." Hadley went on to remind him of concepts they'd talked about in dealing with such a low. Once he got off the phone, Wade prayed again, then went back to the bedroom and sat on the edge of the bed.

"What's wrong?" he asked gently, pushing her hair back off her face.

"Same old thing," she said.

"Is there anything I can do before I go?" he asked.

"No, I'm fine."

"Don't lie to me," he said. "I would think if you were fine, you would have gotten up by now."

"Okay, I'm sorry. I feel . . . discouraged."

"Do you think staying in bed will make you feel better?"

"Not likely," she admitted.

"Well, that's good, because I've got to go, and I need you to take care of Rebecca." He kept his voice kind but firm.

She looked mildly alarmed, as if she would like any excuse in the world to be able to relinquish the responsibility to someone else. But he stared her down, and she said nothing. "Is that a problem?" he asked.

She hesitated, but said, "No, of course not."

More tenderly he said, "If you need to have a down day, that's fine, Laura. Stay in your pajamas if you want to. Beyond caring for Rebecca, anything else can probably wait a day or two. But don't let it overtake you. Promise me."

Her chin quivered before she said firmly, "I promise."

"Okay," he said with confidence in his voice. "I'll see you later then. I love you." He kissed her quickly and left the room, fighting his own fears and negative feelings all the way down the stairs. He paused for a moment to gauge if he was being guided by the Spirit to do something more, or different, or if he was just giving in to fear. He took a deep breath and knew he was doing the right thing before he went into the kitchen where Jane was looking through a recipe book and Alex, dressed in his scrubs, was drinking some orange juice, obviously soon on his way to work. Wade looked at Jane and simply said, "Whatever you do today, do *not* help with Rebecca. I don't care if you have to fake feeling sick, or whatever it takes, but don't rescue Laura from that responsibility."

"Okay," Jane said, looking a little taken aback. But he knew that both she and Alex understood the principle, because they'd been present in the counseling session where it had been discussed. They all knew that while it was good to offer compassion and support to a person dealing with depression, rescuing them from their responsibilities would only enable them and contribute to their feelings of uselessness.

"Thank you," Wade said. "Call and leave a message if you think there's any reason for concern. Otherwise, I'm going to do my best to give it to God and not think about it until I get home."

"Okay," Jane said again. "I think that sounds like a wise plan."

"Let's hope," Wade said.

"Try to have a good day," Alex said.

"You too," Wade replied and hurried out to the car.

Later that morning he checked his messages and heard Jane's voice saying, "I told Laura I had some errands and I was taking Ruthie. She seemed fine when I left. She was out of bed. Keep smiling. Bye."

On his lunch break Wade called home, as he often did, just to tell Laura he loved her. When he asked how she was doing she told him that she'd had better days, but she and Rebecca were reading lots of stories. He knew that was one of Rebecca's favorite things, and he could hear her chattering in the background. So far so good.

Chapter Twenty

When Wade got home in the early evening, he found Laura still in her pajamas, but she was sitting on the floor in Rebecca's room, playing a haphazard version of Old Maid with her and Ruthie and not seeming terribly down.

"Hi," he said. She looked up and smiled. "How's it going?"

"I'm losing," she said, and he bent to kiss her just before Rebecca jumped into his arms for a hug, and Ruthie followed her example, as she always did.

Wade hugged them and sat on the floor near Laura. "How was your day?" she asked.

"It was tolerable," he said. "And you?"

"The same. I'm afraid I didn't do much beyond taking care of Rebecca."

"That's okay," he said and kissed her again. "Obviously I wasn't here to do it, so I'm grateful."

"You don't have to be grateful for my taking care of her, Wade. I took on the responsibility of being her mother when I married you." She sounded angry, and he wondered why.

Before he could ask, Barrett appeared in the doorway, saying, "Mom said dinner's ready."

"Okay; thanks, buddy. We'll be there in a few minutes. Go ahead and start."

"Do you want me to take the girls?" he asked.

"That would be great—thank you," Wade said, and Barrett

cheerfully urged Ruthie and Rebecca to come with him to the kitchen.

"Why don't you tell me what you're thinking," Wade said once he was alone with Laura.

"I . . . guess I just . . . wish I could be a . . . better mother."

"You're a good mother, Laura."

Her anger became more evident as she said, "I was not even *here* for her *or* you, for weeks!"

"And we both know why," Wade countered, his voice kind but firm. "So, are you going to beat yourself up for what's past and keep holding onto it, or are you going to move on?"

She sighed loudly. "I'm sorry, Wade."

"For what?"

"For . . . everything." She shook her head. "You're so good to me. I'd be nothing without you."

Wade felt an underlying message in her words and knew he was being guided when thoughts flowed into his mind, and he hurried to speak them. "You don't need me in order to feel worthy, Laura, or lovable. What if I were a jerk? Would that have any reflection on you? Maybe I *am* a jerk; I don't know."

"You're not a jerk."

"Well, I try not to be. But I'm human, Laura. I'm not perfect. I'm not always going to say or do the right things. I try, but you have to find the strength inside yourself to know that in spite of what anyone else says or does, you are worthy of God's love and His every blessing. You're worthy of His love simply because you are His child; no conditions attached. And you're worthy of His blessings because you've made the choice to live a righteous life. But you can't rely on me for those answers. What if something happened to me? What if you were on your own? This is between you and God. You do *not* need another person to make you happy and whole. Do you hear what I'm saying?"

"But you *do* make me happy, Wade. Having you in my life is the best thing that's ever happened to me."

"Laura." He took her hand. "Being together allows us to contribute to each other's happiness, but I can't *make* you happy. Do you understand the difference?" She nodded but didn't comment. He could only hope that something of what he'd said would penetrate her spirit and start to make sense where it really mattered.

Wade touched her chin and tilted her face upward to look into her eyes. "Laura, why are you so unhappy right now?"

"I don't know, Wade. I've been trying to figure it out. I really have."

He didn't want to, but suggested it anyway, "Maybe you need to go back on the medication."

"No!" she insisted, then said more softly, "I hate the drugs. I really don't want to do that."

"Okay. I don't really want you to, but we may have to accept that it's necessary. Maybe we should at least give it some thought—and prayer."

"I'm not sure I even know how to feel the answer to a prayer, Wade," she said.

"Is it just me, or have you forgotten how to say *anything* positive whatsoever?"

She hung her head and sighed dejectedly. Wade sensed an overload in the conversation and simply said, "Let's go have some dinner, and we'll talk later."

"Okay," she said, and he helped her to her feet.

Laura didn't say much during the meal, but she did seem a little more cheerful. When they were done eating he got up to help load the dishwasher, and she washed up Rebecca, then started helping him. Later that evening, after he'd bathed Rebecca and put her to bed, he purposely sat down, facing Laura directly, and took both her hands in his.

"Talk to me," he said.

"It's just the same old thing, Wade. And I don't know how to fix it. But . . . I want you to know that . . . I'm working on it. I did some reading today, and I'm trying. I'm not feeling even remotely suicidal, and I don't want you to worry."

Wade allowed her words to sink in, along with everything Hadley had reminded him of this morning. He told himself to trust in God, have some faith in Laura, and let go of his fears. "Okay," he said. "Just . . . promise me you'll talk to me if it starts to get worse . . . even a little bit."

"I promise," she said, and kissed him.

Over the next several days, Laura got out of bed and did everything she normally did to care for Rebecca and contribute to the household. But Wade sensed that she was down, and he felt concerned. Still, he often found her rereading articles that Hadley had given her, and also reading in the journal she'd been given where she'd recorded many positive thoughts. She was listening to uplifting music and often reading the scriptures. He knew she really was trying, and he let her know how much he appreciated it. He told her regularly how much he loved her and all that she meant to him. He only wished that she could fully believe it. Through his own prayer and introspection, he knew that the biggest problem was the need to alter her deepest core beliefs. Instinctively he believed that for Laura, medication wasn't the answer. In fact, he felt strongly she should avoid medications from this point on. If it was necessary, then he knew they would take it on the best they could. But she'd been on the drugs long enough to even out what the severe depression had done to her brain chemicals, and the present situation was not chemical; it was based in her emotional beliefs. He just didn't know how to change those beliefs. Knowing that he couldn't fix it—as Hadley had told him—he just prayed very hard for her and did his best to take it one day at a time.

Wade was pleased one evening when his father called to see if they could meet for lunch the following day. Neil made a habit of an occasional lunch with Wade, just to keep in touch and catch up. And for Wade it was always a pleasure to spend time with his father. They made arrangements to meet at a place not far from the clinic where Wade was working so that they could visit as long as possible during the time Wade had off. Once they were seated across from each other, Neil's first question was, "So, how is Laura doing? She's been on my mind a great deal lately."

Wade told his father about the present situation, expressing his concerns and frustrations. He was grateful for the understanding he had with Laura that it was alright to discuss their challenges with close family members within reasonable parameters, so that he knew he wasn't breaking any confidence with her. Neil just listened and offered compassion, assuring Wade that he was doing all that he could, then the conversation went on to other things. They talked about Rebecca, and Wade's sisters who lived out of state, and Wade's present rotation, among other things.

The following day Neil called again to ask if he and Roxanne could take Wade and Laura out to dinner.

"That would be great," Wade said. "Why?"

"Why what?"

"Why dinner? We just had lunch." Wade recalled many times when Neil and Roxanne had taken both Alex and Wade and their wives to dinner, but he couldn't recall ever being singled out this way.

"I thought it would be nice to get out with our wives," Neil said, "and I think that you and Laura could use an evening out. I've already asked Alex if they would watch Rebecca. What do you say?"

The fact that Neil had talked to Alex left Wade wondering if there was some kind of conspiracy here. It wouldn't be the first time that Neil or Roxanne had maneuvered a situation in order to try and help solve a problem. And since Neil had been alerted to the problem the previous day, the timing made Wade suspicious, but not necessarily concerned. Neil and Roxanne were sensitive, caring, and wise people. He felt sure that whatever Neil's motives were, the offer was genuine, and their efforts certainly couldn't hurt. "It should be fine," Wade said. "I'll check with Laura and get back to you."

Laura was a bit hesitant, but Wade reminded her that it was good to get out even if she didn't feel like it, and she agreed. Wade called his father back and said they would love to go out.

On the specified day, Wade arrived home late in the afternoon, glad to be getting there a little early so he could freshen up and spend a little time with Rebecca before Neil and Roxanne came to pick them up. When he entered the bedroom he was startled to hear sounds coming from the bathroom that indicated that Laura was sick to her stomach. He heard the toilet flush and water running, and a moment later she opened the door, startled to see him there.

"What's wrong?" he asked, deferring any other greeting.

She looked almost guilty, and he wondered what she wasn't telling him. He reminded himself not to jump to conclusions just before she said, "This isn't exactly how I'd imagined this moment to go."

"What do you mean?" he asked, and she lifted her eyes to meet his.

Something sparkled in them as she said, "I'm pregnant."

Wade took a sharp breath, then a one-syllable laugh came out of his mouth. "Are you sure?" he asked. "How long have you known?"

"One question at a time," she said, and sat down on the edge of the bed as if she felt a little woozy. "I did a test, and that was about three hours ago. I didn't even suspect until I woke up feeling sick this morning. Jane picked up the test for me, so she already knows. But she said she would let you tell Alex."

Wade sat down as well. "But . . . how can this be?"

"Surely I don't need to explain," she said with a teasing smirk that was more like herself than he'd seen in days.

He chuckled and said, "I mean . . . well . . . forgive me for stating the obvious, but . . . we've been trying to prevent this until we knew you could manage without the medication."

She shrugged. "Obviously it didn't work. Provided I don't miscarry again, I would have to assume that it's the right time for this child to come."

Wade scooted closer and wrapped her in his arms. "Oh, Laura." He took her face into his hands and looked into her eyes. "Tell me how you feel about this."

She gave a subtle smile. "I don't think I need to ask how *you* feel. I haven't seen you smile like that in a long time."

He chuckled. "Okay, so . . . I'm ecstatic. What can I say? And you? But don't give me a peer-pressure answer. Tell me how you really feel."

"Nothing could make me happier than to have your baby, Wade." Tears came to her eyes. "Losing the last one was hard."

"I know it was."

"I just hope that . . ."

"That what?"

"That . . . I can be a good mother and . . ." Her words faded.

"Laura, you are already a wonderful mother. Everything's going to be okay."

She nodded and hugged him tightly.

"Are you feeling up to going out?"

"Yes, I'm fine," she said. "Jane gave me one of the pills she took for nausea earlier in her pregnancy. She asked Alex, and he said it would be okay. It should be kicking in soon."

"Okay," he said, and kissed her. "I love you, Laura. I love you more every day."

"I love you too, Wade," she said, and touched his face.

A short while later when they were ready and waiting for Neil and Roxanne to arrive, Laura said, "Oh, Hadley called this afternoon to check on me."

Wade knew that was standard a couple of times a week. "And what did you tell him?"

"I told him I was still struggling with the same stuff, but I was working on it. And I told him I was pregnant."

"And what did *he* say?"

"He said that could explain part of the problem. He said my hormones could be out of whack with the pregnancy, and it could be the cause for feeling more tired and down. I think it could explain why it's felt a little worse the last couple of weeks, but I think there's more to it than that."

"I would agree," Wade said.

"He also said that I was probably inspired to get off the medications and stay off. Maybe he's right."

"Maybe he is."

"He said to take good care of myself and let him know if I felt worse at all."

"Okay," Wade said, and kissed her hand. "I agree with that, too."

A minute later Wade's cell phone rang. It was Neil calling to say they were in some bad traffic, and they wondered if Wade and Laura could just meet them at the restaurant, which would save time. In the car, Laura was especially quiet and Wade asked, "What are you thinking?"

She sighed loudly. "I'm really trying to figure this out, Wade. I don't want to feel this way."

"That's good . . . that you're trying, I mean."

"I don't know. Maybe I could feel like a valuable human being if I hadn't been brought into the world under such deplorable circumstances."

Wade felt something prickle inside of him before he consciously internalized what such a statement meant to him. He tried not to sound terse as he asked, "So . . . are you saying that a person's value is measured according to the situation they're born into?"

"Maybe." She sighed again. "I mean . . . why would God send me into this world into a situation that just feels so . . . tainted?"

Wade knew she was referring to the fact that her mother was an alcoholic, and her parents had a horrendously dysfunctional marriage. But how could he not take what she'd just said and personalize it? Maybe, if nothing else, it was the means to make a point.

"So, I assume, if you believe what you just said, that you consider me to be a human being of no value."

She turned toward him, alarmed. "No, of course not."

"But I came into the world in a situation that was clearly tainted. Would you not say that being conceived in sin is classified as deplorable circumstances? In theory you just reduced my existence to something completely base and negative."

"That's not what I meant," she insisted.

"Oh, but you did," he said, trying to sound insulted if only for the sake of impact. She started to cry, and he hoped he wasn't overdoing it. He hurried to say, his voice more gentle, "Why is it different for you than for me, Laura? Do you think I'm a valuable human being?"

"Of course," she said, and sniffled. "Your parents are wonderful people and—"

"My parents have *become* wonderful people, and I'm grateful for that. And just for the sake of clarification, there was a time when I believed exactly what you just said. That's why I tried to end my own life. I truly thought that my existence was completely base and negative. But I lived long enough to realize that it doesn't matter how I was conceived, or into what circumstances I was born. God is no respecter of persons, and His love for me is unconditional, regardless. It doesn't matter how a child comes into this world, that child still has equal value in God's eyes. He sent you into a situation that He knew you had the strength to rise above, and He knew that your triumph over your struggles could be a strength and an example to other people." She looked thoughtful, and he repeated, "Why is it different for you than for me? Why can you not look at yourself in the mirror and see a woman of great value?"

He took her hand while she pressed a tissue beneath her nose with the other. "You know, Laura, we're cautioned against judging others unfairly. But I wonder how your Father in Heaven feels when you judge yourself so unfairly. You are His daughter, Laura, His creation. Would you belittle God's power and judgment that way?"

She said nothing, but she looked stunned, as if the idea had penetrated deep in her. Wade let the silence stand until they had arrived at the restaurant. "Are you okay?" he asked.

"I'm fine," she said before he opened his door, then she took hold of his arm to stop him from getting out. "Forgive me. I did not mean to imply that you . . . were anything less than the incredible person you are."

Wade kissed her quickly and said, "The theory works both ways, Laura. One of these days you're going to have to admit that *you* are an incredible person. No matter who you were born to, how you were raised, or what kind of garbage life has dealt you, *you* are an incredible person. So get used to it."

He got out and went around to open her door. When she stepped out of the car she wrapped her arms around him, hugging him tightly. "I love you, Wade."

"I love you too, Laura," he said, returning her embrace. Then he took her hand and walked toward the restaurant. "Come on," he said, "I bet that baby's hungry. I know I am."

Laura laughed softly, and they went inside to find that Neil and Roxanne had already been seated. They stood to greet Wade and Laura with tight hugs, then they were all seated in a booth, with the two couples facing each other. After they had ordered their meals, Neil looked directly at Laura and said, "I asked

Wade the other day how you were doing, and he told me a little bit of what's been bothering you. I hope that's okay."

"Of course," she said, but she seemed uncomfortable. Wade sensed it was more being the center of attention as opposed to caring that he knew about her struggles.

"There's something I haven't been able to stop thinking about since then; something about myself. I really feel like I'm supposed to share it with you—if that's okay."

"Of course," she said again. "But you didn't have to take us out to dinner just to tell me something."

"Oh, that's just an excuse. We all needed to get out anyway. So, I'll just say what I need to say, and then we'll enjoy a nice meal together."

"Okay," she said, and took hold of Wade's hand beneath the table.

"I'm certain you must know something about my past," Neil said. "You can't know that I'm Wade's father without knowing that I made some less than admirable choices in my life. I don't know how much Wade has told you about my reasons, so you'll have to forgive me if I'm repeating something you're already aware of, but I would like to make a point." His gaze intensified on Laura as he said with compassion, "I'm thinking that perhaps you and I have a great deal in common, my dear. You see, the home I grew up in was abominable. I'm not going to share any details of that, because I came to terms with it a long time ago, and it's just not something that needs to be talked about. Just let me say that the attitudes I was raised with were grossly distorted, and my perception of myself in coming out of such a home was much the same. I tried very hard to rise above all of that and make something valuable of my life. I worked hard to get an education and to find avenues to be successful in my career. When I married Ruth I believed that my problems were solved, and my life was good. We were happy and had three beautiful children, the youngest of which is Alex. Now, I didn't realize it at the time, but during those years something ugly was festering inside of me, and eventually it drove me away from my family and lured me to do something that in my conscious mind I never would have thought myself capable of doing."

He took a deep breath and leaned a little closer to Laura as he went on. "With Wade's mother, her reasons for leaving the marriage were . . . well . . . it wasn't a good marriage. At the time, he treated her very badly and wouldn't give in to her pleas to make some effort to change. I'm sure you knew all of that. They've come far beyond that now, and Brad and Marilyn are wonderful people. But in *my* case, the only thing Ruth did to drive me away was to treat me far too well."

"I don't understand," Laura said when Neil paused.

He intensified his gaze on her and said firmly, "I didn't feel worthy of her love, Laura." Wade discreetly took a sharp breath at the same moment he felt Laura's hand tremble in his. He knew this story; he knew it very well. But in the present context it pierced his heart.

Neil continued with an austerity that offered a glimpse into the gut-wrenching heartache he'd gone through as a result of his past mistakes. "I *sabotaged* our relationship, Laura, because I had nothing inside of myself that could believe I deserved how very blessed I was. So I left her and the kids, made choices that hurt myself and everyone I loved, finally hit absolute rock bottom, tried to end my own life, and spent months in therapy before I finally understood. But even in understanding, I realized quickly that it's no small thing to take a lifetime of thinking and alter it. Such a project is somewhere in the realms of digging the Panama Canal, I think. But it's *possible*. Don't do what I did, Laura. Don't throw away a good life just because the negative voices inside of you tell you that you don't deserve it."

"How?" Laura asked, her voice cracking. "How is it possible?"

"Well, the important thing to remember is . . ." He stopped when salads and bread were brought to the table, along with their beverages. Once everything was settled and the server had left, Laura looked at him expectantly. Wade was pleased to see affirmation that she was truly *hearing* his father's message. Perhaps the timing was right for his wisdom to be absorbed.

"What's the important thing to remember?" she asked when Neil didn't speak.

Neil looked thoughtful, then said, "Let's go at it this way. There's a battle taking place here, Laura, and it's real. We talk about the war in heaven, the plan of salvation, the temptations of evil that we're up against, but sometimes I don't think we stop to consider how real and powerful those influences can be. The battle taking place here and now is for our souls, Laura. We need to understand the opponent in order to conquer him. Satan and his followers are very good at what they do. I believe they know our every weakness, our flaws, our experiences—and they use them against us. I learned a great deal about this by reading second Nephi, chapter four, over and over. Nephi talks about being weighed down by sins and temptations, but he was a prophet of God. I don't think he's talking about what we commonly look at as sin and temptation. I think he's talking about his own discouragement. But the answers to countering it are very clear. He says, 'Nevertheless, I know in whom I have trusted.' And that's one of the essential keys. Who are you going to trust?"

Neil took a bite of his salad as if to give her a moment to think about it. She countered, "What do you mean?"

"Well, I see it this way. Someone shared this with me once, and it stuck. Fear is a belief in something you can't see, and faith is a belief in something you can't see. If you have fear, you're giving your power to Satan. If you have faith, you're giving your power to God. When you hear voices and thoughts in your head, which ones do you listen to? Which will you choose to follow? Who will you trust?"

A couple of minutes passed while they ate, and Laura's expression indicated she was letting his words sink in. She then said, "So . . . are you saying that my thoughts are controlled by one or the other? All the time?"

Neil smiled at her. "I certainly don't have all the answers. I can only tell you my own personal experiences combined with what I believe the gospel teaches us. Obviously your thoughts are your own, as are your memories. But the Holy Ghost *will* speak to you through your thoughts, and Satan will do the same. They both work very subtly, and you have to learn to discern the difference."

"*How* do I discern the difference? It just . . . feels like there's . . . so much noise in my head so much of the time. How do I sort it out?"

"Now, remember," Neil said, "I said that it wasn't easy, but it's possible. And the more you practice, the easier it will become. The answer is simple, but not necessarily easy. And the answer comes from the scriptures, my dear. Every good things comes from Christ. If a thought does not encourage something good, it is not from Christ. Simple as that."

Again Laura took a couple of bites and looked thoughtful. Wade assimilated the concept as well, wanting to be able to do everything he could to help her get beyond this.

"Okay," she said as if she meant to argue his point, "but . . . my conscience is there to keep me humble and mindful of my weaknesses, right?"

Wade heard the words and thought they sounded reasonable, while something about them didn't feel right. His heart actually quickened when he saw his father lean over the table, and his eyes took on a piercing quality. "Laura," he said with gentle intensity, "your conscience is the light of Christ. It is there to help you become a better person. If there is something out of order in your life, then it will show you your guilt and guide you to making things right. If your thoughts are not inspiring you to become a better person, to be happy, to feel joy, then it is *not* your conscience." His gaze became even more intense as he added, "Do not allow Satan to disguise his voice as your conscience. He will only tempt you to belittle yourself, to focus on your weaknesses and mistakes in order to weigh you down with them and hold you back. Laura," he took her hand across the table, "he knows your weaknesses and he will use them against you. But *you* have the power to fight back. *You* are more powerful than he is, because you have the knowledge that puts you in partnership with God in combating his influence. God is on your side, and in the name of Christ you are capable of brushing Satan's influence aside as if he were nothing more than a pesky fly." His voice broke with emotion as he went on. "I have felt Satan's influence in my mind many times to the point that I felt utterly helpless and on the brink of destruction. And I have felt it flee in haste and become replaced by light and understanding. The only thing you really need to understand, Laura, is that the power is within you—as you rely on the power of the priesthood and your knowledge of the Savior's power over the adversary—to fight this battle and win. Hour by hour, day by day, line upon line, one thought at a time. Just ask yourself, 'Is this thought doing me any good? Is it helping me feel better? Become better?' If the answer is no, then get rid of it. Replace it with a positive alternative. Use the concept of opposition in all things to your benefit. Replace the dark with light, the negative with positive. If the thought comes that you're a failure, push it aside and tell yourself something you've succeeded at. If you think you're not lovable, remind yourself of all the people who love you. And if it's just a mass of negative thoughts and feelings that make no sense, remember that you are in charge of you, and make it clear who you trust. 'Get thee hence, Satan.' It's not just a great line from a great story, Laura. It's instruction! So use it. Don't be afraid to ask for a priesthood blessing, and don't be afraid to call on the light and power of Christ that are within yourself." He leaned back and sighed. "Forgive me if I'm sounding overvigilant here, but . . ."

"No," Laura said, and dabbed at her eyes with her napkin, "I think it's exactly what I needed to hear. I'm certain you were inspired." She sniffled, and Wade put his arm around her. Roxanne smiled at her husband with tears in her eyes as well. Her love and respect for him were readily evident.

"Does it ever get better, easier?" Laura asked.

"Yes," Neil said easily. "With time and practice, it certainly does. But enduring to the end is part of this life's purpose. I'd be lying if I said it had ceased being a challenge for me. There are still times when Roxanne has to remind me of who I am and what's important and true. Sometimes my children help keep me on track." He tossed Wade a tender smile and said, "There was a day when I thought I would drown in the despair of my own poor choices, and it was Alex who talked some sense into me and gave me a priesthood blessing and sat beside me in the temple, the combination of which got me back on track."

Wade felt curious but didn't know if he should ask. Neil seemed to pick up on this and said, "That was the day I found out that you existed, Wade. It was shocking how quickly Satan moved in to remind me of my every shortcoming, of everything I'd ever done wrong throughout my entire life. But Alex reminded me that once repentance was complete, there was no need for me to burden myself with those things. And he was right. Even when we make mistakes and commit sin, we repent, we give it to God, and then we need to forgive ourselves and keep moving forward instead of wallowing in past issues that will only hold us back in our eternal progression."

Again silence prevailed except for some small talk while they finished up their salads, then their table was cleared and they waited for the main course. Neil then said to Laura, "Forgive me if I'm being too overbearing here, but . . . I just have to say that there's no shame in relying on medication if you need it. I've gotten beyond that now, but I never would have survived without it. We need to remember that God inspired the creation of these things to help His children deal with some of the challenges they face in this life, and some people just have to rely on those things throughout their *whole* life. And that's okay."

"I'm actually off all the medication now, and . . . I've wondered if I should go back on it. We've talked about it, but we both felt like it wasn't right. Instinctively I believe that I'm capable of fixing this, that it's more situational than chemical. I've just wondered what I was missing. I think you've just answered that question."

"Well, I hope it helps," Neil said. "And I'm glad to hear that maybe I wasn't too far off base in thinking I needed to share those things with you."

"Not at all," Laura said. "I'm grateful and . . ." She got teary again.

"What is it?" Neil asked.

"It's just that . . . I love my father . . . because he's my father. But he was never the kind of person I could rely on, or turn to for advice. I'm just . . . grateful now . . . to have a father like you."

Neil gave her an emotional smile, then took her hand and kissed it. "You are precious, Laura, my dear. And we are all grateful to have you as part of the family."

She chuckled without humor and looked down. "Now, when I hear things like that . . . I have to admit that my thoughts turn to wondering how that could be true when I've been such a mess, and—"

"Laura," Neil said, "we all have low points in life. We all have challenges. The purpose of life is to help each other get through those times. Your challenges do not make you unworthy of *any* blessing in your life." Neil motioned toward

Wade. "Look at him." Laura turned to meet his eyes. "Do you see how much he loves you? You have been the light in his life since the day he discovered that you really were available." Neil chuckled. "How could we not love you, simply for the love you give to him?"

"It's true," Wade said, holding her gaze. "You *are* the light in my life."

"I think I'm starting to really believe that," she said, wiping at new tears.

"Good," Wade said, "you just keep believing, Mrs. Morrison, and we'll get through this."

Their main entrees were brought to the table, and the mood lightened with casual conversation. Wade sensed that Laura actually *felt* more light and cheery than she had for a long while. At a lull in the conversation, he whispered to Laura, "Is it okay if we let the cat out of the bag?" She just smiled and nodded. Wade looked across the table and said, "We think there's more than one reason that we felt Laura shouldn't go back on the medication. Of course, we're hoping she doesn't need it anymore at all, but . . . either way, she won't be taking any for at least nine months."

Neil and Roxanne both looked momentarily expectant, as if they sensed Wade was trying to imply a deeper message. Then enlightenment filled their faces in the same moment. Roxanne chuckled and asked, "Are you saying what it sounds like you're saying?"

"If it sounds like I'm saying that we're expecting a baby, then that's what I'm saying."

"That's wonderful!" Neil laughed. "We'd better order dessert, too. We're celebrating."

The remainder of the meal was filled with pleasant conversation, while Laura participated and seemed happy. When the ladies when to the restroom, Wade said to his father, "Thank you. I'm absolutely certain you were inspired."

"Hey," Neil said humbly, "if my grief can save her even a little bit of grief, I'm only too glad to help. She's a wonderful woman."

"Yes, she is," Wade said firmly. "And one of these days, I believe she'll come to accept that."

When they were finished with their meals, Neil insisted they all get dessert to go along with the containers that held their leftovers. Outside the restaurant they all exchanged hugs. Neil and Roxanne congratulated them once again on their forthcoming arrival, and Wade and Laura each thanked them for their love and support. Wade felt especially touched when Laura hugged his father and said, "You're the best dad a girl could ask for. Thank you."

Neil smiled and kissed her cheek, saying, "And no father could ask for a sweeter daughter. You take care now, and remember what I said."

"I will," she said.

"If you need a pep talk, or a shoulder to cry on any time, you know my number. I mean it."

"Okay," Laura said.

They started to walk in opposite directions, then Neil turned and said, "Oh, one more thing." They all walked back a few steps to face each other again. Neil gave Laura one of those penetrating gazes and said, "I can't believe I forgot the most important thing of all. The Atonement makes up for everything, Laura. Wherever or however we might fall short, after the best that we can do, it's there to fully compensate. Ironically, it's the only thing that can truly make us worthy in spite of all our human weaknesses and imperfections, and that's why it's the very thing that Satan will try to convince you that you are unworthy of. But you're entitled to that gift, and you need to ask for it and claim it in your life. You must remember that God loves you unconditionally, Laura. You don't have to be *worthy* of His love. It's just there. We can talk more about that—or anything else—later if you want."

"Okay," she said, and kissed his cheek. "Thank you."

The drive home was mostly silent until Laura said, "Do you think Alex would help you give me a blessing?"

"I'm certain he would," Wade said.

"Okay. I think that might help give me a fresh start, and then I'm really going to try to do what he said, Wade. I could feel the truth in it, and that alone makes me realize that maybe I'm not past feeling, that the Spirit really is close to me."

"I'm certain it is."

"And what your father said . . . it all goes right along with everything Hadley taught me. But . . . maybe just hearing it put in different words, or . . ."

"Or the personal experience behind it?" Wade guessed.

"Yeah, I guess that's it. To know that he's actually risen above the same kind of things I've been through . . . and to see how amazing he is . . . it gives me hope."

Wade took her hand and kissed it. "I love you, Laura Morrison."

"And I love you. Thank you . . . for not giving up on me."

"Never," he said, and kissed her hand again.

Wade and Alex gave Laura a blessing that simply reaffirmed very strongly the concepts she had been taught. She was reminded of her value in God's eyes and admonished to hold fast to the knowledge and power that were at her disposal through the gospel. She was also told to rely on the love and support of those around her in difficult moments, and to press forward with diligence in replacing the darkness within herself with light and a perfect brightness of hope.

News spread quickly that Laura was expecting, and everyone was thrilled. Since she didn't feel well, she made it clear she had no desire to try to keep it a secret. Wade hoped and prayed that she wouldn't miscarry again, and that the things she had recently learned would make a difference in her emotional healing.

A few days after their dinner out with Neil and Roxanne, Laura asked Wade if they could go to the temple. They'd been there many times since she'd come back home, but he had always initiated it, and she'd seemed mostly indifferent, as if the experience was not penetrating her spirit. He eagerly agreed, and couldn't help looking forward to it. After going through a session, they sat in the celestial room for a long while, holding hands, remaining mostly in silence. Reminiscing about their surroundings, he turned to her and whispered, "Remember the day we were married here?"

"Of course," she whispered back. "It was the happiest day of my life."

"Mine too," he said.

She looked hard at him and said, "I've wondered a thousand times if you regretted it. We got married so fast, and . . ."

He pressed his fingers over her lips. "I knew after that first date you were the one, and I know it even more today. No, I do not regret it, and I never will."

She smiled and touched his face. "Well, that's good," she said, "because I certainly don't regret it. You're the best thing that ever happened to me, and I'm going to stop questioning that and just try to enjoy it."

"How delightful," he said, and hugged her tightly.

Laura felt her husband's strength flow into her from his embrace. She put her head on his shoulder, and he left his arm around her, pressing a kiss into her hair. Tears came to her eyes as the obvious evidence of his love mingled with their surroundings, and she felt truly grateful. In that moment she actually found it possible to believe that she *was* worthy of all she'd been blessed with, and with such feelings came a determination to work very hard to heed the advice she'd been given to win the battle taking place for her soul.

Leaving the temple with Wade's hand in hers, Laura prayed that she could hold on to the peace she felt inside herself and be able to conquer the opponent. She wasn't certain if the opponent was her own negative thinking or Satan's evil design to undo her—probably some of both. Whatever it was, she wanted with all her heart to triumph and be truly happy.

In the car, Wade said, "Hey, we got done earlier than I expected. How would you feel about stopping by to see my parents? I've been feeling overdue for a visit."

"That would be great," she said. "Let's take ice cream."

"Okay," he laughed. "Is this for emotional eating?"

"Maybe."

"And the emotion of the day would be . . ."

"I don't know. I'll have to think about that."

"When you figure it out, you let me know."

Wade called Jane to be sure Rebecca was okay and to let her know they'd be a while longer. She assured him everything was fine. Alex was taking charge of the kids while she was taking it easy, and they should stay out as long as they wanted. A short while later they knocked at the door of his parents' home, even though he usually just walked in. Brad answered the door, and Wade said, "Hi, we brought ice cream."

"Well, hi," Brad laughed, hugging them both. "What a nice surprise—even without the ice cream. Come in."

As soon as he closed the door, Marilyn came to see who had rung the doorbell. "Oh, hello!" she said brightly. "And I was just thinking it was a boring evening and I should go to bed."

"Oh, don't do that," Wade said, kissing her cheek. "We brought ice cream."

"Wonderful," she said, and they all gathered around the kitchen table. Wade helped his mother get out fancy dishes and long-handled spoons while she said to Laura, "How are you feeling, dear?"

"Oh, tired and nauseated off and on, but it's not so bad."

They had a nice visit over ice cream, leaving the extra in the freezer, then they moved to the front room and visited some more, catching up on all that was going on. They talked for a few minutes about Brian, and they all expressed a certain amount of surprise at how well they'd done in coming to terms with his death. They all had moments of missing him, and even bouts of grief, but the peace they felt was evident. They all agreed, as they had many times, how grateful they were for the gospel and the understanding it had given them.

While the conversation ran on, Laura kept feeling drawn to the framed print hanging over the couch where Brad and Marilyn were sitting. She'd noticed it right away on her first visit here, and Wade had told her he'd bought it for his mother. It was a beautiful artist's depiction of the woman taken in adultery when she'd been brought before the Savior. Laura kept looking at Marilyn, and the painting on the wall, pondering the significance for her—and the message of the story from the New Testament. Even though this woman had committed a grievous sin, the Savior had not condemned her. He had expressed love and compassion. It then occurred to Laura that Marilyn was a brilliant example of taking hold of that love and turning her life around. She too had been subjected to a difficult upbringing, and Wade had told her that initially she hadn't possessed the skills to appropriately deal with the problems in her marriage, and so she had left her husband, and Wade was the result. Brad and Marilyn had both come far in unraveling the dysfunctional circumstances that had once entrapped them. Laura had known all of that almost as long as she'd shared a relationship with Wade. But in that moment, the present conversation became distant as the situation before her took on new meaning. She could almost hear the Spirit asking her to recount any grievous sin she might have committed in her lifetime. Her thoughts wandered through many weaknesses that she struggled with, but she honestly couldn't come up with any time when she had willfully committed sin—especially anything huge or grievous. But she knew that even if she *had* committed some horrible sin, or *any* sin for that matter, repentance was part of the plan. She knew that because of the power of the Atonement, it would be possible to put it behind her, fully and irrevocably, just as Marilyn had done. Laura's desire to take her own life stood out strongly, but as soon as it came to mind she also knew beyond any doubt that her state of mind had influenced her behavior. She had asked God to forgive her, and she knew that He had. Laura then felt the question appear in her mind: *If Marilyn has risen above her challenges and poor choices to be held in high esteem as a noble daughter of God, why can you not see the same in yourself?*

Laura gasped softly, startling herself back to the fact that she was not alone in the room, and that she had become oblivious to what the others were saying.

"Are you okay?" Wade asked, looking concerned.

Laura felt a burning in her chest that she felt certain would soon erupt into tears. She forced a smile and said, "I just . . . need a minute." She hurried out of the room, hoping they might credit her hasty retreat to a bout of nausea. In the bathroom on the other side of the house Laura gasped for breath and allowed a rush of hot tears to overtake her. She felt hot and cold all at once, but more importantly, she felt filled with light. She knew then that whatever the future might bring, in that moment she had absolutely no doubt about one simple fact. God loved her. He loved her without question or condition. And she knew it.

For a few minutes Laura just held the feeling close and pondered it while tears flowed. Then she regained her composure, checked her face in the mirror, and returned to the front room.

"You okay?" Wade asked when she entered. Then he did a double-take as if he saw something different in her face.

"I'm fine," she said, and sat close beside him, taking his hand. He kept looking at her while Brad was talking about something. She just smiled and whispered, "I'm fine, really."

"Okay," he said, but he was smiling, and she felt sure he suspected that something had changed inside of her.

During the drive home, Laura pondered all she had felt in the temple and in the time since, mingling it with all she had learned since the day her ex-husband's visit had pushed her over the edge. She felt overwhelmed with gratitude and in awe of all she'd gained. And while she still felt some trepidation about pressing forward into the future, knowing that the normal challenges of life would continue and that the reality of overcoming her tendencies toward depression could be difficult, she instilled her present state of mind into her memory, knowing that she could rely on this moment to carry her through.

Once they were home, she went straight to the journal Dr. Hadley had given her, even before she changed into her pajamas, and she wrote down what she had felt and learned this evening, right beneath where she'd recorded in detail the things that Neil had told her not so many days ago. Both events fit well into Hadley's purpose for the book, which was to write anything that would help her replace the negative with positive, and to help her in difficult times.

Wade came into the room and removed his tie just as she was finishing up. She knew he'd been talking with Alex about some medical procedure he'd witnessed earlier that day, and he would have peeked in to check on Rebecca, who was sleeping soundly.

"Hey there, gorgeous," he said. "What are you up to?"

"Just . . . writing something down that was . . . well, worth writing down."

"Okay," he said, and she held the book out toward him, silently offering to let him read what she'd written.

Wade sat on the edge of the bed right next to her, and she watched his face while he focused on her handwritten words—in purple ink. After a minute he looked up at her, his eyes sparkling with awe and amazement. "Yes, that really came from me," she said, and he continued to read. His love for her was reinforced once again as tears came to his eyes before he closed the book and set it aside to take her into his arms. He held to her as if he might die without her, then he kissed her cheek, her eyelids, her other cheek, before he looked into her eyes, murmuring, "I love you so much, and I'm so proud of you. You've come far, you know. And it's going to keep getting better. I know it will."

"I believe that," she said, and then she wanted to tell him how grateful she was for his love, his support, his acceptance, and for all he'd done for her. But a knot gathered in her throat, and she couldn't find any words to fully express all she was feeling, so she just settled for, "I love you too." And then she kissed him.

When their lips reluctantly parted, she smiled up at him and said, "I think . . . this moment calls for . . ."

"More ice cream?" he asked with mock excitement.

She smiled. "Ice cream always works, but . . . I was thinking more of a dance."

Wade grinned. "What a marvelous idea." He stood up and put on an appropriate CD, then he dimmed the lights and held out a hand for her. While he held her close and gently swayed her back and forth to the music, Laura felt as if time had momentarily stopped long enough for her to connect this moment to every good moment she had shared with him. She recalled the first time he'd danced with her on their second date, and the waltz rehearsals they'd shared in preparation for the waltz they'd shared at their wedding. She felt a twinge of sorrow to recall how he'd danced with her this way at the facility when she had been so lost inside her own anguish that she had barely been aware of his presence. And she thought of the dances they'd shared here in this home when she'd only been here for the evening, attempting to work her way back into a normal life. And now they were here, together, in love—and she was alive.

Looking into his eyes, she felt more grateful to be alive than she'd ever imagined possible.

"I figured it out," she said, smiling up at him.

"What?"

"The emotion of the day."

"And what is it?" Wade asked, his smile lighting his eyes.

"It's happy," Laura said. "Just plain . . . happy."

Wade laughed a perfectly happy laugh, and they just kept dancing.

Epilogue

After an ultrasound made it clear that Jane and Alex were having another boy, Barrett came to Wade with a seriousness far beyond his years and asked if it would be alright with him if his parents named the baby Brian, after Wade's brother.

"Why are you asking me?" Wade said. "It's up to your parents what to name the baby."

"I told them I thought it should be Brian, and they said I should ask you, because . . . well, they said you might want to name *your* son Brian."

Wade smiled and hugged Barrett. "You know what? I think Brian is a wonderful name for your new little brother, if that's what your parents feel his name should be. I already know what my son's name will be, and while I certainly like the name Brian, I know that's not his name."

Barrett seemed pleased. "Is your baby going to be a boy, too?"

"We don't know yet. But I think I'll have at least one son eventually. We'll just have to see."

Before Jane's baby was born, Rebecca turned three, which meant Ruthie did too. Wade couldn't help but feel struck by the passing of time in realizing that Elena had been gone three years. And soon afterward, he and Laura celebrated their first wedding anniversary, and they were also able to maneuver taking a second honeymoon, which was especially nice since the first one had been so brief. It felt like a huge landmark for many reasons, the most significant being the evidence of how far she had come in a year. The happiness they had shared in their early marriage had returned fully to their relationship, only now there was the undeniable absence of her discomfort over certain issues. Her struggle to overcome her past had been tough, and it still crept up occasionally, but they had learned to talk about it and work it through, and she was getting steadily stronger. Her episodes of discouragement were becoming farther apart, and more easily overcome. And he felt deeply grateful. Pondering his impatience during the long weeks of Laura's initial rehabilitation, he realized that he'd learned something about trusting in the Lord's timing. For all intents and purposes, Laura's healing had been miraculously quick and thorough compared to the challenges faced by many people with depression.

Alex and Jane had their fifth child in the fall, and he was officially named Brian Wade Keane. While the name *had* been Barrett's idea, his parents had both agreed it was the right name for this baby. Wade loved seeing Laura help with little Brian, and he loved seeing her growing excitement—along with his own—for their baby to make its grand entrance into the world.

When it came time to do another Christmas tree for the Festival of Trees, Jane declared that she was considering skipping it while she was dealing with a new baby. But Laura insisted that she would help, and everyone else agreed to pitch in. And that's when Barrett declared that it should be a Batman tree. Wade knew the boy loved Batman; it was one of many things they had in common. But the look on Jane's face in response to her son's suggestion was something he had trouble not laughing over.

"Honey," she said to Barrett, "something else . . . might be more appropriate."

"Oh, Mom," he pleaded, "I've seen all kinds of things on trees up there. And people *love* Batman. If they don't, they should. He's awesome."

"I have to agree with that," Wade said, and Jane scowled at him.

"Oh, come on, Mom," Barrett said, and proceeded to explain the type of ornaments they would make and the colors they would use. He'd obviously thought it through very carefully. Jane was still hesitant, until Barrett said firmly, "I'm the one who almost died in that hospital you know, and I think we should do a Batman tree."

"He's got a point," Alex said.

Jane just laughed and said, "Well . . . since you put it that way . . . a Batman tree it is."

The project was a great deal of fun, and ended up being a huge success. When the family all went together to the festival, Wade couldn't help thinking of how far they'd come in a year.

While Wade progressed with his education, enduring some rotations and enjoying others, Cole and Rochelle continued to keep company with each other, and they all got together every week or two, becoming more close than family in many respects. The changes in Rochelle became steadily more defined, as did the growing romance between her and Cole. Around Thanksgiving they finally announced their plans to be married—soon after Cole would baptize her. The waiting period following her excommunication was drawing to a close, and the miracles and healing in all of their lives were worth taking notice of. Wade thought of his own mother having gone through an excommunication, and how Brad had baptized her when the time had come. He thought of what his parents' example of repentance and acceptance had meant in his own life. The relationship that Cole and Rochelle shared certainly had the same ingredients.

The holidays were some of the best Wade ever remembered in his adult life. He couldn't recall ever being happier. Laura hit an unexpected low in January, but following a session with Dr. Hadley and going through the process of careful steps to counter it, she was able to navigate through it and move on. By

Valentine's Day she was doing much better, and they were both greatly anticipating new landmarks in their lives.

Bradley Neil Morrison came into the world on a cold, rainy afternoon, weighing in at eight pounds, five ounces, bearing a strong resemblance to his father.

"But he doesn't have a beard," Laura said quite seriously.

"Not yet," Wade countered. "Maybe I should shave mine off, and we'll look more alike."

"You have more teeth than he does," she said. "But . . . I don't know if you should shave or not. You've now broken your tradition of only wearing a beard when life is hard, you know."

"So I have. I hadn't even thought about it. One day I might just . . . surprise you."

Rebecca immediately took to her new little brother, and the two of them together were absolutely adorable. And seeing the way Laura loved them and took such good care of them left Wade feeling more complete and content than he ever had.

Little Bradley was only a few weeks old when Wade officially became a doctor. He'd met the requirements some time earlier but had chosen to go through the graduation ceremony at a more conventional time. His timing had been off somewhat due to the semester he'd taken off the summer that Elena died, but now that he'd gotten this far, the challenges of those years didn't seem nearly so horrible as they had at the time. Now he felt prepared to take on the future, knowing that he and Laura could probably survive just about anything—even having to leave Jane and Alex's home and venture out into the world. Wade felt good about the internship he'd been offered at a cancer clinic in Omaha, even though it was a thousand miles away from the family members they were so close to. But they knew it was only temporary, and he was already praying that an opening for a residency position at Primary Children's Medical Center would bring them back to this place he loved so that he could embark on the career he felt so passionate about.

When the time came to say goodbye, it was even harder than Wade had anticipated. Brad and Marilyn and Neil and Roxanne had all gathered at Alex and Jane's home for this tender farewell. While everyone else was occupied elsewhere, Wade found himself facing Alex, knowing that this was it—the last minute they'd have together before Wade took his family a thousand miles away. He wasn't necessarily surprised by the emotion that burned in his throat and between his eyes, but he wasn't quite sure how to handle it. He felt a little better when he saw Alex's eyes turn moist.

"Wow," Alex said, clearing his throat loudly and looking down, "I knew this was going to be hard, but . . ."

"Yeah," Wade said, "I know what you mean." He chuckled tensely. "You know, not so many years ago, you didn't even know I existed."

"And vice versa."

"Yeah," Wade said again, then his voice cracked. "How did we ever manage?"

"I can't begin to know," Alex replied. His voice became forcibly lighter as he added, "Dad just told me they're submitting mission papers. I'd like to know how I'm supposed to get by without him *and* you. Who will meet me at the cafeteria for lunch?"

"You might have to find a new friend," Wade said.

"Not likely." He looked hard at Wade. "Not like you."

They hugged each other tightly and said nothing more before their families surrounded them and the final goodbyes took place. There was nothing more to say; it had all been said before. They would talk on the phone regularly, make good use of email, and arrange vacations to see each other whenever possible. But it just wasn't the same. The only real comfort came in knowing that it wasn't permanent. Wade couldn't imagine wanting to settle down anywhere but here, within close range of the people he loved and counted on the most: his parents—all of them—and his brother, who came with a wife and kids that had given him more love and support than he could ever measure. It was as hard to say goodbye to Barrett as it had been his father, but they already had plans for Barrett to come and stay with Wade and Laura for several days during his summer vacation.

When the farewells became torturous, Wade helped buckle Rebecca and Bradley into their seats. Wade would be driving the rented truck and would keep Rebecca with him while Laura followed him in the car. Thankfully, the baby was young enough that he would sleep a great deal, but they'd already figured out that their driving breaks would be determined by Bradley's need to be fed and changed.

Once they were on the road, Wade kept Rebecca happy next to him with a well-prepared supply of storybooks, toys, and snacks, while he kept an eye on Laura in the side mirrors of the truck. He called her cell phone from his and said, "Hey, Mrs. Morrison, I just thought of something."

"What?"

"This is almost like . . . the trek the pioneers took . . . only backward."

"So it is," she said. "I'm grateful we'll be arriving in much better time than they did. And I'll think about that every time I start to hate the trip."

"Good plan," he said, and the journey began.

They arrived at their new apartment in Omaha thoroughly exhausted, but they were greeted by ward members they'd met on their visit here to rent the place. The truck was unloaded in record time, and a nice meal was brought in by the Relief Society. They were nearly finished eating it, very late, when Laura looked around at the piles of boxes and haphazardly placed furniture and said, "It feels like home."

"It does?" he asked skeptically.

Laura focused her eyes on him, then glanced at Bradley sleeping in his infant seat and Rebecca asleep on the couch. "All the right people are here. Home is with you, Dr. Morrison, wherever that takes me." He smiled, and she added, "There's only one thing we really need to do tonight to break the place in."

"And what's that?" he asked.

Laura stood up and held out her hand. "Dance with me," she said.

He laughed and stood up, eagerly heeding her request. "I have no idea which box has any music in it."

Laura looked into his eyes. "Who needs music?

ABOUT THE AUTHOR

Anita Stansfield, the LDS market's number-one best-selling romance novelist, is a prolific and imaginative writer. Her novels have captivated and moved hundreds of thousands of readers, and she is a popular speaker for women's groups and in literary circles. She and her husband Vince are the parents of five children and reside in Alpine, Utah.